# THE UNUSUAL
# LIFE OF
# TRISTAN SMITH

A NOVEL

PETER CAREY

ALFRED A. KNOPF   NEW YORK   1995

THIS IS A BORZOI BOOK
PUBLISHED BY ALFRED A. KNOPF, INC.

Copyright © 1994 by Peter Carey

ISBN 0-679-43888-2
LC 94-078479

Manufactured in the United States of America
FIRST AMERICAN EDITION

For Alison, Sam and Charley

# Acknowledgements

I would like to thank Kenneth de Kok who guided me through the shoals of Dutch and Afrikaans, translated some of my dialogue, and provided me with the name Voorstand; Charles Poulbon of Perth, Western Australia, who first alerted me to the joys of pigeon racing; Ronni Burrows of Ronni Reports for her highly efficient research on a number of arcane subjects; and Dr Brian Waldron who read a very early draft and was therefore Tristan Smith's first diagnostician.

I owe especial thanks to Alison Summers, my wife, whose careful reading and thoughtful questions helped me to discover, chart and report the emotional and geographical territories of this novel.

# Contents

# BOOK 1

## My Life in Efica

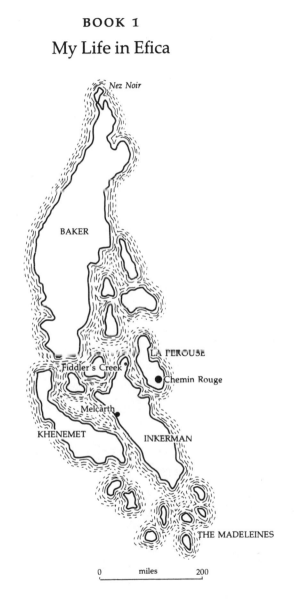

Nez Noir

BAKER

LA PEROUSE

Fiddler's Creek

Chemin Rouge

Melcarth

KHENEMET

INKERMAN

THE MADELEINES

0    miles    200

Republic of Efica

'In foreign countries,' Bruder Mouse said, 'they put animals in cages and keep them locked up and kill them.'

'You can't frighten me,' said Bruder Duck. 'There's a great world out there and I plan to see it. I'm going to fairs, and puppet shows, and I'm going to cross oceans and have all sorts of adventures.'

'You want to be fat and rich,' said Bruder Mouse. 'You want to find gold.'

'It's true,' said Bruder Duck, 'that if I chanced to stumble over a nugget I would thank the Lord for my good fortune and if I found an object of value I might buy cheaply, I would not refuse the blessing.'

'But what of the issue?' said Bruder Mouse.

'What issue?' said the Duck, who was busy eating the cheese pudding again.

'That they have Sirkuses in foreign countries, where they put God's creatures in cages. They have butcher shops where they sell our Bruders' flesh.'

'If what you say is so,' said the Bruder Duck, 'then I would change their minds.'

'How would you do this?' asked the Mouse.

'I would do doody and fall over,' said the Duck. 'I would make them laugh.'

From Bruder Duck's Travels, Badberg Edition

The Dog, the Duck, the Mouse

The Dog, the Duck, the Mouse
They lived their life in a tent
The Duck played the fiddle
The Dog had a piddle
The Mouse ran off with the rent.

Oh God we laughed till we cried
We sighed and wiped our eyes
We kissed the Dog we cuddled the Mouse
With the Duck right by our side.

The Dog, the Duck, the Mouse
Came in braces and baggy pants
They were no moles
But they purchased the holes
We had been left by chance.

Oh God we laughed till we cried
We sighed and wiped our eyes
We kissed the Dog we cuddled the Mouse
With the Duck right by our side.

Efican folk song *circa* 351 EC (Source: *Doggerel and Jetsam: unheard voices in the Voorstand Imperium*, Inchsmith Press, London)

# 1

My name is Tristan Smith. I was born in Chemin Rouge in Efica – which is to say as much to you, I bet, as if I declared I was from the moon.

And yet if you are going to make much sense of me, you have to know a little of my country, a country so unimportant that you are already confusing the name with Ithaca or Africa, a name so unmemorable it could only have been born of a committee, although it remains, nonetheless, the home of nearly three million of the earth's people, and they, like you, have no small opinion of themselves, have artists and poets who are pleased to criticize its shortcomings and celebrate its charms, who return home to the eighteen little islands between the tropic of Capricorn and the 30th parallel, convinced that their windswept coastline is the most beautiful on earth. Like 98 per cent of the planet's population, we Eficans may be justly accused of being provincial, parochial, and these qualities are sometimes magnified by your habit of hearing 'Ithaca' when we say 'Efica'.

If I say 'Voorstand' to you, that is a different story entirely. You are a citizen of Voorstand. You hold the red passport with the phases of the moon embossed in gold. You stand with your hand over your heart when the Great Song is played, you daily watch new images of your armies in the vids and zines. How can I make you know what it is like to be from Efica – abandoned, self-doubting, yet so wilful that if you visit Chemin Rouge tomorrow morning we will tell you that the year is 426* and you must write your cheques accordingly.

If you were my students I would direct you to read *Efica: from penal colony to welfare state*,† *The Caves of Democracy*,‡ and Volume 3 of

---

* 426 by the Efican Calendar, sometimes written as 426 EC, but most commonly as 426. The calendar begins with the discovery of Neufasie (later Efica) by Captain Girard.
† *Nez Noir University Press, 343 EC.*
‡ *Macmillan, London, 1923.*

Wilbur's *The Dyer's Cauldron*.* But you are not my students and I have no choice but to juggle and tap-dance before you, begging you please sit in your seats while I have you understand exactly why my heart is breaking.

<h2 style="text-align:center">2</h2>

My maman was one of you. She was born in Voorstand. She was able to trace her family back to the 'Settlers Free' of the Great Song. Had things been different I might have been a Voorstander, like you, and then there would have been no trouble. But when my maman was eighteen she came to Chemin Rouge to be a model in a fashion advertisement.

She became famous, within Efica, for her role in a local soap opera, and then she was notorious as a founder of the Feu Follett Collective, a small radical theatre group which was always in trouble with our local authorities for its opposition to the country of her birth.

Let us say it straight – Felicity Smith was very critical of her own people. It was because of this, she changed her name from Smutts to Smith: she did not want to be a Voorstander. She was outraged at the way Voorstand manipulated our elections, meddled with our currency, threaded all that shining cable we never understood, miles of it, great loops of it, through the dry granite caves which honeycombed our southern provinces. She did not like the way your country used us. If this is offensive, I am sorry, but it was her belief. It was honestly held. Indeed, it was passionately held. She was not reasonable or balanced or fair. Yet for all the *passion* she expanded, for all the ceaseless *paranoia*, for all the very real Efican government agents who came snooping round the theatre, their electronic pencils dancing like fireflies in the dark, it is hard to see how the Feu Follet Collective was a threat to anyone – it was a small, dirty, uncomfortable theatre at the back of that warren of bachelor flats, stables and dressage rings which had once housed the Ducrow Circus School.‡

When, at the end of her life, my maman found a way to really

* *Artcraft Press, Chemin Rouge 299* EC.
† *Pronounced* Foo Follay – *Ed.*
‡ *Jacques Ducrow (245–310), former cavalry sergeant and then equestrian, later proprietor Ducrow's Efican Circus and (302–9) Ducrow Circus School. Ducrow claimed to be one of the English circus family which produced the equestrians*

threaten the status quo it was not through the theatre but in the dirty old fairground of baby-kissing politics. In comparison the notorious Feu Follet was toothless. It had no money, no advertising, too much boring Brecht. My maman sometimes said that if it had not been for the spies, who after all paid full price for their tickets, they would have long ago gone out of business. That, of course, was a joke. The unfunny truth was that the Feu Follet would never have survived if it had not been for its circus matinées and Shakespeare productions, the latter chosen to coincide with the selection of that year's high-school syllabuses.

I was born in the Scottish Play, at the end of a full rehearsal.

There was no great rush of fluids, but there was no mistaking what was happening when her waters broke and my maman quietly excused herself and walked out of the Feu Follet without telling anyone where she was going.

When she came down the brick ramp in Gazette Street, things started happening faster than she had expected. Oxytocin entered her bloodstream like a ten-ton truck and all the pretty soft striped muscles of her womb turned hostile, contracting on me like they planned to crush my bones. I was caught in a rip. I was dumped. I was shoved into the birth canal, head first, my arm still pinned behind my back. My ear got folded like an envelope. My head was held so hard it felt, I swear it, like the end of life and not its glorious beginning.

My maman had never had a child before. She did not understand the urgency. She walked straight past the line of empty red and silver cabs whose Sikh taxi-men, unaware of the emergency taking place underneath their noses, continued to talk to each other from behind their steering wheels, via the radio. As she crossed the Boulevard des Indiennes to the river she already felt distinctly uncomfortable, as if she were holding back a pumpkin, and yet she would not abandon her plan, i.e. to walk quietly, by herself, along the river to the Mater Hospital. She had long ago decided on this and she was a woman who always carried out her plans.

It was a Sunday morning in January and the syrupy air smelled of dried fish, sulphur and diesel fuel.

The year was 371 by our calendar. My maman was thirty-two

---

*Andrew, Charles and William and the clown William. There is good reason to doubt this.*

7

years old, tall, finely boned. No one watching her walk along the grey sandy path beside the river bed would have guessed at what her body was experiencing. She was an actress of the most physical type, and for the first half of her journey her walk was a triumph of will. She wore a long bright blue skirt, black tights. On her back she carried a black tote bag containing an extra shirt, another pair of tights, four pairs of pants, a pack of menstrual pads and a life of Stanislavsky she had always imagined she would read between contractions. This last thing – the book – is a good example of the sort of thing that irritated people, even members of her own company who loved her. They sensed in her this expectation of herself, that she could, for Christ's sake, read Stanislavsky while she had a baby.

She had a rude shock coming to her. They did not say that, hardly had the courage to think it in the quiet, secret part of their minds, but it was there, in their eyes, fighting with their sympathy. She had obsessed so long about this birth, not publicly, or noisily, but she had done the things that sometimes annoy the un-pregnant – eaten yeast and wheat germ, chanted in the mornings.

No one from the Feu Follet saw her walk across the Boulevard des Indiennes. Had they done so, they might have been tempted to see it as evidence of her will, even her pride, her belief that she could walk while a lesser woman would be in an ambulance calling for the anaesthetic, but Felicity was someone who liked to celebrate the milestones of her life – birthdays particularly – and she had imagined this moment, this walk beside the river, for too long to abandon it.

My maman was a foreigner, but she loved Chemin Rouge with a passion barely imaginable to the native born. She believed it was this provincial city in this unimportant country that had saved her life, and if she had believed in God it was here she would have kneeled – on the grey shell-grit path beside the river. If she had had parents it was here she would have brought them to show them what she had become. She had no God, no parents, but still she celebrated – she brought me here instead.

She had been a resident for fourteen years. She had been a citizen for ten. She had her own theatre company. She was going to give birth. It was so far from where she had been born. All these sights – this ultramarine sky, these white knobbly river rocks, the six-

8

foot-tall feathered grasses which brushed her shoulders – were unimaginable to anyone in the great foreign metropolis of Saarlim, and they were, for her, at once exotic but also as familiar as her own milky Hollandse Maagd skin.

This small, slightly *rancid* port city was her home. And her feelings for the Eficans, those laconic, belligerent, self-doubting inhabitants of the abandoned French and English colonies, descendants of convicts (and dyers who, being conscripted by Louis Quatorze, were as good as convicts), grandchildren of displaced crofters and potato-blight Irish, were protective and critical, admiring and impatient. It was no small thing to her that I should be an Efican, and she betrayed her foreign birth in the way in which her ambitions for each of us, the country and the child, were not humble.

Although the theatre was appreciated for its rough colloquial Shakespeare, she and the actors also devised a sort of agitprop, part circus, part soapbox, in which they attacked our country's craven relationship with yours. There were people who valued the Shakespeare but found the agitprop unrewarding, and others who never set foot inside the Feu Follet who imagined the famous actor-manager to be both strident and humourless. It was half true – she was capable of being both of these things occasionally, but she was also a softly spoken woman with warm eyes. No son was ever so cherished by a mother as I was by her.

The hospital where she had planned that I would be born was half a mile to the south of the theatre. It was built on the banks of the Nabangari* river which, being wide and blue on the maps, was usually a disappointment to visitors, who were likely to find it empty, dry, full of blinding white round stones, with no sign of the waters whose crop gave the Central Business District of Chemin Rouge its controversial smell.

When the famous river flowed into the port it raged not blue, but clay-yellow, filled with grinding boulders and native pine logs which drifted out into the harbour where they floated just beneath

---

* *Those Voorstanders only now acquainting themselves with Efican English may notice, from time to time, place names like Nabangari which seem to owe nothing to either English or French. The Nabangari was so named by the 'lost' Indigenous Peoples (IPs) of Efica. The names of these long dead people litter our islands – tombstones in a lost language.* [TS]

the surface, earning themselves the name of 'widow makers' with the pilots of the sea planes to Nez Noir. Every four or five years the Nabangari broke its banks and more than once filled the basement of the Mater Hospital, and then the front page of the *Chemin Rouge Zine* would carry a large photograph of a hospital administrator netting perch on the steps of the boiler room.

Felicity had a striking face. She had long tousled copper hair, a straight nose, a fine 'English' complexion, but as she came to the bend of the river where she should be able to see the hospital, her mouth tightened. What lay between her and the hospital was a Voorstand Sirkus in the process of construction, more different from our own indigenous circus than the different spelling might suggest.* The giant vid screen was already in place and high-definition images of white women with shining thighs and pearlescent guitars had already established their flickering presence – 640×200 pixels, beamed by satellite from Voorstand itself – shining, brighter than daylight, through the immobile yellow leaves of the slender trees.

The incredible thing was that she had forgotten her enemy was there. She had opposed its importation as if it were a war ship or subterranean installation. She had fought it so fiercely that even her political allies had sometimes imagined her a little fanatical, and when she said the Sirkus would swamp us, suffocate us, they – even while supporting her – began to imagine she was worried about the box office at the Feu Follet.

As the great slick machine of Sirkus rose before her, her muscles came crushing down upon my brain box. Her mouth gaped. She backed a little off the narrow path, her arm extended behind her, seeking the security of a pale-barked tree trunk. She got the base of her back against the tree and propped her legs. She breathed – the wrong breathing – hopeless – but she did not know I was now ready to be born. When the contraction was done, she limped through the confusion of the circus, which lay in pieces all around

---

* *The Efican circus has its roots in English circus – lions, elephants, equestrian acts, acrobatic performance, feats of strength. The Voorstand Sirkus began its extraordinary development, not as the powerful entertainment industry it is today, but as the expression of those brave Dutch heretics, the 'Settlers Free', who were intent on a Sirkus Sonder Gevangene – a Circus without 'prisoners', that is, one without animals.* [TS]

her. She stepped over coloured cables as thick as her arm, limped past wooden crates containing the holographic projector. The road crews, working against punitive clauses in their service contracts, had their pneumatic tools screaming on their ratchets. They wore peaked hats and iridescent sneakers which shone like sequins. They danced around the woman who was, by now, almost staggering through them.

My maman made it up the front steps of the Mater Hospital, whose staff, in true Efican style, responded instantly to her condition. Within three minutes of her arrival she was on a trolley, speeding along the yellow line marked Maternity 02.

The birth was fast and easy. The life was to be another matter.

3

On the afternoon of my birth, as the clock in the Chemin Rouge Town Hall struck three, an actor named Bill Millefleur sat down on one of the moulded plastic chairs in the Mater Hospital Maternity waiting room and began to peel the wrapper from a doigt de chocolat. My mother's lover was very young – just twenty-two, but tall and handsome, olive-skinned, dark-eyed, with finely chiselled, beautifully shaped lips. He ate the chocolate bar quickly, hunched over, as if he were alone.

There were, at the same time, two other men waiting in the same room, and they were there for the same reason Bill was. One of them – Wally Paccione – was the production manager of the Feu Follet. The other – Vincent Theroux – shared with Bill the distinction of being my maman's lover.

Bill worked with Wally every day, saw Vincent at least four times a week. Yet he managed to finish the chocolate without acknowledging either of them. He could not make them go away. Indeed, he feared they had some business being there.

As he wiped his pretty lips carelessly with the back of his hand and folded his arms across his broad chest, he told himself again what he believed to be true.

My mother had been with *him* when she conceived. It was *him* she loved. She had been with *him* when her waters broke. It was *his* speech she had walked out of, turning the great noisy latch and laying a jagged white knife-blade across the circle of his con-

11

centration. He had seen her, no one else had. Vincent had been at his office. And Wally, who was now acting in so pathetically paternal a way, had been up in the booth, and from the booth you could not see the door.

It therefore seemed impossible that they should be here now, unless – and the very thought of this betrayal made Bill's smooth cheeks darken – my mother had telephoned them.

My maman had a curious network of loyalties, it is true, but in this case she had no time to telephone anyone – it was Bill Mille-fleur himself who sent the signal, by leaving the theatre without waiting for compliments about his work.

When Wally Paccione learned Macbeth had disappeared before notes,* he knew I was about to be born, and he slid down the narrow ladder with a grin on his face which Bill – had he been able to witness it – would have found at once grotesque and threatening.

Wally was fifty years old. He had big pale lips, a craggy nose, pale grey eyes, ginger bushy eyebrows, a tall freckled forehead, a receding hairline.

When he strode across the centre of the stage the curve of his broad back suggested excitement, furtiveness, urgency, secrecy. He checked the 'foyer', then ran, hunched over, elbows tucked in against his ribs, up one flight of stairs, down three steps, and up another flight to the tower which had once housed the office of the Director of the Circus School but which was now my mother's apartment. The tower was empty. He skittered down the narrow steps to the second floor. He knocked on the bathroom door and disturbed – not Bill, not my mother – but the notoriously con-stipated Claire Chen.

While Bill was running across the Boulevard des Indiennes towards the Mater, Wally was using all his charm to persuade Claire to slide 5 dollars out under the door. He did not run to hospital. He went by cab. Thus he was already in the foyer when Bill came striding in. The two men, both six foot tall, rode up in the lift side by side staring at the numbers above the door.

* *The critique of an actor's performance normally offered by the director and, sometimes, the playwright. In the leftist Feu Follet these critiques might be offered by other actors, assistant stage managers, the house manager – by any member of the company.*

When they opened the Maternity waiting room door they found Vincent Theroux – forty-six years old, not very tall, wide in the shoulders but now plump, even portly. He was sitting in a plastic chair, still wearing his broad-rimmed black hat, smoking an Havana cigar. Like Bill, he had a remarkable mouth – a rose-bud which shone like a flower in his neat sandy beard.

'Cigar?' he said.

Bill turned his back without answering. Wally nodded, took a cigar, and tucked it in the pocket of his iridescent pink shirt.

Bill inspected the water cooler, looked out the window at the sky. Wally selected a chair on the long wall, facing Vincent.

Bill also sat. He folded his arms across his chest and watched Wally flipping through a zine. Though he did not like Vincent being there, he was *offended* by Wally's presence.

Wally claimed to have been raised in a touring circus and to have spent his early years as a 'Human Ball' being thrown in an act from mother to father, but this cut no ice with Bill, to whom he was nothing more than a small-time crook, one of those Efican facheurs who hang out in artists' bars, carrying books of poetry for the purpose of attracting middle-class women. Certainly he had done time. He did not deny it. He talked like a crim – said 'violin' for jail, 'musico' for con-man, 'riveter' for homosexual. He was now the production manager – a good one – but he had become so attached to Felicity, during the pregnancy, that he had begun to give the impression that he had been responsible for it.

So Bill found his presence impertinent.

Yet when the santamarie entered the waiting room and asked, 'Which of you gens is the dab-to-be?' Bill could not publicly lay claim. He began to fear that someone in the room knew something he did not.

He felt his neck burning. He folded his shirt cuffs. He began to button his red and black plaid shirt.

'It's you,' the santamarie smiled, locating him by his high colour. She touched his sleeve. '*You're* the dab.'

He moved sideways.

'You're Mr Smith, right?'

Of course he was not Mr Smith. He drew further away, pressing his back against the window. His brows pushed down over his dark eyes and his blush spread right behind his pierced flat ears and disappeared down the collar of his work shirt.

13

'The doctor,' said the santamarie, 'says Mr Smith might as well go home and rest.'

'Actually, Nurse' – Vincent put his fat backside on the window ledge; it touched Bill's elbow – 'there is no Mr Smith. There is a Ms Smith, but no Mr. It's Felicity Smith,' he said.

Bill tried to make eye contact with the santamarie.

'Felicity Smith,' Vincent said, 'the actress.' He unbuckled his two-inch wide belt and tightened it an extra notch. The gesture was worldly, confident, sexual. 'There is no *Mr* Smith. There is only us.'

The santamarie smiled at Vincent, nodded. 'I see.'

'What I see about our situation,' Vincent persisted, 'is that it's vaguely ludicrous. The three of us, all smoking cigars.'

'OK,' said Bill, who just wanted the santamarie out of there before something embarrassing was said. 'That's nice of you. Thank you.'

'All right,' she said. 'Class dismissed.'

'Was I brusque? I'm sorry.'

'I don't know what *brusk* is,' the santamarie said. 'But I know when I'm not wanted.'

'Why don't *you* leave?' Wally turned to Bill. He folded his zine and returned it to his back pocket. 'If you can't be decent you'd be better off not being here.'

'*I'm* here,' Bill said, 'because my son is being born.' He turned back towards the Sirkus in the park. A giant mouse with a white stick was dancing on the video.

'So you *are* Mr Smith,' the santamarie said. She opened the door to the hallway. 'The water closets are one floor down or one floor up.'

'I sympathize with your enthusiasm,' Vincent said, as the door slammed shut behind the santamarie. He laid his hand on Bill's shoulder. 'I sympathize, but you don't know it's a boy, and you don't know it's yours.'

'You should go home and check your diary,' Bill said. 'If you're the father you must have put your pecker in the post.'

'Go home,' Wally repeated. 'Just like the doctor says.'

'Maybe *Wally* is the father.' Bill held his palms upwards in appeal. 'Now there's a vision.'

Wally had pendulous ear lobes, soft like wattles, fair-haired arms with small round scars where no hair would grow. Now his austere face contracted a fraction more. 'I have not had the pleasure,' he said.

Bill whooped.

'You petticon,' Wally said. He sprang from his chair, stepped on to the coffee table, and launched himself at Bill, his neck tendons tight, his pale lips stretched across his teeth, his right fist raised like a hammer.

Bill leaped over a row of blue plastic chairs, yelping with pleasure, his teeth white, his eyebrows arched high.

'For Chrissakes,' Wally said. 'You didn't even ask why we can go home.' He let his scarred and tattooed hands hang limply by his side. 'You didn't even ask her how she was.'

He went to stand beside Bill, to look out of the window at the Sirkus. In a moment Vincent joined them, his large black hat silhouetted against the bright arc lights in the park. Vincent put his arm first around Wally's shoulders, then Bill's. 'She's going to be all right,' he said.

It was the first time it had occurred to Bill that she might not be.

As for Tristan – not a word about me. I did not exist for any of them – I was a thing, an idea, a ripple on the other side of a beautiful woman's large white belly.

But by this time, just after noon, I was, regardless of what the santamarie had said, already two hours old.


4

My three 'fathers' were treated badly, as if their alliance with my maman were unnatural or perverse, and they were separately and jointly responsible for my peculiar condition. They were lied to. They were given to understand the labour was long, that the labour had not begun, that there was a C-section to be performed, that Ms Smith had been shifted to another hospital. They were told, bluntly, to go away, to wait at home for a call, and what is incredible is that they tolerated this treatment. They were not meek men, but they were men, intimidated by birth, and so they went meekly, and with so little idea of what was happening to Felicity that they could not even answer each other's questions in the street outside.

Five storeys above their heads, in a small windowless examination room, two doctors were nervously trying to persuade Felicity that it would be better, although they did not use so blunt a word, for them to kill me.

There was nothing much in the room: a metal cabinet with one thin drawer and two fat ones, a bright red bin labelled 'Sharps' and another, larger one, marked 'Bio-hazard', the chair on which my maman sat, the paper-covered couch on which Dr Eisner perched.

Marc Laroche, the obstetrician, leaned against the door and folded his long thin arms across his chest. He had known Felicity for ten years, had seen every play she had appeared in or directed,

'You don't have to decide anything now,' he said, but he could not look her in the eye or pronounce the illegal act he was silently advocating.

My maman turned to the paediatrician. She had not known him three hours ago. His name was Eisner. He was very young. He had dark beautiful doe eyes which were now filled with pity. 'You can take as long as you want,' he said.

Marc Laroche jammed his hands deep into the pockets of his trousers. 'God damn it,' he said.

Felicity had given birth less than an hour before. She was weak, frightened, in shock.

'I want to see him,' she said.

'What?' Marc Laroche said. Then, 'Of course.'

He left the room. Dr Eisner smiled at her, frowned, fussed with the slippery paper on his examination couch, then left the room as well.

Felicity was abandoned to the hum of the lighting. She thought: this is not happening to me.

A long time later the two doctors returned, rolling a small perspex crib. Tristan was lying in the crib. She did not look at him directly, but saw that he did not take a lot of space. He was swaddled in a bright patterned cloth.

'Unswaddle him.' She heard herself say it. She was aware of removing herself from herself, of becoming a character whom she could watch. She closed her eyes, breathed a little – in–out, in–out.

The young men did not say when they had done unwrapping, but she could tell from the stillness in the room. She opened her eyes. She had no distance from herself, or not sufficient. When she saw the baby's face again, she put her hand across her mouth. A noise came out, a noise so painful that Marc Laroche's anxious face contorted in sympathy.

'God damn,' he said.

She thought: I am the mother.

But she did not want to touch Tristan. She made herself. Her *character* touched me. I was naked, defenceless, frightening.

'Damn,' said Marc Laroche.

'Shut up,' she said.

She held her finger out and touched my hand. I grasped the finger and held it with an intensity that surprised her. I was barely human. I was like some dream she might expect to stay forever hidden in the entrails of her consciousness. She tried to jerk her hand away. I would not let go.

The feeling – she had felt this before: it was when you held the worm in your fingers before you baited your hook, the way the life shrank from the hook, the way you responded to it, that strong demand within your fingers. It was not your personality or your character. It was something more basic than character. Now she held her hand against the little thing's chest where you could see its beating heart. She did not know what she felt. It was like the bomb blast at the theatre when Suzi Jacques lost her leg – flesh, blood, screaming. I wailed and my awful face shrank up in fear as if I could smell the harm floating in the sterile air.

Felicity heard herself make mummy-noises.

When the hovering Marc Laroche came to her side, she saw his intention was to take Tristan away.

'Show me how to wrap him,' she said. And when he hesitated: 'Please.'

She was aware of how she looked. She was an actress. She had been a model. People were always stirred by her beauty. It was the first thing anyone would write about her. She was 'tall and willowy', had 'stunning cheekbones', a 'mass of curling coppery hair' which framed her 'slightly triangular face'. She could see the doctors being moved (Marc Laroche to tears) by her beauty, my lack of it, by what they would describe as 'love'. But what she could not say to them was that it was not anything half so noble. It was not anything she could help or alter.

'I think you should let us have him now,' Marc Laroche said when he had swaddled me, not expertly.

'I'm OK,' she said. She took the bundle and sat with me on the straight-backed chair.

'Just the same,' he said.

She looked at his long bony fingers as they stretched towards her. She shook her head.

'OK,' he said. 'Just take your time.'

But no one moved. They stayed like this, not speaking, for the best part of half an hour.

'Well . . .' Marc Laroche said at last. 'I think we might put him in the nursery now. What do you think?'

My maman shook her head. 'I want him in my room.'

'Listen,' Marc Laroche said, 'you've got to face it, Felicity . . .'

'In my room,' my maman said.

'It will be even harder for you later.'

'In my room.'

My maman got her way. She kept the crib hard against her bed. In the night there were feeding difficulties because of deficiencies in my lips.

She tried to stay awake all through the night, but finally she could not keep her eyes open. She slept with an arm and a leg placed protectively across the top of the bassinet.

I was safe. Laroche and Eisner were home in their beds, relieved, you can bet, not to have jeopardized their careers with an illegal action, but at seven o'clock the next morning, just as the night staff were leaving, when the first floor-polishers and vacuum cleaners brought a level of confusion into previously calm corridors, a santamarie tried to move Tristan to the nursery. There was no evidence that the woman meant to kill me, but my maman was not taking any chances. She picked me up – I weighed only four pounds – and walked out of the hospital.

There had been no time to try to find her tote bag – she arrived on the street in her hospital wrap. But although she was nearly naked at the back, she held herself in such a way that you would never think the wrap was more than just a summer dress. And as, walking to the hospital, she had hidden the feeling of the pumpkin between her legs, she now hid the fact that she was aching and sore from labour and everything in her wanted to shuffle, not along a public street, but in some quiet protected environment with shiny floors and pink-faced women in white uniforms.

She barely noticed the alien Sirkus. The river bed existed like some bright white over-exposed photograph. She carried Tristan along the sandy path in a kind of daze, and when he vomited an acrid substance the colour of summer grass, she wiped the muck with her finger. There was not much of it – but it was bright and inexplicable and she was frightened.

The Boulevard des Indiennes was filled with large trucks loaded with reinforcing mesh. She got caught for a minute on the traffic island before limping across to Gazette Street which was, at this hour, dominated by dull corrugated walls of metal shutters and roller doors and lined by bright red and silver taxis, all double-parked, driverless, complacently illegal. Her destination was number 34 – the Feu Follet. The posters on the cracked concrete wall outside advertised the Scottish Play with previews beginning on this first Monday in January. In normal circumstances Felicity would have played Lady Macbeth, but she had taken the part of First Witch in respect of her condition.

Between the striking black and white posters was a rusty roller door. Above the roller door was a second floor with six high, gracefully arched windows. The building was topped by the tower in which I had been conceived (and in which, in the time of the Circus School, the great Ducrow was said to have seduced the contortionist Gabrielle Dubois). The rest of the company lived in little monks' cells scattered through the building. There was no nursery ready. Everyone had been too busy getting ready for the Scottish play.

Felicity walked carefully up the brick ramp and let herself in through the small door inside the big rusty roller. Holding my soft head protectively, she edged through the dark dusty space which was called 'the foyer', and walked painfully – her inner thighs hurt, her vulva hurt, every step hurt – up the wide wooden stairs to the second floor where the air was scented with patchouli oil, dirty laundry, incense, cigarette smoke, musk, and the insidious but persistent odour of a blocked toilet which was the subject of

19

dispute with both plumbers and debt badgers. The poky cells in which the great Ducrow had once housed his students were now covered with posters both political and theatrical, the brick walls with spray painting, the frosted glass with glass beads, cane blinds, folk prints.

When my maman arrived on the second floor she was already beyond exhaustion. She had no plan. She began the narrow splintered stairs up to the tower thinking only about the impossibility of the next step, and once she finally gained the safety of the tower, she did something she only did when making love – she locked the door.

Then she laid me on the bed, lay down beside me, and began to cry. I woke and vomited – more green stuff. Sobbing, she wiped me clean with a pillowslip. She had no tissues, no bandocks, nothing but a bottle of eau mineral for herself to drink.

When the company, alerted by our crying, came tapping on the door, she would not let them in or even whisper through the door.

Afterwards she pretended that this had all been part of her plan – her dramatic announcement later in the evening of that day. This was how she liked history told, but the truth was, she lost her nerve.

Bill and Vincent were called. They left gifts at the top of the stairs – a pack of bandocks, a tape of meditation music, a cellular telephone – but she stayed behind the locked door, ashamed, frightened, shaken. When the hospital sent a pair of doctors and a Gardiacivil demanding that the baby be handed over for special treatment, she left them hammering on the door.

Vincent tried to talk to them, but he had no status with the authorities and so learned nothing, only that there was something possibly illegal about the baby's care.

The company did a line run for the show in the afternoon. I slept from two until six-thirty, and when I woke Felicity was already putting on her make-up.

5

Wally had first fallen in love with my maman from a theatre seat. To say he worshipped her is not hyperbole, but although his love was not requited he carried his sorrow without complaint, revealing it only in the slight widow's hump that began to show across his shoulders. It was a load, always present, a pain, a pressure, and it was this which drove his engine, which kept him moving, dancing, talking, joking, as if the sheer pain would be too much if he sat down and let himself feel it.

No matter what went wrong, he was always positive. He believed, or said he did, that what happened was always for the best, that you could triumph through the expenditure of will and optimism. He spent his days and nights in ceaseless motion across the cobbled floors, through the labyrinthine corridors, running up the stairs, down the stairs, fretting, sweating, and he spent my first day on earth being positive, not merely about my maman, or the Gardiacivil who were ominously knocking at her door, but about all the things which will concern a small theatre before press night – the First Witch's absence, Macduff's sore throat, the props list, the hot weather, the noisy air-conditioning, the bookings. At half past six he was in the first-floor office, manning the telephones.

On the ground floor, the doors of the hot little theatre were already open and a few of the actors – Banquo, Lennox, the Porter – were on the sawdust stage, pacing, whooping, publicly performing all the normally private activities that go under the name of 'warming up'.

Wally found the ASM smoking in one of the old stables and sent her out for bandocks for 'the baby'. He filled two jugs with water and ice. And in all of this he kept up a manic, snapping sort of fret, a hand-clapping, irritable, sometimes sensible commentary. When the ASM returned, Wally took the bandocks, the jugs, and personally delivered them to my maman's door. A moment later he was back in the office, slipping a red usher's waistcoat over his white T-shirt. He kicked off his rubber thongs. The white phone rang. Claire Chen took it. The black phone rang – four more seats. Wally took the credit card details and smoked a cancerette right down to its fat white filter.

He put his elbows on the long bench and looked out through the high arched windows, across the rusting rooftops, the trawler hulls beached at the end of concrete driveways, the dense shows of bougainvillaea, the wind-torn palms, all the way to the wide mud-flats where his great-great-grandparents had met, ankle deep in mud, their backs bowed by the weight of 'blue briques', the little gastropods which the Imperial Dye Works bought for a penny a sack.

It was in Gazette Street that his grandparents' union had been 'gazetted' in a weatherboard government office – number twenty-eight – which was now the site of a bankrupt panel-beating business in front of whose closed roller doors the cast of the Scottish Play was presently demystifying itself. Macduff – tall, anachronistically bespectacled, cadaverously thin – was playing cricket with . . . a busload of noisy giggling schoolkids who had somehow got themselves tickets to a press night.

'Shit,' said Wally. 'Rug rats.'

Claire Chen put her plump little hand across the phone and looked down into the street.

'Get rid of them,' she said.

'Yes, your majesty.'

'Get rid of them *please*.'

'Get rid of who?' It was Bill Millefleur in his Macbeth costume – pale, nervous, sweating inside the sculpted foam rubber.

'It's not who,' Wally said. 'It's what. Get rid of what. Ask me.'

'Tsk,' Bill said.

'Paper-clips,' Wally said, kneeling to pick up one from the floor. He took Bill's arm and drew him away from the window to a place where the actor would not be upset by the sight of schoolchildren. As Wally had a much caricatured tendency to furtiveness, a habit of bringing his mouth up to your ear to communicate to you the most public facts, his behaviour did not seem unusual. 'We've had a major problem with the paper-clips, frere,' he hissed to Bill, still holding his arm tightly. 'I wondered if I could get your advice.'

'You want to talk to me about *paper-clips*?'

'You don't have time for that sort of stuff? OK, I understand. So how is the suit? Is it too hot?' He began patting at Bill's sculpted foam rubber like a tailor, shifting the shoulders, smoothing the chest.

'Stop it, frere. I've got to talk to you about the set.'

'The set. Of course. Let's get out of here.'

Bill didn't move. 'I don't like that platform. It's lethal.'

Claire Chen placed her phone on the cradle. 'Oh great . . .'

Wally winked at Claire and made a face and pushed his hair back from his hair line so it stood high on his head. He raised his ginger eyebrows at her, rolled his eyes, trying to signal that he did not want Bill looking in her direction.

To Wally, Claire said, 'What?'

To Bill, 'Who was the macho man who didn't need the rails?'

'It's OK,' Wally said. 'Just leave this stuff to me.'

'It is not OK,' Claire said, 'to say one thing at a company meeting and then come in here half an hour before the curtain in a funk.'

'A what?' Bill said, stepping towards her.

'A funk,' she said, picking up a phone. 'Hello, Feu Follet.'

'It's OK,' Wally said.

But it was not OK – Bill was staring out the window past Claire's bare back.

'Oh, I see,' he said. 'Very nice. You've got rug rats. I see. So,' he said to Wally, 'get rid of them.'

'Frere, you know that ain't possible.'

'Well I'm not playing to them.'

'Talk to Felicity,' Claire said, her hand across the mouthpiece.

Bill looked at Wally, his black eyes fast and anxious. 'Please, frere. This is *press night*.'

'Talk to Felicity,' Claire said, holding the phone under her smooth round chin. 'Sorry, could you hold. It's not just rug rats,' she said, 'it's other stuff. For God's sake, Bill, surely *you* can go into her room. *Please*?'

'What's that meant to mean?' Bill said. You could see his colour glowing through his make-up. The second phone began to ring. Wally answered it and put it on hold.

Claire took the phone from Wally. 'I want to know,' she said, 'is Felicity playing First Witch or not? If I have to do her lines as well, I want to know. Surely you can go in and ask her. Isn't that clear enough?'

'No.' Bill found a paper-clip and began twisting it. 'It is not clear.'

'It's your baby, isn't it?' Claire said, and held his eye.

'Hello,' she said, still looking hard at Bill. 'Hello, Feu Follet.'

'No,' Bill said to Claire as she hung up, 'it's *not* my baby – not necessarily.'

'Not *necessarily*?' Claire said.

Wally stared at the strong body, the intelligent face with its sensual lips, at this young man who had been graced by God in so

23

many ways, not least with the pleasure of holding Felicity Smith in his arms.

'*What?*' Bill demanded of him. His lips had lost their shape. 'What's so weird about that? It's true. All I said was, not *necessarily.*'

Wally hesitated. 'Did you talk to the Gardiacivil? Did they frighten you, mo-ami?' he asked. 'They don't know anything. They're only penguins. They're not doctors.'

'No one frightened me,' Bill said. 'What's everyone acting so weird about?' He picked up a paper-clip from the floor and handed it to Wally. 'If anyone is frightened, it's you two. Look at you.'

'The curtain's up in fifteen minutes,' Claire said. 'If you want to change the platform you've got twelve minutes to do it.'

'You want to talk about this platform?' Wally said.

'Sure,' Bill said.

'Well come on, mo-ami.' Wally cuffed him lightly on the head – he could not help it. 'We'll sit up there together.'

'I don't have a problem sitting on it,' Bill said, rubbing his head and frowning. 'I have a problem fighting on it.'

'I know,' Wally said, 'I know.' As he walked out across the cobbled path and pushed through the velvet curtain into the sweet pine smell of the deep, sawdust-covered stage, he took his tension in his shoulders, pulled his biceps in against his ribs, and when he began his ascent towards the platform he was a production manager going to fix a problem. He had no intention of quarrelling with an actor before a curtain.

# 6

To picture Bill and Wally as they climbed up the set of the Scottish Play, you need first to know that the theatre was constructed in the largest of the old Circus School rings. The ceiling was a good forty feet from the sawdust ring and around the ring were seats – not the original bleachers, which had been termite-infested, but in the original configuration, that human circle which the Voorstand Sirkus abandoned but which gave the much humbler circuses of Efica their live, electrically charged audiences.

Many of the Feu Follet actors had some sort of connection with the indigenous circus and my mother used to like to shape her plays so that they used or developed, wherever possible, these disappearing skills. Our Shakespeare had tumbling, slack ropes, posturing, trapeze and general acrobatics, and in the case of the Scottish Play she had designed a kind of jungle gym which could suggest a room in the palace, say, but also a scaffolding on which some fight scenes could be choreographed.

The idea was that Macbeth would work himself into higher and higher and more 'dangerous' positions until, on a platform just under the lighting rig, in his final conflict with Macduff, he would tumble and fall, not into their normal safety net – there was not room to stretch it – but into an eight-by-eight footer they had borrowed from the Theatre for the Deaf.

Wally, as everybody knew, was never happy with heights. He, the 'Human Ball', was observed to avoid long ladders and lighting rigs whenever possible, and even though he had been aware of the safety problems with Bill's platform, he had not climbed to inspect it himself, but had sent Sparrowgrass Glashan to deal with it instead.

But now, of course, he had no choice. He climbed, following the glow-tape in the gloom.

On the platform, forty feet above the audience, breathing the hot air under the cobwebbed corrugated roof, he searched for the new black safety wires he had ordered to be strung around the perimeter of the platform. With the lights on pre-set, it was gloomy up here. There was glow-tape marking the platform perimeters, but the wires were painted black. He searched for them with his hand, a little giddily.

'How's that?' he said, finding a wire and twanging it, as if he were touching it only for the purpose of demonstrating its strength. 'Does that solve your safety problem?'

Bill ran his hand over the wires. He knelt so he could inspect the point where they were anchored to the wall. He leaned against them, gingerly at first and then more aggressively. He bounced once or twice, like a boxer against the ropes, but when he had done with his tests he withheld his judgement. Instead he turned, and looked down into the gathering audience.

'There's no point you being angry,' he said at last. 'Obviously, there's something wrong with that baby and denial isn't going to help anyone.'

'How's the wire, mo-ami?'

'Tray bon, thank you.'

'That's good,' Wally said, and turned to leave.

'It *might* be Vincent's baby,' the actor said. 'No one can say it isn't.'

Wally was kneeling on the platform, getting ready to descend.

Bill said, 'You needn't look at me like I'm so weird.'

Wally rose. 'Listen, frere – you've got a show to do in ten minutes.'

'What's the matter with you?' Bill said. 'Who are you to look so fucking righteous?'

Wally knew better than to argue with him, especially not now – he was like a drunk, full of chemicals – ten minutes before the curtain on press night.

'Mollo-mollo,' he said.

'Mollo bullshit,' Bill said. 'Why is everyone pretending there's nothing wrong?'

'If there's something wrong, mo-frere,' Wally said (gently he hoped), 'she's going to need you. You can't afford to be afraid.'

Bill stared at Wally, his black eyes suddenly brimming with poisonous emotion. The look was intense, unwavering.

He jumped. The platform shook. Wally put his hand out to hold the wire.

'Look at you, you old twat,' Bill said. 'Don't lecture me about fear. You're too piss-weak to even check the scaffold. You sent the Sparrow here instead.'

'You knew it was fixed? You knew?'

'Don't lecture me about fear.' Bill jumped again. The whole platform kicked and swayed, listing over nearly twenty degrees before coming back to a shuddering horizontal. 'What ever made you think you had all this wisdom to impart to me?'

Wally put his arms out, found a wire, steadied himself, looked down into the half-full house. There he saw a familiar beard-fringed countenance scowling up from the front row. It was Vincent, stewing in his own negativity.

When he saw Vincent's defeated face, something changed in Wally. He was still afraid, it's true. He hated heights, feared the giddy emptiness of air. But when he realized that Vincent had already abandoned me and my mother to the whims of fate, he went a little crazy.

Wally loved my maman, and it was this powerful and secret emotion that moved him now. When he began to speak to Bill he no longer cared that they were only minutes from the curtain.

'It's true – I don't like heights,' he said to Bill, and something in his manner transmitted itself to the actor who extended a placating arm.

'Come on, mo-ami . . .'

'What is love?' Wally said.

'I'm sorry . . .'

'When you love,' he answered, 'you don't care. If you're thinking about your own prestige, your own position, that's not love.' Wally was grinning now. He was bright red and sweating, he had purple fungicide between his toes. The long hair on the back of his head was lifting off his neck. He went to the edge and stood with his toes sticking out over the edge of the platform. Down below, directly below, was the eight-by-eight foot net he had finally 'borrowed'.

'Give me your hand,' Bill said.

Wally's big pale lips twisted in a smile, a kind of grimace. 'I'm here for the long haul.'

'Sure you are.'

'You want to know what love is?' Wally said.

'Wally,' Bill said, 'don't do this to me.'

But Wally did do this. Showed him exactly what his love was made of. First he grinned, showed his two gold teeth to Bill, then he winked, then he knelt and slipped under the bottom wire.

That's how it is when you have three men around one woman – a general excess – passion, foolishness, misunderstanding – the half-assembled audience, imagining the show had begun, stood in their seats and cheered.


# 7

When Wally leaped, what Vincent saw was suicide, gentian violet between its naked toes. He saw the red waistcoat, the huge bunioned feet daubed violet, the violiniste production manager descending like some dreadful cock from heaven.

If he had been previously aware of the eight-by-eight foot safety net, he now forgot it, and he was in any case too depressed to accommodate the notion that the leap might be a declaration of love.

When the audience applauded, Vincent was shocked. When Wally bounced off the net and bowed to him, Vincent felt out of joint, confused, angry. The violiniste's arm was broken – it was hanging like a rag – but he was grinning and running from the stage like some *space creature*. Vincent could not hope to understand. He looked around, surprised to see the *Neufzine* critic, a woman not normally sympathetic to the Feu Follet, smiling broadly and applauding. Then the drums started and Vincent gave himself over to his greater fear – the one that had obsessed him all afternoon, the one that had hung around him like a cloud since he had seen the Gardiacivil banging at my mother's door – that his 'son' was somehow monstrous.

It is clear enough by now that I am not Vincent Theroux's son, but at the time nothing was so simple. My maman had imagined both of her lovers to be, in different ways, my father. Bill, her public man, was strong and beautiful. Vincent, her secret lover, was rich and intellectual. And if she had conceived me with Bill, it was Vincent she had discussed me with most often. Vincent was married already, but he wanted me, more than anything he could imagine. Bill was only twenty-two, but Vincent *wanted the role*.

My maman wanted me too, but after *Lear*, after *Mother Courage*, after the tour to Nez Noir. She scheduled me, rescheduled. She named me Tristan* in the summer of 366, even as she postponed me. I was Tristan before my egg was hit, Tristan before they knew if I was a boy or a girl.

The moment I was conceived, I was Vincent's little liefling.† He treasured me, the idea of me, just as he might a folk painting, offered by a dealer by transparency, purchased on recommendation, presently being crated in another country. Ever since the day he had seen the small phial of urine turn a gorgeous lilac colour, he had drawn on this reservoir of wonder and joy which was nothing less than my existence.

---

* *Published speeches of Felicity Smith suggest that Tristan Smith was named after Tristan Devalier, the leader of a calamitous strike at the Imperial Dye Works in 137 EC.*
† *'Liefling' is a common Voorstandish endearment, meaning 'darling'. It is unusual that Vincent Theroux, an ardent Efican nationalist, should use the term.*

And he had maintained this feeling until he had – one hour before the curtain of the Scottish Play – met the Gardiacivil knocking on my maman's door. I am not suggesting that the sight of uniforms alone depressed him, but the Gardiacivil were no friends of the Feu Follet and he knew they were not delivering flowers. Indeed, they brought with them an administrator from the Mater Hospital and, it was this gen, kneeling on the top step so his fat lips were level with the keyhole, who gave Felicity Smith, actor-manager, a legal warning – that she would be held legally responsible for the death of the child should she refuse to provide it with the proper care for its condition.

'What condition?' Vincent asked.

But the three men had that dull, flat-faced look of policemen at murder scenes. They drew a line around themselves and their terrifying secret.

'Are you the father, Mr Theroux?'

Vincent was a married man, a public figure, the chief executive of Efica's largest pharmaceutical manufacturer.

'No,' he said. 'Of course not.'

The deputation wished Mr Theroux and Mr Paccione good day. As their footsteps echoed along the corridor below, Vincent heard a high warbling sound from the other side of the peeling brown door.

It was me.

It seemed to Vincent's ear that the noise I made was 'singing'. Not singing as in a song, but singing like a warble, not a new-born noise, something rather unusual.

One step lower, Wally was combing his hair excitedly. 'Listen,' he said. He slipped his comb back into his shirt pocket, and winked at Vincent. 'It's Tristan.'

But the hair on Vincent's neck was standing on end.

He turned and pushed past Wally, and fled into the theatre, and there he sat in his starbuck* for a whole hour, brooding that he could never love me. He was there when the actors began their warm-ups. He was there as the schoolchildren streamed into their

---

* Traditionally the Efican circuses offered the first two rows of seats with back supports. These seats, named starbucks or starbacks, were marked by one or a number of stencilled stars. In Voorstand, of course, all seats have backs and there are no starbucks. [TS]

29

seats, sunk in deep depression, and you can see, straight away, why it was necessary for my mother to choose two fathers.

Vincent's great fear about his own character was that he was too much of an aesthete, a perfectionist, that he had such an addiction to things beautiful that he could not go and buy a simple tea cup without returning with an object he would have, finally, to lock up in a museum case for fear that his breakfast tea would stain its delicate eggshell glaze.

It was this flaw in his character, he believed, which had wrecked his marriage. In his version of the story he had captured Natalie Lopale and 'installed her' in that beautiful modernist house on the banks of the Nabangari. The house had seamless transparent walls, and it stepped down towards the river in a series of platforms, each one artfully supported on the great round Pleistocene rocks by stainless-steel pegs.

It was conceited to make himself responsible for his wife's character, and crazy to imagine that his beautiful house could turn a warm and loving woman into a status-crazed neurotic with a twenty-by-thirty foot wardrobe. Vincent, however, believed both these things.

He gave great weight to his single two-dimensional flaw. And he sat in the dark believing he could never love me if I was not perfect. He was such a good man in so many ways, humane, generous, humble around artists, passionate about justice and equality, but really – what a weasel.

He sat in his seat as the drums beat louder, waiting for the darkness to descend.

# 8

In the darkened theatre you could smell the freshly disturbed sawdust and know the actors were taking up their places.

Then a lightning flash: two witches, Second and Third.

The Witches held a six-by-three foot sheet of shining gauge iron between them.* They made thunder with it. As the drumming reached its peak bright lights bounced off the flexing metal to make lightning.

* *Gauge iron is known to you in Voorstand as galvanized iron, an essential building material in many colonial countries including Efica. In Chemin Rouge we grow up*

30

The storm raged. As the lightning flashed, the First Witch appeared and disappeared in different poses – her birth-sore body wrapped in foam rubber, a laser gun across her back, a gas mask perching on her forehead, her face painted greasy red.

The Second and Third Witches threw the gauge iron to the sawdust-covered floor. When the drumming stopped, Vincent leaned forward in his starbuck, his hand underneath his ear.

He was convinced my maman had me with her on the stage, and he listened for my 'singing' beneath the text like you may listen for a burglar's footsteps under the noise of the vid. He waited in this strained, intense way throughout Scene II.

Then the drums came back. Then the Witches. The First Witch stood off to upstage left, in what was, technically, a weak position. Somehow she used it to dominate the stage. The Third and Second Witches leaped and screeched, but the First Witch was immobile, wrapped in rubber.

Then Macbeth came in with Banquo, one red, one blue, both of them sweating in their airless suits.

When the Third Witch went to say her line ('*Thou shalt get Kings, though thou be none*'), the First Witch stepped across and stole it from her.

'Thou shalt get Kings,' she said, and then revealed Tristan Smith in his hiding place, inside the cloak against her sweating breast. She held me up, high, turning slowly so I could be seen on all sides. She had one hand between my legs, the other behind my neck and head. A boy behind Vincent gave a grunt of fright.

Macbeth said, 'Oh God.' It was clearly audible.

The First Witch's eyes were opals, burning.

'Thou shalt get Kings, though thou be none,' she said, and thrust me out into the world.

ENTER TRISTAN SMITH – a gruesome little thing, slippery and sweating from his long enclosure in that rubber cloak, so truly horrible to look at that the audience can see the Witches must struggle to control their feelings of revulsion.

He is small, not small like a baby, smaller, more like one of those wrinkled furless dogs they show on television talk shows. His hair

---

*listening to deafening tropical rain on gauge-iron roofs, knowing what it is for roofs to rust, to leak, to lift in cyclones, to gleam in the sun.* [TS] is fair, straight, queerly thick. His eyes are pale, a quartz-bright white. They bulge intensely in his face. He has a baby's nose – but in the lower part of his severely triangular face there is, it seems, not sufficient skin. His face pulls at itself. He has no lips, but a gap in the skin that sometimes shows his toothless gums. He has, as make-up, two blue dots, one on each cheek.

Vincent saw him. His son. He saw the ghastly rib cage, saw his shrunken twisted legs, bowed under him, heard him make that noise he had called 'singing'.

Vincent put his hand up to his open mouth.

Tristan's forehead mirrored his, wrinkling like a piece of cloth. Then, from the depths of his turbulent stomach, he brought forth the business that was bothering him – yellow-green, strongly sulphurous. His mother did not notice it for a full minute, but when she did she smeared it on her cheeks – one stroke on each like a decorative scar – and blew kisses to the fellow in the front row dressed in black.

I did not come back on stage, but for Vincent the aesthete, who felt he had invented me, it was a kind of hell. He was left alone with his thoughts and theories in the dark – a two-hour production with no interval.

## 9

So let me ask you, did you notice, in the theatre, how the witch's suit was red? A slightly plummy red? Did it signify something political – the red, also the blue?

Meneer, Madam, forgive me – but if you had a little more knowledge of the countries whose destiny you control, I could get on with my story. I am eager to let you see how my mother and I abandoned the stage and retired to the tower apartment, but it is now obvious you know nothing of Red and Blue and therefore nothing about Efica. As you yourselves were once subjects of the Dutch you will understand my passion to set this right before we move on – it is the periphery shouting at the centre, and you will forgive me, I hope, for surmising that you know even less about Efica than the British and the French who colonized the eighteen islands, murdered its indigenous inhabitants, set up dye works and prisons, and then abandoned us as being an unsuccessful idea.

In the dreadful years of 90, 91, 95, our population nearly starved – French dyers, English convicts – it made no difference. We were left with little seed grain, no ships, abandoned like a folly three thousand miles from home. In the great European Exhibition of 102, none of our European parents devoted so much as a bioscope image to our existence, while we, even while our children's bellies swelled and our mothers' breasts dried up, *comforted* ourselves with Shakespeare and Molière.

Three hundred years later the same habits persist on both sides. And even you – literate, liberal, students of the Sirkus and the pages of the *Saarlim Verlag* – will need a little assistance in spite of the fact that we both speak, more or less, the same language.

If you follow foreign affairs you may know that we are a country whose southern islands are granite, that the granite is filled with caves which the English once found attractive as ready-made prisons, and that you, from the year 358, have found useful as a place to lay your miles of 'navigation cable.'*

Whatever this navigation cable does, your government will not say, not even to our government, but you value it immensely, and value our 'Red' governments which let you keep all this shiny metal lying in our guts. Red? Did I say 'red'? I did, Meneer, Madam. It is red I wish to speak of now.

If you make anything red in Efica, it means something particular, but not what you are presently imagining. It was red dye-stuffs the French came to get, the reason they shanghaied the master dyers of Rheims and shipped them to Chemin Rouge, the reason you will sometimes find Efica on old French maps named 'Rouge Asie'. It was red that Louis Quatorze wanted, and red he found in the little yellow-flowered cactuses which grew on Efica.

Even after Louis found easier ways to get red at home, the red dye works continued to do business with Europe and the colour

* *The Voorstandish Navy's ELF-FOLK (ELF for Extra Low Frequency) PROJECT has remained a mystery to the Efican people until 427, as we go to print. We now know that 2,400 miles of insulated cable was threaded through our nation's belly. The cable was grounded at each end in the dry bed-rock of Inkerman, thus turning our most populous island into a giant antenna. The low conductivity of Efican granite allowed for the more efficient generation of extra low frequency waves and enabled the Voorstandish Navy to communicate with its* SNEEK 77 *submarines at depths of 400 feet.*

red begat its own establishment in Efica – the owners of the so-called *Imperial* Dye Works who produced it. It was these local capitalists who called in European armies on three occasions to help them put down the Blue factions.

You may have noticed that poor Banquo wore blue. It was the colour blue that Wally's great-great-grandparents were collecting, out on the mudflats with their jute sacks. The colour blue, extracted from shellfish by a stinking process, was the poor people's dye, harvested originally by ex-convicts. Blue has been the party of idealism, of reform.* Blue governments have given women the vote, a thirty-five hour week, a national health scheme.

To be consistent, my mother should have made me up with red – after all, I was a witch's child – but she could not put that hateful colour on my skin, hence the two blue spots. And although many of the company found the symbolism confusing, and some others were critical of the manner in which she had introduced me to the world, it was – they all agreed – just like her.

It was not like her to limp up the stairs after Scene III and leave her comrades one witch short for the remainder of the play, but that is precisely what she did. She laid her sweating baby in the crib. She lay down on the bed herself, curling up, her knees almost touching her chin. Her red make-up was still on her face. Her body was still clad in foam rubber, strapped with canvas. She pulled a pillow across her eyes and lay still, but only for a moment. Almost immediately she began to forage amongst the rumpled sheets, finally finding what she had been looking for – a small plastic bag of very dry marijuana (not like her either – she had stopped smoking on the day she knew she had finally conceived). Then, with her make-up still caked on her face, she rolled what was not the first cigarette of that particular day. It was a small cigarette, but the ganja was from Nez Noir, the northernmost island, and was therefore very strong.

In a short while the entire company would come up the stairs and enter the tower. It was what happened after each production.

---

* *The Blue Party is formally known as the Efican Democratic Party, or EDP. Its supporters are more familiarly referred to as Blueys or Muddies, the latter term providing a direct link back to the men and women who gathered those 'briques bleus' in the mangrove mudflats in the early days of settlement.*

Unless she was to be a total coward, she would have to unlock the door.


## 10

Vincent skulked around the windy little cobbled courtyard, while all the cast and half the audience pushed up the noisy staircase to the tower to see exactly who I was. It was the tradition at the Feu Follet that anybody could come up to the tower on opening night – audience members, critics, visiting actors, spies from the VIA and DoS* – and anybody could give notes – Moey Perelli's dad, for instance. Vincent too, and this was a privilege that he relished. He was the theatre's biggest single patron, but on opening night he always sat on the dusty floor in his good black suit. He drank wretched wine from paper cups without ever puckering his fastidious lips. He seemed so confident, so worldly, wealthy but hip. He had such a detailed knowledge of theatre history, an excellent eye, a real feeling for the moment when a scene lost energy or focus. No one but my mother knew that each opening night he had to steel himself to face 'them', to win the respect of actors of half his age, wit or taste.

And because of these windmills he felt he must dispense with, the sessions in the tower had always been the high points of his life – first the discussion, the exercise of his considerably theatrical education and sensitivity, and then, some time before dawn, his secret love-making with the leading lady beneath the turning ceiling fan. He was addicted to the whole process, and no matter how he anguished over the deceitful phone calls to his wife, he could not bring himself to give up either my mother or the theatre.

On the press night for *Macbeth*, however, he stayed down in the foyer. He pretended to read the tattered hand-written notices on the walls. He jiggled his car keys in the big pockets of his fashionably baggy black trousers.

He could not love his child – he was clear on that. It was not

* *Voorstand Intelligence Agency and Department of Supply, the latter being the Efican secret service. The two services worked closely at all times, it sometimes being said that the DoS's loyalty lay with the VIA, not with the elected government of Efica.*

that he would not *like* to, but that he could not. It was his flaw, his weakness, not admirable, but beyond him. And if he could not love the baby – one step led to the next – Felicity would not love him. He had seen it in her eyes on stage when she pasted that vile green muck on to her cheeks and pointed at him. It was not to do with text or character, but to do with him and her – he understood her perfectly.

But he, also, understood himself – he could not walk up the stairs. Nor could he leave the building, for if he left the building now, tonight, then that would be it, the end, and he would not permit it to be the end. He went to the open door and looked balefully at the last of the theatre patrons, a man and woman, standing in the middle of the street and talking in the sweet salty air.

'Croco cristi,' he said to himself, but more loudly than he intended. The man turned sharply to look at him, and Vincent thrust his hands deeper into his pockets and turned back to face the bleak little foyer with its ragged self-important notices.

'Croco cristi,' he whispered. He undid his wide leather belt in that elaborate way of his which always suggested a man about to undress for bed.

'God damn.'

He tightened the belt a notch.

What happened next was not very much – his mouth tightened a little. But a second later he was crossing to the staircase in three strides.

Next he was ascending the stairs. Next, revealing a more athletic frame than his bulk might have promised, he was striding along the deserted first-floor corridor. His squeaking crepe soles echoed in the empty couchettes, and then receded as he climbed the steep narrow stairs which led to the roar of conversation.

The tower room was small, ten foot by ten foot six, and by the time the chief executive officer of Efica's largest aspirin manufacturer had reached the top there were fifty people crammed inside. One step below the door sill, his courage failed him. He stopped, marooned it seemed, jiggling his keys.

He could not see Felicity, but he could hear her. There was a stirring in the crowd – the tall, gaunt Sparrow Glashan stepped aside, and there she was, totally alone, exhausted, with the spooky white-eyed baby on her crumpled bed.

36

How he loved her, loved her at that instant, beyond anything he had known before.

Felicity saw him. She caught his eye. He did not know how to look at her. His own eyes wobbled, then dropped. He stepped into the room and busied himself at the drinks table. He took a paper cup and filled it brimful of dark red wine.

When he next looked up, the crowd had blocked his view again, and he could hear Felicity asking someone to phone the hospital again to see when Wally's arm would be attended to. Her Voorstand accent was clear and crisp. It cut through the humming, sighing Efican voices like a silver knife.

He stepped back into the doorway and raised himself on his toes. Someone had, at last, taken pity on Felicity – Claire Chen. Vincent had always thought of Claire Chen as a limpet on Felicity's life – low-life dramas, breakdowns, abortions, bail money. But now she was the one who sat on the bed and laid her ringed hand on the baby's foot.

When she did this, the room quietened.

She began to stroke the baby's twisted foot. 'Isn't it amazing?' she said. You could hear her nerviness. 'All the bones and skin,' she said.

Felicity asked Claire, 'Would you like to hold him?'

Sparrow Glashan moved sideways and blocked Vincent's view again. Vincent left the doorway and pushed in past Annie McManus.

'Sure,' Claire said, 'I'll hold him.'

As the baby passed from its mother its spindly arms sprang out like a spider and Claire flinched and screwed up her face. The actors watched. Vincent watched. He could see by the way she pulled her chin into her neck – everything in her wanted to thrust the child away.

Claire did the thing Vincent knew he was expected to do himself – touched the lipless little tragedy, stroked its gaunt little praying mantis head. It was very quiet in the square, high-ceilinged little room.

'See,' Felicity said, speaking generally, smiling, fondly, like a mother.

'Feel,' Claire invited, her little brown eyes flicking about the room – she had done the brave thing, but she did not want to do it a second longer. 'It's so amazing.'

Vincent felt the crowd stir and shift. He imagined eyes looking for him.

'Feel,' Claire repeated. Vincent looked down at the floor, avoiding her eyes.

Annie McManus turned and looked at him. Her pretty face had no expression – she did not know he was Felicity's lover, no one did – but Vincent was convinced the opposite was the case and he pushed forward, to escape her. He bumped into the critic for the *Neufzine*, who turned, and then, misunderstanding his intention, stepped to one side to let him through. A path then opened up before him, and he walked it – what else was he to do? – squeaking on his crepe-soled shoes.

At the bed he looked into my mother's eyes, and gave a melancholy kind of shrug which gave no indication of the wild, confused state of his emotions.

But then he held out his square, soft hands – their palms soft as the underbelly of an animal – and fitted them around Tristan's chest cage, hooked under my arms, and lifted me out of Claire Chen's sweating embrace, slowly, smoothly into the air.

When he had me held aloft, all he could think was that he was going to faint.

No one spoke, no one made a sound. They left him there, alone, teetering on the edge. He glanced around the room, his eyes weak with need, his mouth oddly shapeless. Only Moey Perelli gave him any sign – pushed his own mouth into the shape of a grin.

'He has intelligent eyes,' Vincent said. 'He's not beautiful, but he has intelligent eyes.' And then he embraced me. He was harsh and awkward – pushed his beard into my eyes and ears, grazed my skin, held me too tight, nearly tripped as he tried to walk a little closer to Felicity. He landed heavily on the bed. Felicity stretched out her light, tense hand and grasped at his knee.

Moey began to talk, very loudly, about his security dossier (which he claimed to have seen), and somebody pulled a cork from a bottle of case-latrine.

'He has extraordinary eyes,' said Vincent. It was not easy for him. It took everything he had. He sat beside Felicity and made a little seat for me with his fat hairy arm. He supported my head with his fleshy pectorals.

38

Felicity held his knee and smiled and bit her lip.

Moey came – his head shining now he had removed his wig – and held out a long finger with wide tombstone fingernails.

Vincent took Felicity's hand – not something he normally did in company. 'He has a strong grip,' he said.

Felicity nodded, and blew her nose.

'Whose turn is it to pick up the reviews?' she asked.


## 11

What Bill could not stand was: why must they deny there had been a tragedy? Why must they all smile and coo? When Felicity put out her hand and tried to hold Vincent's old fat knee, he felt he was in an alien country where you could not even guess what might be going on. So while he believed he could *feel* the horror running through the room like a shiver, all he saw was smiling faces. All these actors – not one of them in touch with what they felt.

'I'll get the zines,' he said.

'No, mo-chou. You should be here with us.'

'It's no trouble,' Bill said, his eyes full of poison. 'I need the air.'

Felicity frowned at him. He saw the need in her eyes, but she was sitting next to Vincent and Vincent had his fat valsir where he was so clever at placing it – on the moral high ground.

Three minutes later, alone on the ramp in front of the theatre, Bill unscrewed his hip flask and took a long swig, spat the wine out on the bricks.

The Feu Follet bus, a three-ton Haflinger with big slab sides and small decal-spotted windows, was parked right in front of the theatre. He found Felicity's sandals sitting on the dashboard. He picked up and flung them deep into the dark body of the van.

He let the clutch out so hard you could feel the prop shaft thunk and he accelerated out into Gazette Street in loud metallic first gear, shifting noisily into second as he passed the brightly illuminated taxi base. He pulled across the tram tracks and turned right, away from the Voorstand Sirkus and the Mater Hospital down towards the port.

He thought: that's it, I'll keep on driving and never come back, but the truth was, of all my maman's admirers, he was the one

39

who needed her the most. She had altered his life. She had taken him into the company when he was nineteen years old, a cambruce. He had fallen out with a travelling circus over his wages. Fearing a beating from the proprietor and his brothers, he had run away to Chemin Rouge and there he had wandered down Gazette Street and discovered a free Wednesday-night performance of *Hamlet*.

He was dirty, starved, down to 120 pounds when he saw my maman play Ophelia. He sat in the dark, Row P, and fell in love.

That night he slept in the lane behind the Feu Follet. Next day he walked out into the suburbs and stole roses, hollyhocks, snapdragons, whatever he could find, and next evening he brought them to my maman at the Feu Follet. It was the same the next night, and the night after that.

At first she joked about him, teased him, said she was too old for him. But she never seemed too old to him. He loved the language she used, the language she knew. He told my maman he was the best voltige* artist in the southern hemisphere. And although he had never been inside a theatre until he walked into the Feu Follet, he told her he was going to be the best actor in Chemin Rouge. He asked her for books about acting and she could not refuse him. She gave him her precious first-edition Stanislavsky with her neck tingling and her eyes feeling loose and unfocused. He read the whole three volumes of *An Actor Prepares*, one volume a day. He argued with it. He was very handsome. He had a long flexible back, and dancing passionate eyes that never left her face. He was nineteen, a baby, but she could not withstand it.

The first time they made love he told her he would die for her and she wept in his arms.

Later, she read him *Paradise Lost* in bed, her head resting on his smooth and luminous chest. She bought him two dictionaries, the big two-volume Oxford and the smaller Efican University edition with its creolized French and English prison slang.

He took her to a dressage ring in Goat Marshes and taught her voltige. She learned it too, without the benefit of a meccano.† She

---

* *In the Efican circus, voltige describes a broad series of acrobat acts performed from and around horses – voltige infernale, voltige Tcherkesse, voltige à la Richard etc. etc.*

† *Invented by Spencer Q. Stokes to aid in training bare-back riders. A central post supports an arm like the jib of a crane from which the student is suspended.*

was twenty-eight, knew nothing about real circus, but she had such guts, such style. Within a week they were performing 'two men high', round and round, no one watching.

He took her out into the cantons to the petites tentes. She did not see the meanness of the circus, the lying proprietors, the stinking caravans, the brutal beatings Bill had suffered. She saw instead the discipline, the lack of affectation, the highly critical audiences who could compare a given performance with others from a hundred years before. Seeking to invent an Efican national style in drama, she began then to incorporate circus skills into her shows. Not too much later she bought this old Haflinger bus and began to take her circus-theatre back into the little towns.

It was the only vehicle the Feu Follet owned. There was nothing lighter or easier to use when they went shopping or, as now, to collect the zines. Bill bounced over the train tracks, and followed the old Ridge Line Road down into the port of Chemin Rouge. He drove past flour mills, catalytic convertors as pretty as cruise ships decked with lights, oil terminals with their long pipes running out into the night. He drove, thinking of Vincent.

He never had liked Vincent. From the very beginning, even when he had thought he was usurping him, he had been threatened by his wealth, his educated accent, his confidence. Tonight in the tower, he had let Vincent win again. Bill had walked away. He always walked away. He didn't know any other solution. He felt sour shame come to take his cooling skin. He was sorry at the injuries he caused, the toxic things that had passed between them, in their eyes.

He loved her. He could not bear to see her with Vincent, the fucking patapoof. He had been counting on the baby to change all that. It was his baby, *necessarily*. He was the father. He had built domestic pictures he dared not even name himself. But when he saw the real child – on stage, in the middle of his performance – his first feeling, in the middle of the horror, was outrage, the sense of theft, as if his happy life had been stolen from him.

Then – for ten, twenty seconds – he was capable of anything. He wanted to hurt her, break her. He was a frightened soldier in a burning village.

For a moment, in front of one hundred and eighty people, he was mad. And then, slowly, a bit at a time, he turned his rage away from Felicity, and turned it back into his performance.

The wind was warm down in the port. It smelt of heavy oil and sea salt. He drove with the window rolled down, clattering past the bleak waterfront bars with their yellow tiled walls and used-car-yard bunting, heading towards the *Zinebleu* sign where the review of *Macbeth* was already rolling off the presses. It was the quaint habit of the *Zinebleu* to adopt what it imagined was the Voorstand practice – they would not send a reviewer to 'press nights', only opening night. So they held the theatre page till half past ten and the poor suck-arse reviewer either scribbled his review in the dark, or – as Veronique Marchant had obviously done tonight – wrote most of it before the show began.

He picked up the zines and headed back up the Boulevard des Indiennes. He could not run away. He had to go back. But he was not going to lose to Vincent Theroux.

When he arrived back in the tower he had not only the zines but a brown paper bag full of bottles, and as he entered the little room he was pleased to learn that Vincent had been called home to wifey.

Felicity looked up and smiled, but he saw, already, the distance he had lost. He did not know how he knew this – a flattening of the cheeks, a tightening of the upper lips, a lack of animation in the eyes.

He threw the zines on the bed. The normal praise-addicts – Moey, Heather, Claire – all leapt upon them, but Bill kicked off his moccasins and sat cross-legged on the quilt, going through his bag of bottles.

'I have Rosemary oil,' he announced, 'Apricot Kernel, and Scented Olive. I think Rosemary is appropriate, don't you?'

'No, sweets,' Felicity said. He could see her trying not to offend him while she was, at the same time, shocked by what she thought he was suggesting.

'Come on, Flick, I'm not going to massage *you*.'

His own hands, when he held them out for the child, felt as dull and heavy as lead.

Felicity tucked the wrap around the child a little tighter. He was left with his hands held in the empty air.

'Come on,' he said.

Felicity's reluctance hurt him like almost nothing he could

remember. He felt his lip tremble, and when she gave him the child he actually wanted it, but could not bear to think she had given it to him because she saw this weakness.

His son was so light: a parcel of bad dreams.

'He's asleep,' she said.

If she meant *don't do it*, Bill did not get it.

'He'll like this,' he said.

He laid the parcel down and unwrapped it. The child had woken and was looking at him with those disconcerting marble-white eyes.

'Is it OK to massage him?' Felicity asked.

The chest cage did not seem right somehow. The skin seemed to hang there like rag on wire. The legs and feet were all wrong too. He could not look, but it seemed as if the heel was missing. Bill felt sick. He poured the oil into his hands and blew on it. It was warm anyway. He had stolen the oil from Annie's room. Annie had gone to visit Wally in the Emergency Room. She would not be happy if she knew he had done this.

'Of course it's OK,' said Moey. 'Look at him, he's smiling. He sees me.'

'He's too young to smile,' Bill said. 'It's not a smile '

The little creature looked at him. It scared him shitless. Bill put his broad-palmed hand across the fragile chest, and spread the oil.

'You have to take his bandock off,' Felicity said.

He did not want to. He feared there would be something horrible there as well, but when Felicity had undone the bandock the penis looked quite normal. He began to massage. He could feel the little being inside his hands, some sort of life-form not your own. He was half repulsed, half attracted. He could feel Felicity beside him now, felt her red hair brush his neck.

He looked at her. She leaned across and kissed him. Now she was not withdrawn from him, he was really angry with her – she had forced him to play the musico, to out-Vincent Vincent in his admiration of this tragedy.

The more he massaged, the more the child cooed, and kicked his malformed limbs, the more angry Bill became. The company began to press around, and it made him sour and cynical to see how they now wanted to massage too, and he gave up to them, gave up gladly, listening to everything they had to say. It was an orgy of denial. It disgusted him.

43

He looked from this to see Annie standing at the door alone. She raised an eyebrow at him and held up a bottle of case-latrine. He looked at Felicity. He turned, before he could stop himself, and followed Annie down the stairs.

12

Wally claimed to have been born 'on the sawdust', to have grown up in a circus family, to have been the 'Human Ball' from ages one till three.

When he first arrived at reform school he had still been able, so he said, to fit himself, together with twenty-four green soda bottles, inside a box measuring 24″ × 12″ × 12″. It was this which bent his back the way it was.

Furthermore, his father had been a contortionist so extraordinary that he had been able, whilst still alive, to sell his skeleton to medical science. He had travelled around Efica with a coffin already addressed James Hazzard, MD, Boulevard Raspail, Chemin Rouge, Efica.*

'My old dab was a dreadful gambler,' Wally said. 'If it had not been for the need for money, he would never have done it – it was a shocking inconvenience to be always toting that coffin about.'

All his life Wally had been around the circus and the theatre. He had been a roustabout, a tent-staker, a stablehand, a farrier, a driver, a turnboy,† a carpenter, a production manager, but the truth was – this leap into the safety net was his first performance ever.

Now he wished he had never made it. He wished he had died instead.

He sat in Casualty and held his throbbing arm while the flesh swelled like yeast dough around the fracture.

He waited for the visitors he knew would arrive after curtain time at the Feu Follet. He waited with trepidation, embarrassment, imagining Bill Millefleur impersonating him to the people in

---

* Students of the Efica circus may recognize the story of Petit Paul who, having died in 335 EC, was probably still performing when Wally was a child.
† Originally a chauffeur, but later a mechanic. Probably originates with the job of starting an engine with crank handle.

the tower, repeating his speech, mimicking his accent, revealing all his very private feelings about my mother.

On a different night it might have turned out as he feared (some cruel things sometimes went on in that little tower), but Bill had other matters on his mind and the whole question of Wally's motivation was overshadowed by the *Zinebleu*, which had noted the leap ('inverse levitation') and had seen it as setting the tone of the production – 'the Smith forte – the Efican vernacular'.

So the hospital visitors, all actors, came to celebrate the review as much as to commiserate about the injury.

'I was just testing the rig,' he said. 'Jeez.'

He sat on the plastic bench with a forbidden cancerette cupped in his palm, his arm resting across his thigh, and listened while the review was, once again, read out to him. To have his performance admired by actors was worth anything to Wally.

'Bill was a bit worried,' he said. 'I just tested it is all.'

His veined face flushed and his ears burned red with pleasure. He sat on the plastic bench, his cancerette hidden in his palm, and listened to repeated readings of the review. It was not until the sixth recitation that he noticed the mention of the 'Witch's homunculus'.

'What's a homunculus, for Christ's sake?'

'A foetus,' Moey said.

'A baby,' Claire said. 'It means a baby.'

'The Witch doesn't have a baby.'

'Felicity does,' Claire said. 'You both made your début the same night.'

'Jeez,' said Wally. 'Hope it looks like Bill.' He winked at Moey. 'Hope it doesn't look like you.'

'It's a boy,' Claire said.

'How is it?' he asked Moey. 'Who does he look like?'

'He's got very intelligent eyes.'

Wally registered the tone. They were like actors talking about a performance they hated. They would never call another actor a ringhard. They'd say, oh, I loved your business with the tea towel.

'What does he look like?' he asked Claire Chen.

Claire fiddled with her big silver death's-head rings and told him Flick's baby was *amazing*.

45

Wally stared at her with his still grey eyes until she said it was time for her to go and lock up the theatre, and Moey said he'd better walk with her across the park. When they said goodbye they looked mournful and depressed. They gave the review to Wally – just a scrap of paper – but it was the first time he and I were linked together. I found it among his papers when we were leaving Efica, just before his death. It was folded inside his driver's licence – as dry and fragile as something from a flower press.

At one o'clock in the morning Wally was alone in Casualty waiting for the results of his X-ray. He knew something was very wrong with me. His arm was throbbing. His leap now seemed no more than a vulgar joke, a raspberry in the face of fate. There was something wrong and he knew he had to be with my maman.

He tried to go to her. They would not let him. In Saarlim you could have walked right out the door, but this was Efica – more humane, more bureaucratic – there were forms to sign, the forms were missing, and thus it was nearly three in the morning when he walked out the door, with his unset arm held in a Lasto-net, and that was how he was – with that knobby white material on his arm and that slight ammonia smell – when he first held me.

The lights were all out except an Anglepoise on the floor beside the bed. Felicity was asleep on her back in a long white T-shirt, her hair spread out on the pillow, snoring ever so softly, and Tristan Smith was placed between her legs.

Wally approached me with his neck craned, squinting, his lips compressed in a pale grimace.

He saw – loose-skinned puppy – marsupial not ready to leave its mother's pouch – skin folds, wide staring eyes.

'You poor guy,' he whispered. 'You poor little guy.'

Felicity, in her sleep, put her hand across her mouth and moaned.

'Flick?'

Her lips were dry and cracked. She made a small whistling snore.

Wally leaned over and managed to scoop me up with his good arm. He held me against his shirt, one-handed.

'It's OK,' he said. 'I'm here now.'

He sat on the edge of the bed. Felicity listened to him. She heard him sniffling.

46

'They mean well, mo-rikiki,'* Wally said, 'but they don't know anything.' He held my puppy-skin against his old veined face.

Felicity began to sob. Wally knelt on the bed and, jerkily, panicking, tried to return me to my resting place.

'No, no,' she said. 'Hold him, hold him.'

'I'm really sorry.'

'Hold his head, hold his head.'

'Flick . . . I'm sorry.'

'No, no.' She was rubbing her running nose with the sleeve of her T-shirt, but her whole beautiful face was wrung like a rag.

'I'm just an ignorant old violiniste. I should shut my mouth.'

'They rose to it, they really did. I was proud of them.'

'I'm putting him in his crib. He'll be happier there.'

'Do you know about babies, Wally?'

'Oh Flick,' Wally said, as he laid me on my back in the crib and tucked a sheet around me as smooth and tight as any matron at the Mater. 'I'm just an old pea and thimble man.'

And then Felicity was crying again. This was the first time she let herself really cry in company. Bill was downstairs in bed with Annie. Vincent was at home with his wife. It was Wally who came to hold her. My second night on earth was the only time he ever held my mother's body.

He was wide awake. He was so shaken, so sad, but at the same time he knew this was his moment, his time. He had seen himself, he told me later, in my eyes. While my maman and I slept, he made the promise, said the words, out loud. He was going to be the father, the one who would really do the job.

## 13

It was my fourteenth day and I woke to the noise of heavy rain thundering on the tower's thin roof. My first Moosone had arrived. The Nabangari had begun to flow again. Outside you could hear the river roaring, the muffled noises of boulders and logs crashing against the river wall. Slowly I became aware that my mum and dab were already awake, talking to each other. We lay, the three of us, on the same hard mattress I had been con-

---

* 'My little one', or 'my little finger'. Rikiki can also refer to a 4 fl.oz. glass of beer.

ceived on. My mum was on the telephone side, Bill on the window side. I lay between them, staring up at the pressed metal ceiling whose fat-bottomed little Cupids must have dated from the time when old Ducrow brought Solveig Mappin* into his bed.

'It's your life,' my mother was saying to my father. 'You've got to live your life.'

My bandock was wet. My stomach burned me. A bitter taste was in my mouth. While I grizzled quietly, my mother stroked my head, ran her little finger down into the soft indentation at the base of my skull.

'If I go to Voorstand now,' Bill said, 'I know I'm going to lose you.'

'You can't lose me, sweets,' she said. 'I'll always be here.'

'You want me to go,' he said.

'No, I want you to stay.'

'Tray bon. I'll stay.'

'If you stay, mo-chou, that's your business, but if I persuade you to stay you might hate me for ever.'

'I guess,' Bill said, lying on his side, stroking his chest with the back of his fingernails.

'You guess? You're not meant to agree with me.' She started tickling him. He squirmed and tried to still her. As they bumped and rolled, I lay there between them, a concrete fact of life. I kicked my legs and farted.

'Watch the baby.'

They came to rest with Bill lying on my mother. She put her hand out, just checking me.

'It's your life,' she said again, but she had become sad, and the animation had left her face.

'Oh Flick,' Bill said, 'I feel so bad, mo-chou. I get offered a part and all it does is make me feel like shit.'

My mother smiled wanly. She had sore breasts, cracked nipples. She did not mention them.

'I know it is an honour.'

My mother stroked my head. There was a clap of thunder.

'It's a great honour,' my dab repeated, a little petulantly.

---

* *Solveig Mappin (271–336), the young wife of Henry Mappin, Red Prime Minister of Efica (240–307).*

'Sweets, you must not make a meal of it,' my mother said. 'You have been cast in a show, that's all. Now you have to decide if you want the part or not.'

My father rolled off my mother.

'Croco cristi,' he said. 'I'm the first Efican actor to be cast in a Saarlim Sirkus!' He stood up by the bed and looked down on us. There was a second clap of thunder. The rain intensified.

I went to sleep. When I woke – hours later – buttery sunshine was shining on the rain-splattered windows. My mother was wearing a large white T-shirt and Bill – bare-chested, dressed only in white canvas frippes – was sitting on the end of the bed. Their argument had not developed.

'It's only a fucking Sirkus,' my mother said, 'for God's sake. You're not about to invent penicillin. Do it or don't do it.'

'All right I will.'

'Will what?' my mother said, kneeling beside me, flipping me on to my back and removing my bandock.

'Do it,' Bill said.

'Well, if you want to . . .'

'No, I don't *want* to, but the company can use the money.'

'Hand me the wipes.'

'Please?'

'Please.'

'It's a lot of money,' Bill said. 'More than anyone in the Feu Follet was ever offered.'

My mother picked me up and pulled up her T-shirt. I was hungry, but I also knew that each time I fed on those hard white breasts it made my stomach hurt again. To make things worse, she was not concentrating, and although you would not detect it in her tone she was agitated.

'Don't be frightened of the company meeting,' she said to my dab. 'They'll tell you what a hypocrite you are, but in the end they'll agree that it's a good thing to get thirty per cent of your salary. It's never any different.'

'You're the one who hates the Saarlim Sirkus.'

'Sweets, I hate it here, not there. In Saarlim, the Saarlim Sirkus is just the Saarlim Sirkus. I don't hate it in Saarlim.'

'It's so tedious,' Bill said, staring at us distractedly. 'There's always the same posturing, and then they accept.'

What he was talking about was the collective policy – those who got 'straight' jobs contributed 30 per cent of their salary or fees to the company. Each job offer had to be considered by the company as a whole. So when Sparrowgrass Glashan, for instance, was offered a part in an ice-cream commercial everybody gathered to weigh up the public benefit and the moral damage. You never heard such long and protracted deliberations.

Bill, it turned out, had called a company meeting for ten that morning. You need a certain sense of your own importance to call a theatre meeting at that hour. My mother, who might normally have advised him to have the meeting later, withheld her counsel. It was as if she had decided to let the dice fall as they would.

The dark theatre had a smell which was never present when a show was on. Perhaps the big casseroles burnt away the odours of damp and dust and poverty, but when Bill stood before us on the sawdust and frowned and rubbed his denim shirt against his pectorals, the casseroles were dark and a single 100-watt work light provided the illumination.

As he delivered the news, he made himself – in spite of the arrogance of the hour – small before us, belittled his talents (as he was expected to) and talked about the moral and artistic consequences of the role in terms that may strike you – someone for whom Efica is small and unimportant – as grandiose, if not comic.

What this poor theatre saw itself doing was inventing the culture of its people. So even while the rain leaked through the ancient roof and ran in a rippling wash down the back wall, the young man who paced back and forth on the sawdust stage presented himself as someone involved in a moral judgement which had the highest consequences. He was going to work in the interests of – please do not take this personally – the enemy. I do not mean your country, but your Sirkus. In its celebration of the individual, in its inequitable rewards for luck, in its invitation to have the audience be complicitous in the not infrequent death of performers, it ran counter to everything we Eficans held so dear. The Saarlim Sirkus was thrilling, spectacular, addictive, but also heartless. Was this all? No it was not, but it is enough for now.

My father was impressive. Despite his lack of education, his mind was the most classically inclined of all the actors. He had an almost Jesuitical sense of argument, and when he came to the conclusion of

50

his formal statement, my mother squeezed me hard in her lap.

On that stage on that long ago Sunday morning, Bill Millefleur shone, a star already, and the members of our collective, sitting under that dark and distant canopy, were happy for him, jealous, relieved to hear that such substantial funds would be brought into the Feu Follet.

Just the same: when he concluded that the immense size of the salary meant that he was obliged, on moral grounds, to take the part – they smiled, some more cynically than others. When he said that he was frightened of the role, and, indeed, might still refuse it, his obvious excitement made him appear disingenuous and his colleagues' laughter had a harder, less patient edge. Those who stood to speak afterwards were harsher than they might otherwise have been. They could not imagine he might really say no.

## 14

To reach your great capital, Bill would have to fly for three hours above the long island chain of Efica and then for five hours more across the landlocked web of lakes and inland seas, the great green and gold hinterland of Voorstand dotted with the mushroom shapes of Sirkus Domes – and what he said was true: he *was* frightened, not only that he would lose my maman, but also that he would somehow lose himself at the other end of this great muze.

We Eficans, generally speaking, were frightened of Saarlim. It may make you smile to think how much: how we rubbed and burnished our idea of its cruelty and ruthlessness.

My father was a colonist, an islander, an Efican. He was, by definition, not a Voorstander. When he spoke his lines in Saarlim, he would need to abandon his soft, self-doubting Efican patois – *Shapoh, mo-ami, mo-chou, cambruce* – learn to speak with a clip to his consonants, give up his Feu Follet habits of irony and self-mockery. To you he would be an exotic performer introducing live animals into the Sirkus.* But to himself (and to us) our circus boy

* *One hundred years before, this act of Bill Millefleur's – an historical enactment which involved performing with horses and monkeys – would have been regarded as blasphemy in Voorstand. As recently as 255 EC one Piers Kraan was sent to prison for lion taming and the lions transported, at the expense of the state, to 'that place where God intended that they dwell'.*

51

would be acting out, with his own body, the surrender of our frail culture to your more powerful one. He would be singing your songs, telling your stories, and this went strongly against the grain, undercut the whole notion of who he thought he was. So even though the collective had told him, *go*, he could not let it be so easy.

Back in the tower, he said the same things he had said before.

My maman also: 'Listen to me,' she said. 'It is your *life*.'

It was perhaps the twentieth time she had said it, but this time something different happened. Bill began to comb his thick black hair with both hands, rapidly. 'What does that mean, Felicity?' He used only a slice of his great booming actor's voice, a whisper, thin and nasty as a piece of wire: 'What exactly does that *mean*?'

It was now three in the afternoon. My maman lay down with me on her unmade bed, fully dressed. She pulled the blanket up over us, and looked up at my father with her green eyes.

'*What*?' he said.

She pulled her hair back from her forehead and held it at the nape of her neck. She was the mother of a scary child with special needs, the owner of a theatre whose existing debts would easily consume Bill's 30 per cent.

'What?' he insisted.

'I didn't say anything,' she said.

'What you *thought*.'

She turned her head aside, exhausted.

'You thought . . .' Bill insisted.

'You have to go,' she said. She felt sick in her stomach, but she was an actor, too – she smiled. 'Take the part.'

'Take it?'

'You *have to go*, mo-chou,' she said, sitting up. It was not so hard as you would think – this moment. 'You'll see the best theatre in the world, every night. You'll do voice with Fischer and movement with Hals or Miriam Parker. You'll be a great *actor*. You'll never be a great actor here.'

'Flick, you know this isn't acting. It's a fucking *Sirkus*.'

'The Sirkus won't last for ever,' she said. 'You won't be seduced by Sirkus. The Sirkus is mechanical and manipulative. I wouldn't love a man who could be seduced by Sirkus.'

If her eyes now slid away from his, it was because she was not telling the truth and she was ashamed. She could not stop thinking about the money he would earn. She coveted it almost as much as she feared losing him.

She was a woman who owned only three dresses, two pairs of shoes, who was always scratching around for extra in order to pay her mortgage, or her actors, or build the sets, or repair the ancient lead plumbing. If you had asked the actors, still gathered in the theatre downstairs, they would have said my maman was rich. And it was true that she owned the crumbling bricks and powdery mortar of the Feu Follet and she had capital invested which returned her a small income, but not enough, not nearly enough, and the future of the theatre was always in doubt. The thought of all that Sirkus money drove her crazy with guilt and longing.

'You *want* me to go,' Bill said.

'*No*,' she said. 'How could you say that? I don't *want* you to go, sweets. I *want* you to stay.'

'It is a lot of jon-kay . . . '

'Never do anything for money,' my maman said. 'Never, ever.'

'That isn't what you said before.'

'It's what I'm saying now,' she said. 'It's your life, but if you want to know what I think – you're an Efican actor. You belong here, with us. We have important work to do. We have a whole damn country to invent.'

The light was behind Bill when she said this. She did not see him start to cry, and it was a moment before she caught the sheen of the tears on his beautiful high cheeks. She left the bed and put her long pale arms around his neck.

'Don't cry, Billy-fleur.'

'Just let me go,' he said. 'Please, just let me go.'

'Darling, darling,' she said softly, standing on tip-toes. 'Do whatever it is you want.' She kissed him with her mouth soft and open, kissed his big rough salty face.

'You're right.' He withdrew from her to carefully blow his nose. 'If I stay, I'll always regret it.'

She took his handkerchief from him and threw it on the bed. She stretched up to kiss his lower lip. 'If you stay, you stay. Baby,' she said, smiling, but retreated to the bed, to the other baby. 'Your son has thrown up on the blanket,' she said, but neither of them did anything to remedy it. They sat, and waited, as if something would happen.

53

And, indeed, something did eventually happen.

As the yellow street lights flicked on and the rain began again, my father appeared to choose. My maman saw him do it. She watched him as she might have watched an image form on a sheet of photographic paper. She saw how he tried to hide his decision from her. He ran his hand through his hair and then across his face. He got himself engaged in a bit of business with a handkerchief which occupied his whole attention from the window, where he had been standing at that moment, to the bed, beside which he now knelt.

He placed his big hands flat on the white linen cover and looked at my ugly wrinkled face. His eyes were glistening, and there was a small smile on his archer's-bow lips which my maman was familiar with from more intimate circumstances and which now made her believe that he had decided to stay.

She felt dull, anti-climactic.

'Goodbye little boy,' he said.

Then she saw – he was going.

As my maman's head bowed, as her beautiful face began to crumple, he kissed the crown of her head and walked away, out the door, down the stairs. When she looked up towards the door, he was already passing through the foyer. She stood in the gloom and watched him run through the Moosone rain with a small black rucksack he must have had already packed and waiting since the day before.

She rested her face against the glass. 'You bastard,' she said.

The drains were overflowing. A plastic rubbish bin was blowing down the street. My father ran gracefully away, his head back, his white shirt already black with rain.


## 15

When Bill left us, it was as if he had died, and life in the tower became tearful and depressed.

My red-eyed mother read the foreign bank advices – pale yellow slips with her name misspelt 'Smit'. She entered the amounts into her ledgers, but could not bring herself to spend the money as she had planned. Instead, the company went out to play agitprop at fish cannery gates, at street fairs, in the streets around the mudflat suburbs like Goat Marshes where no one had money to spend on such luxury as a theatre ticket.

There was no Efican playwright, none of any talent, who shared our passions or our politics, so the company devised its own material. These little plays were crude and funny. There was juggling and feats of strength and acrobatics, but everywhere with both a story and a purpose. We mocked our snivelling 'alliance' with Voorstand, publicly libelled the silk-shirted facheurs who ran the Red Party. We dressed one actor as an obese Bruder Rat, another as randy Oncle Duck. We had our audience write down the phone numbers of top DoS agents and sometimes had a little fun telephoning them from the stage. We broke the obscenity laws, the alliance laws, the secrecy laws, all in one act with two posturers.*

Life in the Feu Follet was passionate, paranoid, sometimes dangerous. I did not understand it was not normal. I was picked up, put down, rushed into cars and trucks and up the stairs of net lofts, down alleyways to rooms behind hamburger restaurants, back to Gazette Street where, by the time I had survived another eight weeks, the Feu Follet was in rehearsal for a very athletic production of *The Caucasian Chalk Circle*.

I was to play THE BABY. There are not a lot of roles for babies in the theatre, and *The Caucasian Chalk Circle* is not really one of them, but it was my mother's way of keeping me with her while she performed. Of course, it didn't work. I was often in pain, I cried and grizzled and distressed my fellow actors. Felicity, already guilty and depressed about my father's absence, became so stressed that her milk refused to flow.

It was not a good time for me – by the night of the first dress rehearsal I had lost not only my first father, but also my first role to a straw dummy, and, worst of all: lost my mother's breasts.

I know I complained about them – hard, white, made my stomach hurt etc. – and I spoke truly. Also, you might as well know, they spurted too much, hit the peristaltic button at the back

---

* At this time we had, in our company, Ernest Gibbs, an Englishman, who could disjoint almost his whole body. He could produce at will, without aid of cotton wadding, forms as diverse as Quasimodo and the president of your great country. He was a political cartoon made flesh, and was with us until his death in a boating accident in 374. [TS]

of my throat so I gagged and vomited. But finally these breasts and I had reached an understanding, and I was (just as you were, Meneer, Madam, in your own time) happy there.

There was no warning that these pink and slippery friends were also to abandon me. One minute my world was centred on the soft spurt and trickle, the apple-scented skin against my nose, the next it was prosthesis: rubber, plastic, the chlorine-heavy smell of sterilizing solutions.

I did not take it lightly. Indeed it changed what was previously a pacific disposition. I became irritable, devious, needy, capable of blazing fits of rage. It was at this stage, an hour before curtain of the dress rehearsal, that my maman telephoned Vincent.

## 16

Vincent was a busy man. He was not merely the chief executive of a large company, he was also an important strategist for the Blue Party. He spent a great deal of his waking life plotting ways to expose the servility and cynicism of the Reds, to somehow, with one stroke, produce the kind of crisis that can unseat a corrupt and gerrymandered government. The week in which Felicity's milk stopped was also the week before an important by-election to which he had personally contributed both money and time.

It was a dramatic Moosone. There was flooding and a cyclone which swept away the old sea wall and sank a ferry in the Madeleines. Vincent spent his days at his downtown office, his nights driving from meeting to meeting in his Bentley Corniche, negotiating flooded streets in Berthollet, fallen trees and power lines in Goat Marshes. He drove with his nose pressed up against the windscreen, with loud music blasting from the speakers.

He believed that the history of Efica was about to change direction. The weather intensified his passion. He drummed tom-tom beats on the steering wheel, and whooped when he saw the lightning strike the earth. He imagined Efica would soon be free of Voorstand influence – its spies, its cables, and of the Sirkus which was then threatening to wash across us like a tidal wave.

He wanted Efica to be free of Sirkus. But also – he loved the Sirkus. This was what the VIA never understood about him. He was a serious scholar of Voorstand culture, painting, music, literature. He was also, in a country whose people were not usually aware that the Sirkus had an ethical and religious history, something of an expert on the theology of the 'Settlers Free'.

Vincent loved to read. It was the thing that bonded Vincent and Felicity – the belief that talk was not just talk, that what you said mattered, what you *thought* could change society, that a book in a foreign language, a meeting above a pizza parlour in Goat Marshes, a theatre production in a decaying circus school, could be the thing that made the river of history break its banks.

And, indeed, he was on his way to one of these meetings (above an oyster lease in Swiss Point) when my mother called him on his car phone in a state about the baby.

Vincent turned down the Pow-pow music,* spoke softly into the receiver. He was already late for a strategy meeting, but when my mother could not be calmed he detoured across the Narrows Bridge (which already had one foot of yellow water rushing over it) and drove the Corniche right up to the door of the Feu Follet. It was now six-thirty and he was late for his strategy meeting.

He put on his black hat, tightened his wide leather belt, smoothed his beard with his metal comb, and walked slowly up the ramp through the Moosone rain and into the foyer.

Here he was astounded to find a whole team – edgy electricians, sound techs, production managers, soup servers for the most part – seemingly all waiting for him. They had bags of bandocks, bottles, a carrycot, written instructions, which they all seemed to want to transmit the minute they saw him. Behind them, on a folding chair which wobbled on the cobblestones, sat my mother – pale, stretched, tense.

'I cannot carry him on stage,' she said, when Wally had finished explaining how to sterilize a teat. 'I tried, but it can't work.'

Now Vincent loved the theatre. He was, in some ways, the original stage-door Johnny (loved to be around actresses, loved to watch Felicity on stage, was moved by her courage, aroused by the sight of her long legs in the public gaze). But the Therouxes traced their lineage back to the first century of the Efican Calendar, and his great-great-great-grandfather had been forcibly

---

* *The peculiarly rhythmic music created by POWs – prisoners of war – in Voorstand.*

57

shipped from Marseille by Louis Quatorze and sent to practise his foul-smelling craft in hell. Vincent had drunk politics from his mother's breasts, and he was flabbergasted to realize that he was being asked to disrupt a major strategy meeting for ... baby-sitting.

'You know I've got a meeting,' he began. He paused, imagining it. His *brother** would be there. He could not do it.

'Vincent.' She smiled and held out her hand. 'You don't need to be ashamed of him.'

Vincent looked at my mother – the eyes sunken with weariness, the mouth small and down-turned, the arms thin and white – and knew she had pushed her idea of herself to a place where it would soon publicly collapse.

He took her wrist with his left hand, and with his right then silently handed over his car keys to Wally.

As Wally and the others hurried outside with the baby under their umbrellas, Vincent was a curious mixture of sympathy and anger. He drew my maman to him, kissed her.

'Sleep,' he said to her, 'meditate.'

'For God's sake,' she said, hearing what he imagined so well disguised, 'he's your son. Is it such an ordeal to look after him just one night?'

'No,' he said, 'not for one night.'

When he went out into the night he could hear me screaming through the loud drumming of the rain. He found me in his car, my face like a flapping crumpled rag, my pale eyes bulging, all my skin wet with snot and sour milk. I was strapped into a safety seat right next to the driver.

Vincent felt he could not endure the smell. He opened the windows, then shut them because the rain was blowing in on me. He set the car in gear and drove.

Before he had even arrived at the first meeting I had thrown up on his velour upholstery and left tell-tale white formula stains on his black collars, but Vincent was, again, a better man than he feared. He endured the smell, the noise, the slime coating on his collar. He walked on to his own stage with me in his arms. He did

---

* *St John Theroux,* b 332 EC, *General Secretary Efican Postal Workers Congress.*

not introduce me, but he held me, and continued to hold me – partly because this was the only way I would be quiet.

No one commented on my appearance, but Vincent's brother – a quiet, conservative man, five years older – showed him how to pin a bandock and then touched him with uncharacteristic gentleness upon the shoulder.

Vincent did not take this moment to say: this is my son, Tristan. Indeed, for Vincent, that moment never came. However, he established, silently, that his relationship with me was intimate, and as *The Caucasian Chalk Circle* continued its previews this relationship improved.

He was so happy that week, manic, exhausted. The prime minister had been accused of taking money from the VIA. There was a paper trail that led all the way from Saarlim via Berne and Amsterdam. Vincent had faxes, photocopies, statutory declarations.

'We've got them, mo-poulet, we got them with their parsley showing.' Vincent was high.

I began to enjoy the rides in his car, the green-glowing dials, the rented car phone which could talk to other countries.

I went to sleep to music, woke to music. I was lifted from the car, cried on cold stairways, interrupted meetings. Though I was never named in public, I was changed and powdered by famous names. I was touched, caressed, tickled.

But then it stopped.

I woke up one afternoon – no tickle, no car, no green dials. The by-election had been lost.* Vincent had shrivelled, collapsed, disappeared. He had gone home to Natalie, depressed. This, everyone knew, was typical of him. But Tristan Smith did not know, and there was no way for them to tell me.

## 17

It had not occurred to anyone that the violiniste with the small round burn scars on his arms might secretly wish to be a father. He was the production manager of *The Caucasian Chalk Circle*.

---

* In 371 the Red Party had a bare one-seat majority in the lower house, and this by-election (for the seat of Swiss Point) could have brought down the government.

Right up until the dress rehearsal, he was trying to get a grandiose set built with a two hundred dollar budget, and on the stormy night I first went off with Vincent, he was still trying to 'locate' eighty yards of canvas. How he finally did this, at no cost, no one liked to ask, but as usual his ingenuity saved the show, and my maman said – as she had said a hundred times before – that the Feu Follet could not have existed without him.

When he was praised, Wally hid his feelings of pleasure. Likewise, he never hung around my crib, but hovered around the periphery of my life, watching everything. If he sometimes changed my bandock, my maman was grateful, yes – but it did not occur to her that he was *practising*.

On the night the by-election was lost, he seemed as depressed as anyone at the Feu Follet, but he was a poker player with a winning hand. He knew how Vincent would behave. So when, next day before the curtain, my maman was trying to locate a baby-sitter, Wally stepped forward.

While Felicity watched him, he expertly changed the sodden bandock. I was ten weeks old. He was already fifty, his flaming red hair gone mostly grey and nicotine brown, his skin marked by old cigarette burns and (two) knife slashes, his skeleton – if you could have seen it – showing the marks of three mended fractures, a man so damaged by life, so secretive and suspicious, that he had long ago stopped dreaming that he would find someone to love.

'How do you know how to do this?' my maman asked.

'Rest,' he told her, as he expertly pinned my bandock in place. 'You have a show to do.'

'Dear Wally,' she said. 'You really are amazing.'

'Don't you worry, ma'am.' He picked me up and felt my soft skin against his prickly cheek. All his ears – those great fleshy wattles – suddenly red with blood. 'You do your show,' he said.

He already had my dinner in the fridge.

He took me down the stairs to the cavernous old brick-floored kitchen. He had a brand new bright red high chair, which he had 'located' that afternoon.

'There,' he said, turning the chair. 'Look at the pretty tree.' He

---

*Whatever evidence Theroux had of government corruption, there is no mention of it in the zines of the time.*

faced me towards the courtyard under whose flowering oak, it was believed, Ducrow had tethered the ancient lion that finally caused his death.

Then, with his face shining, immobile, his mouth compressed under the weight of his pleasure, he took one of his very sharp knives and began to fillet the fish, a playing card he had bought for my dinner. It was precise work, and he was good at it, just as he was good at soldering and using a key-hole saw. He separated the delicate white flesh from the pink and pearly skeletons. He placed two delicate fillets on a pale blue plate – and I know, Madam, a ten-week-old child does not eat fish, but Wally did not know. I was his first.

When he had the fillets done, he wrapped the bones in paper, placed the fillets in the fridge, opened a beer, poured a bride. He flicked on the gas and quickly, deftly, cooked the delicate fish fillets in a little milk. Then he mashed it with a fork and, worrying it might be too hot, placed it in the freezer to cool.

I, of course, did not know what fish was. So when, at last, he offered me the meal he had so lovingly prepared, I rejected it. He called me Rikiki, but it made no difference: I wanted Vincent. I wanted my bottle. Wally gave me a cup. I had never seen a cup. I knocked it over. Wally yelled at me. I cried. And that is how it was always to be with us – Wally was the one who made the rules and was angry, the one who cooked breakfast and lunch and yelled at me when I didn't eat it.

Amongst the actors, he was famous for his sentimentality, but in spite of all the 'Rikikis' he was not soft and conciliatory like Vincent, who had often, in his euphoric pre-election mood, stroked his baby's cheek with the back of his pudgy hand. Wally brought no gifts, like Bill would. He was not full of compromise and sweet smells like Felicity. Indeed, he did not bathe enough. And when no one was around to see him do it, he would scream and yell like a maniac, particularly at the end of a long weekend.

Wally loved me, but he did not find this prayed-for state to be the blessing he had imagined. Love aged him, made his forehead taller, his shoulders a little more hunched, his brow increasingly hooded.

It was Wally who confiscated the toy laser gun which Bill sent – this was a year or so later – for my birthday. It was Wally who

61

stopped me going to the country with Vincent because Vincent had been drinking and could not figure out my new safety seat. And it was Wally – later still, when I was just over ten – Wally who told the doctors about my penchant for climbing. He wanted it stopped, and hoped to invoke a greater authority than his own. He knew Tristan was their precious thing, their cracked and mended pot, and that they would not want it shattered, and it is true – from the moment I was born, the doctors had not been able to keep their hands off me.

Felicity, who had begun so independently and who was, anyway, a great one for homeopaths, naturopaths and iridologists, unexpectedly capitulated to what she called 'straight medicine'. She still, at bedtime, dropped sweet little grains of Silica (for mucus) into her son's lipless maw, but once *The Caucasian Chalk Circle* was over it was 'straight doctors' who began to deal with Tristan Smith's 'anomalies'. They began with the duodenum, which had a partial blockage. At eleven months of age, they put me to sleep, cut me open, sewed me up, resuscitated me in sterile rooms where I found myself held down like a frog in a dissecting room, pinned at the legs and arms. They had catheters up my porpoise, tubes down my throat, drips in my arm, and when that was over and my temperature began to rise, they did not give me Panadol but took samples of my blood, spit, shit, urine, often by the most painful methods.

At eighteen months, they pinned me with their soap-smelling hands and took marrow from my bones. I shrieked and screamed and begged for them to let me be.

Vincent was squeamish around hospitals, but Bill – to his credit – came flying in to sit beside me on more than one occasion. He was nice to me. It would be years before he would be able to act as if he were responsible for my existence, but he could look me in the face and touch me. He was less than a father, more than an uncle. He arrived with tricks up his sleeves – wind-ups, frogs that blew bubbles, geese that farted, fake vomit, gross picture cards. He flew back to Saarlim. He sent postcards.

Wally was always there. He argued with the santamaries about his cancerettes. He held me down.

And this was my childhood: Dr Tu slid me into dark tunnels; Dr Fischer strapped me on steel platforms and tilted me upside down.

They tortured me, not just in that first year, but on and off for the first ten years of life. They mended the hole in my heart, but took three goes to get it.

The doctors (Dr Tu, Dr Fischer, Dr Wilson, Mr Picket-Heaps, Dr Ayisha Chaudry, Dr Brown etc.) were able to tell my mother exactly what operation they wanted to do next, but they could find no pigeonhole to shove me in, and the summation of all of their investigations was 'Multiple Congenital Anomalies'.

They had wanted to give me lips, but my mother chanced to see their 'similar case' and was so distressed by this poor man's goldfish pout, she would not let them touch my mouth. Either way, there was no chance I would ever have a smile you would recognize. Nor was there any hope that they might make me taller. But these ingenious Efican toubibs made me function better, stopped the green bile bubbling out of my mouth, stopped my heart walls leaking, repaired my faulty duodenum, and although this was not a pleasant way to begin a life, consider this – Tristan Smith had a loving mother, an entire company of actors who cooed and cosseted him and tickled his tummy and took him for rides on their shoulders. Plus I really had three fathers – Bill and Vincent, sometimes, and Wally every day. And if Wally did shout at me he was also the one who bought me chocolate and ice-creams, the one who tried to sneak me into the Voorstand Sirkus when I was five years old. My mother nabbed us at the entrance way.

One minute we were standing in line outside the bulbous free-form 'tent', already inhaling the pervasive odours of spun sugar and ketchup, watching the projected twenty-foot high shadows of Bruder Dog chasing Bruder Duck around and around inside of the luminous pink shell;* the next we were trudging back along the river bank and my mother's pretty face was spoiled by that disapproving expression which is described in Chemin Rouge as being 'like the ass of a hen'.

After that, I did not get to the Sirkus for another another seven years. Wally went alone on Saturday afternoons and came back with beer on his breath and a perroquet in his hand.

---

* From the very beginning, the Voorstand Sirkuses in Efica had laser clowns. By the time the Sirkus came to Chemin Rouge the days when performers put on animal suits were

'For Bruder Rikiki,' he would say as he set the sugary green drink before me, 'with the compliments of Bruder Mouse.'

Later he would 'tell' me the whole Sirkus, describing the spectacles, the falls, the injuries, the songs. It was our secret, the thing that bonded us more than any other. I would fall asleep dreaming of the cheeky Bruder Mouse or the clever Bruder Duck, whose laser images I, probably alone of all the children in the eighteen islands, had never seen in life.

## 18

I grew up preferring the dry season, and not just because it was in the Moosone that I always had my operations. In the dry season the company hired a little one-ring tent and went out into the countryside with the Haflinger bus, a horse float, a rented truck, and an ever-changing show my mother named *The Sad Sack Sirkus.**

More circus than Sirkus, and more revue than either, *The Sad Sack Sirkus* was a patchwork of tumbling and posturing, skits, Shakespearean speeches, and – best of all – equestrian displays which country people always loved to see. *The Sad Sack Sirkus* made a little money; it got the company out of the city; and – thanks to the occasional egg-throwing of Ultra Rouget fanatics – it gave a sense of urgency to the company's political agenda.

My mother now scheduled these tours to coincide with the summer recess of the Saarlim Sirkus. Thus Bill was able to come back for every tour and he and Sparrow Glashan and my mother rode three-men high and Bill performed flip-flaps, round-offs, pirouettes and somersaults on the back of a cantering horse, just as he

---

*gone. We never saw a 'live' Bruder Dog or Mouse. As for Simulacrums, we read about them, but there were none in the eighteen islands. [TS]*

* *To the Voorstand reader the disrespectful conjunction of 'Sad Sack' and 'Sirkus' may seem to indicate an ignorance of the meaning of Sirkus, but it was exactly this conjunction that made the name so appealing to my maman. [TS]*

† *These political thugs published various pamphlets and news sheets which revealed a perplexing mixture of ideas – Efican nationalism, anti-semitism, a passionate attachment to the alliance with Voorstand. While their often extreme actions were always criticized by the government, it now seems certain that they were funded by right-wing elements of the Red Party.*

did under the big Dome in Saarlim where the tickets cost 100 Guilders each.

Vincent, of course, could not come on tour. He stayed in the city, running his business, dining with his wife, waiting for his life to start again. When he could not stand the separation any more, he would visit, stumbling out on to a southern beach from the belly of an ancient aluminium-bodied aircraft with one colossal engine and oil streaks on its wings. Vincent was an urban animal, never at home in the countryside. He was nervous around the horses, and obviously disconcerted to feel himself disadvantaged with 'Young Bill', who had quickly become an international star.*

I liked Vincent better in the dry season. He was less sure of himself, often melancholy.

What he was suffering from – I see now – was sexual jealousy. When we were on tour, Bill shared my mother's bed. In the turmoil of his unhappiness, Vincent turned his tenderness on me. He gave me gifts, taught me to hold a crayon, to form my quivering big letter 'S'. He sat next to me, his shampooed beard occasionally brushing my neck, and spoke to me in French, a language I did not understand.

'Mon petit, mon pauvre petit,' he would say.

But finally the dry season smelt, not of Vincent's shampooed beard, but of sweet hot horse-shit, chaff, dust, tick drench. Each day dawned clear and painless, long sweet gravel roads, chalk-grey dust, singing actors packed into the old Haflinger bus, the horses and the rented truck bringing up the rear. Wally drove the bus. He liked to drive. If he could have done it, he would have driven the float and truck as well.

The tours were long, covering not only the (formerly English) main islands which were all to the north of Chemin Rouge, but back south through the whole 'Granite Necklace', and the old dye towns of Melcarth and King's Coat. I knew the granite caves beneath our feet were often filled with your government's navigation cable, but the truth is, I did not think about it.

---

* Bill Millefleur, as Voorstand readers will be aware, was not as famous a name in Saarlim as we all imagined. In Efica he had become a star. Everyone watched Vids of his Saarlim performances, particularly his part as Franco Hals in The Black Stallion Gallops into the Burning House. [TS]

When we were on tour, my mother devoted herself to me with an intensity few parents could have sustained for long. She listened to my every sound, brought to my taut malformed face the full focus of her curiosity and attention. Even though Bill was there, she brought me into the bed before she finally went to sleep, and I was in child-heaven. I woke to – no doctors – the sound of magpies carolling and the smell of warm sheets and my mother's sweet musky skin-smell. Almost every day we woke up in a new place – rock-walled fields of brown grass thatched with rust like Harris tweed, ravines, dry rivers with stones like prehistoric eggs, a chalky coastal estuary where, even when I was ten years old, my mother would strap me on to her body and we would slowly, quietly, gather oysters and mussels at low tide.

The southernmost islands (the Madeleines) were like cake crumbs on the map, and on our way back up to Melcarth* we would spend almost as much time on ferries as on roads. The roads themselves were mostly dirt, bordered with century-old cairns commemorating famous deaths by starvation, 'rot', spearing, typhoid, pig-headedness and folly.† This was the country everybody felt was Efica – mostly wind, water, sky. There was an emptiness, a refusal to charm, an edge of terror in the air which cut us to the bone. The landscape was dotted with failed attempts at European enterprise – bauxite claims, farmhouses, abandoned rusting windmills. The skies were a huge and empty ultramarine.

Of course I often repulsed strangers in those isolated estuary towns, but when I say this did not affect me you have to see the crowd that I was travelling with: men with tattooed fingers, women with tinted leg hair, crushed velvet, aromatic oils, ornamental face scars. By the time I was two I had become their emblem, their mascot, and I shared with them their sense that we were an avant garde, not only artistically, but also morally. Thus I remained as swaddled and protected under the bright southern

---

* *Named, as every Efican schoolchild knows, after the God of dyeing.*
† *All European deaths. The deaths of the IPs (Indigenous Peoples, the eighteen tribes of Efica) remain essentially uncommemorated and unresolved. Even Vincent Theroux had difficulty resolving the notion that his great-great-grandfather may have been party to a genocide.*

skies as I was inside the rank dusty womb of the Feu Follet.

I was, indeed, a curious-looking child – strong in the shoulders, withered and tangled in the legs. My hair was dense and blond, and the irises of my eyes – although no longer white as they had been when I was born – were now milky, marbled, striated with hair-line spokes of gold. They were my best feature, and were sometimes thought to be quite beautiful.

Naturally my maman worried continually about her deformed little boy's self-esteem, but the truth was, I was being privately tutored not only in my schoolwork, but in the radical's conceit, that I was different, but superior. To cause upset in motel dining rooms – something which would later be the cause of such shame and anger – was no ordeal to me. My comrades placed me in a new high chair which Wally had built for me, and when we played Ultra Rouge towns I would sit with a crushed velvet shawl around my shoulders and bring my intense eyes to stare accusingly at anyone I imagined was the enemy. Few could hold my gaze – bristling Ultras with their shirtsleeves cut high and their elastic-sided boots red with bauxite dust: they grimaced and looked down at their barley soup.

## 19

It was never my mother's plan that I should be an actor, and if she had not been desperate she would not, I am sure, have permitted the seed to be planted by Bill Millefleur: he had always been, until now, an amateur as a father and – you only have to look at the handwriting, the spelling, the eccentric capitalizations to know this – an unlikely expert in the field of formal education.

Until January 381, when Bill's postcard arrived, my education was conventional enough. Between the ages of six and eight I had a Korean tutor, a Mr Han, a delicate old man who finally died of asthma. He was succeeded, in my ninth year (380), by Claire Chen, who, despite her erratic personal life and slovenly dress, had an almost tyrannical code of behaviour in the class room – that formerly pristine little tower room which was now a wilderness of broken chalk, torn theatre programmes, half-assembled rak-rok blocks, the Great Works of Literature, old horseshoes, and French coins I had found while playing truant in the labyrinthine underworld of the old Circus School.

The chubby Chen had an MA from the University of Nez Noir. Her field was the classics – Plato, Horace, Seneca – but she also made me understand the principles of algebra. She was both clever and impatient, and – having had a convent education herself – not above striking me on the knuckles with a wooden ruler.

It was in response to one of these attacks that I bit her on the thumb, and this, in turn, got me into big trouble with my maman, who began, that night, to shout and scream at me in such a frightening way.

Was she shouting at me about the bite? No, she was not.

Madame, Meneer, she was shouting at me about the *bandage* on her actor's thumb.

Chen was meant to teach me in the morning and be available for rehearsal in the afternoon, but when she had returned from the Emergency Room that afternoon, she would not act before she knew – why did her character (Clytemnestra) have a bandage? What should Clytemnestra's attitude towards the bandage be?

Chen was an anxious actor at the best of times, with a negative intelligence that could readily destabilize a cast. Now she wished to know – should her bandage affect Orestes' attitude towards her character? Should the bandage be so white and bright when all the costumes were so bloodied and brown? Should she paint her bandage red? Could she perhaps apply other bandages to other parts of her body, and so on?

The production was frail and complicated anyway, very 'techy', and the actors had still not found their characters and were trying to fix their problems by rewriting their own lines. Also, the problem with Chen and her bandage arrived in a period when my maman was in crisis with her taxes, her loans, her repayments, her applications to the funding bodies, her medical insurance claims. It was, in addition, the end of the wet season, which meant she was trying, once again, to raise funds for *The Sad Sack Sirkus*.

My maman came back from rehearsal and asked me, calmly, why I bit my teacher.

Instead of saying that Chen had hit me with the wooden ruler, I said that I did not like her and I would not have her for a teacher any more.

My maman said there was no other teacher she could afford.

I said I did not need a teacher. I said I would be an actor instead.

My maman then turned nuts. She screamed at me in a way I had never seen her scream before. She tore her hair. While I shivered and snivelled in the corner she told me I was beyond her, that she was a working actress and I was a child with Special Needs.

I said I was sorry, but she was lost, beyond herself. She said that she was going to find a Special School for me.

I said Wally would never let her.

That sent her totally crazy, ripping corks out of bottles and drinking wine like water. She said Wally was an emotional cripple. She said she would fire him if he said a word about it. She wept and said she was going to die. I went to sleep behind her great wall of shuddering back.

She frightened me, I'll admit. Damaged me, even. And yet this truly dreadful night, which gave birth to the fearful notion of 'Special Needs', also produced the following message from my father which came into my life like a golden ray from God on High.

*'My advice to you, liebling,'* Bill wrote to my maman in a postcard that arrived two weeks later, *'is to relax – excuse him his lessons. All the education anyone could need is available just through the work you do. Let him watch Orestes instead. Also: we have a* Sad Sack Sirkus *coming up, Let him play a PART,'* my dab wrote on the back of the card, which my mother straight away locked in the third drawer from the bottom. *'Obviously I am not suggesting he top the bill but why not give him a CHARACTER? I myself am rather taken by the idea of* The Hairy Man.* *Give him the* exercise *– develop character's ACTIONS for himself.'*

---

* *A Voorstandish character often used in the Feu Follet to represent Voorstand as a whole. It seems likely that the character has its roots in the animistic culture of the Native People of Voorstand – the famous 'Suit of Goose-feathers' in the Saarlim Museum bears a striking resemblance to early artists' representations of The Hairy Man. It is only after two centuries of Christian settlement that we find The Hairy Man used as a synonym for Moloch or Satan. Even the church-sponsored Badberg Edition of* The Tales of Bruder Mouse *suggests an identity more like a 'Bogey-man' than the devil. These two identities, folk character and Christian demon, co-exist to the present day.*

69

When my mother finally decided to read this to me, I grunted and said that that would be OK, but I was so excited that I developed diarrhoea.


20

I had become a furtive, even sneaky child, one given to wild and dangerously unrealistic dreams. I devoured histories and fictions, personally identifying not only with revolutionaries but with figures like Napoleon whom I was expected to despise. I wrote: *'J'y suis une grande Destinée'*, on a cigarette paper and watched in silent satisfaction while Wally ignited and inhaled my words.

At ten years old I believed books would be written about me.

And although I said, and will say again, that I was not aware of my monstrosity, the opposite was also true: I knew exactly why I could not be an actor, and I was equally determined to become one. I also knew that if my maman saw how excited I was she would become fearful for me and send me back to Chen.

That is why, when she offered me my part in the *Sirkus*, I affected a passive, pathetic, half-defeated attitude, and when the actors were called the following day, I did not push myself forward amongst them. Instead I sat in the dark and watched them argue about *Orestes*. When I finally came into the light, it was to complain about boredom. I sat on my mother's lap and whined and fidgeted, until finally she gave me what I had wanted all the time – a rehearsal room in one of the old stables.

There, with no one watching me, I was an egotist in the great theatrical tradition. I declaimed. I leapt into the air and landed. I scrabbled around the dirty brick floor roaring like a lion. I did my own version of 'warm-ups' and 'breathing exercises' until my clothes were covered with mud and straw and my knees were cut and bleeding.

Stanislavksy says that in order to build favourable conditions for creativeness, an actor's organism must be prepared. The Master of the System would have clucked his lordly tongue not merely about my face and body, but also my voice – the failure of fusion in my mid-line structures meant that I would always, all my life, have trouble enunciating my words so a stranger could understand me.

To hell with that. I would make my Hairy Man a mute,

70

something scary that jumps at you from the dark. I would base him on a spider.

This was not original, of course. I had watched my father building a character.* He would say: This character is a crab, or that character is a mole. And he would cut himself some sandwiches and go off to the zoo or the aquarium to study.

I therefore crawled around the stables, clawing at loose bricks with my broken nails, trying to find a spider so I might study it. The spiders I caught were not easy models for my instrument to follow. Their legs were fine and supple, mine were twisted, and my feet – although I hate to use the term – were clubbed. When I walked, my ankle had to do the job normally done by the sole of the foot. I had developed thick calluses all over my ankles, but to walk this way for ten minutes put strain on the knees and the hips that could cause me pain for weeks. In short, I could not do a character that walked.

My biceps were not large, but the pale blue-ish skin covered healthy muscle and I knew that muscle could be made to grow. My Hairy Man could climb and drop free-falling out of the dark sky.

There was a rusty steel ladder fixed to the courtyard wall outside my stables, and by the time the company was hammering and sawing at the new set for *Orestes*, I had taught myself to climb, to hang upside down for fifteen minutes. As a student I was known for my squirming and impatience, but as an actor I had that quality by which great men are often marked: their ability to endure tedium in pursuit of their obsession. By the time my absent father returned to Chemin Rouge I had calluses behind my knees, across my palms. But I could hang upside down for half an hour.

Without revealing my reason, I had found out exactly what time Bill's flight would land. I knew when his taxi should arrive. The company, which imagined me an amiable sort of pet, would have

---

* *Although I had heard the other actors mock this process behind his back, I knew without being told that it was not to do with the process, but his fame in the Sirkus. Sirkus stars, it was commonly thought, could no more act than singers in an opera. They said their inane lines, but it was not acting as we did it at the Feu Follet. You, of course, will know that this opinion is born of jealousy and, further, that the assessment of Sirkus acting is ignorant and ill-informed. It is true that the standard of 'acting' in certain of the high-risk Saarlim Sirkuses is not high, but this is the exception, not the rule. As a Voorstander you will quickly see the inability of these provincial actors to 'read' a tradition of performance which is closer to Kabuki than their own.* [TS]

been surprised at my deviousness. But when, at six o'clock that night, my father finally entered the theatre, he saw the Hairy Man, spotlit precisely, hanging from the ladder on the back wall of the theatre, right up near the lighting rig.

I saw Bill Millefleur, upside down, loose and handsome in his grey silk suit. He looked up at me, light reflected from his skin, his suit, his hair.

'Hairy Man?' he called. 'Am I right?'

My limbs were crying out with pain, but my heart, as your great poet says, 'was all over the heavens'.

'He's a spider, right?' Bill called. 'Your Hairy Man's a spider?'

Beneath my blood-filled head I heard my father walk softly across the cobbled floor. He climbed up the rusty old ladder to where I hung – closer, closer – he smelt of fame, of foreign spices and dry-cleaning.

'I'm very proud of you,' he said, and caught me just in time. He lifted me off the rung. He held me to him, thirty feet above the floor, not worrying about the snot streaming from my nose.

'Just be careful, OK?'

'Thanks . . . Dab,' I said.

My words were not clear and he did not understand me, but I did not care.

'Floor-work,' he said when he had got me to the ground. 'I'd work on that.' Then he ruffled my hair and went to find my maman.

There were now ten days before the tour began. Sparrow, Bill and my mother were busy rehearsing with the horses. Wally was flushing and pressure-testing the radiator on the Haflinger, assembling his mammoth tool kit – vice-lock, brake-adjusting tool, centre punch, hacksaw, heavy hammer, side-cutters. Once I would have been by his side, under his legs while he fitted tubes inside the tubeless socks, collected brass rivets, clips, blades, rubber rings, corks, bits of wire. But all these activities which had once so interested me now seemed mundane, and I abandoned Wally for my more glamorous father.

I have no excuse. I knew it hurt Wally. I saw the pain when I ate my lunch sitting in Bill Millefleur's lap.

In the last week they brought the new horses into the Feu Follet and began to run the show. Without giving away the more spectacular part of my performance, I made my character visible. I hung upside down from the ladder where Bill could see me. And in the middle of the animal and human chaos which now filled the whole theatre, and spilled out amongst the taxis in Gazette Street, he would say, 'Good work', or, 'That's coming along.'

Having been so often and so publicly blessed, I was furious to be informed that the collective had decided not to let me perform the spider action.

Typically it was not Bill who broke this news to me, but tall, cadaverous Sparrow Glashan. He was widely known to be a decent man. It was what everybody said about him, and yet he took my action from me casually, not even noticing what it was he did.

'But . . . Bill . . . told . . . me.'

'Bill told you?'

'It's . . . much . . . better . . . than . . . he . . . saw . . I . . . fall . . . from . . . heaven.'

Sparrow smiled and patted me.

'Fuck . . . you . . .'

'What?'

'FUCK . . . YOU . . .'

Maybe he understood me. He pretended not. He said that it was only in Saarlim that they risked an actor's life for entertainment. He said that was why it was better to be an Efican.

As for my father, I could not believe what he had done to me. I watched him, smiling, joking with the other actors.


### 21

Eight weeks later, three hundred miles from Chemin Rouge, Bill came around the corner of Shark Harbour Parish Community Hall, and saw THE HAIRY MAN – already five feet off the ground.

At first he did not know it was the Hairy Man. All he saw was me, snotty, white-eyed Tristan, doing something dumb and dangerous. He started hollering my name.

This drew Wally out from under the half-erected tent, his head thrust forward like a turtle. He was followed by my maman, crawling on her knees, carrying a mug of coffee.

'What is it?' she called to Bill. 'Are you OK?'

Wally tried to grab me by the leg, but I was the Hairy Man, and

73

he was only human. I pulled away from him. He tried to follow, and you would think he was made to fit a tree – his legs were Louis Quinze, and his biceps prominent – but he scratched and scrabbled and could not hold.

'No, wait,' Bill said to Wally. I heard this. I heard it clearly. 'Wait, I know what he is doing.'

Whatever joy this understanding unlocked in my heart, it produced the opposite effect in Wally's. He had been polite to Bill until this moment, but now all the passions he had bottled up came rushing out, and he was so mad – at Bill, at me, my mother – he picked up pine cones and hurled them up the tree. 'You're never here,' he said to Bill. 'Don't play the father now.'

A pine cone hit my ear.

'Come down, you little prick.'

'Wally,' my maman said. 'That's enough.'

By then the Hairy Man was already fifteen feet above their heads. I dragged my running nose upwards, past lines of ants. I pressed my cheek hard against the corrugated bark as if skin alone might keep me stuck there, and watched, from an inch away, the ants congregate around the snot-smeared bark.

I now waited for my maman to understand my action. Not a word came up to me. Her silence went on and on, pushed me up and up. When I finally looked down, I was perhaps forty feet from the earth.

My audience was all spellbound – Wally pale, my father smiling, but my maman was so still, so *intensely* still. She held her wind-blown curls back from her eyes, squinting up at me. My arms were an agony. My legs hung like tails. But there was nothing I would not have done to maintain the private look of admiration that I found in her face. So although I dared not hang as I had planned, I turned and climbed.

I will not easily forget the boiling green ocean I found up that tree, or the blustering easterly which swept the sea spray up the cliff face and stung my broken skin as delicately as Vincent's eau de Cologne, or the resinous sap, rich in pine or the mouettes, their wings white, their eyes orange, who came squalling around me as I, unknowingly, approached their rough-stick nest.

Everything smelt of salt and seaweed. It was as if I had finally ripped through the Glad wrap that had always separated me from my true history.

Far, far below me was my silent mother. She stood beside the grey weather-board hall, her eyes creased but still young and beautiful, her red anorak wrapped tight around her, her black skirt flapping like a flag against Wally's bent grey flannel legs.

'Watch him,' I heard her say. And felt, even from that distance, that she and I were in communion.

Wally said, 'For Christ's sake.'

The wind blew her answer away.

All I heard Bill say was, '. . . kid.'

'He knows,' my mother answered.

What did I know? I knew nothing. I knew only that I was weak, in pain, delirious with fear and pleasure, that the branch I was edging out along was bending, that I might die a famous death, that the sky was a brilliant cobalt blue, that the birds were hitting me with their wings, that the wings did not hurt, that I did not know how to go backward. I froze. 'Just watch him,' my mother said. 'He knows what he's doing.'

Just the same, I was very pleased to hear Bill say, 'Maybe we should get a ladder.'

I began, obligingly, to shift into reverse. But my legs would not go backwards. The birds were coming back. I shut my eyes, opened them. I could see their nest ahead of me, a bundle of sticks with a toffee wrapper woven into it. If I were a Famous Actor, what would I do? I had no choice but to perform my action, to edge towards the nest. There were four eggs, pale blue with brown spots. I would stay in character, till the death.

'What good is a fucking ladder now?' Wally shrieked. 'What would I do with a ladder?'

The branch was dipping and swaying. I leaned forward and pressed my face deep into the nest.

THE HAIRY MAN took one egg in its maw. He held it there, trying to breathe around it.

'You should listen to me,' Wally shrieked. 'Not wait for this to happen.'

THE HAIRY MAN wanted to throw up. He could taste bird shit in his mouth.

I breathed through my nose and managed to make my arms go backwards. I knew I wasn't going to die my famous death just yet. I began to experience the feeling of what I would later know when

I did my first show in Saarlim – a feeling of intense well-being which was not contradicted, but rather amplified by the pulsing pain in my arms. I came down the tree, my arms feeling warm and sticky with blood, and shrugged myself free of my mother's eager embrace.

"Ah,' I said. 'Uh-uh-UH.' Finally she saw it: the egg in my mouth.

She held out her palm, her eyes bright, that bright, bright look, love-bright, nothing like it, and started laughing. Her coat was marked with my blood, her cheek pink from my blood.

'You can start a collection,' she said. 'I'll buy you a book about birds.'

'You're insane,' Wally was saying. I thought he meant my maman, naturally.

He grabbed me and held me so hard it hurt – chin, zipper, arms too tight around the chest – tobacco, stale sweat, rubber, liniment oil for his bad knee. 'You're crazy,' he said as he released me and patted down my snotty hair.

'Relax,' Bill said. 'It's the circus in his blood.'

'You keep out of this,' Wally said to Bill, and then, to my maman, 'I never want to see something like that again.'

'I don't think you're going to have a choice,' my mother said.

She put her hand on my head and stroked me. 'Do you want to see how to keep the egg?' she asked me. And she showed me there, beside the old rusting tank stand. She made a small hole in each end of the egg and blew its contents.

'That is the mouette's baby,' Wally said. 'Is that what you want to teach him?'

'I want him to be strong and brave,' Felicity said.

'You can't teach that,' Wally said. 'It's how he is. He is, anyway.'

'That's right. He is.' And she gave me back the egg, now light and as slippery with egg white as my own skin was with blood.

## 22

Two weeks before the Hairy Man climbed the tree, my father had gone to find a Saarlim newspaper in a provincial mall.

He had left my mother sitting on the bumper bar of the Haflinger, eating vanilla ice-cream. He had walked down into the shining wet-floored mall, dressed in rumpled faded dungarees and a plaid shirt, but he carried with him still, in spite of the ordinariness of his dress, his stardom – the softness of his skin, its sheen.

As he walked along the deserted early-morning mall he was very happy to be exactly where he was. There had been a full house the night before. There was another full house tonight. The day was clear-skied, eighty degrees. He planned to spend the morning fishing from a clinker boat.

Bill returned to Efica in the summers as other actors, his colleagues in Voorstand, went off to climb mountains in Nepal, to retain touch with something basic which his real life made impossible to know.

Here in the islands of Efica there were circus, theatre, horses, solitude, conflict, battles you could imagine might be won. Here, working for peanuts in a shitty little tent on the edge of the crumbling coast of Inkerman, playing to hatchet-faced oyster farmers, you could forget the franchised Sirkus Domes and the video satellites circling above the ozone layer, and you could imagine that theatre could still change the destiny of a country. In Efica you could have the illusion of being a warrior in a great battle, and when you toured you lived with others who shared the same illusion. When you toured, you performed as if art mattered. Doing agitprop under a petite tente you were inventing your nation's culture.

And he was – although he was to forget this in a moment – pleased to see his face in the large blue *Sad Sack Sirkus* poster at the news stand, pleased to be important in his own country. And when the voice called out his name, 'Bill Millefleur,' he turned, as an actor turns towards the light.

He saw two youths in their teens, conservatively dressed in three-button suits.

'Hi, fellahs,' he said.

So convinced was he of the scenario that when the button-nosed one drew out a box cutter, Bill's brain insisted that it was – against all the physical evidence to the contrary – a pen.

He smiled.

'Muddy,' the man said, and seemed to wave the 'pen' across Bill's cheek.

77

'Tapette,' said the other, and spat.

There was no pain, and when he felt the wet on his cheek he thought it was the spittle. The two young men did not run. They turned and walked quietly in amongst the nylon underwear on sale in Lucky Plaza, and then Bill's face began to sting and then to burn, and then he knew he had been slashed by members of the Ultra Rouge.

As he watched the blood drop in fat warm splats on the tiled floor of the mall, he thought what a fool he had been.

He was an actor, disfigured, for what? For what good reason? To play-act at politics? He walked through the mall, a rueful smile on his face, bent forward to keep the blood off his shirt, but by the time he reached Felicity on the street his face was shiny with it. She was sitting cross-legged on the fender of the company truck still eating the ice-cream from a cone, but when she saw him he thought he saw a flash of excitement in her bright green eyes.

Trust was always a fragile commodity with Bill, and when he saw, or imagined he saw, my mother's excitement, he thought it was a Voorstandish response – the excitement over risk, danger, blood. It was the same look you saw in the lines in Saarlim every night. It was what made Voorstand Voorstand, kept it alien no matter how long he stayed.

He blamed her then. He blamed her, silently, secretly, for placing his face on the poster, for using his fame to sell tickets for something that was, to his taste, distinctly mediocre. And now this damn scar, this wound.

She staunched the blood with her silk scarf, cancelled the night's show, flew him back to Chemin Rouge to see a good doctor, but somehow the cut changed things for Bill, and when he saw her blow the egg beneath the pine tree, he decided it was typical.

What he could not say to her was: wattle-eared old Wally had acted like an Efican, not timidly, but with respect for life. She was an alien, a foreigner, no matter what passionate speeches she made about culture or navigation cable, and he was surprised – lying beside her that afternoon, naked, squeezed in next to her on the twin bed in the Shark Harbour Motor Inn – to recognize the degree of hostility be felt towards the woman whom he had always thought of as his only love.

'He was not bird-nesting,' he said.

'Sweets, he brought me *eggs*.'

'It was the Hairy Man. It was his action.' He turned on his side and raised himself on his elbow. 'He was showing you his action. He was showing you he had the guts to perform his action. He did not plan the eggs. He made them the character's aim.'

She smiled. 'You're turning this into a story about you.'

'I'm not.'

'You're saying he climbed the tree because you wrote him one postcard.'

'All I'm suggesting,' he said, 'is that it would not be peculiar if that was what it was. We gave him a role and then we took it away from him.' But before he had finished speaking she was shaking her head, and he collapsed on to his back and stared up at the water-marked plaster.

In his mind's eye he could see how she would be in ten years' time, slightly hawkish, gaunt, her eyes still alight with that amazing life, and he knew he would certainly not love her then, not because of her looks, but because that force he saw there was distilling, intensifying, changing from something sexual into something cold and controlling.

'This isn't to do with you,' she said. 'Besides, it would be ludicrous for him to be an actor.'

'Please,' he said, 'I'm not nineteen any more.'

'No,' she said, and looked at him, and he wondered, was she thinking what he was thinking – that long-ago day when she had finally asked him to come in from the lane and eat with the collective? He had wanted to schtup her, he had such a hard-on – the way she carved the leg of lamb, the way she stood, her legs firmly apart, her fine-boned shoulders leaning in towards her work, the way her small hands grasped the implements, the thick slices of red meat, the blood pooled in the bottom of the dish. She scared him. He could not take his eyes off her.

He had imagined he was stealing flowers for a vegetarian, but she had heaped his plate with meat and looked so intently at him – it was always messed up with blood, from the beginning.

He was crazy about her, from Ophelia on. She slept with him, but she never said she loved him until she saw the voltige, and then she called him those names, Brave Billy-fleur etc. The insides of her thighs were glistening wet.

Thirteen years later, Bill lay beside her in the bed and realized that he wanted to be back in Saarlim. He stroked her side, caressed her in a gentle line from under her arm to her hip, and as he did so he allowed himself to know all the things he was angry about – that he had let himself be used in the publicity and poster, that he was identified with her cause, that he had been used, and disfigured, perhaps temporarily, perhaps not, that she was so committed to being right she could not even listen to a different point of view.

'Please don't be angry,' she said, looking over her shoulder at his face which, he knew, had revealed that little fault line in his brow.

'I'm not angry.'

'Don't you see – it would be ludicrous for him to be an actor.'

'I wasn't recommending it,' he said, and kissed her.

'You know how much I love him?' she said. 'You don't think I don't love him?'

'Don't worry,' he said, and made a small laugh – there was a sort of *mania* in the way she loved their son.

'I know I lose my temper with him. I've said terrible things to him,' she said, 'but I do love him.'

For Tristan she would deny herself, thwart herself, go places that bored her, go without sex, eat food she loathed, touch and caress him as if he were exactly that perfect child everyone had expected her to have when she named him Tristan. Her expectations of herself were so high that, after six weeks on the road, the pressure always showed. Bill saw the way she dressed him, almost brutally sometimes, pulling the tight polo-necked sweater down even though he screamed inside it. She would bang his head with the prickly hairbrush and tug the knots with the comb.

She did not want to be like this, and the kid did not either. He watched them both trying. They both apologized to each other. It was moving to see the little creature with his pale wet eyes stroke his beautiful mother's cheeks. It was also slightly pitiful to watch the way he tried to keep out of her way, to amuse himself, to ask for nothing, to curl his alarming limbs up into his body, to occupy a corner of the bed where he would not kick her in the night, but in the end they could – neither of them – stop it. He dropped a book, or broke a glass, or wet the bed. Bill, having drifted off, would wake to find Felicity screaming at Tristan, Tristan vomiting, Tristan crawling down the aisle to sleep in Wally's tent.

'Do you really think he was being an actor?' She shivered. 'Oh God.'

'How could I know?' Bill said. 'Like you say – I hardly know him.'

The northern summer was nearly over. Soon Saarlim City would be habitable again.

'You're very important to him,' my maman said.

Bill disentangled his legs from hers. 'Kids bird-nest,' he said firmly. 'It's what they do.'

## 23

As he drove the Haflinger towards the old dye town of Melcarth, Wally spied on my mother in the vibrating mirror above his head. He watched the shuddering reflection of her lips as she read to me from *The Birds of Efica*.

He knew the book – all those speckled eggs and out-of-register colour plates. He imagined Tristan Smith seduced by it, could not know that I was bored, worse than bored. I was DEPRESSED. I was an ACTOR not an egg-sucker. I had performed my ACTION and not a thing I could say would make this clear to either my mother or my father. They did not want to know.

Wally watched us from the driver's seat. He imagined me embarking on a dangerous career of bird-nesting and his mind whirred as he tried to find an antidote. As he drove, his eyes flicked from the road to the water-temperature gauge and his face appeared blunt, hollow-cheeked, vacant. It was, in fact, all sucked in around his feelings, and those feelings, although diffused and transferred out across the landscape, were centred on the back seat of the crowded bus – Tristan Smith, Felicity Smith, Bill Millefleur, the latter with a rich red scab running upwards from his chin.

Wally stared out through his dirty windscreen at the grey dusty road, a lumpy cigarette adhering to his bottom lip. From time to time he had a vision of my injured body, snapped bones, closed eyes. It came out of nowhere, like a tear in the film of life. He flinched from the sight, squinting shut his bloodshot eyes. Meanwhile my mother turned another page. She could not see the broken bones, but then she would not be the one to find my lifeless body amongst a bed of pine cones. It would be him. It would be him, because he would be there.

He had spent more hours, more *minutes*, with me than my mother or my father, than anyone on that bus. He was the one who fought with me, who forced the medicine down my gagging throat, put me to bed at nine o'clock on opening night. He was the one who had to scream and threaten me. He was my baby-sitter, my nanny, my paid companion. When we were in the street alone, the pair of us, he moved within the aura of my mighty stinks. He held me against his palm-treed rayon shirt and pushed the supermarket trolley and my life burned into his. My calloused ankles were imprinted on his chest. He understood my language without its being repeated. He imagined he understood my soul. That was his belief. He could never be one of those who said how beautiful I was. Indeed, he carried, in his speckled light grey eyes, a silent contempt for all of those who did.

This was a shy, fierce man with his passions all burning underground. The only way you might intuit his emotions was by the ferocity of his temper, by the way he had shouted at my mother about the ladder. She understood him well enough to pat his shoulder and then, when she boarded the bus at Shark Harbour with that brand new book, to kiss him lightly on his cheek. God damn, she pulled his strings, pressed his buttons. But still she was the same person who blew the mouette's egg yolk. She left it where it landed, like snot or come, like a poor spent life clinging to the grass and thistles by the tank stand of the Shark Harbour Mechanics Institute.

He had tried to talk to Bill about it, but Bill – he saw it happening – was already distancing himself from the child he had spent so much energy seducing.

'Kids bird-nest,' he said. 'It's what they do.'

He thought Bill had no right to call himself a father. They had no right to a child, either of them. But he had no power over them, only their frigging lives in his hands as he drove them. He thought about that: the road. He sought peace there, in the soft grey sand.

Wally enjoyed driving, and particularly enjoyed driving across the islands of the French Necklace where Captain Girard had found the *Cactus Ottomania* plants to grow the thickest. Wally liked the road itself – the real Efica, he thought – a soft grey unmade road with long straight stretches broken by rutted unbridged sandy-bottomed streams. He liked the rippling passage of the big old-fashioned steering wheel through his dry hands. He liked the way the sand softened the feel of the big-cleated tyres. But he liked most of all the idea that a foreigner could pass through this land-scape of countless dreary little cactus plants and see nothing – that you, Meneer, Madam, might dismiss them, belittle them – think them dull, impoverished, stupid – and not know that there was a second parallel chemical landscape in which the tinctures of the plants blazed crimson.*

None of us, sitting in the back seat, none of the actors and soup-servers playing cards and sleeping in the middle, guessed that the uneducated driver was travelling through the mirror of his soul.

Melcarth itself was no one's mirror, *pace* Captain Girard who had proclaimed it the capital of Neufasie.†

The caves, as usual, were illustrated on the drink coasters at the Melcarth Motor Inn, but Wally did not have drink coasters that night. When he had the bus parked between the tight ugly concrete columns which held the motel above the dun-coloured river, he washed the truck. It was Happy Hour, a time he normally spent in the bar, adopting life stories that might provide him with 'a little company', but he wanted to be alone and he spent Happy Hour finding a garden hose and a pair of demi-bottes and then he washed, not the float or the rented truck – he did not think these his responsibility – but his beloved Haflinger, slowly, carefully, think-ing all the time about ways to thwart my mother.

In the first century (EC) Melcarth had been a famous dyeing town, and even though the works had long ago closed down, the

* The cactus plants of Efica – Cactus Tinctorum, Nez Rouge, Poor-man's Back – once dyed the tunics of Italian soldiers, the robes of French choirboys, the ceremonial cloaks of the kings and queens of England. On the first Monday of every month, you can go to the museum in Chemin Rouge and see the ancient red clothes stacked high – crimson, madder, rose, carmine, ruby, vermilion. There are also two skeins of red thread, once the property of the last of the IPs in Nez Noir, but little is known about the provenance of this exhibit.
† 'Here there is a high mountain, out of which the finest blue is mined. There are veins in the earth whence silver is mined. The little cactus plant is everywhere so abundant that one might, had one the cloth, provide red tunics for all the king's men from now until the end of the world. The fowl is abundant and the fishing good. Once again we chose a splendid little house in a cave and gave thanks to God for leading us, after so many misadventures, to this Eden.' Girard, Journals, vol. xv.

river still had the poisoned look for which the dye works had originally been responsible. Its banks were lined with chemical storage tanks, and old warehouses which had once hoarded red cloth like Persian carpets but which were now half derelict, carrying silvery ghosts of signs for Hellas Aspirin. At sunset, Wally removed the tent poles and guy ropes which were stashed along the aisle of the bus. He took them out one by one, and laid them in the next parking bay. He laid them all neatly parallel, the six-inch aluminium poles, the one-inch thick ropes.

He swept the bus, emptied the ashtrays, folded the blankets, shook out the ganja butts and biscuit crumbs and chocolate-bar wrappers and swept them all neatly into a dark corner of the car park. Then he squatted with his back against the stained concrete wall of the car park, adding the smell of Dutch tobacco to the riverside odours of cold mud and flying foxes.

The river caught the sun and shone a bright bilious copper colour before sliding into ash-purple and – as the neon lights flickered on above Wally's head – a deep and definite black.

It was at this point, when all the poles and ropes were still lying on the floor, that Roxanna Wonder Wilkinson came bouncing into the car park, broke, abandoned, stinking of spilt kerosene. She bottomed-out on the culvert, squealed her tyres across the shiny concrete floor and squeaked to a stop almost in front of him.

She was just like Irma.* That was the first thing that struck him – the spitting image. She had the blonde hair, the red dress. She was plump, buxom. She had the peaches and cream complexion, the pert nose.

She was trying to park the car and little caravan behind it. He watched her swing the wheel from lock to lock. He was no longer thinking about eggs. The tyre rubber screeched unpleasantly against the concrete. She edged forward, she edged back. Wally shifted on his haunches, and flicked away his cigarette.

He stood. He wiped his hands carefully with his handkerchief. He combed his hair, two flicks. He dropped his comb in his shirt pocket and walked across the neon-bright concrete forecourt,

---

* *The role of the little blonde ingénue who recites the 'Great Works' in the Saarlim Sirkus has always been known as 'Irma' in Efica. Why it should be Irma here and Heidi there, no one can tell me.* [TS]

shading his pale eyes with a freckled hand which would, within ten minutes, be cupped around Roxanna's pigeon.

## 24

'Can I be of assistance?' Wally said.

He put his freckled hands on the edge of the car door and Roxanna considered them thoughtfully: the stranger's wide pink nails hooked over her wound-down window.

She turned off the ignition, leaving the car stuck where it was, its wheels askew, poking out into the entrance lane. 'Got a light?' she asked. This time yesterday she had been a married woman.

Wally's lighter was silver, with a windshield. When it flamed it was red and smoky, and Roxanna – fresh from her own adventures with kerosene – held back her fringe to stop it getting burnt.

'It's the Happy Hour,' he said when she had exhaled. He just said it as a fact. As if it were the Happy Hour and therefore dot dot dot.

Until this moment Roxanna's only plan had been to check into the motel, eat on room service, and leave without paying. Now she looked at this man and considered him. She had done worse things in the old days, but the truth was – yuk – she no longer had the stomach for the life.

'Could you tell me what day the local zine comes out?' she said, and hid from his insistent eyes in her handkerchief, blowing her nose wetly, unattractively, deliberately. She found her dark glasses in her bag and put them on. 'I need to put an avvert in.'

'What are you selling?' he said. He had a high forehead like a clown, and sad grey freckled eyes.

'Pigeons,' she said, very level.

'What sort of pigeons?' Wally said. 'I got a young fellah might be interested.'

'Racing pigeons,' she said.

'Start him off with a couple of street-peckers.'

'These aren't street-peckers,' she said. 'They're racing pigeons. They have *pedigrees*.'

'I had a grandpa who raced pigeons,' the punter said. 'He won a lot of races, but he never had any pedigrees. I had a *dog* once.' He smiled: he had wide pale lips. 'Now that fellow had a pedigree.'

'So are you interested or what?' She took the keys out of the ignition. She wiped her hands with her handkerchief. 'I've got other people interested.'

'I could be *persuaded*.'

'What do you think I'm talking about, mister?' she said.

He opened the door for her and stepped back politely so she could get out of the car. 'Not doves,' he said, and grinned.

'They're expensive,' she said, lowering her eyes as she locked the door. 'That's all I meant. It isn't like an impulse buy.'

As she walked back to the caravan, she sensed Wally Paccione's freckled hand, imagined it half an inch away from her pleated red skirt, as insistent as thrip, a fruit fly hovering, but when she looked over her shoulder she saw he was not even looking at her, but back towards the chalky green motel doors.

When she opened the van for him the smell came flooding out.

'Sorry,' she said.

That smell used to drive Reade crazy. He always asked her – every morning before he drove away – please clean the loft. When she was under the impression that pigeons made BIG MONEY she had cleaned – brooms, scrubbing brushes, disinfectant. She had been a fanatic in the cause. She laid out brown-eyed peas, ground millet, butcher's seed. She checked each hen once every day – eyes, throat etc. But when she saw what Reade's idea of BIG MONEY was, she gave up on the pigeons.

If she had bought a gun and pushed him into a bank, Reade would have thought she was a genius. But when she wrote away for books, he laughed and farted and spilt his drink back in his glass.

'Your lips move,' he said. 'Your fucking lips move, Roxanna.'

She let him laugh. It made him look so pitiful.

She sat in the kitchen in her dressing gown, toast crumbs embedded in her elbows. She read about things that bewildered him: the production of tin soldiers in nineteenth-century Europe, for instance. His lip curled, but his eyes looked frightened. He could not imagine the pay-off. He was not meant to. She read slowly with a wooden ruler held under each line.

He came home with beer on his breath and snatched the ruler away. She knew he was hanging round with that Voorstandish widow up at the cashier's office. He did not look beautiful any more. His sexy red lips had got all twisted and his eyes were bulging, like someone with a thyroid condition. He was her husband, but she looked at him from far, far away – one more bozo going to hit it big with greyhounds, pigeons, possum furs.

Rich people did not mess with things that shit or made you ill. Only poor people did that. Reade already had bronchitis, fancier's lung, all that bloom which came off the birds, white clouds of it, every time they settled.

The weird thing was that when he split, he abandoned the pigeons too. Now they were her only asset.

'Can I hold one?' the punter asked her at the Melcarth Motor Inn.

She folded her arms across her chest and watched him as he lifted out the cage and opened it without being shown the tricky latch. He took the bird – hands up and down its chest, down around its neck, like a fancier.

What she could not know was that the only two truly happy years of Wally's childhood had been spent with his maternal grandfather who was exactly that character that Roxanna now despised – the working-class man with a passion for pigeons, a man making twenty-five cent bets, upgrading his stock, crossing street-pecker with street-pecker, dreaming of the big bets, the famous birds.

She watched him running his nicotine-stained finger down the back of the bird's head and thought he was just like Reade looking at ties in an expensive shop. She was deep within herself. She did not hear the five members of the Feu Follet cross the yard and stand behind her. What she was thinking was: she was back at square one – if he did not buy these birds, she was going to have to have sexual intercourse for money.

Then she heard the scrape of shoe behind her. The hair on her neck stood on end. She spun around and saw tattoos, face scars, ripped shirts and sweaters, a bald-headed man with bright blue eyes staring at her tits. Sweat pooled in the tight creases of her hands.

There was a woman with an accent like a Sirkus star. She was striking, pale-faced, copper-haired, holding a blond-haired child who was hiding himself under a patchwork shawl.

'We all wanted to see the clean bus, Wally.'

'Here, Tristan,' Wally said to the fair-haired boy. 'Hold this.'

A pair of surprisingly large hands emerged from the tatty shawl, and as the child took the bird she saw his face, my face.

*Jesus fucking Christ Almighty.*

It was hard to look, hard to not look – my triangular head, my dense blond hair, my frightening lipless mouth, my small regular white teeth, my striated marble eyes – terrible, beautiful – flecked with gold, like jewellery.

'Feel its heart,' the punter said. 'You can feel its heart beating in your hand.'

Everything was happening for Roxanna in slo-mo. She saw Tristan Smith hold her pigeon with his normal hands.

'You feel that?' Wally said. 'That's its heart.'

The boy cupped his hand around her pigeon's breast.

He said, 'Air . . . atter.'

'OK, you're an actor,' the punter said. 'I never said you wasn't.'

'Ah . . . don . . . hellet . . . ehh.'

'That's right. You don't collect anything yet,' the punter said. 'I'm not saying you're not an actor. I'm asking you, would you like to breed pigeons, race them? Feel its heart, feel it on your face.'

'Ah . . . don't . . . hellet . . . ehh.'

'You don't collect their eggs. You let the yolk stay inside, then you get birds out of them.'

The boy held the bird so tight Roxanna feared he was going to choke it.

'You like the pigeon?' the woman asked. 'Would you like that?'

The boy's eyes were big, swimming, alive, all those fine gold stripes flashing in the artificial light. His legs were twisted, wasted, pipe cleaners inside his striped pyjamas. He nodded.

'Is this OK?' the punter asked the beautiful woman.

The woman turned to the boy. She smiled and stroked his soft white neck. 'Is this instead of climbing trees?' she asked him.

When the punter turned back to Roxanna his face was blazing red. His eyes had changed. They had been all sleepy and slitted but now they were bright, prickly, absolutely awake.

'How much?' he said.

Roxanna did not know what it was, but she saw something was happening.

'I don't sell them individually,' she said.

'All of them,' the punter said, his colour still high.

He held the bird's beak open and looked inside – checking the cleft.

'That's Apple Pie,' she said. 'He's famous.'

'How much is all I'm asking.'

She thought 300. She thought 5000. 'You couldn't afford it,' she said.

'Wally,' said the beautiful woman, swinging Tristan Smith on to her other hip, 'where would we keep pigeons in Chemin Rouge?'

'Chemin Rouge?' Roxanna asked. (There was an antique toy exhibition in Chemin Rouge next week!) 'Are you going back to Chemin Rouge?'

'We get the right price, we're going to buy it,' the punter told the boy. 'We're going to have pigeons.' To the woman he said, 'Is this OK?'

'They're educational,' Roxanna said. 'Maths, genetics, dot dot dot.'

The punter could not hear her. He was looking straight into Tristan Smith's wild unnatural eyes. He was like a man proposing marriage – still, intense, a coiled spring.

'A thousand,' Roxanna said.

The minute she said it, she knew it was too much. She saw his Adam's apple move. He grinned at her, a little foolishly.

'Oh, for heaven's sake,' said the beautiful woman.

'I'd set you up,' Roxanna said to Wally. 'You know what I mean?'

That was how sex got mixed up with it again. She hadn't needed to say this. It was habit, insecurity.

'You know what I mean?' she said. 'For a thousand, I'd be prepared to come down to Chemin Rouge and set you up, get everything in nice working order.'

'We're actors,' the woman said. 'We haven't got that kind of money.'

'Three hundred,' Wally said.

In the end Wally paid 650 dollars and my mother was aghast, bewildered. 'Was this about what I think it was about?' she asked Bill Millefleur.

## 25

The last day of the tour found our party camped at Fiddler's Creek, waiting for the next day's car ferry to Chemin Rouge. Bill had spent the late morning in sleep, or pretended sleep, and now he lay in the back seat of the bus, reading and rereading the first page of *Dead Souls*, wishing nothing more than for the time to pass, the sultry day to go, for tomorrow to come so he could catch his flight back home to Saarlim City.

My maman, however, had other plans for the last day.

She appeared at the window by his head, tapping, beckoning. 'What?'

When she saw his face through the dusty window – the great ridged scar from mouth to chin, the anxious eyes – Felicity knew something was up, but she did not know how serious it was.

Bill held up his book.

She shook her head and beckoned.

When he appeared at the bus door, he looked strangely shy, and she took him by his hand and led him past the dusty horse float, through the hash-sweet campsite, along a rather melancholy avenue lined with dead black mimosa trees and shoulder-high blackberries whose leaves were now grey from dust.

'What is this?' he said.

'You'll see,' she teased him.

Around the bend Bill saw his best linen suit, clean and pressed, shrouded in plastic, hanging from a low mimosa just off the track. He felt a dull kind of dread.

'Some fancy joint?' he asked. 'Out here?'

'Sssh.' My mother made her eyes go big, fluttered her lashes, began to undo the buttons of her khaki shorts.

'Some joint with cha-cha?' Bill whispered, rolled his eyes.

'Ssh.' My maman slipped out of her shorts and into the deliberately crumpled blue silk overall she had carried in her handbag. 'They'll hang us if they find us out.'

There was nothing for my father to do but get into the suit.

When they were both changed, my mother took him by the hand and set off, not along the road, but along a narrow path of the sort made by cattle. She had played this kind of game before – birthdays, anniversaries – and Bill guessed they would soon come to a village or at least a filling station where she would have arranged a rent-a-car.

Their destination, however, turned out to be an unprepossessing building 200 yards away. It was larger than the little fishing shacks beside it, but just as rusty. It was only as they came to the steps of the wide veranda that he noticed the details, the crispness of finish, the spare teak-framed doorways cut into the thickly insulated corrugated skin.

It was a small hotel, very Efican in its modesty – expensive, of course, but affecting, in its skin, the artful camouflage of rural decay.

Bill's hand went to his slashed face, feeling the raw, rough ridge.

'You don't like it.'

'No,' he said. 'Good heavens, no. The opposite.'

And as they walked to their suite he gesticulated and congratulated, admired the view of the mudflats, the red and blue hangings of old Indienne, but he could not keep the shadow of depression out of his eyes.

'It's a lot of money, I know,' she said when the concierge closed the door to the room and they were at last alone. 'It's very bourgeois.'

'It's wonderful.' Bill held his arms wide. The room was white and spare, the floor teak. 'It's very tasteful.'

'Tasteful?' She raised her eyebrows.

'Wonderful. Truly wonderful. It's such a treat.'

'It'll be our last night for eight months, mo-chou. I wanted it to be nice.'

'It's wonderful.'

When Bill and Felicity lay in bed after their bath, she said, again, 'I wanted you to remember Efica like this.'

They could look down their long pink naked limbs and see, behind the rifle sights of their toes, the inky blue clouds of a thunderstorm, the low lines of brilliant green mangroves, the long flat mudflats glistening pink in the late sun and the spindle-legged birds gathering their evening meal.

They had soaked in the hot tub and soaped each other, but now they lay naked, side by side, neither sought the other.

'Are you OK, Billy-fleur?' Felicity turned on her side and began to slowly rub his smooth wide chest with the flat of her hand.

'I guess.'

'Depressed?'

'Nah . . .' He held his hand over his eyes. 'I'm OK.'

'What's the matter?'

She peeled the hand back from the eyes, playfully.

He pulled his hand away with a roughness that surprised even him. No sooner had he done it than he was stroking her hand and apologizing.

Felicity stroked his neck but her hand came clumsily close to his face and he turned his head away from her.

'Is it your face?' she said suddenly. 'Of course, I'm sorry. You're upset about your face.'

In his late thirties, interviewers, women particularly, would like to ask the question about the small pale line that ran from the corner of Bill's mouth to the point of his chin. There would be something sexual about this mark whose story the Sirkus performer would never tell. They would extend a finger sometimes, as if they would have liked to touch it, and he would rest his own forefinger on the pale silky little path of tissue, and smile.

But when Bill smiled at my mother, the scar was ridged, raw, purple, and destroyed the symmetry of his archer's-bow lips.

'Let's have a good time,' my mother said. 'It's our last night for a year.'

Bill held up his glass, smiling. My mother filled it. Bill sipped the champagne and placed it carefully beside the bed, but once that was done, he was quiet and she could feel nothing had changed. She put her hand out to the scar and this time touched it deliberately.

'You know how you've *worked* to convince me that this didn't matter to you?'

'So think: why would I act like that?'

'Well, it's not so crazy . . . '

'. . . so you'd admire me.'

She looked across at him. He turned his head towards her, his mouth loose, his chin a little soft.

'So you'd *admire* me,' he repeated.

She shook her head. She could feel all his upset broiling and churning away beneath the surface.

He lay on his back again, staring up at the carefully finished teak ceiling. She lay propped up on her elbow, watching him. He said, 'Your whole life you are surrounded by people doing things so you'll admire them. Moey does a high-wire act. Your son tries to kill himself in a pine tree. I pretend this doesn't matter.'

'You get yourself slashed . . . for me.'

'That isn't what I said, but still: who put me on the poster?'

'Bill, that's not even logical. You're so angry.'

'I'm not angry. I'm not angry at all. This has been happening to you all your life,' he said. 'You should let yourself see it.'

She sat up again and sipped her drink. 'This is nothing to do with me. It's all to do with you.'

'What?' He also sat up and raised his eyebrow at her.

'You're angry. You're looking for something to let your anger out on.'

'Of course I am fucking angry. You would be angry too. I got my face slashed for nothing.'

'Hunning, it's going to be fine. It looks horrible now, but you told me what the doctor said . . . '

'A tour like this. What's it for? If there's an election tomorrow . . . '

'There's one on January 22 . . . '

'All right. If there's an election next month, what have you affected?'

My maman looked at him a long, long time, her forehead creasing, a shadow appearing in her eyes.

'People come,' she said at last. 'They laugh, they cry, their minds are engaged.'

'Why are you so wilful? Why are you so deliberately not understanding? You know who these people are that come. They're converts. You come down out of the sky like some angel of fucking light. They love you before you get there. Nothing changes.'

'So why are you here?'

'I don't see that it is worth it,' Bill said. 'I said a group of performers who feel they are beyond criticism, who elevate sloppiness to a style of acting.'

'You think our work is poor?'

'It's perfectly fine.'

'Don't patronize me.'

'I'm not patronizing. I'm saying: it is perfectly fine. It's like this champagne . . . '

'You don't like the *champagne* . . . '

'Well, actually it is not champagne . . . You cheer up the lonely liberals, you annoy the fascists. It entertains. It educates.'

'But you despise it.'

'No, I don't despise it. It's just not worth getting myself slashed for. I feel a fool. I feel like I've been in a theme park, acting out some heroic role, and now it's time to go home and . . . '

'Have I become provincial?'

'All art is provincial.'

'That's an evasion.'

'Well, what do you mean?'

'I always thought I'd know if I was becoming second-rate.'

He shrugged. It took only a second. She did not ask him to explain it. She did not need to.

'I always thought I'd know.'

He took her hand and held it. 'You know what you should do? *Tartuffe*. Costumes, the works. Have some fun. You might even make money. There's a great French video of Bernstein's *Tartuffe*. It's a little campy, but very nicely done.'

'You've thought this, all through the tour?'

'You're too smart to waste your time like this.'

She looked at him, her brow furrowed.

'You thought all this, when you were giving notes?'

'I've fooled myself,' he said. 'It's like some kids' game. I got too excited and let myself believe it was real.'

'You little snot,' she said.

'What?'

'You little snot. You shallow, vain, posturing little snot. Don't you dare act out your vulgar Sirkuses and come and tell me that what we do here does not matter.'

'I don't think you should talk to me like that.'

'Why? What will happen to me?'

'I might not be interested in coming back.'

'Why would I want you back?'

'To fill the seats,' he said. 'You had me on the fucking poster, so don't you curl your lip and say "Oh dear" to me, and *never*, not *ever* do I want you to use that word about me again.'

And so on.

Some time before dawn Bill and my mother stumbled back along the narrow cattle path, dehydrated from the wine, heavy with sleep, trying to avoid blackberry tangles in the dark. At the camp site, they felt their way carefully through the tethered horses and crawled into the bus.

94

'Are you OK, Billy-fleur?' she asked him.

'I'm fine,' he said.

'Did you kiss your little boy goodnight? He's been so happy to have his father home.'

'I didn't mean it,' he said. 'The work is really wonderful.'


## 26

I boarded the Haflinger next morning ignorant of my future. I sat next to Bill Millefleur and put my hand in his. I had no idea, as I fiddled with the ornate silver ring on his left hand, that he was breaking up with my mother and therefore ipso facto was breaking up with me.

His eyes were puffy, his mouth disconsolate.

'Are . . . you . . . tired?' I asked him.

'Yes,' he said.

Then my mother came on to the bus.

I knew she had woken with lank dirty hair and a headache, but now as she came down the aisle of the Haflinger she had changed herself into a bride in a satire – beautiful, golden, funny, drunk on oxygen. She wore the long white loose-fitting dress and sandals she always wore in *Hamlet*. This item was now thirteen years old. It was patched, threaded, had yellowed patches round the hems.

I did not know what it meant. I simply clapped her. She looked so beautiful. She kissed me very sweetly and smiled at Bill. Her fury was odourless, invisible. She sat herself between us, tucking her legs girlishly under her.

'We're going to do *Tartuffe*,' she told the bus of actors as the Haflinger lumbered out of our camp site. 'It's the new season. Just Molière.'

None of these actors had ever played Molière, and not one asked her what she meant, but her delivery was so fast, funny, and everybody picked up on *Tartuffe*, and as we headed for the ferry along the Road of Broken Bridges the bus was filled with *Tartuffe* jokes.*

---

* Felicity later told me that she thought **Tartuffe** *a very political and 'appropriate' play, and one which she could have quite happily adapted for the Feu Follet, but that she was using the title in the way that Bill, in 'all his splendid ignorance', intended.* [TS]

'Will . . . I . . . have . . . a . . . part?' I asked her.

'We'll all have parts,' my maman said carelessly.

I clapped again.

'Especially Bill.'

But when I wished to talk about my part, she would not hear me.

'What . . . about . . . my . . . part? . . . What . . . about . . . my . . . part?'

Finally she hissed in my ear, 'It's a joke, there's no *Tartuffe*.'

It was, you can see, complicated weather in that bus, and no one could have guessed that *Tartuffe*, this word she continued to throw around so lightly, was a knife, and that my maman was using it to saw at the bonds that tied her to my father.

I watched my maman laugh and felt unhappy. I did not know why I should. All I could see was that Claire Chen was now the driver of the Haflinger and I had lost Wally to Roxanna and her pigeons. I doubt that this would have mattered to me if the air had been less poisonous, if my maman had not been so agitated about *Tartuffe*, but in the course of a few hours the pigeons became the basin into which I poured all the bilious liquid of my distress. I came to dislike them like you come to dislike the last meal before an illness. I was repulsed by the memory of their nervous fibrillating hearts, the way they squirmed and made my fingers oily. On the bus I became nauseous. On the ferry I threw up – raisins and apple juice all down my front.

'Would you?' my maman asked my dab.

Bill took me to the bathroom and cleaned me up, roughly, impatiently.

He felt he had *outgrown* his relationship with us. He had come out on the flight, eager to be with us, to be a proper father. Now he had decided we were hicks, cambruces. He brought me back on to the deck with raisins still sticking to my shirt.

'Oh look,' my Maman beamed at me. 'Don't you have a lovely father.'

All the way up, across the Straits of Shanor, up Highway 1, Bill lived in a morass of sub-text. Nothing, even my mother's hand on his thigh, meant what it seemed to mean. And this white dress, the same one he had seen her wear as Ophelia thirteen years before, was a bitter reproach whose meaning, being unable to be discussed, could never be exactly clear and was, in all its ambiguity, all its possible meanings, like one of those barbarous bullets which fragment inside the body.

Bill wanted to be out of there. He could not wait. He thought of women he knew in Saarlim, young, sophisticated, very pretty. He thought of shops he might visit. Restaurants where he was known.

On the outskirts of Chemin Rouge, he announced that he would not travel all the way back to Gazette Street but catch the airport bus at the Ritz. My maman did not argue with him.

When the Haflinger stopped, my father shook my hand. He wished me well. I had no idea of the damage that had been done. None of the actors watching Felicity kiss Bill goodbye outside the Chemin Rouge Ritz guessed how urgently he wished to leave or how badly they had hurt each other. She kissed him lusciously, softly, sensuously, but carelessly too, like you might eat a peach in the middle of the season.

'Stop it,' he said, gripping her shoulders.

'*Tartuffe*,' she told him, and slipped away, laughing. From her seat in the bus she blew kisses and waved and the bad feeling did not break through the sea wall until she was inside the tower again and the actors were running in and out of the building, shaking the floor joists as they unloaded the remnants of *The Sad Sack Sirkus*.

## 27

Gabe Manzini arrived at the Chemin Rouge Ritz at the same time as Bill Millefleur got down from the Feu Follet bus, and if it took him a moment to recognize him, it was not just the fresh scar, which was certainly disconcerting, but the fact that Manzini was just off the flight from Saarlim.

It was not exactly culture shock that the short athletic man with the trimmed grey-flecked hair was suffering from. He came here too often for shock. It was something softer, more diffuse that he felt, a sort of mosquito net between himself and life, a dulling of some senses, a heightening of others, an almost sexual response, not unconnected to women, but also related to the place itself, the wide sleepy straight streets, the fragrant mangoes, the dried biche-la-mar hanging in racks in the old godowns by the river, the river itself which would, with luck, soon be filled with thunder-borne water, raging, turbulent, clay-yellow.

Gabe Manzini loved the taste of the air at this time of year. He was alive to the taste of mould spore amongst the fresh-mown grass. It was all so far from the great Sirkus Domes of Saarlim City and when a tall dark-haired man in a crushed light suit brushed past him, it took a moment to place him properly.

'Mr Millefleur,' he said.

The Sirkus performer turned, blinked.

'You don't know me,' Gabe said. 'I just love the way you handle horses.'

The young man frowned, nodded, and something in the way he did it, his embarrassment, made Gabe remember that he was indeed an Efican and, rather than being annoyed by his gracelessness, as he once would have been, he privately celebrated it. He liked Eficans, their lack of slickness, their sense of privacy, even their disconcerting habit of calling their superiors by their first name. He liked their lack of bullshit, their pragmatism, their sense of realpolitik. And as he walked across the soft grey carpet to check in, he began to think how he might use this Efican actor with strong ties in Voorstand. It occupied him as he signed in, as he went up to his room, and when he was finally alone he dictated a short note which would sit in the computer casebook all through the exercise.

In the end he would not try to recruit Bill Millefleur – he would not need to – but the actor's name would sit in the secret action book of Voorstand's chief undercover 'vote-dokter'* for the following six weeks, and when the elections were finally over he would look back at this moment, when he crossed paths with Bill Millefleur, and marvel at the symmetry.

## 28

It was the smells that got my mother, I was sure of it. She had forgotten the way they pile up – dampness, mould, the leaking gas, rodents in the walls, rotting wood in the sills, the rust-and-grease odour from damaged plumbing. These are things she had lived with, shaped herself to, but when she re-entered her old life,

* *The author is aware that your PM claims that no such position exists in the VIA.* [TS]

which was, in the afternoon sun, as unlovingly lit as a stage under work lights, overly warm, bright, malodorous – it reminded her of everything that was unsatisfactory about her existence.

The tower had become smaller than her memory of it. It smelt of mouse and mouldy paper. Yellow sun entered through a screen of rain-spotted dust. It made her whole life seem second-rate.

'I'm sick of this,' she said.

'Really?' I said, but I was already shot through with panic.

'Yes,' she shouted, tugging at the sleeves of her Ophelia dress. 'Really. Totally, completely sick of it.'

I unrolled my mattress and lay down on it and folded my arms behind my head.

'I'm . . . not.'

My maman walked to the window where she looked down at Wally and Roxanna, who was unloading pigeon cages on to the vert-walk.

'Funny old Wally,' she said.

'It . . . always . . . smells . . . like . . . this . . . when . . . we . . . get . . . back . . . Open . . . the . . . window . . . the . . . smell . . . goes.'

'Tristan, your maman is too old to live like this any more.'

I pulled my knees up to my stomach. She sat down on the mattress beside me. She stroked my head, but there was something actorly in the way she did it and I flinched from her.

'Don't!' she cried.

I took her hand and kissed it.

'We could live in a proper house,' she said. She touched my hair, again not hard, and even though it still felt false, I let her do it. 'You could have a yard,' she said. 'With trees. We could be in a proper house tomorrow.'

'Hate . . . trees.'

'Oh,' she tried to tease me. 'It must be another boy who liked to climb them.'

I opened my stony-white eyes and stared into hers. 'I . . . need . . . a . . . *theatre*,' I said softly. 'Maman . . . I . . . have . . . a . . . destiny . . . '

My poor mother. She put her hand up against the place on her chest where you could see the bones beneath the skin. 'Tristan, listen to me.'

I knew what she was going to say.

'I . . . know . . . I . . . am . . . not . . . handsome.'

'Don't kick.'

I shut my eyes, squinched up my face.

'I . . . will . . . play . . . Richard . . . the . . . Third.'

Felicity put her hand across her mouth. 'You know who Richard the Third is?'

'A . . . mighty . . . king.'

'Who set you up to this?'

'Now . . . is . . . the . . . Winter . . . of . . . our . . . discontent.'

'You *cannot* be an actor,' she said. 'You would not *want* to be.'

'You're . . . an . . . actor.'

'Not any more,' she said.

'The . . . smell . . . will . . . go . . . you'll . . . get . . . used . . . to . . . it.'

'I don't want to get used to it,' she said.

She leaned out the window to where Wally was unloading the pigeons and stacking them along the street.

She called, 'Wally.' Then, 'Come up.'

'He . . . knows . . . what . . . I . . . want,' I said. 'He . . . loves . . . actors . . . when . . . he . . . is . . . reincarnated . . . he is going . . . to . . . be . . . an . . . actor.'

'Re-what?'

'When . . . he . . .lives . . . after . . . he . . . has . . . been . . . dead.'

'Do you really think I'd ask Wally's advice about acting?'

'Why . . . you . . . asking . . . him . . . up?'

'We could let him keep his pigeons here,' she said brightly. 'This could be a perfect pigeon loft.'

'NO.'

'Tristan, what have we ever done for Wally and what has Wally done for us? He loves you so much, I think he would die if anything happened to you. He only bought those pigeons because you liked them.'

'Birds . . . in . . . our . . . HOME? . . . No . . . one . . . will . . . let . . . you . . . do . . . it.'

'No one will *let* me?'

'The . . . collective . . . won't . . . let . . . you . . . REALLY.'

She came and sat down beside me on the mattress. 'You want to know what's bad about being an actor?'

Her skin looked white and tired, but her eyes were dangerously active – angry and demanding.

'When you are an actor, you are so dependent. You're a baby. You stand in line. The director and the producer look at you (look at me if I let them) like you're a worm. They know less about the play than you do. They have the most superficial understanding of the material, but they turn you into a lump of nervous jelly, even the most pathetic specimens, just with their power. They talk about the character you will play as if it is nothing to do with you. They talk about your body like it was a thing. They give someone else the role. When you are an actor your normal state is unemployed. It is so hard to even have a reason to get up in the morning.'

'You . . . are . . . an . . . actor,' I insisted.

'No,' she said. 'I'm an actor-manager, and if I want to put pigeons in my tower, then that is going to be my pleasure.'

## 29

All my mother's misery was now focused, not on Bill or his comments about the company's work, but on the tower. My father had left us, but it was the tower that was the demon. Once she had decided this, she could not stay still. Even though it was a Sunday, she had to act.

She rushed out to the cavernous old Levantine shop on the Boulevard des Indiennes and came back with *Zinebleu*, the *Argus*, the *Herald*, the *News*, *Chemin Rouge Zine*, *L'Observateur*, *Le Petit Zine*, and took to them with a big pair of dress-maker's scissors. She covered the slippery floor with sheets of expensive cartridge paper and on each sheet she wrote the name of a street or an area she imagined might be pleasant to live in. Then she cut out the little avverts and glued them to the paper.

Wally arrived twice to invite me to come and feed the pigeons, but I would have nothing to do with pigeons. I stayed on my mattress ostentatiously reading *Theatre Through the Ages*.

I wished Vincent would come and look after my maman. But Sunday was Natalie's time and my mother could not even call him at his home. The only thing she could do is what she did – stay up all night cutting up the sheets of paper and arranging them in different ways. When I took her Voorstand first-edition Stanislavsky from her shelf, she did not try to stop me. I read it, pointedly, waiting for her to take it back.

Some time in the night she woke me to give me a chocolate bar. She touched my hair, tenderly. I was very hungry, but I knew that eating chocolate would somehow weaken my hold on the tower. I picked up the Stanislavsky and left the chocolate, unopened, on the coverlet.

The next thing it was six-thirty a.m. The Stanislavsky was sitting on my maman's desk. She was talking to Vincent on the telephone. She was bright, alert, positive, but her bed had not been slept in and she was still wearing the same long grey dress with the white collar. While she talked I tried to find the chocolate bar but could not see it anywhere.

At half past nine we left the theatre, walking past the pigeons which were piled up in the gloomy foyer in their wicker cages. Vincent tried to persuade me to fondle one but I drew my fingers back into a fist and wrinkled up my nose. Then he took us for breakfast in a booth at the Patisserie Jean Claude where I ate two plates of scrambled eggs and bacon and drank three hot chocolates. By half past ten I had a stomach ache and we were touring property in Vincent's Corniche. These were not the properties advertised in the papers, but properties owned by Vincent and his brother.

I had no intention of leaving Gazette Street, I told my mother. She listened to me carefully, nodding her head and seeming to give weight to my objections, but I knew she thought she could bring anyone round to her point of view.

Each new property made her more animated, talkative, 'girlish', and Vincent spent the day with his neck glowing pink above his collar, a sure sign of what was happening below his belt. Yet when we returned to Gazette Street she did not, incredibly, ask him in.

She kissed him on the street, in public, and carried me inside.

The minute we were inside the Feu Follet, everybody wanted Felicity Smith – they set upon her in such a hungry way that I barely had space to notice the pigeons were gone from the foyer – but we stopped for none of the supplicants. We went up to the tower, shut the door, and locked it.

There my mother walked up and down, loudly noticing how small the tower was, talking about the big house we had seen on

Cockaigne Place, the two bathrooms on Hellot Road, but mostly about the little house Vincent had had Belinda Burastin build for him in the bushland fifteen miles away. She said I would be more cheerful when I was not constricted by 'this wretched place'.

'What . . . wretched . . . place?'.

'Oh darling, you'll see – there's so much more to life than theatre.'

My mother smiled and kissed me.

In defence, I picked up the Stanislavsky. I opened the musty pages. This is what I read:

There are those who think that nature often works poorly. To some aesthetically minded people, taste is of greater consequence than truth. But in the instant that a crowd of thousands is being moved, when they are all swept by a feeling of enthusiasm, no matter what the physical shortcomings of the actors who cause this emotional storm. At such times, even a deformed person becomes beautiful.

I did not tell her. I did not take the chance that she would say something sarcastic which would weaken it. Instead I took the book and quietly wrapped it in a pillowslip.

Soon, I was pleased to see, she changed her clothes and announced she was having 'supper' with Vincent at the Chemin Rouge Ritz. She made me eat some vitamin pills and wrote her hotel room number on a slip of paper and pinned it to the door.

She kissed me. I kissed her back.

The minute she was gone – before Wally came looking for me – I stole the Stanislavsky. I dragged it downstairs – thump, thump, thump – thinking I would hide it under the bricks in the stables where I had rehearsed for *The Sad Sack Sirkus* tour.

The pigeons, however, had got there first. They whispered and fluttered in their wicker baskets in the very corner where I had planned to hide my (now slightly damaged) Stanislavsky. It was only then I realized I might really lose my tower.

I stood in front of their baskets, staring at them with my white quartz eyes. If I were Napoleon, I would have killed them. Even a lesser spirit, like Jango, would have opened the door and let them fly away. In the histories I had read there was always the defining moment when the hero had to act wilfully, selfishly. The man of destiny would have grasped the thistle, bitten the bullet. But I was only a kid. I was afraid of Wally.

I retreated into the dark space under the raked theatre seats.

Here, in my oldest hide-out, it was dark and safe, but also melancholy and rather damp. I thought of heroes HOLED UP in mountains. Above my head I heard the actors' footsteps and imagined GUARDS. I thought of ROBERT BRUCE and the SPIDER. But there were no spiders, only scuttling cockroaches which I attacked with a wooden block until it was covered with their black slimy insides.

I already had a blanket here, also a flashlight, and a clasp knife I had stolen from Chen. I had a tartan blanket my mother used in *Hedda Gabler* and a whole series of crowns, bowler hats and helmets which had since been replaced in Wardrobe.

Also, as soon as the next show opened, more stuff would fall from overhead – sweets and coins particularly, but not exclusively – and I knew that I could find, after almost every performance, something edible or valuable. Once I had found a ten-dollar note, once a condom in a plastic packet, once a phial of what I now realize was heroin but which I kept for years imagining it was a medicine I could cure my mother with if she were going to die.

Now, I unwrapped the Stanislavsky from its pillowslip. I laid the pillowslip on the dusty floor and placed the Master's text on top of it. I placed my left hand on its cover and my right hand on my heart. And there I vowed that I would never desert the theatre.

## 30

The collective had already begun its normal 'development' stage for their new show – a deconstruction of *Uncle Vanya*. They were pre-occupied and hardly noticed me as I made the many trips around the circular stage, bringing the items I would need for my siege.

This was a reputedly physical company, with actors always at the osteopath because they had pushed their body the wrong way. I was an actor with a shape that was *already* interesting. I passed them TWELVE TIMES, walking on my knees, but they did not seem to see me.

I was in my hiding place an hour before one of them came to speak to me – Sparrowgrass Glashan, he who could make himself a

'Human Wheel' and recite a comic version of 'Tomorrow and Tomorrow and Tomorrow' while spinning round the stage and grinning. This Sparrowgrass Glashan, six foot five inches tall, with big comic bug eyes and his skeleton showing through his skin, was squatting outside the tiny triangular hole through which I had egress to my lair.

'What's cooking, mo-frere?' he called, squatting at my doorway, his bright white bony knees level with my eyes.

I held up the Stanislavsky

'Wally's looking for you, ' he said.

'I'm . . . reading . . . Stanislavsky.'

'You know he bought those pigeons for you, son.'

'I . . . didn't . . . ask . . . him . . . to.'

Sparrowgrass did not argue with me. 'You're a good kid, Tristan,' he said. 'You know what's right.'

'He . . . bought . . . them . . . for . . . me,' I admitted.

'That's the boy. You know what's right.'

'I . . . didn't . . . know . . . he . . . would . . . keep . . . them . . . in . . . the . . . tower.'

Not unusually, Sparrow did not understand me.

'You know what's right,' he said. 'It's all the money he has.'

'In . . . the . . . TOWER . . . my . . . home.'

'What?'

'Pigeons . . . in . . . the . . . tower.'

'T-o-w-e-r?'

'SHITTY . . . BIRDS.'

Sparrow didn't tell me not to swear. He didn't say anything for a moment.

'In the tower? Felicity won't let him do that, son. Don't fret.'

'Her . . . idea,' I said.

He looked into my hole and grimaced and screwed up his eyes.

'She's . . . changed,' I said. 'She's . . . all . . . upset.' And, without knowing I was going to do it, I began to weep. 'I . . . AM . . . AN . . . ACTOR,' I said, but I was now crying so hard not even Wally could have understood me.

Sparrowgrass did not know what to do. 'You're a funny little bugger,' he said. 'It's a shame you don't have other kids to play with.' He found a crumpled tissue and passed it in to me. Finally he went away and there was no point in continuing crying.

I began to cut my tartan rug with Wally's clasp knife. I ran the knife down the yellow lines so that the cut was hidden in the depth of the colour. I stayed in my hiding place for two hours. I became hungry again. I skirted around, looking for crumbs, but the theatre had been dark all through the summer and all I got on my wet finger was bits of dirt and dust. The actors moved from the stage to the seats above my head. They did not drop anything interesting.

At last Wally came for me.

'I got your dinner,' he called. 'I made special chicken.'

The actors above my head stopped talking. I thought this was to do with me, but then I heard Sparrow's stage cough and everyone became quiet.

Wally placed the plate of crumbed chicken and fried banana two feet from the opening. I stayed inside in the dark, looking out at it.

'All right,' Sparrowgrass said. 'Quorum. Definitely a quorum.' It was a stage voice, more appropriate for Gogol. 'For those members who have just come in, we have one item of urgent business.'

Someone coughed. A chair creaked. I pulled the chicken into my cave.

'We are a collective,' Sparrowgrass said. 'It says so on that blue piece of cardboard inside the front door. Anyone who comes in from Goat Marshes can see it. Anyone, even if they have a stretch limousine in the street outside, can see how it is that we live and work here.'

No one interjected. No one called to get off his high horse. I picked up the chicken thigh and began to eat it. It was sweet and greasy, just the way I liked it. I alternated bites of chicken and plantain.

There was applause above my head. Wally was a wonderful cook. He had beans and onion sautéed together, and little eggplants dry-roasted from the oven.

Claire Chen was speaking. Her voice was tight and a little shrill. She also said something about limousines in the street. This was the collective's normal way of speaking critically of Bill and Vincent.

I returned to work on the rug. I cut out a slice of yellow from the middle. My mother shouted out something – I had not even known she was there.

That was not like her, to shout. She did not like to interrupt, but now Claire Chen shouted her down. Somebody was thumping their boot nervously above my head.

I put the clasp knife in my pocket and slipped out through the high narrow canyon between the raked seats. *Vincent* was talking. I crept close enough to the ring to see him. He had been called away from a downtown office and was wearing a conservative pinstripe suit and pale blue shirt and tie.

'It is her vision,' he was saying. 'None of you would have had the vision to do this.'

'Capital,' Annie McManus called.

Vincent put his hands in his pockets. It made him look like a Conservative politician. 'Annie thinks capital and vision are the same thing,' he said. No one laughed.

Still intent on proving myself to everyone, I did not appreciate the nature of the catastrophe that was befalling us. I crawled to the back wall and began to climb up the steel ladder which ran up beside the booth.

My mother took the stage as I began to climb. I was beyond the third circle of her concentration and she did not look at me. She was frightened of the audience. I could see it in her smile, the way she engaged with them, one by one.

I was up with the lights now, as high above the floor as Wally had been on the day I first came into his life. The lights had not been stripped and rerigged since the dry season started. There were spider webs, sticky ancient gaffer tape, curling coloured cells. I swung out around these obstacles, hoping to find my way to the other ladder backstage left.

As I moved out across the audience's heads, Moey Perelli stood. He began talking from his seat before my mother had a chance to speak. Vincent, apparently, had left his Corniche in the street. There was a chauffeur behind the wheel and the engine was running. Moey was talking about the exhaust emissions, waste. He called Vincent Carbon-rich. Vincent tried to explain that he was only staying for a moment, but everyone started laughing at him. He walked forward to the edge of the circle and shouted about the amounts of money he paid to the collective each month. I was edging around a Leko with a loose gel filter; my mother tried to say that she had given her life to this theatre.

I was now above her. She seemed so small on the stage. I could see a small round white patch on her scalp, the size of a 20-cent piece.

'There are landlords everywhere,' Claire Chen said (she did not bother to stand – she was sitting, cross-legged, in the audience).

'Claire, please,' my mother said. 'What are you talking about?'

'You'd rather house pigeons than people,' Claire said. 'You want me to sleep next to a blocked toilet and you want the pigeons to sleep in the best place in the building. Fuck you!'

My mother looked at Claire. 'Claire, it's me you're talking to.'

'I know who I'm talking to,' Claire said. 'It's all become very clear at last.'

My mother began crying. Vincent stood to one side. He thought it was the right thing, the feminist thing, to not take her light, her position, to let her shine. He was fine at all this stuff, but this time he was wrong: he should have been beside her and I – I knew what I should do – I should have dropped on Claire Chen, hurt her, but even though my arms were in agony, I was frightened of dying. I counted to ten but at the end I could not let go my grip.

'Get out,' my mother said to Claire.

Claire stood at last. She brushed her purple hair back from her eyes and looked around her and smiled. 'I'll go if the collective votes it.'

Sparrowgrass Glashan stood up in his front-row seat and looked back at the seated company who had only yesterday made jokes about *Tartuffe* with my mother. 'Show of hands.'

'Get out,' my mother said to Claire Chen. She stepped out of the ring and stood in front of the empty starbucks. 'Get out of here, and don't come back.'

'All those in favour,' said Sparrowgrass. No one was putting up their hand.

'No,' my mother said, 'it doesn't matter.' Claire Chen was shaking her head and snorting through her nose at my mother. 'You get out of my theatre. Go.'

She owned the Feu Follet building. She had spent years persuading everyone that, in some fundamental spiritual way, this was not so. She had done a damn good job of it, but the fact remained – it was her name on the title. It was hers in her secret heart, and not because it was her money that had purchased it, but because she made it, dreamed it, spun it out of herself. Perhaps she was an anarchist, as the police later claimed, but she was not a socialist saint.

'Go,' she said to Claire Chen, with the result that Moey Perelli was already walking towards the door, and other members of the company looked like they were going to join him. 'Try the real world,' she said.

I clung to the lighting rig.

Vincent came to put his arm around her, whether to restrain her passion or to comfort her, it was not clear. She shrugged him off and climbed back into the sawdust ring, white, shaking with passion. She was Nora, Hedda Gabler. She no longer cared what happened to her. She shook her tumbling curls back out of her eyes and put her hands upon her hips.

'Go,' she yelled to no one in particular. 'Go – audition.'

Only as the actors left did I realize what it was I'd done.

## 31

Roxanna was walking on ice, on thin glass, high-heeled shoes, one step at a time. She had no house, no husband. But she was not dead. She was not falling apart.

She had no money yet, but she did not need money yet. Nothing creepy had happened.

She had no clothes: she had torched the lot of them, knickers, kerosene, black carbon. She had nothing, just these shoes, a red dress, a black skirt. She was very light.

Quite nice feeling.

He had pale, pale lips, scars along his arms, hurt in his eyes she did not know whether she should fear or trust.

When Wally had begun to shift the pigeons from the draughty foyer, she had followed him. He had not asked her to, but it was not her kind of place and she had not liked to stand around alone. He had not invited her, but she had followed closely behind him, her high-heels clacking on the duckboards. When she realized that he had led her into the theatre, that actors were performing, she was no longer sure of the protocol. She tried walking mostly on her toes, like church.

A pretty actress with long black hair and kohl-ringed eyes was calling out, 'Oh Vanya,' over and over.

The tall streak of Sparrowgrass, the one who had driven the horse float, had made himself into a Human Wheel. He spun round and round in a circle crying, 'I love you,' while the actress followed him with a little hoop-stick, striking him on the backside and singing in a foreign language.

Wally stopped, and put his leg up on the little wooden ring curbs, balanced the wicker crates on his knee.

Roxanna folded her arms across her breasts.

'Is it different from what you thought?' Wally asked her.

She did not answer him.

'It's different,' he insisted.

The woman and the man were trying to make a double wheel – the woman in the centre and the tall streak of Sparrowgrass wrapped around her like a floppy retread. It was like one of those seedy little circuses that make a living out of hokey towns, raising money for the volunteer fire brigade.

The man and woman stopped and fell apart and the other characters gathered around them and abused them.

'Is this an old play or a new play?' Roxanna whispered.

'It's an old play.'

'It doesn't sound like one. All those f's and c's.'

'They're not the words in the play itself.'

'Why don't they learn the real words?'

'You want to go to the *Comédie*, you can see that kind of acting. This is what they call the avant garde.'

'The words of this play,' she asked, 'they're no good?'

'You're kidding. It's Chekhov.'

'So,' Roxanna said. 'Dot dot dot.'

'What?'

'So dot dot dot – what's wrong with the frigging words?'

'Nothing's *wrong* with the words.' Wally smiled.

She slit her eyes and looked at him.

He stopped smirking – which made him smarter than Reade.

'I've got a pretty face,' she said. 'It doesn't make me stupid, mo-frere.'

'My apologies,' he said. He looked so serious, so respectful, she suddenly wanted to laugh. He had a boner in his pants, no way he didn't.

'This is a very artistic theatre company.' He looked her straight in the eye. His eyes were grey and velvety, the softest thing about him. 'They don't like to use the original words.'

'Let me get this straight.' She cocked her head and squinted, because now she had the picture of the boner, she had to stop herself from laughing at his solemn expression. 'The words are fine?'

'The words are fine. I didn't mean to say they weren't.'

'Then they should learn them and use them.' And she put her hand out and touched his shoulder. First time she actually touched him. He was hard as a brick.

'They're deconstructing it,' he said, looking down. 'That's what they call it. It's tray artistic.'

Roxanna had studied many aspects of art – tin soldiers, art-nouveau crystal. The theatre was not outside her range of possible interest. It met many of the right criteria, and she really did try, for a moment at least, to be respectful of what she saw here in this little circus ring.

'The minute I saw the maman,' she said at last, 'I knew she wouldn't like me and I wouldn't like her.'

'You'll like the theatre, in the end.'

But it smelt like poor people, musty, old. 'Allow me to know, mo-frere.'

'It's like drinking green wine.'

'You like to drink, mo-frere. Let's drink.' He had pale, pale lips, scars along his arms. 'Let's get these birds dry and quiet and then you can go to the bank and get your money, and then we can dot our i's and cross our t's.'

She could feel her smile lying easy on her face. She looked him in the eye, asking him to show his own, and when he was shy and combed his hair back from his forehead she was pleased.

A week ago she had a new washing machine, a new gas drier. Now she was walking side by side with this frere, bumping shoulders. She knew exactly what she planned to do eight days from now, but she had no idea what she would do in the next minute. They walked down into some little dungeon then up some steps and into a little sweet-smelling courtyard where an old Efican oak was dropping its sappy petals on the damp green bricks. She felt fantastic, for a moment, free, young.

Then he stopped again, and looked at her. When he opened his mouth she thought, I don't know what he is going to say. It hit her with a jolt. She saw the pale lips parting and was scared.

'You ever hear of Ducrow?' he asked.

'Look.' She hardly heard him. 'I didn't say I was going to be your friend, OK?'

'All I asked was – did you ever hear of Ducrow's Circus?'

'Ducrow's Circus, of course.'

'You ever hear of Ducrow's lion? *Ducrow's lion/ sadly sighing/ ate his nose and foot . . .*'

'He died and his own lion ate him,' she said. 'Everyone knows that.'

'This is where it happened, on this spot, under this very tree. This was Ducrow's Circus School where he had the romance with the prime minister's wife,' Wally said.

'Solveig Mappin was her name.'

'Solveig Mappin, yes.'

'So,' she said, 'dot dot dot.'

'I worked with Ducrow. I never knew him here. He was here when he was an old man.'

'Everyone knows about Ducrow.'

'I knew him when he was trying to have a real Sirkus. Not just the horses and bears and the birds. He bought a laser projector. Our pay cheques always bounced.'

'He had a bird rode a bicycle,' Roxanna said. 'I saw that.'

'He had an eastern parrot ride a bicycle, and the toucan jumped through hoops. I trained those birds myself.'

'I saw those birds.'

'Get out with you. You're too young.'

'It was in 372. In Chemin Rouge, at Gaynor's Paddock at Goat Marshes.'

'They were my birds in 'seventy-two,' Wally said. 'I caught that parrot myself in a wicker trap not two miles from here. Its name was Linda.'

'Get on with you.'

'The show Ducrow did that year. Remember? He had the Royal Hussars. He had the Moroccans.'

'Of course I remember.' She had just run away from the convent. She was fourteen years old and her picture was in every Gardia-civil office in the southern islands. She sat alone, her hair dyed red, jealous of the families around her.

'He had the idol in the middle. Like a god. This is Ducrow, this is how he tells them what to do.' Wally started placing wicker baskets around the courtyard and began to talk to them. He got a wild sort of energy, his hair rising and falling, his eyes flashing, his arms thrashing. She started laughing, watching him. 'He says, now look here, you chaps, you see that lump of smoking tow, that's the idol, and you, Mohammed, stand here with the knife between your teeth. Now when Hussars come in here you chop chop chop, and that is how he spoke to them, the Great Ducrow. He was better with horses.'

'You taught that bird to ride a bicycle?'

He shrugged, and began to stack the wicker baskets. 'You could have done it.'

'I really liked that bird,' she said. 'I don't like birds, if you want to know. I don't like pigeons. I'm very pleased to have them out of my life.'

'You can make money with pigeons.'

Roxanna chose to say nothing.

'You can,' he insisted.

'Listen,' she said, 'if you got them for the boy, that's really sweet, that's very nice of you. And even if he's not too excited now, he'll come around.'

'He'll come around.'

'He'll come around. He doesn't look too interested right now.'

'You got any kids?'

'Do I look like I have a kid?'

'You have a good figure.'

'You're full of shit, you know that. You don't really think . . .'

'Have I lied to you yet?'

'I don't know whether you lie or don't lie. I can't imagine getting into the situation of wanting to know. I don't have kids, OK. I don't know what kids do, least of all this one. Let me tell you who I am, Monsieur Pigeonnaire: I am someone who is going to make money. It is the only thing I am interested in: money. I don't like this place here. I don't like how it smells, or looks, or feels.'

'Then go,' he said.

'You haven't paid me.'

'I'll pay you.'

'OK,' she said, 'when you pay me, then I'll go.'

She brushed the fallen flowers off the bench under the tree and sat and watched him as he stacked the pigeons into the old stables. It was too dark in there, and damp. She did not say anything. What was it to her?

When he had finished he came out and washed his hands under an old wide-mouthed tap. 'Take some advice,' he said, as he flicked the water off his hands. 'Don't say things with double meanings unless you want the second meaning took.'

But she was not listening to him. She was thinking of toy soldiers, a group of them, turbaned, moustached, a marching musical corps of the French Zouaves, one of eighty lots to be auctioned in Chemin Rouge on 11 January, eight days from now.

This thought made her feel so good, she reached out her hand and took his. It was wet and cool with tap-water.

## 32

My mother, in real life, was always neat. Her white blouses were always white and spotless. She was as ordered as her desk top, graceful, clean. But on the evening when the actors walked, she filled the paper cups carelessly, sending sticky bubbles cascading over her friends' hands, forcing Roxanna (whom she had hitherto referred to as that little spin drier) to retract her red shoes quickly into the shelter of her dress.

'Cheer up,' she said to Wally, 'you've just got yourself a pigeon loft.'

Wally shook his head and mumbled.

'What?' my mother said.

Wally looked down at the silver foil ashtray he had placed on the floor, between his feet.

'I'd rather kill the birds,' he said.

Roxanna murmured. My mother ran her wine-wet hands through her hair and shook her curls. Vincent held out a handkerchief. 'No thanks,' she told him. She then wiped her hands on her red velvet dress.

'I'd rather kill the actors,' she said, and laughed uproariously. 'Not you,' she said to Sparrow – the only person standing in the

114

tower – tall, thin, bug-eyed. 'Not you.' She laughed until her face was red and her eyes running. Vincent took her pale white hands and she watched him while he wiped them as though her fingers belonged to someone else.

'That's enough,' she said, and tugged them out of his grasp.

Wally said, 'I don't want to be remembered for closing the Feu Follet.'

My mother smiled at him vaguely.

'You haven't closed down anything,' Sparrow Glashan said. 'They'll be back. No way they won't be back.' He winked at me.

'Take it from me,' my mother said, all humour suddenly leached from her voice, 'they won't come back.'

There was a longish silence which ended only when she picked the dripping magnum from the red plastic ice bucket and over-filled Vincent's paper cup. 'Come on,' she said, 'drink up. It's not every day I change my life.'

She turned to me and ruffled my hair. I looked her right in the eyes but she would not accept the heavy weight of remorse I tried to press on her.

She patted my legs with her sticky hands.

'Cheer up, buster.'

But all I wanted was to undo what I had done, to never have crawled under the seats in the theatre, to never have spoken to Sparrow Glashan, to never have destroyed our lives.

She tousled my head. She stood and wrapped the magnum in a black and white checked tea towel. She poured champagne into Roxanna's paper cup, filled it right to the top like a waiter in a Chinese restaurant.

'So will you hire new actors now?' Roxanna asked.

'I'll have pigeons instead,' my mother said. 'Much, much nicer.'

'I don't even like the birds,' Wally said. 'I'm just so sorry I ever bought them.'

Roxanna pulled her dark glasses down from her hair to her eyes.

'You'll get another company.' Sparrowgrass held out his empty cup towards my mother and watched her fill it up. 'It's not as if there aren't good actors looking for work.' He looked for my mother's response but she had moved on and was trying to find a Pow-pow station on the short wave. While she did this, everybody else talked, but they were aware of making conversation. 'There are elections coming up,' Sparrow Glashan told Roxanna.

Roxanna slitted her eyes. 'I know that,' she said. 'I'm not from Mars.'

'I meant – people really want to work in political theatre right now. There's nowhere else but the Feu Follet. It's an institution. The Blue Party should do something.' He looked at Vincent.

'Claire Chen never worked on that voice,' Vincent said. 'It was always tight.'

'Claire's voice is not great,' Sparrow agreed, 'but she can use her body well. She's very physical.'

'It wasn't their acting.' My mother had found her Pow-pow station. She turned the music up, then down so low I wondered why she'd bothered. 'It wasn't even yours,' she told Sparrow. 'You got to be an actor, but you weren't one when you came.'

Sparrow made a show of being offended, but my mother was not playing games. 'When we were on the road at Melcarth,' she said, 'what did you think of our work? Really.'

'It was good,' Sparrow said. 'It was great.'

'But compared to something *really* good.'

'People laughed and cried, and now it's gone.'

My mother dropped her eyes. When she looked up her face had become the colour of her arms.

'Didn't it ever look second-rate to you?' she asked.

Sparrow looked so stung I felt sorry for him. 'No, why? I'm sure not.'

'But what would be first-rate?' my mother insisted. She had come temporarily to rest and was now leaning against an open window, her arms folded across her chest, a paper cup in her hand.

'She means Brecht directed by Alice Brodsky,' Vincent said, 'at the Saarlim Volkhaus, something like that.'

'We've lived by our principles,' Sparrow said. 'I think that's first-rate. We've played towns like Melcarth and Dyer's Creek where people never took a show before. That's first-rate. We've got something to say. We make people think, and laugh, and cry.'

'But what did we change?' my mother said. 'At the end of the day?'

'That's a different question,' Vincent said.

'Did we even begin to define a national identity?' Felicity said. 'No one can even tell me what an Efican national identity might be. We're northern hemisphere people who have been abandoned in the south. All we know is what we're not. We're not like those snobbish French or those barbaric English. We don't think rats have souls like the Voorstanders. But what are we? We're just sort of "here". We're a flea circus.'

'You mean, you wish we were more famous.'

'No,' Felicity said, passionately. 'No, you know I don't mean that. I mean, I don't know what we are. Or maybe it's just me, still a Voorstander after all.'

The bright nimbus of saline across her eyes did not break into tears, but it was perfectly clear to me then that, for whatever reason, my mother was now finished with the theatre.

She sat down on the bed again and snuggled into Vincent. He put his arm around her and she closed her eyes. She was shivering. Wally took off his sweater and draped it on her shoulders. Vincent slipped off his jacket and arranged it round her.

I put my arms around her too, as far as I could reach. I was very frightened.


# 33

Roxanna had this flash – it came to her that night, marooned in the draughty tower in Chemin Rouge drinking warm champagne. She saw the blood, like in a horror film, a wall of it, wet, liquid, with a sheen of blue licking around its edges. She should kill the shitty pigeons now.

The moment passed, like a clear frame in a film, like the brief mad moments when you think you will throw yourself off the bridge or swing the wheel into the oncoming traffic – a tic, a shudder, not real life but something parallel, something that could only happen if the thin muscled walls between the worlds of thoughts and things got frayed or ruptured. She was not, *Deo volante*, the woman with the knife, chopper, axe. But she was the person who innocently carries the plague, like that woman Rebecca (whoever she was really) they named Rebecca's Curse after – just a pretty red and yellow flower, and now it raged through the pasture of half of Efica and every schoolkid, even the little rag-mouth here, knew it was called Rebecca's Curse.

The pigeons were like that: like dog-shit sticking to her name.

They had been in Chemin Rouge for only thirty-six hours but already the famous Apple Pie and his twenty-six fellow pigeons had brought down this theatre company. The pigeons were like some spore, some sexually transmitted disease, and when she thought of the night Reade brought them home she knew that her first sense about them (before her bending, obliging, smiling, head-nodding personality got in the way) had been the right one.

It was not just that he was mistaken about their money-making possibilities. She had not liked the way he *touched* them, with his big horny hands around their chest and neck. She damn well *made* herself think she liked it but it was bullshit. It made her jealous – that was her true feeling. She wanted him to act like that to her, not to a bird. She told herself how nice it was to see a man acting gentle, but that was shit, she knew it even then.

She did not like those pigeons' eyes, not that pair, nor any other. She never did see a pigeon's eye that did not frighten her a little. She told Reade that. He was patient with her at first – he said it was because they had an eye each side of the head which made them sort of stare, and she tried to buy that, except it wasn't true. It was something in the eyes themselves she did not like – stupid, nervous, demanding – and it did not matter whether they were speckled or plain, the condition was the same. They scared her.

As for money – forget it. It was the pigeons caused the rift with Reade. It was the pigeons ipso facto lost her the joint bank account, the $105,023.56. They lost her shelter, protection. She should have killed them in Melcarth when she BBQ'd the house. Now she was in Chemin Rouge, they were still with her. She could chop their heads off with a tomahawk, have them run around Gazette Street with the blood squirting in the air like a poulet. She could see it, she really could. She could see the blood pooling in the bluestone gutters. It was most realistic.

She blinked and drank champagne. It was perfectly clear that Madame here would now lease or sell the building and then Wally would have lost his home, all thanks to pigeons. She did not care. She refused to care. She should BBQ them before they did the next thing.

*Don't even think it, Roxanna.*

She held her breath but the lack of air made the flames burn brighter. They were carbon-hemmed, orange-skirted. There was soot, kerosene, a sweet hot singeing smell. She grinned at Wally. He smiled back at her. She went to the bathroom and splashed her face, then she turned and walked down into the street, hoping the air would make this feeling go away.

The air in the street smelt cold and damp. The wind was from the east and it carried, not the salt of the port, but a sweet mouldy smell, the smell of gullies and rotting leaves from twenty miles away. She stayed out there, just leaning against a car, looking up at the moon, listening to the sarcastic voice of the dispatcher coming out over the taxi radios. She saw Vincent Theroux open the door and stand at the top of the steps. He raised his arm. A car engine started and then a low expensive car – she did not know the make – pulled up in front, and Vincent, having checked his jacket and trouser pockets, carefully descended the stairs, got into the back seat, and was driven away. *My God,* she thought. It was as if she had splashed cold water on her face.

Around ten o'clock she saw Sparrow Glashan, made hunch-backed by the rucksack under his poncho, slip quietly out of the door, and walk down to the dark end of the street, away from the taxi base. A moment later Wally sauntered across the street with his hands in his pockets.

'You OK?'

'The patapoof, what's his name?'

'That's Vincent . . . did you see his car?'

He stood in front of her grinning, as if he knew that she was excited by a wealthy man.

She shrugged. 'What of it?'

She turned back towards the theatre. Now the actors were gone she would have, she hoped, a better place to sleep than a mattress in the corner of Claire Chen's room.

The pigeons were no longer in the foyer although, imagining she could still see their bloom hanging in the air, she held her nose as she passed through. It was only eight more nights. She would buy a padlock for her door.

It was a rabbit warren, a flop-house. She went looking for a room she could make lockable. The doors were ply. Most of the locks and many of the knobs were missing. The rooms themselves were dead, curtainless, creepy. The floors were covered with litter created by the actors' flight, the sort of things rag-pickers might have fought over and left behind when alcohol or thunderstorms changed what they thought important – empty vid cases, print-outs, T-shirts, bras, single socks.

In eight days' time she would turn up at the Chemin Rouge Antiquities Fair, a butterfly emerging from a shit-heap – no one who looked at her would ever imagine the chain and padlock on the door, the ice-cream container for peeing in at night.

She went from room to room, looking at the doors. Wally accompanied her, but hung back, did not enter the rooms, occupied their doorways.

No way was she going to fuck him. No way at all. When she caught his eyes, he smiled at her.

'What's so funny?' she asked, but before he could answer she walked past him, out into the corridor. Her high heels were loud. She hated that sound. The rooms were all insecure. The windows opened on to verandas and roofs. There were no latches.

Wally leaned against the wall behind her and began to roll himself a cigarette. 'You don't want to worry about them pigeons,' he said. 'I'll build them something.'

'Better you than me.' She turned to face him. 'Pigeons are a mug's game,' she said. She took a cigarette out of her bag and lit it. You could hear the front door swinging open on its hinges – that was two chains, two padlocks she would have to buy.

'My grandad had pigeons,' he said, reproachfully.

'So you told me.'

He pulled a comb out of his shirt pocket and dragged his long hair back from his high forehead. Then he leaned across and, without asking permission, lifted her dark glasses from her face. 'I paid you six hundred bucks for them.'

'It was a fair price,' she said, but she slipped out of her shoes.

'Seems to me you were offering a little more than pigeons.'

She bent down and picked up her shoes. She refused to be guilty.

'It seems to me you were offering something tray specific.'

She held out her hand for her dark glasses. He hesitated a moment, but then he gave them back to her.

'What I said was I'd set you up, OK?'

120

'That's right.'

'I know you think that's a double meaning, but it isn't. I meant I'd get you the seed for them to eat, show you how to set up the automatic watering.'

He shook his head. His eyes had that hurt look men got – she didn't know whether to pity him or fear him.

'I'm sorry if I gave the wrong impression,' she said carefully. 'I'm also really sorry I put the hex on you.'

'You didn't hex me. I like you being here.'

'I hexed the theatre. The pigeons did. I wrecked her theatre for her.'

'You don't know Felicity,' he said.

She snorted.

He cocked his head. 'What did you do that for?'

'What?'

'Laugh.' He folded his heavy freckled arms across his chest.

She shrugged.

'Why did you laugh?' he demanded. He tightened his mouth. She did not want to look at all that dangerous hurt dancing in his speckled eyes.

'I was thinking you don't know her,' she said. 'That's all. I'm probably wrong. It was my impression.'

'How would you know if I knew her or not? How could you even have an opinion on the subject?'

'You're a man.' She smiled and touched his forearm with her hand. 'That's all.' And she turned and headed up the corridor, before it got any more intense. She hurried into what had been Annie McManus's room. It was the room she had planned to commandeer, but now she saw it had a door opening on to that spooky little courtyard.

'You're saying I don't understand women?'

'Look at you,' she said, suddenly angry. 'You're hanging round me like a dog. You want to fuck me, you don't do it like that. I'm sorry. I'm really sorry. You've paid a fair price for the pigeons, but that's all you did. You bought some pedigree pigeons, OK? Enjoy them.'

He leaned across and held her arm. The maman and the boy were up in the tower. They were all alone on this floor. He was hurting her.

'You think you know who I am, Roxanna. You think I am some

sort of creep, but you don't know shit. You want to know about me, go upstairs and ask her. Do you think she'd have me here if I was a creep? I'm a good man, Rox. You're too scared to see that. You're so jumpy you think you have to rip me off. You're so nervous you don't know what to do. But I'll promise you this and you can trust it – you can sleep in my room, in your own bed. You'll be safe. No one's going to bother you in any way at all.'

She looked at his face – the velvet grey eyes – and believed him.

'OK?' he said.

'You want to go to the bathroom first?' She put out a hand to touch his forearm but he moved away a little as if by accident.

'I went,' he said.

When she came back from the bathroom, he was lying beneath a quilt on an old mattress which he dragged in from somewhere, one of those mattresses with off-putting brown stains on their black and white ticking. He lay beneath the quilt so still, on his side, his back to her. She did not completely trust the integrity of his stillness. He was a good man, maybe, but he was a man and this was a standard male act – to get to fuck you by pretending they did not want to fuck you.

She looked at Wally like she might have looked at an alarm clock, something ticking quietly which would, sooner or later, no matter how quietly it ticked, start ringing in her ear.


# 34

French toast was a treat in our house, something I was permitted to have only once a week. Yet in the days following the actors' departure, I had it three days in a row. Twice was a treat. But when, on the third morning, I found Wally beating up the eggs and milk, I knew all my fears were well-founded – something seriously bad was going to happen to me.

I climbed up on to the kitchen chair and watched him apprehensively as he pulled a yellow seed-sprinkled semolina loaf from its bag and cut three slices, each one a good inch thick.

'Did . . . I . . . have . . . french . . . toast . . . yesterday?'

He turned to look at me, hollow-cheeked, poker-faced. He took a pack of Caporals from the pocket of his black and white checked cotton trousers and lit one on the gas jet, jabbing his nose and lips towards the neat blue flames.

'Who knows?' he said.

This was not like him.

He now dipped the bread into the beaten egg, one slice at a time, and dropped three slices of delicious slimy yellow into the sizzling pan. He picked up a dishcloth and wiped a little spilt egg from the blue iridescent surface of the kitchen table.

'I . . . had . . . it . . . yesterday,' I said.

'I thought it was your favourite food?'

'You . . . said . . . it's . . . bad . . . for . . . me.'

Wally lobbed the dishcloth on to the draining board and winked.

Then he placed the jug of sugar syrup right next to my elbow. Now I was really afraid – he had never let me control the syrup jug before.

'Is . . . Sparrow . . . coming . . . today?' I asked.

'He's looking for a job,' he said. He turned the slices in the pan, watching them intently while he smoked. 'You know that.'

'She'll . . . change . . . her . . . mind.'

'She's going to stand in this election,' Wally said. 'You heard her. You saw those gens in their suits. You know who they are.'

'She'll . . . change . . . her . . . mind.'

'Eat,' he said, flopping the first slice on my plate.

I flooded the plate with syrup. He did not criticize me. All he said was, 'You clean your teeth afterwards, you hear me?'

'Yes.'

'Why?'

'My . . . teeth . . . won't . . . look . . . like . . . yours.'

He stubbed out his cancerette. 'That's right.'

He cooked the next two slices until they were mottled brown and yellow like the melted tiger in the story. When he had served them, he washed the pan, dried it, and stacked it neatly inside his wooden crate. Then he wiped down the counter top. Finally, he brought me my blue mug full of hot cocoa and sat opposite me at the table to watch me eat.

He placed a box of tissues on the table beside his ashtray. He lit a second cancerette and I looked up from my plate to watch the way the smoke rose up past the grey tips of his ginger eyebrows.

'Taste good?'

'Very . . . good,' but the truth was, I was ill with apprehension. Everything my maman had done for two days had made me nervous. She had said no more to me about the new house, but on the other hand she had 'tidied up', stacking all her belongings in wine cartons.

'I'm . . . not . . . leaving . . . here.'

Wally shrugged. 'I yell at you a lot, don't I?' he said, not looking at me.

'Yes.'

'You know it's because I love you, don't you?'

I don't think he ever used that word to me before. Now I nodded my head, unable to look at him.

'Sometimes I laugh, don't I?'

'Yes,' I said, but in truth I could not, at this moment, remember him laughing. All I could feel was his sadness.

'What would you say was the most memorable thing about me?' he asked me.

'I . . . don't . . . know.'

'You're a smart kid,' he said. 'You're going to do fine.'

'I'm . . . staying . . . here,' I said. 'Not . . . leaving.'

'You maman's worn out with theatre. Don't make it hard for her. This election is just what she needs.'

'I'm . . . not . . . going . . . to . . . that . . . house.'

'You maman needs a change.'

'Please . . . sell . . . the . . . pigeons.'

'For Christ's sake. The pigeons are not the point, Rikiki. From what Vincent tells me – it's not the pigeons – it's your dad.'

'My . . . dad?'

'They had a falling out, Rikiki. It's not the pigeons. She's gone right off your dad, the theatre too.'

'No . . . no . . . they . . . did . . . not . . . fight.'

A car horn tooted – four short blasts.

Wally stood and stubbed out his cigarette. 'Are you finished eating?'

'NOW?'

'I'm sorry, Rikiki. I couldn't tell you.'

'TODAY?'

I was not ready. I had not expected this. I expected change to come gradually, in a long slow slide. I slipped from my chair. I was not going. I turned towards the door, my secret place.

But Wally lifted me up before I made it to the door.

124

'Please,' I whimpered.

I clung to his hard shoulders and pushed my face in against his rough bristly neck.

'For Christ's sake,' he said, his bloodshot eyes already rimmed with tears. 'Don't blubber.'

I did not even fight him. I let him carry me down the steps and into the harsh light. When I looked up from the shadow of his neck, I was not surprised to see Vincent in the driver's seat of the Corniche, but I was very surprised to see that all my rebel's armoury, the stolen Stanislavsky, the mutilated tartan rug, all the secret things I had hidden underneath the theatre seats were now packed in three cardboard boxes in the back seat.

Wally kissed Tristan Smith an unhygienic, tobacco-smelling kiss. And then put me on the seat next to the boxes. He clipped my seatbelt and tugged it extra tight. He depressed the door lock and slammed the door. He began to wave but then turned abruptly away.

## 35

Four o'clock that afternoon found me in the isolated Belinda Burastin* house my mother had decided was to be our home.

I sat on the highly polished floor looking out across a melancholy sea of khaki and olive forest to the dusty roads, palm trees and rust-streaked roofs of the distant port. Thirty feet below me: broken logs and small rocks with their sharp edges softened by thick green moss. Behind me: Vincent and my mother squeezed into a small black leather chair. She was half on his lap, half off. He had his wide square hand resting on her knee.

'This will turn out to be the best thing that ever happened to you,' he said. 'For both of us. You'll see: big things will come of

---

* Belinda Burastin (341–90), the celebrated Efican architect, whose domestic dwellings perfectly reflect the liberal post-colonial conundrum. Every Burastin house carries an obvious sub-text – that it would be better for everyone if the house were not really there. Burastin's houses barely penetrate the soil. They tiptoe on their sites. They are as light as thoughts, prayers, wishes that history had been otherwise, that cloven-footed animals had never been brought across the sea in ships, and that those who live there now should disturb the place as little – to quote – 'as those early colonizers who inhabited the dry cool granite caves'.

this, for both of us. Bill should never have said what he said about your work, but when it's all over we'll print postage stamps with his face on them.'

'I think he'd rather like it,' my mother said wistfully. 'Don't you?'

'I'd like it too,' Vincent said. 'I'd like him on a postage stamp.'

I listened to him, filled with animus. I did not like the way he talked about my father. He had a soft plump lower lip. He spoke softly, quietly, with much patting and stroking. 'The Feu Follet will be like a chapter in your life,' he said to my maman, 'when you are a senator.'

My mother laughed but I thought she was too frail for the wild things he was saying – her veins too blue, her skin too white, her lipstick too red for her complexion.

'There is no reason why you shouldn't be a senator, a minister.'

For me, listening to him, he was a jackal, poking, prodding, moulding, demanding, preying on my mother's weakness for political influence. But of course he knew what I did not believe: Bill had abandoned her, and my maman was unexpectedly adrift, drowning. This unseemly rush into politics was the only life raft Vincent could offer.

'You know everybody,' he told her. 'You have a following. You're prettier than the competition.' He turned her face with the flat of his hand. 'Even your accent might help you.'

I was three feet in front of her, costumed in a blue iridescent dress-up hat, a silver waistcoat, a sequined belt, a red cap. I wanted her back in the theatre, but I could not compete with Vincent who was already writing her future in his little notebook. They had already phoned this person. He had called in this favour, had lunch with that opponent. One was 'flattered to know you'. Another had 'his heart in the right place'. One more was an 'amiable ditherer'.

My mother rested her head on his shoulder. Vincent talked to someone on the telephone about progress on the 'one hundred thou' for 'the candidate's slush fund'.

The house was built on delicate thin poles, bright yellow like an egret's legs. The whole thing flexed and moved, and when the wind gusts started from the west you could feel the house rippling and shuddering under you like canvas. I hated it. It felt as if our lives would blow away.

'I'm hungry,' I said.

When I saw my mother look expectantly to Vincent, I thought this was his Achilles' heel.

I closed the Stanislavsky and placed it carefully on the floor.

'A . . . restaurant,' I said, thinking that this, at least, would get my maman back closer to the theatre. 'Let's . . . go . . . back . . . to . . . town . . . and . . . eat.'

Crows rose from, and settled back into, the canopies of *Enteralis*. I listened to the crows and imagined them to be cold, goose-pimpled below their oilslick black feathers. I wrapped my sequined silver waistcoat around me.

'What have we got to eat?' my mother asked.

I looked at Vincent, his startled eyes. I thought I had him in check, but not checkmate.

'First,' he said, 'we need wood for a fire.'

The hill on which the house sat was steep and slippery with stones, logs, fallen leaves and *Enteralis* seedpods. I lay flat on the cold hardwood and edged myself to the outer rim of the floor. I looked down and watched Vincent and my mother try to gather wood. They were not suited to this new life. My mother had sandals. Vincent had bright black slip-ons with a little gold chain across the top.

Vincent slipped and fell on his fat backside. He tried to break long sticks but his shiny little feet kept sliding off. Felicity dragged a big log half up the hill.

'I can't burn that,' Vincent called. 'I've got no axe.'

My mother dropped the log. It slipped then rolled. It hit a large projecting rock and then catapulted itself into the air, narrowly missing Vincent's head. The log crashed into the woods below, without either of them knowing what had happened.

Vincent and Felicity came back to the house and tried to start the fire with bits of torn-up cardboard, toilet paper, dead leaves. I knew it was not the time to discuss my own future, that Vincent had dirty hands, that they both felt incompetent and angry with themselves. So I waited, a really long time, until there were smoky yellow flames licking around the brittle green sticks.

I thought they had no food. I did not mention food. I knelt next to my mother and dropped little bits of broken leaf in amongst the smouldering twigs.

'I . . . need . . . the . . . theatre,' I said.

My mother looked up from the fire. Her eyes were red. There was a streak of ash on her cheek. 'Do you, sweets?'

She carefully lifted a charred and smoking stick and inserted it so it was against a feeble little yellow flame. Then she stretched out her arm to stroke my head. 'There's plenty of time for you to decide. Lots and lots of time.'

'I've . . . decided,' I said.

'Sweets,' my mother said, her eyes red from smoke, 'I've made you imagine it's a happy life.'

'It's . . . not . . . happy . . . here,' I said. I looked back at Vincent when I said it. He stared straight back at me.

'It's a beautiful house.' My mother stroked my hair. 'It's actually the most perfect house for bird-nesting. Did you think of that? Think how many birds must live here.'

She knew I did not care about birds or bird-nesting. I tugged myself away from her.

My mother squeezed her eyes shut. 'For Christ's sake,' she said, 'you are ten years old. You have serious problems you are going to have to cope with in your life.'

'I . . . know,' I said.

'You don't know,' she said. 'It's my fault. I protected you too much.'

'I . . . know,' I screamed. 'I . . . know . . . I'm . . . ugly.'

'Darling . . .'

I pushed her away. She sucked in her breath. 'Sweets-ki, I'm doing my best to help you, but, please, help me too – just accept that I can't go back to the theatre.'

'Why?'

'Shush,' said Vincent.

'Why?'

'Come on,' Vincent said. 'Cool it.'

I glared at him. 'I . . . want . . . Wally.'

My mother opened her eyes. 'Listen to me,' she said, speaking very quietly and slowly, 'Wally has a job. His job is to build a pigeon loft.'

'You . . . can't . . . afford . . . that,' I said.

Vincent stood behind my mother and began waving his finger and shaking his head at me vehemently.

'It's Wally's job,' she said. 'That's all. It is his job to do that.'

'Who . . . pays . . . Wally? How . . . will . . . Wally . . . pay . . . rent?'

'Your mother can afford whatever she wants,' Vincent said. 'She can fill the tower with ping-pong balls if that's what she wants to do. Just let her rest.'

'YOU . . . LET . . . HER . . . REST,' I said. I looked at my mother. She was grinning at me, but there was a wildness, a real craziness about her. 'YOU'RE . . . CRAZY,' I said.

She slapped my hand, hard, so it stung.

I looked at Vincent, who just nodded his head, as if to say, you had it coming.

'I'm . . . an . . . actor,' Tristan Smith said. I was crying, but my mother did not comfort me. She broke a stick across her knees like a woman in a fable and then put the two pieces on the fire

## 36

I was betrayed, abandoned, slapped, broken like a stick, smouldering, oozing bubbling sap.

My maman fiddled with the smoking fire, thinking what a problem she had with me. She never guessed how serious it was. She did not imagine that I was planning to run away. But why would she? I had never walked further than a hundred yards. My legs were twisted like old pipe cleaners. My only wheels were on my skateboard. I was ten years old, knew nothing, had no money. But once I saw her break that stick and throw it on the fire, I had to confront the fact that I would have to fight to earn my right to occupy a higher category of life.

I had, of course, been wrong about the food. They had plenty. It was tasty, but I ate the moist grilled skipjack thinking of the tower being filled with ping-pong balls, and later, as my mother read me the Voorstand folk tale of the duck riding the dog to market,* I did not listen to the words in case I softened. I lay on my mattress and held my anger tight to me. I was the son of two actors.

Not long after my maman turned out my light, a wild wind-storm arrived, slapping the canvas walls beside my bunk. I lay on my back

---

* 'Bruder Duck Rides to Kakdorp', from the Badberg Edition.

with my eyes open and listened to Vincent and my mother running round pulling ropes, closing hatches and shutters. When the rain eased I realized they had moved to the bedroom. I could hear my mother crying and Vincent murmuring. I imagined she was remorseful. My heart softened.

But then, just as I was about to go to her, the weeping turned to moaning and all my anger was alive in an instant. She had broken the stick. He had filled the tower with ping-pong balls. I hated her cold green eyes, her little mouth, the tired line at each of its edges, and I hated Vincent most of all, and I curled my lip in the dark as I thought of his talcum-dusted flab, his bearded mouth between my mother's legs.

I got out of bed. The rain had stopped. The moon was out, projecting images of trees weaving and waving like thick grass stalks across the walls and floors.

I crept down into the living room and looked out across the wild shaking tops of sclerophyll scrub to the glowing buildings of Chemin Rouge and the golden light of the forbidden Sirkus Dome which was less than a mile from the abandoned Feu Follet.

The idea – the vision – of my journey to reclaim my theatre now burst from the tight little place I had been keeping it and gushed, bubbling like lava, towards my destiny. At that moment, I should have been afraid, but what I had instead was a feeling so intense you could almost call it ecstasy. I lapped at the cold spring water from Belinda Burastin's terracotta pipe. I strapped on my knee pads and tucked folded newspaper underneath for extra protection. As I stuffed Vincent's treasured driving gloves with newspaper and then pulled them on to my own hands, I did not know what roles I would play, but I imagined them as great ones, not the parts written for Fools or Jugglers, but those for Kings to whose own loves and tragedies, misfortunes, weaknesses of spirit, I would lend my own peculiarly expressive form. I could be their spirit, manifest, their pain made three dimensional, their tragedy got up to walk around.

To be inside the house, to feel it shudder and shake in the wind, was unnerving, but to pursue this action, to crawl and walk up the path to the road, to feel the wind envelop my body, swallow it, hold it, was thrilling. The resistance of my body, the immediate and early declaration of its limitations, was nothing – the stretch of my abbreviated hamstrings was, not quite pleasure, but certainly not pain.

Tall dry grasses brushed my face. I thought: *I can do this*.

The moon was bright, and everything was very clear. (*I can do this*.) I had imagined myself stumbling and falling and I was ready to accept that, but there was a tamped dirt path which more or less followed the tree-lined driveway up to the road. Yes, sticks scratched my face, and my breath, so early in the journey, was rough in my lungs, but I did not fall and I carried my skateboard under my arms and walked uphill on my knees, like a pilgrim, and all above my head the great tree canopies whipped and waved, tossed like hair, like showgirls' feathers.

Now, recounting this, I know more. I have travelled through dangerous tunnels in foreign countries, climbed steel ladders where bats are used to roosting, and my imagination, thinking of my younger self, is filled with the possibility of rats, brush-hogs, tree-adders, but that liquid silver night was free of them. No tree-adder jumped on me, no brush-hog collided with me. I dealt with my life one knee-step at a time.

Every ten yards or so I stopped, caught my breath. I looked back down at the shining roof of the house between the wild tossing umbrellas of foliage.

After the driveway there was a street. It was wide, and hard. It was here I confronted, in that broad shining black macadam strip, the size of my decision, and yes, sure, I was frightened there. Yes, I wanted my maman and my bed a moment, but then I remembered my maman and the twisted anger of my bed, and I had to proceed, one knee-step, then another, along the pebble-littered concrete gutter – it was too steep for a skateboard – down towards the rumble of the freeway, towards the theatre. The forest roared like a river in flood on either side of me.

I will not say that some self-pity did not smear the glassy brightness of my earlier jubilation, but the thing is – *listen to me* – I kept on going. *My mother was right – it was how she brought me up*: I had no idea of how I looked.

I had no real conception of my effect on others. Had you told me this then, I would have argued fiercely. I would have described myself to you, unflatteringly, in more detail than you could possibly have observed, and I might have convinced you. But I had no *idea*. And although no one ever spelled it out to me, I was really led to believe that it was only BAD PEOPLE who found me repulsive – supporters of the Voorstand Alliance, racists, fascists, not ordinary decent folk.

And when, on that long-ago midnight, I came knee-walking down that moon-bright concrete gutter with my white hair fluttering and my torn-rag mouth loosened by the wind, I could not know how my wave would appear to the driver of the first oncoming car.

The car stopped. There was nothing in my education to make me fear it. It began to make that slow, whining noise so beloved of hitch-hikers – the sound of reverse gear, fully engaged. It came to a stop right next to me: high, mud-splattered, vaguely white.

There was a radio playing Pow-pow music – rough field-hand voices, long sad dissonances, violin, cello.* It switched off. I knelt beside the door, waiting to be let in. Then the passenger-side window came down a little, about an inch.

'What you want?' a man's voice said.

'The . . . Feu . . . Follet.'

'Wha?'

'Foo' – I spoke slowly – 'Folll-ay.'

The car backed some more and then drove directly at me, so slowly I could hear individual pieces of gravel crunching beneath its rolling tyres. Hot urine washed my thigh. The car's headlights shone full on me, so brightly that, when I turned to face them, I had to hold my arm across my eyes. My left leg was wet and warm. I could also feel the heat of the car's radiator. I could hear its tappets singing. I took my hand down and stared into the lights, but then the car backed off, swung out, and slowly drove past me. I watched its red lights slowly drop over the rise and descend to the freeway on the plain below. Soon my trousers were wet and cold, sticking to my legs.

I began to crawl back up towards Belinda Burastin's house, but it was just too steep. That's the truth – it was easier to go on down,

* *Visiting Voorstanders are always surprised to find Pow-pow music so popular in a foreign country. If you are a child of the Hollandse Maagd it is possible that you find Anglo-French Eficans more enamoured of the music than you are. And it is true, we do not always appreciate the nuances of race and class, but we know the words, can hum the melodies.* [TS]

towards the freeway. The skateboard was more a hindrance than a help. Finally I grasped it with my hands and crawled behind it, using my knees as brakes when it went too fast, skidding and scraping my way down to the bright ribbon of macadam whose carbon-rich emissions I could now smell, in brief bursts, upon the wind.

An hour later, my belly swollen with nervous gas, my fingers bloated, my knees red raw, I finally climbed down the side of the ramp and slipped down a rough grassy bank to the freeway verge. I lay there, in the shadow of the overpass, for perhaps an hour, feeling the buffeting of big wheat trucks coming down from the north, their sirens blasting as they exceeded the governed speed limit.* I would have gone back to my bed if I could, but I no longer had that option. I just lay there in my pee-wet trousers, shivering, lost in space until the cold became worse than the fear and I edged my way slowly out of the overpass shadow and into the bright stage-light of the freeway. There I managed to stand on my feet and hold out my thumb. I don't know what I expected. No longer something good.

I don't know what make the car was. It was a small car, silver, no longer new. It screeched its brakes on so hard white smoke came flying out – I'd seen that sort of thing on vid – and came reversing back towards me at high speed.

The driver did not wait for me, but came right out to meet me, eagerly, it seemed. He was a big fellow, tall, broad-shouldered, sort of squeezed into that little motor car. He came holding a big black metal flashlight in his hand. He had long straight blond hair like mine, blowing in the wind.

'You just stay there,' he shouted. 'Don't you move.'

He was scared, of course, but I did not figure that. I trusted his hair. He came towards me, crouched a little like a fighter. His high forehead was a sea of wrinkles, and his mouth was oddly pursed as if he had eaten something bad but had not yet spat it out.

He shone that damn light right on me.

'Jes-us,' he said, and coughed.

Well, I thought he coughed. But when he did it again, I realized

---

* *Efican trucks are fitted with a siren which sounds when the vehicle exceeds the speed limit.* [TS]

he was retching. It did not occur to me that it was my appearance that made him ill. When he had finished spitting, he scuffed up the dirt with his boot and wiped his mouth with the back of his hand.

'Just be cool,' he said. He was just a boy, really, less than twenty. He looked so jumpy and nervous I began to be afraid of him.

'Be cool,' he said, looking up and down the freeway, which was, at that minute, empty.

'I'm . . . cool,' I said. I held out my goose-fleshed arms. I was just trying to calm him down, to stop him staring at my piss-stinky pants and my bloodied bright green knee-pads.

He squatted in front of me. I shuffled back a little. I started to take off Vincent's big gloves. He tapped the torch against his palm but did not turn it on.

'Well, hell,' he said. He had blue eyes but they were an old man's blue eyes, full of worry. 'Well, hell and Christ, where did you come from?'

If I had known Belinda Burastin's address I would have said it, but I could not. 'Foo . . . Folll-ay.'

He was not listening properly. He kept looking at my face and then up and down the highway.

'A . . . famous . . . theatre,' I said.

He hit the torch against his hand.

'Who left you here?' he said.

'No one . . . *left* . . . me . . .' I was insulted. 'I . . . came . . . here.'

'I don't know what you're saying.'

'Mah-ter.' I said, thinking that if I could get to the Mater Hospital I could find my way from there.

'Mater? Mater Hospital?'

I nodded.

'My grandpa died there.' He started to walk toward the car, then stopped and looked back at me as I started to crawl after him.

'Should I carry you or what?'

'Open . . . the . . . door . . . please.'

He did not understand me, but I climbed through the driver's door and across to the passenger seat. I did up my own seatbelt. Then we took off down the freeway and in a minute, inside his warm dusty car, with the high buildings of downtown ahead of us, my crazy optimism was back in force.

His name was Wendell. I knew right away he was from the

country – he had that dry sweet dusty accent that always made me see wide tin sheds, chaff floating in sunlit air. He was so shocked by me, he could hardly look at me. He drove, one-handed. Before we had been 0.1 miles on his odometer he had revealed that he had a cadetship with a security agency, although he would not say which one. 'Security reasons.'

I laughed, but that could not have been clear to him.

'Don't you read the news in hospital?'

'I'm . . . *near* . . . hospital.'

'I guess you couldn't join security,' he said. 'You wouldn't meet the height requirement. You know what I'm telling you? You know what security is for?'

I knew all about security. I knew about DoS, VIA, EJIO. I knew they had tapped our telephone, stopped performances, arrested my mother, burgled our tower.

'You know what the alliance is?'

I shrugged.

'The alliance between the parliamentary democracies of Voorstand and Efica,' he said, 'is built on three areas of joint co-operation – Defence, Navigation, Intelligence – DNI.'

I felt I should respond to him, but I could not think of anything to say. I was embarrassed by the smell of urine and would have apologized for that if he could have understood me.

'DNI.' He glanced sideways. 'You should remember that. It's a handy way to remember it.'

We came on to a highway interchange, and he missed his turn and had to go around again. I thought he had finished with the conversation, but he took it up again, a full two minutes later.

'That's what all those Muddies forget. The Big D. It's quid pro quo. You look out for me. I'll look out for you.' He glanced sideways. 'All those wheat farmers should remember that when they're complaining about the price they get in Voorstand. We're getting the benefit of a ten-battalion army, for nothing.'

'Not . . . our . . . army,' I said. 'It's . . . theirs.'

He frowned at me, then shook his head. 'Well,' he said after a moment. 'I suppose you're too young to be political. You like the Sirkus, right? You're a fan?'

I nodded.

'They say it's a real buzz. I'm going this time. By golly I am. Who do you like the best – the Dog, the Duck or the Mouse?'

Of course I was a child of the Feu Follet. I had never seen the Sirkus.

'Irma,' I said. It was how Wally would have answered. 'Ir . . . mah . . .'

'Irma? Well I'll be damned.' He slapped the wheel and laughed and at that moment he sounded like the Dog himself – *Ho, Ho, Hee, haw*. 'You'd like to do the pink Watutsi with Irma? You dirty little bugger. What's your gazette?' he asked.

'Tristan . . . Smith.'

'I'm Wendell Deveau,' he said, 'and I'd give my left ball to do it with Irma too.'

I remember that, clear as day. You would not forget a name like Wendell Deveau. It was the same man who crossed my path later in life when we were both in love with the same woman.

But on this night the woman was still only eleven years old and Wendell, with all his considerable, ill-informed good will, delivered me into the safe hands of the orderlies at the Mater Hospital and convinced them, no matter how I wept or hollered, that it was their duty to detain me for treatment.

Finally, I was held suspended like a bat or bird between the orderlies. The entire Casualty waiting room looked on. Wendell Deveau stood before me, red-faced, out of breath.

'I hope you get better, ami,' he said. 'I really hope you do.'

## 37

In the Voorstand Sirkus, there is no pity. A man falls, he dies. This, you would say, is the point – the reason a Sirkus star is rich is because of the risk he takes.

But when we Eficans watch the Voorstand Sirkus we do not watch like you. We watch with our mouths open, oohing and aahing and applauding just as you do, but we watch like Eficans, identifying with the lost, the fallen, the abandoned. When a performer falls, *c'est moi, c'est moi*.

Our heroes are the lost, the drowned, the injured, a habit of mind that makes our epic poetry emotionally repellent to you, but let me tell you, Meneer, Madam, if you are ever sick whilst visiting Efica you will quickly appreciate the point of view. If you come to the

Mater Hospital with no money, no insurance, even if you stink of piss and have no lips – you will not be sent away, not even if you beg to be.

They asked where my mother was.

I said I had no mother.

Wendell Deveau began to click his tongue. I tried to crawl away. Wendell Deveau tried to stop me. I bit him. The admissions clerk became alarmed for me. She called two nurses, wide fellows with close-cropped hair and big soft hands. I did not want them touching me. When I struggled, they restrained me. When they restrained me, I screamed and hollered and of course it made me look a fright – my hole of a mouth, my dribbling nose, the blood on my knee-pads, my flailing hands – there were people in the waiting room covering their faces, leaving the room, holding their hands over their sick children's eyes. I saw this. I did not understand why it was happening. I pulled Vincent's newspaper-stuffed driving gloves back on, ready to scamper for it. Scraps of torn paper fluttered all around me. It was two a.m. I did not give the impression of mental health.

Wendell Deveau fled into the night to begin his life as an operative with the DoS. The nurses were young, embarrassed. I smeared them with snot and blood. They must have feared hepatitis, TB, viral cancer, but they were calm and hardly bruised me.

It's OK, they told me. It's OK

When people in a hospital tell you, 'It's OK,' it's the same as when they say you're going to feel 'some burning' or 'some pressure'. It means that they are going to do something that will hurt like hell. So when they told me, 'It's OK,' I screamed. I was placed in a wheelchair, strapped in like a lunatic until I just sobbed, passive, pathetic, exhausted, hungry, thirsty, dirty. My big leather gloves stuck out in front of my strapped-down arms like Bruder Dog in the story we know in Efica as 'The Prize-fight Purse'.* I was wheeled along the yellow line, the course of which I knew better – I would bet you – than the people who were pushing me. I knew these departments of the Mater and the short cuts between the fifteen buildings. That blue line led to Digestive Diseases (my bowel). The red line to Cardiology (my septal defect). The yellow

* 'Bruder Dog Kapow', Badberg Edition.

line was to the Burns Unit which contained (Room 502) the Plastic Surgery Unit. I told them I was not from there, but I doubt they understood me.

My captors were polite, but firm.

I myself was not polite. I was in the habit of thinking of myself as – I have said this already – the avant garde, the elite. I associated with anarchists, populists, nationalists, but whatever position we had, we imagined ourselves better informed than anyone who walked outside the big door on Gazette Street.

I called them drool-brains, know-nothings, airheads.

'What are we?' they asked.

'Drool . . . brains.'

'Drool-brains?'

'Yes.'

They started laughing.

I went into a frenzy. (*Cretins. No-bodies. Shit-rakers.*) My mouth flapped. My legs shooks. My nose ran a river. They delivered me to room 502 with tears of laughter down their faces.

In room 502 they did not know what to do with me. They let me keep my gloves on, but they shot me full of Valium, and took some Buccal scrapings from inside my cheek (*It's OK*) to file-check my DNA. It was through this last procedure – once a two-week procedure, now a quick routine – that they located my hospital records.

A chubby young man in a shiny dark suit brought me a document, a facsimile of my birth certificate. He had a square pleasant face with a springy fringe across his mild green eyes.

'Can you read?' this young man asked me.

Of course I could read. I could read from the age of three. I held out my driver's gloves to take the document. 'I'm . . . *eleven.*'

Reluctantly, he gave me my own birth certificate.

I read.

FATHER'S NAME: *n/a.*

FATHER'S OCCUPATION: *n/a.*

I knew what n/a meant, but why my mother wrote this, I could not guess. Perhaps she knew Bill would go away. Perhaps she wished Vincent to think he was my father. In any case: it did not shock me. It was like my mother, like my father too.

'This is you, right?' he asked. 'You're Tristan?'

MOTHER'S NAME: *Felicity Smith Actor-Manager.*

138

'Is this you?' this angel asked me. 'Are you Tristan Actor-Manager?'*

I turned to look at his watery benevolent eyes and believed my period of trial was over.

'Are you he?'

'Yes . . . I . . . am.'

'Your name is Actor-Manager?'

I nodded.

He flicked his fringe back.

'What is your address?' he asked, and then scrunched up his face as he readied himself to understand me.

'Thirty-four . . . Gazette . . . Street.'

'Yes,' he said. 'That's right.'

## 38

When Roxanna woke – at dawn – the first thing she saw was Wally Paccione's freckled arm, bare above the sheets. For the third night in a row he had kept his word – he had not left his own bed – but she was still disturbed by the sense of intimacy, the skin, the smell of his warm sheets, the sound of his feathery breathing. It was one thing to go to sleep in the same room. It was another to wake. She had *slept* with him.

She had her skirt beside the bed, and in a minute she would sneak it underneath the sheets and dress, carefully, quietly.

His life lay all around her. He was a poor man and a neat man – probably a decent man – but apart from that, what sort of man he was she could not guess. A dozen small pine boxes were stacked along the wall beneath the window in such a way as to make a kind of dresser, the kind of depressing life you saw in fishing baches on the Isles Anglais. Inside the boxes he had placed grey plastic crates, each one labelled with its prosaic contents – socks, shirts, trousers. A chipped china jug, a shaving mug, a brush, a comb were laid out neatly on the top of a rough wooden bench. He owned so little. He was over fifty and this was all he had. It made his breath seem so

---

* *Felicity Smith was not the only Efican mother to confront the official lack of curiosity about her profession by linking it in her surname. Witness, amongst contemporary Eficans, Anton Dietrich-Notaire and Billy Marchand.*

frail, so vulnerable, Roxanna could not bear to think about him any more.

She quietly withdrew her auction catalogue from her handbag.

The catalogue was her comfort. It was one inch thick. It cost $50 through the mail. Its glossy coloured pages had a slightly soapy smell which always produced in her a feeling of rather dreamy well-being.

She took out her pen. The pen joined her to the catalogue like a needle to a thread. She brought it back and forth across the pages, pausing here and there, at the seventeenth-century dragoon in the uniform of captain, which she estimated at $350, at the complete eighteenth-century regiment, all in the uniform of the Royal Scots Guards, which might reach anywhere up to $5000. These last pieces were crude and eccentric in design and, although they had 'Made in England' on their bases, they had probably been produced by French convicts in Chemin Rouge in the second century (EC).

It was now six days until the auction. She turned the glossy pages slowly, breathing the smell, thinking of a park with peacocks. She let her lashes down, got herself to the point where she could smell mown grass, hear water falling in a fountain. Then his voice slammed against her eardrum.

'What's the book?'

He was *dressed* – shirt, trousers – had been naked in the room beside her, was pulling on his socks. He had been *watching* her.

She turned to him, her hand to her breast.

'Don't you be so *tense*,' he said. 'No one's going to hurt you.'

She was wearing a T-shirt but she felt exposed, as if he could see, not her body, but what she had been imagining.

He smiled at her.

She tried to smile back but could not.

'You were a million miles away,' he said.

He held out his freckled hand and at first she thought he wanted to touch her, and then she saw that he expected her to show him what she had hitherto kept hidden from him – the catalogue. He had no idea what an intimate thing that was. She was embarrassed – she held the catalogue up, just enough so he could read the cover, but then he sort of *tugged* it from her and sat back down on his mattress and leafed through it.

'This is worth three-fifty?' he said, holding up the plate depicting the dragoon.

She just wanted to ask him: please give it back.

He kept turning the pages of the catalogue, not like the poor man he was, but like a rich man, someone with an education – gently, respectfully, sliding his big hands between the shiny surfaces. But whatever he really thought of it he did not say.

When he gave the catalogue back, she slipped it into her handbag and changed the subject to something less tender. 'What you doing today?'

'I don't know. What are you doing?'

'Sleep. Read. Same as yesterday. There's not much I can do until you get your money.'

'It's just the sort of account,' he said. 'I told you that.'

'I know.'

'If I gave it to you now, I'd lose my interest.'

'I know all that. So what are you doing?'

'Well, first I'm going to clear the stuff out of the tower,' he said, sitting down on his mattress and resting his long wrists on top of his knees. 'And then I'm going to figure out how to build a pigeon loft. No,' he said, although she had not done anything except fold her arms, 'no, just imagine it from Tristan's point of view,' he said. 'It's like a schoolroom. He can learn about biology, genetics, mathematics.'

He was repeating bullshit things she had told him when she was selling him the birds. She felt herself blushing.

'I know you don't like the pigeons,' he said. 'No, that's fine, but you just imagine, how a rikiki like Tristan . . . There's all sorts of stuff he'll learn . . . magnetism.'

'Magnetism?' She wondered if he was teasing her.

'It's how they navigate. You must know that.' Was he sending her up? 'Woman like you, surely you know that? That would be an advantage to owning pigeons.'

'I didn't know that.'

He smiled, but not much more than a creasing of the eyes.

'Well, your big bazooley is tin soldiers,' he said. 'It's more artistic than pigeons.'

'Thank you.'

'Nothing to thank.'

'Tomorrow is my pigeon day,' she said. 'I'm going to help you set up the automatic watering.'

'You don't have to do that.'

'A promise is a promise,' Roxanna said, pulling her skirt on underneath the blankets. 'Ask anyone who knows me. I always keep my word. That's one thing about me you couldn't have known.'

'Oh, I knew it.'

'Well, tomorrow I'll set you up. Soon as I'm finished, you're going to the bank and I'm going to buy a little suit for Rox.' She threw back the covers and dusted down her skirt. 'Next week I've got serious business to attend to. But today,' she stretched and yawned, 'I'm still on holiday. I'm sleeping in.'

Yet as it turned out she helped him clear out the tower, not because he asked her to, but because she had already slept two days and could not sleep any more. There were still six days to go, time to fill without spending her money.

At first she enjoyed the work. All she did was lump wine cartons full of Madam's personal effects down one floor to the next. They did it together. They carried the cartons down the steps and then stacked them in the corridor. At first it was companionable. But as the morning went on, something soured inside her, not toward Wally, whom she had, against her better judgement, begun to like, but – *here she was again, a servant to some frigging pigeons.*

He was a decent man, she did not doubt it, but decent was not what she was looking for. She began to go up the stairs too quickly, her mouth open, the little bracelet jingling on her ankle.

She was doing what she always did – she was attaching to this dump because she feared that if she didn't she would end up somewhere even worse. She had been inside for three whole days. She was attaching to it, to him, one more poor bozo, because he was here. She could feel herself doing it. She became angry with the building, with the birds. She had that feeling again: like bubbles in her blood.

She felt the flames flicking around, tickling the edges of her vision, and God knows where this feeling – itchy, irritating, more-ish – would have led her had she not, in stooping to pick up the twenty-first box, caught her fingernail and torn it to the quick. The pain was like iced water. It snapped her out.

'That's it,' she said. 'That is *it*.'

'What's it?' he said.

Once again: she had not even known that he was in the room. 'I don't have to stay here,' she said.

'No one's asking you to.'

All his hidden hurt was suddenly as clear as freckles. She laid her hand on the back of his wrist, the only apology she could make.

'You could stop right now.'

'I think I will.'

'You could take a break.'

'Yes.'

'You could just do me one favour.'

'What's that?' she asked.

'I need to go out for an hour,' he said, 'and . . . I'm expecting a delivery.'

'I got to be honest – I'm getting tired of being cooped up, you know?'

'It'll be fifty minutes, maybe less.'

'I got to be honest – I just can't baby-sit your pigeons.'

'The pigeons will be with me, sweets. I want to show them to a mo-ami.'

'You'll be back in fifty minutes?'

'I'll be back by four o'clock. I promise. You could sit outside, on the steps.'

She looked at his face, the pale lips, the hurt grey eyes. 'You'll be back in fifty minutes?'

'In an hour, easy.'

She did what he said: sat out on the front steps, in the air. It was not so creepy out there. She bought a sandwich at the Levantine shop across the street. She watched some black ants crawling across concrete.

At half past four there had been no delivery and he was still not back. She was going to take a walk, but then the evening thunderstorm arrived and she retreated inside and sat on the unmade bed and waited for him. There were books there but she did not look at them. There was a radio too, but she was apprehensive about being alone inside the big old building and didn't want anything to interfere with her hearing. She sat cross-legged on her mattress listening for noises. She did her nails, and when they were done she let her hands sit limply on her knees, waiting.

At six o'clock it was pitch dark outside. The bastard was still not back. The rain had stopped and she would have gone out, except now she was scared to walk down the damn corridor alone.

But finally she was more mad than scared. She took her shoes off and crept down the dark stairs to the foyer.

She opened the velvet curtain which shielded the foyer from the theatre and there she found Wally standing on a high ladder, fixing a blue gel on to one of the lights.

'Want to know what I'm doing?' he called down.

She could have had great satisfaction in pushing his ladder over. Once upon a time she would have done it, and he would have found out, faster than a blink, what he had not noticed about her in the two days until now. But she sat down instead and he could not guess, grinning down at her from the top of his ladder, his great good luck.

'Guess,' he called. 'Three guesses.'

She shrugged. There was a six-pack at the base of the ladder. She leaned forward and ripped one off.

'Setting up a show,' he said.

'That's nice,' she said. The beer was warm.

Six nights from now, all this would seem like a bad dream. She would be in an auction room with all her funds invested in a nice dress and some shoes.

'Will you come into the ring a moment, sweets?'

'Why?'

'Please. Just be careful of the wires. I've got the mixing console up there.'

She shrugged, and stood up and stepped on to the damp saw-dust in her bare feet.

'A smidgin to your right, careful of the wires, now a little further forward. Great.'

He shone the light right in her face. She held her hand over her eyes.

'Now what?' she asked.

'Now go back and sit in your seat. Just watch out for the wires.'

When she was out of the ring, the lights still dancing in her eyes, he sat beside her. Smelled of toothpaste again.

'Here.'

She took the package.

'Choccies for the show.'

And then he was over at the wall, flicking the house lights off.

'Don't do that,' she said. She was scared now. She could see his bare knees shining in the gloom over by the curtain.

'It's a show, Roxanna.'

'Well, come and sit by me.'

'I'm in it,' Wally said. 'It's me.'

And then the theatre plunged to black.

## 39

He had taken off his shirt and put on a white T-shirt, a pair of khaki bloomer shorts, a red pre-tied bow tie. He had knobbly knees showing at the level of his shorts. He had a wooden box which he had painted in brilliant green and sparkling silver stars. At first, as he put his foot delicately on the mixing panel and faded up the lights, she thought it was, like, magic. She was charmed, well maybe not exactly charmed, but touched by what she saw as nerdy but good-hearted. She started to unwrap the chocolates, smiling in the darkness.

But then, before she had the first chocolate in her mouth, he put his liver-spotted hand in the sparkling box and pulled something out. She saw what it was, but her brain would not let her believe it. Her brain did not want to be the bearer of bad tidings. It gave excuses, alibis. Her brain told her the thing in his hand was a glove, or a puppet.

Then she finally realized what it was. *God damn, God damn his fucking freckled eyes.*

It was not a glove – it was a pigeon. HE WAS TRYING TO CHARM HER WITH THE FUCKING PIGEONS.

'Oh no,' she said. 'Oh no no no.'

She spat the chocolate into her cupped hand and dropped it underneath the seat.

He did not know what he was fucking with. He left her locked up in a room. He shoved pigeons in her face. He did not know her *history*. He could not see her for what she was: a bonfire in a starbuck.

'Oh no,' she said, but he was oblivious. He picked up the bird

145

and whispered to it, kissed it, for Jesus Christ's sake, on its bony beak. He looked it in its one mad eye, eye to eye.

It was like something in a crappy cambruce circus. Something the Voorstand Sirkus had long ago driven out of business.

Then he started to fold the bird up in his hand. She could not believe what he was doing. He folded it in half, like origami. He was killing it, for her, on stage. He was *not* killing it, but he *was* folding it. She watched the way he did it – how he held it up and, with his other finger, pointed out into the air above her head.

He threw the pigeon towards her. It was like a yo-yo on a string, except no string. It flew out, up, it rose, tumbled, spread its wings to show bright red undersides. Good Christ almighty, it was like a dream. The bird returned into his hand. He held it, and took out another. He folded it like the other, and did the same. This one looped, arced, tumbled, fell, revealing blue under the wings.

And then he bowed.

She sat with her mouth open.

'No applause?' he said. He stepped forward and, with his toe, brought the house lights up.

She really could not speak to him. She could not believe the stupidity of men.

'Well,' he said, 'say something.'

She shrugged. 'They're your pigeons,' she said with great restraint. 'They're none of my business.'

'No, no.' He held his hand up. 'These are not the pigeons.'

'These are not the *pigeons*?' She felt her voice rising.

He stepped out of the ring. 'Not your pigeons. I got rid of your pigeons. I traded. These are tumbling pigeons,' Wally said.

'You don't know who I am,' Roxanna said.

'I think you're a businesswoman. You can say I don't know you, but I see it in you. You think about money. You're smart about it, so you'll see what we have here. It's the beginning of a bird show, like the one you saw with the toucan. A real old-time petite tente. We'll get another toucan.'

'Stop. Stop right there.'

'No,' he said. 'I won't stop. I know who you are.'

'You don't know who I am.'

'Roxanna,' Wally said, 'we already have a venue.'

She stood up, she started backing away from him, the box of chocolates still held in her hand. 'You don't know who I am,' she said. 'You don't know what you're fucking with.'

'Roxanna.' He reached out his arms towards her. 'I like you.'

She did not punch his nose. She slapped it, with the heel of her hand. She sort of half pushed half thumped it. Blood came out, on to her hand, arm. He came in at her, dripping, in a cloud of tobacco, toothpaste. He held her, hard. She tried to squirm away, to stay clear of the blood. She could smell it, feel it dripping down her neck, fat warm drops of it.

'You're ruining my dress.' She still had the box of chocolates in her hand.

'I'll buy a new one,' he said.

She could not move. She knew that feeling, from her history. His rough skin was against her forehead. He smelled of ash and peppermint.

## 40

Roxanna and Wally sat on the empty stairs while the last Feu Follet posters flapped on the foyer noticeboard, pulling themselves free from their drawing pins. Wally held a deep red tissue against his injured nose.

'Why did you do that?' he said.

She shrugged and gave him a new tissue. 'I said I'm sorry.'

She was too. She watched him dab at his lip but in her mind's eye she saw the wooden crates in his bedroom, the plastic tubs with their little labels – 'Socks', 'Shirts'. She let him pay top dollar for the pigeons. She couldn't have done it if she had seen his room – 'Wool'ns', 'Letters'.

She patted his bare knee. 'We've got to be realistic – we don't even know each other . . .'

'I know I look stupid in these shorts.'

'It's not your appearance, mo-cheri. It's your type. I knew what you were like when I met you in the car park in Melcarth. Believe me.' She poked him in the ribs. 'I know your type.'

'What type?'

'Fifty plus years old, single . . .'

'No, no. Let me speak.'

'No, no – you're an individualist,' she said. 'There's nothing wrong with that.'

'You've got it wrong, Roxanna.'

'I'm not criticizing you.'

'No, you've seen me – I've got a *family*. I've got the little boy. Let me finish. You ask the company. I stick by people. I was married to a woman fifteen years, a dog trainer. She left me. I didn't leave her. You can rely on me. I'm not some young fellow who's going to run away and leave you. I've got a proven record.'

She raised an eyebrow at him, trying to joke him out of all that dangerous sensitivity. 'Dog trainer?' She grinned and combed her thick straw-yellow hair back with her fingers.

He started fishing in his pocket, and for a moment she thought he was going to produce a marriage certificate, but all he brought out was a second wadded lump of tissue which he patted on his injured nose.

'I know your type,' she said. 'It's just not the type I'm shopping for.'

'Do we have a roof, food, cash . . . a way to make more?'

'Wally, I'm sorry. I'm grateful for the free accommodation . . . '

'I know you,' he said. 'I knew you from the beginning.'

'Some shitty birds,' she said. (They were all the same. Lunatics dreaming of getting rich off pigeons.) 'I want peacocks, and fountains. See – you're smirking. You don't know me. You do not have a fucking clue. If we lived together for five years, you'd still be smirking.'

'Would I?'

'Yes you would.'

'We can make a decent life. I trained that parrot you liked. You know I can do it.'

'I was never *decent*, mo-cheri. You wouldn't have hit on me if I was decent. You thought I was a shooting star, admit it.'

'I thought you were beautiful.'

She looked at him, and saw a saline lens building up across his eyes.

'Well thank you,' she said. She put her hand on his wrist. 'That's very sweet of you.'

'I thought you were Irma, that's the truth.'

'Did you, mo-chou?'

He nodded.

'That's sweet of you,' she said. She opened his hand and touched it with her fingertips. It was papery dry, with deep, worried lines across the palm. 'You'll find someone if you want someone,' she said. 'You're actually a very charming man.'

'The pigeons are not the point,' he said. 'The pigeons are what we have available.'

She closed his hand. 'No,' she said.

'Let me finish . . . the pigeons are just what we have.'

'You don't know me,' she said, not looking up at him, her lips compressed. 'I'll cut their heads off with a *pocket knife*.'

But when she looked up the fucking musico was grinning at her. 'It's the Efican tradition,' he said.

She sighed, then laughed in spite of herself.

'We make do with what we have.' He smiled.

'So I should make do with you?'

'Our great-grandparents fought fifteen years of wars* with the poor bastards whose land this really was, and then all the captains and generals sailed away and abandoned them, left them with the ghosts and bones.'

'You're such a *bullshit merchant*.' She removed his cigarette pack from his shirt pocket.

'The French, the English – they thought the land was worthless, but we changed it.'

'Don't you ever give up?' She accepted the light.

'If you have to be poor, better be poor here than England. You have to be sick, better pray it's not in France. You're a woman, you'll get equal pay.'

Roxanna began laughing. She could not help it. 'Look at you. You've got arms covered with cigarette burns. You sleep on a mattress on the floor. You tell me, so confident, this is the best country on earth, and we're about to have the best life imaginable.

---

* *It is a little known curiosity of history that the French and English garrisons, technically at war with each other, mounted combined operations against the indigenous tribes of Efica from 35 to 39 EC and again in 43 EC. The tribes seem to have given as good as they got, and, had it not been for the Chinese influenza epidemic of 49 EC, might have survived long enough to witness their invaders recalled to headquarters. No indigenous records remain.*

Wally, what have you got? You've been robbed. You tell me you're in paradise.'

'Look at me.' Wally held her firm little jaw between his thumb and finger.

'Ouch.'

'If you could see my past, you'd know that my life is a fucking miracle.'

'Let go, you prick. You're at least sixty years old. You've got nicotine stains on your fingers.'

He released her jaw. 'You want me to stop smoking? I'll stop smoking.'

She stood up. 'Why me? What have I done to you?'

Wally stood also. He held out his hand. 'I know you like me,' he said.

'You know I *like* you?'

He grinned at her.

'I know you like me. You've just got to admit it.'

She shook her head, but she was laughing too. She took the big dry hand and held it a moment.

'We're like each other,' he insisted.

She dropped his hand. 'That's not a plus.'

They began slowly to walk up the stairs together. 'When you first met me,' she said, 'I was soaked in petrol.'

'No, I smelled it . . .'

'You *smelled* it? I'd just burnt our frigging house down.'

'See – you can tell me,' he said.

'That's not a plus. I'm telling you, I'm crazy. I burned down the convent.'

'In Melcarth?'

'No, not in *Melcarth*. Of course not in Melcarth. When I was a kid, here, in Chemin Rouge. I'm a pyromaniac,' she said. 'When I get stressed that's what I do. I can't get insurance.'

'We don't need insurance. We'll make something with these pigeons.'

'You want to make something,' she said. 'You can make a pigeon pie.'

She would have said more, but the telephone began to ring. There was a bell mounted at the bottom of stairs – an old-fashioned square black box with two rust-streaked metal hemispheres on top.

150

Wally let it ring. Perhaps he was making some point to her. If he was, she didn't get it. She took her spare T-shirt and her handbag to the bathroom. She took off her skirt and dropped it in the bath. She turned on the cold water and swirled the skirt around to start it soaking. She sat on the toilet and opened her catalogue, trying to get some pictures in her head.

## 41

Unaccustomed to the sounds of the bush at night, the tree rats on the roof, the brush-hogs which came in at the beginning of the wet to forage around the undergrowth, the mother of Tristan Smith slept badly, dreaming angry dreams about Claire Chen.

Some time after the storm had passed, she came out to drink some water from the cistern and then, almost as an afterthought, walked up the steps to my bed to untangle me from my blankets.

When she did not see me immediately, she was not alarmed. I was a small boy in a big sea of bedclothes. She had felt that hard hit of panic too many times before to easily fall prey to it now. She expected, at any second, to touch my elbow, my bony backside, pushed high into the air. But when she had finally removed all of the sheets and blankets, and produced nothing more than the clatter of my second skateboard, she experienced that wild alarm familiar to every parent – that fast beating of the heart, that rising panic in the throat. She lay down on the anachronistically waxed floor and reached with her long pale arms under the bunk, as if I might somehow be squeezed in there, and all the time she was calling out my name, not loudly, but softly, like you call a cat.

She had talked to me like that, inside her womb, *my beautiful baby, my beautiful baby boy*, and would not have an ultrasound in case this sex was unsaid. She had wanted so much for her little boy, had put so much store by his splendid life, and then, when he was who he was, she had vowed to him, made extravagant promises she had not been able to keep.

'Tristan, Rikiki, Tristan darling.'

Soon Vincent was beside her, naked except for his slippers, and the pair of them had all the lights on in the house and were running from closet to closet, and then, on a wild and fearful intuition, out of the house and down the slippery slope beneath. It was three in the morning and they were shining a weak yellow flashlight across the broken sticks and rocks, and then up the slippery trunks.

'We'll ring the police,' he said when they were back inside the house.

'No,' she said, 'not yet, please.'

She saw the look he gave her, silent, judgemental, but she could not bear anyone to know – her son had left her. She understood exactly. She knew she had betrayed him, not just in the incident around the fire that night, but in so many complex ways, not least by carelessly allowing him to fall in love with the theatre.

He could not be an actor. It was no more possible than that he be an athlete. First, his voice – it was not only that he could not project but that he could not be *understood*.

He did not have the instrument. No matter how he exercised, there was so little muscle tissue to develop, and although she was intensely, continually, moved by his courage – and she had had to stop herself weeping when he descended from climbing the fir tree with that egg in his open mouth – courage was not the same as ability.

His father had broad shoulders, a sweeping supple back, long, almost painfully beautiful legs. Bill Millefleur's Coriolanus died in that stunning circus topple, falling forward from the platform so that he dangled, his feet hooked around a rust-streaked water pipe. That was acting. Her son could never do it.

Yet it was she who had allowed these foolish dreams to flourish, and who – when it was too late – had no better answer for him than picture books of birds and eggs.

'He's not in hospital,' she said to Vincent, who sat at the Nagouchi table, the telephone in his hand. 'I know he's not.'

'Flick, you don't know where he is.'

'Why would he be in hospital? We have no reason to think he's hurt.'

'Then let me phone the police.'

'Why would we want the police?'

'Mo-chou, he's never been on his own before. If he's run away, don't make me say it . . . He could be hurt.'

'OK.' She sat down opposite him and pulled her wrap around her. 'Phone the hospitals,' she said. 'But he won't be there.'

'Where will he be?'

'He's at the theatre,' she said.

'Flick, please, I know you're upset.'

'He's back at the theatre,' she said. 'He frightens me.'

## 42

In the morning I woke in the Burns Unit of the Mater Hospital and there I found, not two feet from me, a harelipped man peering curiously into my face.

When my eyes met his, he started.

'Oh,' he said, standing up, and taking a pace backwards. 'He's awake.' He clasped his hands together and looked towards the door.

'Good morning,' he said to me from near the window. He had such nervous, anxious eyes. His lip was split to his nose. His gum was exposed. When he spoke, his words sounded as strange as my own must have. That aside, he was good-looking. He had very white skin, a heavy beard-shadow, a strong jaw, a neatly combed head of black hair. 'Actor-Manager,' he said, inclining his upper body politely towards me. 'What a splendid name!' He looked towards the doorway again and I saw that my little room was full of visitors – five men and women, two standing, one leaning in the doorway, two sitting on chairs. They all wore hospital gowns and they all had missing faces, cleft palates, conditions where teeth penetrated lips, misfortunes so repelling it would have been difficult for me to quietly contemplate them even in the colour plates of a magazine. You may not like me saying it, but my visitors were gross.

Who was I to be repulsed by them? No one, obviously.

But who were *they* to stare at *me* with such jumpy, frightened eyes?

'Can you speak to us?' asked the man with the harelip.

I rolled my eyes in impatience. The effect was obviously repulsive.

'Your maman's on her way,' the harelip said. He was a good enough man, I guess. He was here to have himself made normal. I assume he wanted marriage, children, decent things. He found me disgusting but he was trying to calm me, telling me lies about my mother who was still, at that hour, conducting her own search of the freeway verges.

'So, you can't go home just yet,' he said.

'No . . . I'm . . . going . . . to . . . my . . . daddy's . . . house,' I said.

'He said daddy. Did you say daddy?'

'His daddy's *out*.'

'His daddy's *house*.'

'You're going to your daddy's *house*?'

I nodded. I was going to the Feu Follet.

'I don't think you're going anywhere just yet.'

'I . . . am.'

'Not until you've had your little op.'

They were adults, I was a kid. When they told me there was an operation planned it was difficult, in spite of all the circumstances that had led me there, not to believe them.

'I'm . . . going,' I said.

'Going? Not until you're better,' said a woman who was sitting on the visitor's chair. She had a bright red burn scar down one side of her face. Half her grey curling hair was shaved clean off her head.

'Have you had your pre-op?'

'Mistake,' I said. And again, very slowly, 'Mis . . . take.'

They did not bother to hide their smiles.

'He's here by *mistake*.'

I tried to explain how Wendell Deveau had found me, but they could not understand me. Even as I gurgled and babbled about mistakes I knew it was not true. I was meant to be here. I belonged here. Their faces defined the territory.

'Relax,' the harelip said. I did not like the way he sat so big and heavy on my bed. He was so ugly, perhaps not as ugly as I was, but ugly just the same. He was not like Vincent or Bill. He had bad breath. 'You're safe here. Everything will be OK, little Actor-Manager.'

'Go . . . away,' I shouted.

He could not have guessed how much he scared me or I am sure he would have left. But perhaps he did know, and he was embarrassed, hurt to be, even here, unloved, and therefore he stayed, because he could not admit to being unwanted.

'We're your freres.' He showed his gums to me.

'FUCK . . . OFF.'

The words were clear to them. They splashed around that little room, like boiling water, caused men and women in white gowns to exclaim, leap, stumble in their hurry to avoid the burn.

'Fuck . . . off,' I screamed.

A minute later the room was empty, the door was shut, and I was alone – scared and shaking. All I knew was: I was not them, would not be them, would not be looked at in that way.

There was a nurses' station right outside my door. I could not leave that way. But there was also a window in the room, a chair. I foot-walked to the chair and crawled up on it. My knees hurt more than I expected. Then I noticed that they were bandaged and there was some black blood soaked through on one of them.

The window looked out into a light-well with an open side reaching to a little lane. The drop, the danger, the hit of fear that rushed into my body – all this felt wonderful. I sought the sensation like a tennis champion feels the satisfaction of the racket gripped in his hand, like the smoker seeks the rough, raw feeling of smoke on the lungs. Perched on the window sill, elevated, alone on the eighth floor, I experienced the ecstasy of performance before there was one.

On the opposite wall there were thick metal waste pipes running in a neat daisy chain from floor to floor, five storeys to the ground. I made a very small leap and caught hard on the round, rusty pipe. I stuck there a minute or two, held fast, a limpet on the side of the Mater Hospital.

Watching the performance, you would not have seen the pain, but that pipe was rusty and sometimes rough and very, very cold. Twice there were leaks and, around the leaks, a slippery green mould or slime. The elbows at every level seemed to offer resting places but they proved almost the most treacherous of all. The elbows had inspection plates which were sometimes loosely held, or secured by only one bolt. When I grabbed the elbow, the whole plate swung sideways, and twice I nearly fell. It was much harder than a tree, rope or ladder, and I could not concentrate on anything but what to cling to, one inch at a time. Yet the hands that reached out towards me from the toilet windows were not an annoyance, nor the changing shift of adult voices a soothing distraction.

I did not know what floor I was on at any moment. My arms felt like ripped lead. My hands were numb, bleeding, but I was transformed. I was no longer one of the pitiable wretches I had left behind upstairs. As I descended, I was an actor – Mark Antony, Richard the Third, the Phantom of the Rue Morgue.

So intense was my relationship with that pipe that I only realized I was near the ground when the murmur of voices, of slammed car doors, reached my ears. Finally I permitted myself to look down to my audience. The ground was not more than twenty feet below me. Faces were tilted up towards me. I turned to them.

The faces were all wrong.

They were not faces looking at an actor. Nor were they looking at something as simple as a boy on a pipe. The faces looked at something like snot, like slime, like something dripping down towards them from which they wished to take their eyes and which, the clearer and closer it became, produced in their own eyes and lips such grotesque contortions that I knew – properly, fully, for the first time in my life – I was a monster.

Wally, his mouth tight, his eyes brimming, stood on an oil drum at the base of the pipe. He held his pale freckled arms out towards me. When I fell into his arms he crushed me to him, as if, in holding my snotty face so forcibly against his neck, he could block out everything I had just learned.


## 43

They were a fast-food crowd outside the Mater, sweaty, pasty-faced, overweight, slippery in their ponchos. They shoved hun-grily into the cul-de-sac, pressing in against the ladders and bricks, trampling on the yellow builder's sand. They did not spare a glance for Wally as he rolled the empty oil drum against the wall.

In those years Wally still had a tennis player's grace, a lightness. He did not clamber on to that drum, but leapt so cleanly, in one light bound, that later, when Roxanna realized that the drum must have been at least four feet tall, she began to doubt what she had seen.

He stood on the rocking drum and reached out his long arms towards the small bandaged figure as it edged its way down the wall. He made a kind of cooing noise.

When first he heard this noise, the boy speeded his descent, but then he paused, and looked down, and there was something in the moment that suggested Sirkus to Roxanna – the way he hung out by one arm, like Darnell Dommartin at the top of her slippery pole. His dreadful face was flushed, his fine fair hair blowing in the breeze.

A kind of shudder went through the crowd. It shifted its ground and emitted a little murmur of disgust.

'It's a mutant, Maman,' someone called. 'It's Phantome Drool.'*

The boy heard it. You could see it reach him, like hot water reaching a spider in your sink. He shrivelled.

'Wooo,' Wally said. 'Woooo.' He did not stretch out his hands, but he stood beneath the child in the attitude of an Efican ring-master beneath an aerialiste, ready to catch. Thus, when the boy did drop, it was, for all its speed, not unexpected.

Wally's knees buckled. He staggered, but he did not fall. When he turned back to face the crowd, his eyes were slitted, his mouth thin. His face was a shell, burnished, made almost beautiful with anger.

A child beside Roxanna spoke. 'Yuk, Maman. A mutant.' Roxanna looked down to see who had spoken – eight years old, Anglo features, brown coat, white gloves, little turned-up nose.

'I beg your *pardon* . . .'

'Something bothering you?' the mother said. She was so neat, so fucking Protestant – thin lips, straight white teeth.

'Excuse me,' Roxanna said, 'but she shouldn't call that little boy a mutant.'

The woman looked Roxanna up and down, lingering for an insulting moment on her scuffed red shoes and laddered stockings. Then she smiled and turned away.

'Excuse me,' Roxanna said. 'Excuse *me*. I said she shouldn't call the boy a mutant.'

The bitch did not even turn her head.

'You don't know who you're screwing with,' Roxanna said. She put her small white hand on the woman's bony slippery shoulder and pulled her round. She did not seek violence, only due respect, but when the woman pushed her hand away, Roxanna knew she had to hurt her – she had no other option.

She pulled an eight-ounce vodka bottle from her purse. 'I'll cut that fucking smile right off your face,' she said, looking for a brick to break the bottle on.

* *Efican name for the Voorstand Sirkus acrobatic character of Spookganger Drool.* [TS]

'Shut up, Roxanna,' said Wally. 'Just shut up.'

He moved ahead of her, carrying Tristan. She followed behind, pointing her finger back at the woman. 'You're so *stupid*,' Roxanna said. 'You're so *cowardly*.'

She walked from the cul-de-sac behind Wally and the boy, almost in tears. She was so angry. It was hard walking so fast in her red high-heels. She wanted to touch the boy, hold him, tell him she loved him even though she didn't. She circled. She shadowed. She wanted to tell him he was beautiful, that he had so much guts she could not believe him.

'You're so brave,' she said.

She put the vodka back in her bag. She thought what she could give him, how she could let him know he was loved, how those morons were the ugly ones, not him.

'They're the mutants,' she said.

'Shut up,' said Wally.

She took it too, from him, from them, burnished, welded together. She would take that sort of shit from no one else, but she took it then, from them. She saw that about Wally, that what he had claimed was actually true, he was not a single man at all.

At Gazette Street she took charge, slowly, insisting for no reason other than she just had to.

'Come on,' she said. 'I was a nurse.'

She set Wally to work boiling water, found some bright red disinfectant, sterilized her eyebrow tweezers in the gas jet, laid a clean-looking towel on the kitchen table, and watched as Wally removed Tristan's clothes and exposed his pale peculiar body, criss-crossed with surgeons' scars. It was shocking, but not shocking, it was just, finally, how it was – bones, skin, scars, the heart beating like in a baby's chest. She did not know what to do, had never been a nurse, but she just pushed in, because she had to do something, and she carefully washed his hands and legs with hot water – maybe the water was too hot, maybe she washed too many times – and picked out the rust with tweezers. She knew she was clumsy. He did not flinch or cry out, but all his forehead wrinkled each time she hurt him. His courage made her want to cry.

She had Wally make bandages with a floral sheet which she had found lying in the corridor. It was dusty but folded and therefore probably clean.

'There,' she said, at last, 'he's done.'

Wally dressed him and asked, 'Do you want french toast?'

He shook his head. You could see his shame. It surrounded him like an aura, like Milly when she had been raped by that moron at the Shell station. This one was the same – he had been so brave, but he was ashamed and could not look anyone in the eye.

'Do you want waffles?' she asked. She somehow knew he could not bear to be looked at, that even the air now hurt his skin. She had Wally's money in her purse. She would have gone and bought a waffle iron, but he shook his head.

'You want to watch a Sirkus vid?' she asked.

'Let's watch the storm,' Wally said, and picked him up, and she followed downstairs and out of the dark foyer and into the storm-bright light – all the sky grey but the walls of the garages across the street shining white and yellow – and sat down to watch the high-piled black clouds as they began to bleed in long grey streaks on to the Cootreksea Mountains.

'He likes storms,' Wally told her. 'Thunder, lightning. It's his favourite thing.'

But Tristan crawled off Wally's lap and crept back inside the doorway, and there he stayed, in the shadow, looking back into the gloom of the foyer.

Roxanna put her hand lightly on Wally's wooden shoulder. 'God damn those people,' she whispered. 'God damn their ignorant mouths.'

Wally shrugged. 'What do you expect?'

Roxanna could not be so philosophical. She went back inside the foyer – the boy was further inside now, sitting, curled up, in the middle of the dirty cobbled floor – and telephoned his mother, but the phone rang and rang. She telephoned the Human Wheel, without telling him what happened, but when he arrived, in a minute or two, *he* was depressed. The famously optimistic Sparrow was gaunt and stooped and had begun to smoke again, holding his badly made cigarettes in the cup of his hand.

Roxanna squatted beside him on the steps.

'Come on.' She spoke loudly, so the boy in the foyer could hear. 'I'm going to shout you all the Sirkus. Not a vid. The real thing.'

Sparrowgrass looked at her, and then away, grimacing goofily up at the black sky.

159

'Come on,' Roxanna said, standing up and fluffing her hair. 'I've got heaps of jon-kay. Let's hit the Sirkus.'

She did not know about this taboo on the Saarlim Sirkus. All she wanted to do was make the kid feel better.

'Have you ever *been?*' the Human Wheel asked her. He scratched the back of his bristling haircut, squinted up at her, creased his eyes, pulled lips right back up past the gum line.

'Of course I've bloody *been*. Everybody's *been*.'

'I haven't,' the Wheel said. He screwed his body around to look back through the crack of door into the darkness of the foyer. 'You haven't, have you, Tristan?'

'No,' Wally said, 'he hasn't.'

'Yes,' the voice said in the darkness. 'Nearly.'

'Is it fun?' Sparrow asked.

Wally stepped down on to the footpath so he could shake his head at Roxanna without Sparrow seeing.

Then the boy spoke. 'I . . . understand . . . it . . . is . . . tray . . . commercial.'

'Very unusual?' the Human Wheel asked.

'Comm-er-cial.' Tristan crawled out into the light, squinting. His skin was so *white*.

'Commercial? OK, but is it fun?' the Wheel asked.

Tristan's face tugged and twisted. He turned his big white eyes on Roxanna. He quietly put his hand across his heart. Yes, he wanted to go, of course he did.

'I don't doubt that it's reactionary,' Sparrow said, chewing on the syllables of this last word as if they might be made of very sticky sugar gum. 'What I want to know is: will it cheer me up?'

The boy nodded vigorously.

'Yes?' Sparrow stood. 'But I don't think I'm dressed correctly.' He brushed the cigarette ash from his baggy Army Disposals trousers and straightened the collar of his checked work shirt. 'Should I dress up?'

'No,' Roxanna said, 'it's come-as-you-are.'

But *she* dressed up, as well as she was able. She tried to do it quickly, but by the time it was done the storm had come and gone and the streets were wet and had that sweet jasmine sewer smell, and when they stepped out into Gazette Street you could hear that low gurgle of water in the drains beneath your feet. She wore her

160

same black skirt – she had nothing else – but she borrowed a white shirt of Wally's and put on a geld-band which emphasized her slim waist and her broad hips. She wore her red high-heels and put a little chain around her ankle and a small stick-on beauty spot on her cheek. She did, in short, everything to make her resemblance to the legendary Irma as marked as possible, and she saw how Wally, who had been reserved and silent since their return from the hospital, looked at her, and when they walked around the river to the Sirkus Dome he began to warm up again and told her things she already knew about the rising river, and pointed out the Chinese on the far bank stretching out their big nets on the high poles.

At the entrance to the Sirkus, she took great pleasure in going to buy the seats, by herself, in opening her purse and laying out the big purple notes in front of the casser.

Roxanna loved the Sirkus. The air was sexy and dangerous, smelled like freedom – fried food, gunpowder, ketchup, and the distinctive honeyed perfume of the wet season which emanated from the little bell-shaped flowers of the *Enteralis Robusta*. Of course she was not the only woman wearing a gold belt or an ankle chain. There were dozens of them, but most of them did not look at all like Irma.

When she came back with the tickets she found the boy was in pain. Wally was pressing and pulling at his bandaged knees, trying to locate the injury.

'Does that hurt? Where does it hurt?' He was trying to look at the boy's hands, but Tristan would not unclench them. They were shut as tight as briques bleus and the man had to use his strength to open them.

'What *is* it?' he asked, staring belligerently at the open unmarked palms.

For anwer, Tristan threw himself upon the grass and hid his face.

'OK,' Wally said. 'I'm going to buy you a perroquet.'

Tristan didn't move. Wally turned and walked away.

When Roxanna saw how he lay there, all rolled up and hidden, she knew exactly where it hurt. She knelt on the grass beside him. She laid her hand on his poor twisted leg. He jerked back. She knew how he was – the merest brush of a stranger's eyes would hurt him.

161

'You know it's nice and dark inside that Sirkus.'

'I ... WANT ... MY ... MAMAN.'

'I know what you need,' she said. 'And I'm going to get it.' She turned to the Human Wheel, who was squatting beside her, rolling one more lumpy cigarette.

'Cover him,' she said. 'Don't let no one stare at him.' She headed straight to the souvenir stall. But Tristan did not even see the embarrassed Sparrow. He saw only her and came after her on his hands and knees, wailing.

'Stay,' she said. 'Stay with Sparrow.'

'You,' he said. 'You.' He came on across the bitumen, hard on her, scurrying between polished shoes, jumpy legs, retreating strollers, followed her into a souvenir stand – tea towels, ashtrays, caps, papier-mâché masks of Bruder Duck, Phantome Drool, Oncle Dog. He grabbed her ankles. She kicked at him – she could not help it – she hated people messing with her ankles. He was strong as a scrub rat. He scaled her leg, her trunk, clung to her neck. He smelt of snot and disinfectant. She got the item she wanted and went to stand in line at the cash register as if the bellowing child around her neck was nothing to do with her.

'I ... WANNA ... GO ... HOME.'

'Shut up,' she hissed.

'I ... HATE ... YOU.'

The queue melted before her. She struggled with her purse, the great fat roll of pigeon money. She gave over one more purple 10-dollar note.

Then he would not accept the Bruder Mouse mask she had purchased for him. She dragged him by his arm over to the grass triangle and tried to wrestle him. 'You gotta have this,' she said. 'It'll cover your face.'

But even this he did not hear, and it was Wally, finally, who came and held the shrieking boy still, while the three adults forced the papier-mâché mask on to his face.

Tristan tried to rip it off. 'I ... HATE ... YOU,' he screamed.

Then Wally picked him up and, holding him under his arm, ran to the toilet block. There, he held the kicking, scratching beast up to the mirror.

'Just look. Listen, just look.'

Tristan twisted his head, pressed against Wally, denting the papier-mâché into his face. But, finally, as he struggled to pull the thing off him, he somehow caught a glimpse of himself. *Bruder Mouse*.

He moved his arm. It was the Mouse's arm. Snot dripped from his nose, but out of sight. He cheeks were awash with tears, but no one could see that.

'Happy?' Wally said bitterly, wiping at his own bloodied cheeks. 'I hope to Christ you're happy.'

# 44

I did not stop shaking straight away, but it was warm inside the mask and my own sweet breath enveloped me. I was Bruder Mouse. All around me were other children dressed just the same.

I did not like children. I was jealous of them, frightened of them, dedicated to placing myself in a FAR SUPERIOR CATEGORY of life, but at the Sirkus I had this in common with them: they too preferred to stay inside their masks, to tolerate the tight elastic, the improperly placed eye-holes which impeded views of the great Sirkus sky above us. They, like me, had their heads forever in exaggerated motion.

It was twilight inside the Dome and the ceiling was a deep cobalt blue, alive with stars, not randomly arrayed like a children's fairy book, but in an exact facsimile of the Eflcan night sky. It was my first Sirkus. All my fears dissolved like cotton candy.

As Roxanna led us down the steps of the centre aisle, her geld-band sparkling in the gloom, I watched Sparrow peering and squinting up into the high seats and I was momentarily fearful that his stern moral view would make the Sirkus tawdry in my own eyes. I was not unaware of how it could be seen. It was my own mother who had called it 'a horror made of cardboard, plastic and appalling colours, a death-dealing construction of hardened chewing gum and degraded folklore, a loopy mix of Calvinism and cynical opportunism'.*

But just as I felt my maman's doctrine struggling to take control of my own perception, and as my initial rush of pleasure began to

* *'Actress Miffed with Mouse'*, Chemin Rouge Reformer, 4 April 371.

163

flutter, lose strength, to give way to guilt, Sparrow turned to me and winked. My maman's doctrine instantly dissolved. I lifted my mask a little, just enough to inhale deeply the distinctive aroma of the Sirkus – a mixture of cordite and something like chemically perfumed face-wipes.

But then Roxanna gave our tickets to the usher and my fragile happiness was threatened once again. I had never been to the Sirkus, but I could not believe Roxanna had allowed herself to be given these seats. There was only one column* in our local Sirkus and the usher was leading us straight towards it. This column was, in itself, one of the wonders of the Sirkus, but it also provided its notorious imperfection: an obstructed view.

Looming high above our heads, halfway up its gleaming shaft, was a mixing booth, a glass-walled, air-conditioned cube which Wally described to me each time he 'told' me a Sirkus. I knew it housed the hologram projectors, the computer consoles, the mixing board. The obstructing column also contained a small cylindrical elevator whereby the sparkmajoors ascended to their station.

So this was to be my first and maybe only visit to the Sirkus. I looked up forlornly at the VIP seats – twelve of them – suspended from the underside of the control booth like the basket on a dirigible. Everyone in Chemin Rouge knew exactly what they were like – the seats were red plush, the carpet was deep Efican wool pile. There was said to be a deluxe auto-bar which was operated by cash parole. This was something to dream about, but to those sentenced to sit behind it the column was something to be feared, and as dear Roxanna led us to a place hard against its base I felt my irritation mount to such a height that I wonder I did not actually convulse.

'Calm down,' Wally said, 'or there'll be no damn Sirkus at all.'

I saw the usher push the code keys in the column itself and the elevator doors peeled silently back to reveal the golden walls inside the cylinder.

'Any complaints?' Wally whispered.

And carried me inside.

Was this the happiest moment of my childhood? Can the best

---

* The Sirkus was almost never in the round. In Chemin Rouge, the space was shaped, spectacularly, like a slice of pie, with the stage at the apex.

and worst moments sit together like this? Was I so shallow in my emotions, so forgetful, that this 'horror made of cardboard' could erase the disgusted faces in which I had seen the effect of my own beastly face? Does it matter that it would not last, that it was a good feeling like the good feeling of ice-cream or those burning hot Voodoo Jubes to which both Wally and I were so addicted?

In the glowing golden reflections in that elevator, Heroic Wally, Divine Roxana, Good Sparrowgrass, surrounded me – the Valiant Mouse. We rose silent as air itself towards the twelve plush red seats, only four of which we would personally require.

We sat high above the crowd wherein we might reasonably have felt ourselves to be blessed. Sparrow produced a cash parole – thereby surprising me – and bought us all fresh perroquets, and then the show started.

You are a settler culture, like ours, and all your Bruder tales reflect your church's simple devotion to St Francis (with none of the legal and theological complications created by the Saarlim Codicils*). So you permitted no animals in captivity, but animals thrived everywhere in your imagination, laughing, singing, playing tricks, saving humans, doing good and evil.

The Voorstandish aerialistes put on their squirrel costumes and flew through the air without a net. They could make a furry totem pole twenty feet high. They could produce the most amazing facsimiles of a horse, five men and women – dancers, postureis – working with thrilling co-ordination to gallop, to canter, to walk a slack wire. When these 'horses' fell, the casualties were always terrible.

This first part of the Sirkus had the clowns – hoards of them in cast-off uniforms of conquered nations – preposterous, pretentious. When they emerged from the stage floor they were ragamuffin POWs set free in Great Voorstand. By the time intermission arrived, these buffoons would have become an orchestra playing wild, lonely, funny, Pow-pow music. It was propaganda, of course. The Pow-pows raced the bears, were fright-

* I refer to those of the first years – Codicils XIV and XIX, with their very specific instructions for the care, containment and slaughter of cattle, sheep, ducks etc. By the time the famous Bear Codicil was written, and the hypocrisy of hunting and trapping permitted, the rules of the Sirkus were set. [TS]

ened by the squirrels, awed, teased and pestered by the moving holographic images of the dancing Bruder Mouse or hayseed Bruder Duck.

There was no slow build-up in this show. The pace, from the first drum beat, was extraordinary. It was like being accelerated into the stratosphere. The jokes and the tricks followed each other at a dizzying speed. It was like being tickled. You could not bear the thought that what you were laughing at would be intensified, although it surely would be, and would be again, as tumbling High-hogs flew across the stage chasing tumbling panicking holographic Bruders.

Above us we could see, through the glass floor, the sparkmajoors in the mixing booth. These men and women barely moved all through the show. Once or twice I would see a hand move. For the most part they seemed to sit with crossed arms bathed in soft blue light.

The performers pushed us, until we were breathless from laughter, and Sparrow's great 'Whoo Whoo Whoo' was like the cry of some great goofy owl eager to take its place on stage.

But we were waiting for Irma.

When intermission came, we said nothing of her to Sparrow. We did not want to trigger the sort of political critique we could expect from any member of the Feu Follet collective. We protected Irma's good name by leaving it unsaid.

Sparrow, who had laughed so loudly, was quiet and thoughtful in the intermission, continually passing his big hands over his cleanshaven cheeks and bristly neck. I began to wonder if he felt himself compromised, or even ashamed, but when I looked towards him he took off his glasses and polished them. Once they were clean, he leaned across the rail and slowly surveyed the audience. I thought of Savonarola, a figure my mother liked to evoke whenever her work was attacked by censors.

I turned to Wally, but he and Roxanna were involved in intense and private conversation. I waited for darkness, and made my breath into a warm wind which blew between my skin and the mask.

The second half began, as always, with dancing, both live and holographic. There was the grey furry Bruder Mouse with his iridescent blue coat, his white silk scarf, his cane. Everyone cheered the minute he appeared. It was no good to say what Vincent said, that the modern Bruder Mouse had become nothing more than a logo-type, the symbol for an imperialist mercantile culture. Vincent knew the old folk tales of Voorstand, collected the masks and clap-hands of the first-century Bruders, but he had never been to the Sirkus in his own home town. He did not know Bruder Mouse. He had never seen him *move*.

The Mouse I met at the Sirkus was quick and cocky and as cruel as any animal who has to deal with survival on the farm. He had spark, guts, energy, can-do. We would have liked him, I thought, in the Feu Follet. He had one chipped tooth and one nipped ear. He was a good dancer, had charm, and when Irma, finally, entered the high cone of light that the sparkmajoors erected for her, she danced with him, a quick fast Pow-pow shimmy that had the audience smiling and laughing at once.

The clowns of the first half were now assimilated Voorstanders – they became the orchestra, and as they assembled in their spiffy new eight-button uniforms we knew that we would have to tolerate, for a while, the chorus girls who followed them. Not that we did not think every each one of them to be beautiful, but because none of them was Irma, and by their very existence on the stage they distracted our attention from their queen.

Our Irma's figure was voluptuous, but you can see today from the old vids that she was not perfect. Her rose-bud lips were a little small, her neck, if you wished to consider this, a little short. It is obvious now – it was not really her figure, or her sinuous movements which entranced us. It was her voice.

We waited for her to sing to us. Roxanna had her hand on Wally's knee. Sparrow sat with his mouth a little open and repeatedly pushed his wire-framed glasses back on to his button nose. I took my Mouse mask off and waited for her to recite. In the darkness, I smiled.

She alone, of foreign performers, dared recite our own stories on the stage. It was the mark of the skill of your Sirkus managers to everywhere adapt the show to what was local. We did not know there was no Irma in any of the Saarlim Sirkuses. I don't know if we would have cared. We were flattered, and moved to hear our own tragedies and Pyrrhic victories celebrated in her exotic accent. She did 'Farewell, Sweet Faith! Thy silver ray' and also 'The Story Teller from the Isles'. Her gestures, her movement at such times, were so minimal, her stillness, her small voice, a whisper. Our stories seemed bigger when she recited them, and it is easy enough to attribute all of this to politics and power, except that it takes no account of her enormous talent. You did not think about the individual words but rather the emotion that they generated, like they were so many drops of water, and yet each word was clear, and just as she could put flesh and blood on the bones of our drowned fishermen and make us weep for our abandoned dyers, she could also recite, to a mass audience, the great works of Voorstand literature, moving even that great Voorphobe, Sparrow Glashan, to tears.

When the show finished Sparrow rose with us in our seats and clapped and hooted. As the lights came up, I pulled my Mouse mask back on.

Roxanna and Wally were clapping shoulder to shoulder, and perhaps it was because he saw their preoccupation with each other that Sparrow, his cheeks still shiny, picked me up and held me high in the air. Irma extended a hand in my direction and blew a kiss to me.

## 45

We got in the cab, all of us squeezing in the back seat. Sparrow held me on his lap and bent his head over so as not to hit the roof. 'They're a great people,' he continued doggedly. 'That's what we keep forgetting when we're trying to get their hands out of our guts.* That's what a show like this teaches you. Theirs was a country that was founded on a principle. What you can still see in this Sirkus is their decency. I'd forgotten it. I spend all my time thinking about their hypocrisy. You don't see decency when their dirigibles are bombing some poor country who tried to renegotiate their Treaty.'

'Why does it have to teach you?' Roxanna said. 'Why can't you just enjoy it?'

* A reference to the navigation cable, an issue which divided Eficans. Supporters of the Blue Party, like Sparrowgrass, felt those unexplained cables to be a humiliating invasion, a reminder of our craven servility to another power. [TS]

Sparrow opened his mouth, looked at Roxanna, closed it. Then he turned back to Wally. 'Both countries have old-world parents,' Sparrow said. 'You would think we had so much in common, but we're the little brother – we love them, but they don't notice us. We've got the same colour skin, we speak more or less the same language. We know the words of all their songs. We know Phantome Drool and Oncle Duck. We love their heroes like they were our own, but we keep forgetting that we don't count with them. It's like seeing a Vedette in the supermarket. You know the Vedette like he's your friend, but you're nothing to him. What was unusual about this was . . . whatshername?'

'Her name is Irma.'

'Irma recited "The Story Teller from the Isles". It was like, she'd *noticed* us, or that she knew us. Do you think that's why I was moved?'

'Relax, mo-frere,' Wally said. 'Just say. I enjoyed the show.'

'It was not at all like what I expected. I *did* enjoy the show,' Sparrow said. 'What's confusing is that I know really we're beneath their notice unless they want to use us for something.'

'Shut up, Sparrow.'

'Don't tell me to shut up, Wally.'

'For Chrissakes,' Wally said, 'we just went to the *Sirkus*. Don't bring us down. We went to cheer ourselves up.'

'It was my treat,' Roxanna said.

'Quite right,' Sparrow said. He peered down at me and adjusted my mask. 'What do you say, nibs?'

I was trying to cling on to that vision of Irma, the way she stood in the centre of the great stage, sheathed in her glittering white gown, her arm extended to me. She had smiled. All I wanted to do now was go to Wally's room and find the photographs of Irma he had hidden in his drawer and to look, again, at that magical smile, the memory of which was now being eroded by the acid of one more Feu Follet conversation.

'So what do you say?' Sparrow insisted.

'Give me the mask,' Wally said.

'Now who's being a tight-arse?' Roxanna said. 'Let him keep the mask. It's fine with me.'

'For Chrissakes,' Wally said. 'Felicity is there.'

We were already in Gazette Street. My mother was sitting on the theatre steps, standing, walking towards the cab.

'Give me the fucking mask.'

But I did not want to let go of the mask. I held it. 'No.'

'Don't be ridiculous,' Sparrow said. 'Felicity can handle this.'

But I knew better than any of them that she could not, and as I saw my mother peer into the far window of the cab, I tore the mask off my own face. It was only papier-mâché. It was sickeningly easy to destroy.

# 46

Felicity clambered into the back seat, cut her knee on a broken ashtray, laddered her stocking, squashed Tristan Smith to her. She touched his face, felt his legs, pulled up his shirtsleeves to examine his chamois-soft skin.

I, Tristan, was full of blame. It ran through my veins like bubbling sap, ruled my glands, my limbs, my actions. I pulled away. I crawled to the far side of the seat. My beautiful Mouse mask now littered the shining malodorous back seat like poor grey petals.

'My baby. Are you burnt?'

I thought she was using 'burnt' poetically. I did not know that she and Vincent had tracked me to the Burns Unit.

'Sweets, I'm so sorry.'

While she tried to pull up my shirt and look at my chest, I turned away. I picked up pieces of torn papier-mâché and stuffed them in my pocket.

'Is your mask broken?' she said.

As if it were not her fault.

As if it had not been her *cultural imperialism*, her *hegemony*, her hatred of the Sirkus, which had guided my hands in its destruction.

When I saw the famous cheekbones wet with tears I showed none of the compassion I feel for her now. She was suffering and I was bitterly, triumphantly, angrily, happy.

My poor maman squeezed herself into that tight space between the front seat and the back and – deaf to the taxi driver's abuse, insensitive to Wally's hand on her shoulder – helped me gather the bits of Mouse and place them carefully in her open handbag.

'You can be an actor,' she said.

My heart stopped. I turned to face her. She was wearing Vincent's jacket over her dress. She pulled it tight across her chest. 'OK?' she said.

I could feel my mouth shivering. I held my hand across it.

'I'll teach you, OK?'

I nodded, and then turned away, not wanting her to see me cry.

She gave me a handkerchief. I wiped my face. She wiped her own – even as she did this she was aware of Vincent sitting sideways in his car seat talking on the telephone. She knew she had a meeting with Giles Peterson who was important in her preselection as a candidate for Goat Marshes. This was her new life. She was serious about the elections. But she had her son back, alive.

'Shall we fix up Meneer Mouse?' she asked me.

I nodded. She carried me into the Feu Follet, and left Vincent to untangle the mess she had made.

Felicity rushed through the foyer, squinting, trying not to see the peeling paint, the flapping posters, the rusting drawing pins. She carried me into the theatre, crossed the sawdust ring and entered the workshop – a long brick-walled room divided by three high archways which made the workshop fall naturally into three areas. In the last of these, curtained by a sheet of paint-splattered clear plastic, was a long workshop bench where our designers had their studio.

My mother was a practical woman in all sorts of ways – money, scheduling, the organization of people, the resolution of conflicts – but nailing, cutting, gluing, these were not her strengths, and she knew this, even as she took the designer's chair. Other people – Wally particularly – would have made a better job of fixing the Mouse mask.

She sat me on the workbench. 'I'm so sorry,' she said. 'Do you understand?'

I was not sure exactly what she was sorry about, but I did not ask and I did not soften. I stared at her.

'Maman is going to fix your mask,' she said at last.

Wally had fixed some expensive-looking kitchen cabinets to the wall above the workbench. Inside one of these Felicity found a large jar labelled 'Milliners Solution' and two sheets of white cartridge paper in a brown cardboard tube.

'What we do is lay the paper on the bench,' she said. We both

171

knew that she was bluffing. 'And then we make a jigsaw puzzle. See – there's his eye.' She laid the crumpled Mouse eye on the white paper, but when she looked up her own eye could not hold my gaze. 'And here's a corner of his cheeky mouth.'

'There's . . . his . . . ear.' I pointed. I did not pick it up.

'Did anyone hurt you?' she asked.

'That's . . . part . . . of . . . his . . . head.'

She picked up the piece I pointed at. We progressed this way, for ten minutes or more – me pointing, she placing the crumpled papier-mâché on the white cartridge paper.

'The thing about being an actor,' she said, as I tried to figure where the last few pieces belonged, 'is it's a very hard life. It's OK,' she said hurriedly, 'you will be an actor because that's what you want, but I'm telling you, it'll be hard for you, harder than for other people. Do you know what I'm saying, mo-sweets?'

'This . . . piece . . . is . . . from . . . the . . . mouth.'

'It's very difficult,' she said, 'and that's why I didn't want you to do it. I knew it would be a very hard thing for you to do. Do you understand?'

'I . . . know . . . I'm . . . a . . . mutant.'

She did not look at me when I said that, but I felt her stillness, all the air held in her lungs.

'Are you angry at me?' she said at last. 'Because I made you how you are?'

'I . . . want . . . to . . . learn,' I said. 'All . . . the . . . things . . . you . . . can . . . learn. I . . . want . . . to . . . talk . . . so . . . anyone . . . can . . . understand.'

'Maybe there are some things you won't be able to do.'

'I . . . can . . . learn . . . to . . . talk . . . better.'

'The problem with diction is physical, darling, you know that.'

'I'll . . . *learn*.'

'OK, OK.' She looked at the hateful Mouse, carefully assembled on the bench. Anyone could see it was ruined. 'I'll tell you what we'll do,' she said, not looking at me. 'We'll leave the mask. We'll let it *set* and while it's setting we'll do a workshop. I thought you might like to play the part of Puck. I think I'd like to make you gold and silver.'

I did not ask her about how the mask could possibly set. It was a ludicrous notion, best left alone.

172

'Come on,' she said. 'We'll do it out in the ring.'

She picked me up and put me on the floor. I watched her choose the make-up pots and sticks with my heart beating so hard that a big vein pulsed weirdly in my neck. She sat the pots down on the bench – small tubs with colour spilling down around their white shiny lids. She placed the fat sticks beside them. She opened the tiny closet where the fabric oddments were stored, collected two or three pieces of tat. Then she carried me out into the ring and removed every single item of my clothing.

I sat still on a white enamel chair while she ran back for the make-up, and then again up to the booth where she fiddled with the lights. When she returned she pushed me into a single tight spot. My skin tingled. I felt the pool of black, the heat of light around me. She knelt in front of me. She gave me Nora's little silver-backed mirror from *Doll's House* so I could look at myself as she painted me.

She ran a single line of silver across my forehead. Above it she painted blue, below it green. She put a towel around my neck, splashed water on my hair, and gelled it, teasing it out in long spikes like Efican ragwort blossom. Then she had me hold the towel across my face and sprayed it silver.

I looked in the mirror and saw a creature, a fairy, something from another level of existence, pixie, elf, homunculus.

She painted a single blue spot on each cheek and surrounded this with pink. I thought of butterfly wings.

She made my chest into something blue and black like the night sky. My scars she turned into lightning bolts.

It took a long, long time. I did not mind. It was like being polished into life, like being a statue whose feet are washed with milk and yoghurt every morning.

'You'll have to push yourself against the pain,' she said, rubbing the fatty colourants into my skin. 'Acting will hurt you. All your muscles will ache. Do you know what I mean?'

'Yes.'

'You'll be frightened that you'll break yourself in half, but that is what you'll have to do. Can you do that?'

'Yes.'

'Everyone will want to marginalize you, but you must never allow yourself to take the little parts. When they call you to a

Mechanical, show them how you can play Bottom,' she said. 'Do you know who Bottom is?'

I did not. She told me. 'You must study,' she said, 'so you are more intelligent than other actors, and you must learn to have an open mind, so any director can understand that you will not be difficult to work with, that you are interested in new approaches to the work. You must keep on learning about being brave. This is something you can't learn once. You have to learn it over and over. You must never be frightened to look how you look, and if you can do this, you will always look powerful. You will have to make yourself into something beyond anyone's capacity to imagine you.'

'Yes.'

'You don't have to even understand all this now. But you will learn it, slowly.'

But I did understand it.

'You worked out your action for *Sad Sack* and you thought you could act.'

'No.'

'But it will be years before you can act. You must not appear in *anything* in Chemin Rouge for years. You'll have to work hard, every day. Lots of exercises, lots of reading, every day, harder than anything you've done. And when it's all done you will, if you're lucky, get one role a year. Do you hear what I'm saying? You'll be poor, like Sparrow.'

I was looking in the mirror. I was feeling the heat.

'Uh-huh.'

She dropped a light blue cloth around my shoulders. She stepped back out of the light.

'Look in your mirror.'

I needed no encouragement.

'What do you see?'

I didn't know what she meant.

'An artist?' she suggested. 'An actor?'

I looked so wonderful, so unimaginable, so beautiful that it seemed presumptuous to say anything.

'A mutant?'

'No.'

'And certainly not ugly.' She came out of the dark, held me, one hand on each of my arms.

174

'Would you like to sleep over at the theatre for a few nights?'

'Yes.'

'You're an actor.' She kissed me on the forehead. 'This theatre is for you. Do you hear me? You won't have to be poor like Sparrow.'

'Yes.'

'When you grow up, you'll always have a theatre. Now you can stay with Wally, and I'll come visit you at least once every day. Maybe Sparrow will find time to help you. In any case, we can work out your exercises as we go along. You know I'm going to run for parliament, but I'll make the time to help you every day. Are you angry with Vincent still?'

'No,' I said.

'OK, we're going to scrub up, and we're going to go and tell everyone that you and I are OK. So now you can take one last good look,' she said. 'A good slow look.'

She left Tristan Smith alone in the spotlight. My bladder defeated me before I was bored with my reflection.


## 47

Four days later, my mother was famous.

She had been famous before, of course. Strangers in the street still called her Yvette, the name of her character in the soap opera. Also, she was famous in a different way for the Feu Follet, and a different way again for her role in demonstrations against the Voorstand presence on our soil.

But she had never been as thoroughly famous* as she was when she stood for parliament.

I was woken by Roxanna shaking me.

'Come on,' she said. 'Quickly.' I was always slow to wake, but Roxanna could not wait for me. She picked me up and carried me into the kitchen where Wally was already cooking – not breakfast, dinner. He had shaved, and he had Ducrow's old wood-burning stove alight, something he did in the wet season when the porous old walls were getting too wet. The big pitted yellow and red tiles were freshly mopped and he had set up a large vid on top of the

---

* In Voorstand, of course, you have a word for all these different degrees of public notoriety. In Saarlim you would say that my maman was experiencing vid-glorie. [TS]

old-fashioned copper. A thick blue 240-volt cable ran from the vid out to the theatre power box.

Outside the day was grey, windy, what we call a 'Mongrel Day', hot wind, always changing. Inside: my mother was a flickering luminous vision in her yellow dress, her red hair. The hair had been cut since she visited me the evening before. It was shorter, tidier. She wore glasses, which she most certainly did not need for anything other than her 'Character'.

As I sat down at the table, Wally put porridge and a glass of milk in front of me. He said nothing, but nodded his head towards the screen. His face was aglow with pleasure, Roxanna's too.

'Isn't she gorgeous?' she said. 'Who wouldn't vote for her?'

Rox herself was wearing an oversize midnight blue T-shirt with 'Stand Back Voor Stand' stencilled on the back.

Rox was now alight in the way people get when they are close to fame. It does something to them, smooths their skin, brightens their eyes. Roxanna stood with the remote in her hand flicking channels. It seemed as if my mother was on every one.

'She isn't even formally preselected for the seat,' she said.

'She'll get it,' Wally said. 'Vinny's got it fixed.' He had a pile of pale meat in a white bowl, and as he spoke he was browning it in a big copper pan, four or five pieces at a time. The room was rich with the smell of browning butter, the smell of raw onions.

When the telephone began to ring no one answered it. It was as if this was our family business, us and the vid, the luminous blue and yellow picture, the flickering fire, the sweet hot butter, the frying meat.

'She's good,' Roxanna said. 'Your maman is awful good. Listen to how she speaks.'

The phone rang and rang, and then the actors – for it had been they who had been calling – started to arrive. Sparrowgrass first, but then all the others – Annie, Claire Chen, Moey Perelli. It was only half past eight in the morning but they were all excited to be associated with my mother, offering their services, phone numbers etc. They stood around the table, patting and fondling me like in the old days, already imagining the possibility of a Blue victory. I wanted to tell them I was going to be an actor, but it was not the time, and instead I held my good news, my fortune, held it tightly and secretly against my chest.

'All your maman's friends work on the vid,' Moey said to me. 'All those sold-out hacks and spin driers. You watch the space she gets. You hear the noise.'

Wally put the lid on his copper pan and left it simmering. He washed his hands, lit a cigarette and was leaning against the wall, supporting the elbow of his smoking arm with the palm of his left hand. He had about him the air of an organizer, as if he, through his own secret methods, had put my maman on the vid and encircled me with actors. This was not so, of course, but when the handsome messenger arrived – a young, muscular man, in a body-hugging blue suit – Wally did not look at all surprised but merely nodded his head to where the messenger stood at the open door-way, dimple-chinned, solemn-faced, holding out a silver and blue box.

'Tristan Smith?' the messenger asked.

I turned my face away from the stranger, but Roxanna signed and brought the box to me.

Then she took my chair and I climbed on to her lap and nestled my head into her breasts. She smelt sugary and alien, but she was soft and welcoming. I held the box in my lap, and no one asked me what was in it. They were drinking sweet Efican tea and staring at the vid. It was that sort of day. You could feel the world shifting its axis.

'I wanted to be an actress myself,' Roxanna said, spooning more blackberry conserve into her tea. 'That was my big dream before I met Reade. I would have given anything to be an actress, but my ankles were too thick.'

We both looked at her ankles. As for me, I would have given anything for ankles like that. Her feet were small, perhaps a little flat, but her ankles were full, generous, like her calves. For me, whose own legs were little more than bones, Roxanna's ankles had always appeared to be perfection itself.

'You need thin ankles,' she said.

'I . . . have . . . thin . . . ankles,' I said.

This made Roxanna pause a moment.

'Well, mine are thick,' she said at last. 'And I'm stuck with them until they bury me. Your mother has very nice legs. She could do well in almost anything. Thick ankles are a real disadvantage, for a woman

177

particularly. Today I really have to find my suit for the auction.'

'You . . . don't . . . have . . . to . . . buy . . . a . . . suit . . . for . . . an . . . auction,' I said. 'I've . . . been . . . to . . . auctions . . . with . . . Wally. I've . . . been . . . to . . . lots.'

'For this one, I need a suit,' she said. 'All I'll be thinking about is my boobs and my ankles, make the most of the one, the least of the other. Oh God,' Rox said, 'look at her. How can she lose? She's just so beautiful.'

My mother was now on a panel discussion, surrounded by men in suits.

'Oh God,' Roxanna said. 'Oh God. I didn't know – she is just so beautiful.'

Wally was now separating the small bones from what looked like chicken. He worked deftly, shredding the meat with his big fingers as he went.

'What's for dinner?' Sparrow asked.

'Nothing for you,' Wally said. 'Something special for Roxanna, for tomorrow.'

'For me? For dinner? I won't be here.'

'Oh.' Wally smiled. 'I think you will be when you know.'

I felt Roxanna's body harden.

'What?' she said.

'Mollo-mollo,' Wally said, smiling, but strangely. He turned to place the bowl of meat in the refrigerator and then began to tidy up the kitchen table.

'What?' Roxanna insisted.

It was at about this stage – as Roxanna said *what?* one more time – that the actors began to vanish. They wrote their numbers or addresses on the refrigerator with magic marker. Neither Roxanna nor Wally said goodbye to them. Roxanna slid out from under me and walked across the kitchen to Wally.

'What the fuck have you done?' she asked.

Wally held out his hands, so his fingers touched her elbows. Roxanna flinched.

'What?'

Wally put his foot on the kitchen tidy. I heard the lid fly up, saw Roxanna look down and her chin drop.

I scampered off my chair and looked in too. It was filled with feathers.

'No!' she said, angry.

Wally's face was pale, waxy.

'No!' she said; she touched his face with her hand.

Wally's Adam's apple bobbed.

'I can't eat,' she said. 'I'm going to an auction.'

I was still confused as to what had happened. I put my hand into the bin and plunged in amongst the bed of soft grey and brown feathers – pigeon feathers. When I looked up I saw Roxanna's face, tears flooding her cheeks, her mascara running like spilt ink.

'You crazy man,' she said, 'you crazy ballot . . .' And then, without a glance at me, she took him by the hand and led him from the room. In their absence I could smell the feathers, like wet ashes.

I climbed back on my chair and, in the empty kitchen, with the stove still burning and my mother's image still shining from the vid, I carefully undid the box the messenger had delivered.

There was a small ivory card with hand-torn decalled edging. On it was written: 'For my favourite actor.'

Inside was an object – wrapped in pale yellow tissue paper which, even though I tore it impatiently, did not reveal its secrets easily. What I found was a surface, burnished like a tea pot, lacquered with eggshell white, deep, lustrous blacks and greys.

Only when the last paper fell away did I realize that my maman had sent me not merely a Bruder Mouse mask, but one far superior to the one I had destroyed. It was heavy, not light. It felt like porcelain, or wood, but – in any case – not papier-mâché. It was hard as the fender of Vincent's Corniche, and glazed. On its inside, in the centre of the forehead, was a little red sticker with the phases of the moon in yellow – symbols of a Voorstand import.

I did not know it was a valuable antique.* Indeed, apart from the folk stories in the Badberg Edition I knew nothing about the history of Bruder Mouse, or even my mother's personal relationship with it.† I was already *feeding*, guiltily, greedily, fiddling with its buckles,

---

* *This mask, dating from the first century of Voorstand, had the serrated forehead ridge which distinguishes the Sirkus masks from the Neu Zwolfe settlement. It was atypical in that it had two chipped teeth, not one.* [TS]

† *My mother's childhood, more than thirty years before, was not so different from the life depicted in De Kok's paintings of the previous century – the crowds in Demos Platz, the fat-arsed factory owners rubbing shoulders with the poor and middle class, the*

pulling it over my head. It felt heavy, shiny, and it smelt of pine needles and expensive leather. There was no elastic band to hold it on, but a series of complicated straps and fasteners like the back of roller-hockey pads.

When I had the mask on, I drew up a chair and sat alone in the slightly overheated kitchen watching my mother on the vid. We were in our new lives. I was the actor. She was the politician. I could see her frailty, a very slight tremor in her voice, a slight uncertainty in her hand gestures, but a stranger would not have picked it up – she would appear to be funny, charming and, with her new steel-framed spectacles, rather stern. She was presenting her paper on armed neutrality. She evoked the images of Oncle Dog, Phantome Drool, Bruder Mouse, the whole panoply of Sirkus characters. She painted the Phantome as a spy, the Dog as a soldier, the sharp-toothed blue-coated Mouse as a paranoid – its white-gloved finger hovering above a button which might destroy the planet.

No one who watched the speech would have believed that she had dressed her own son in the visage of the enemy, and that the son now sat, not listening to a word his mother said, dreaming his own flickering dreams, peering at her through the half-moon slits in the back of Bruder Mouse's eyes.

## 48

Roxanna gave herself to Wally, solemnly, gratefully, in his bleak little room where circus apprentices had once spent their nights, stacked three-high in bunk beds, their bodies bruised from falls and Ducrow's English leather boot, young boys still dreaming of their mothers.

Her eyes were brimming, her lips plump and lingering, and all her swiftly naked body – for she shed her dress with a single zip – was baby-soft, newly born, not muscled like an actress, yet not obviously damaged by her life. At twenty-five years of age, she

---

*ex-prisoners of Voorstand's wars, Egyptians, Germans, Ugandans in saris, the makers of Pow-pow music in their Sunday checks, the picnickers, the pretty skaters, the amiable figure of Bruder Mouse, say, extending a white-gloved hand to accept a dollar from a smiling pink-cheeked matron.*

had no scars, no silver marks. She had a small plump stomach, not exactly fat, but with a round curve her lover could, and did, fit in the palm of his hand. When she brought her pale pretty lips to his, her eyes dropped and her small round chin dimpled.

Afterwards, she rested her coarse, tangled blonde hair on his foreign shoulder and rubbed at her kohl-black tears as they fell into the grey hair on his chest.

'What is it?' he asked her.

What could she tell him?

There was a long livid scar beside his lower rib. She ran her fingers over it, the slippery smooth skin, like freshly shaven skin, but silkier. It was a Mongrel Day in Chemin Rouge, yellow melancholy light, the window sashes rattling in their frames. Her tears kept falling, fat and dirty.

'What is it?' he insisted.

It was the pigeons, of course. It made her feel so pitiful to admit the low level of her life – no one had ever done such a thing for her before. She had sucked their cocks, put her tongue up their arseholes, but no one ever did anything for her they did not want to do.

'Tell me,' he said.

'I was sad about the birds,' she said. Then, blowing her nose, 'I know it's silly.'

'They got born. Someone sold them, someone bought them. Life's very sad, don't you think it is? Even for birds.'

She was crying. It was crazy. She was not even worried about the pigeons. She could have strangled them herself, personally.

'I'm not blaming you,' she said. 'I didn't mean to cry and ruin it.'

'Life is a fucking miracle,' he said. He kissed her ear. Why did hard men always have such baby-soft lips?

'Don't talk like that,' she said.

For answer, he cupped his hand again on her straw-coloured mound of pubic hair. He held her. 'You're a miracle, Roxanna.'

'You're an old hog fart,' she said. He lay back and she felt him smile.

'You know I'm leaving. You know that well and truly. I never hid it from you.'

'Don't worry about me,' he said. 'I'm a big boy.'

But he was not, not really, he was quivering with need – such very soft lips, such grey, sad, freckled eyes with the pretty rusty

181

wash flooding outwards from the island of pupil. She said, 'Just remember what you knew first time you saw me . . .'

'Which was?'

She grinned. 'Your dick got hard.'

'Don't kid yourself.'

'You saw a spin drier in high-heels.' She smiled. 'I know what you saw.'

'Don't talk like that.'

'I'm not a nice person, Wally,' she said. 'You knew it then, when you saw me first. Now you're just making up some other story.'

'What I know is, you're just like me. Things have happened to us.'

'Boo-hoo-hoo.'

'I don't need to know exactly what they are.'

'Well, listen to me, please. I'm not sorry I had sex with you. It was really lovely. It was. But you're not the man for me, OK?'

'You can't know that.'

'It's not to do with you. It's to do with me. Honey, I am going to the Chemin Rouge antique fair tomorrow night. There are going to be rich men there from all over the world. I am going to get me one of them. Watch me. I told you what I was. You knew what I was.'

'You want to be rich?'

'Don't say it like that. Say it how you like. I'm going to find someone there who thinks I am a treasure. And I'm not going to cheat them. I'm going to be that for them.'

'You mightn't.'

'Find anyone? I will.'

'How do you know?'

'Because I decided. Because I planned. Because I have worked, and studied, and prepared. BECAUSE I CAN FUCKING WELL DO IT.'

'But what if there is no one there you like?'

'There will be.'

He smiled. It was exactly the same smile that Reade gave when he came home and saw her reading – could not believe a woman could understand a book he couldn't.

'Don't smirk at me, you ass-hole.'

'Hey.'

'You listen to me,' Roxanna said. 'You kill a fucking pigeon, you think you own me. You try and make me *eat* it, well fuck you.' She stood up. '*You* eat it.'

'Rox,' he said, 'you make no sense.'

'Don't you fucking get it?' she said. She was dressing now, stumbling into her dress, reaching for her red high-heels while he was still rising from the bed. 'I'm crazy.'

She ran down the stairs to the foyer and out into the street. Then she stood there, at the steps, smoking a cigarette, tapping her foot, looking up and down the street, knowing already that she was going to go back inside because there was not yet anywhere else for her to go.

## 49

On the morning of the auction there was a fire at the Chemin Rouge Hilton (where the auction was to be held). I watched the fire brigade on the vid screen, but I watched this catastrophe just as I had begun to watch my mother's interviews, or to listen to Rox and Wally as they moved hourly from rift to rapprochement and back again. That is, I watched from within the shell-like face of Bruder Mouse, through peep-holes.

Roxanna had wept when she heard about the fire. I told her I was sorry, and I felt I was sincere, but there was a way in which I was absent from the scene.

Wally made her tea and rubbed her neck. It seemed to work, because minutes later they were arguing about the *Pigeon Patissy*.

Rox, against all the evidence to the contrary, was insisting that men could not cook *Pigeon Patissy*.* She said she was going to have a female chef when she was rich, and that she was going to invite Wally to her home for dinner. Then she said she could not ask him because he was sure to kill her peacocks. Then she said he could be the plumber. Now they were laughing a lot, and fooling around, acting like they were stealing the pastry and doing things behind the other's back, but it wasn't totally joking either. They argued about the marinade and watched a lot of vid-news and

---

* Pigeon Patissy *is a famous Efican dish, something that is bound to arouse strong opinions. Catholics tend to cook it one way, Protestants another. Wally's version tended towards the Catholic: half a teaspoon of cinnamon blended with the sugar which is sprinkled across the top layer of the filo pastry.* [TS]

drank a lot of beer. It was easy for me to slip away to examine that subject which now interested me the most – my new self.

This was not the first time that day when I had gone to check on my reflection in the actors' dressing rooms, but each time I saw myself in the full-length mirror I was pleased. I did not have the proper Bruder waistcoat, but I had a metallic scarf which was almost the right colour and I taped cartridge paper in cylinders around my twisted legs in an uncomfortable approximation of the Bruder's slick white boots.

The doctrinaire actors of the Feu Follet would have died to see wicked Bruder Mouse invade their sawdust ring and pull himself up the inspection ladders with his poisonous blue cloak tangled dangerously around his body. But they were not there. I was. It was my theatre, and when I left the dressing room that is exactly what I did.

I sat up in my own private dusty dark and recited bits of Shakespeare to the empty seats – *Richard the Third* – you would not have understood a word of what I said, but you were not there, Madam, Meneer, and your pity did not tarnish the glamour of my role.

I removed my mask to eat a hearty lunch of herring. After lunch I strapped it on again. Then for a little while I watched Wally and Roxanna as they brushed butter between the layers of store-bought filo pastry.

And when that was done, I waited patiently for the acting lessons my mother had promised – although if you have ever experienced an election from the inside, you may think my hope naïve. Certainly, an election is a difficult time for a candidate to think about her family. But I was the child of an actress, used to waiting for that time when the curtain was down and the last admirer gone home. I waited for my maman with an ease that came from years of practise.

Roxanna, also, was used to waiting, but on the day of the fire she could get no clear news about the future of her auction. She was agitated by her unexpected feelings for Wally. The pigeon pie made her guilty and anxious. Unable to wait calmly or gracefully for news about the auction, she tried to get me to come out into the air with her, tugging at my hand with an insistence that surprised me.

'Come on,' she said. 'Let's get out of this dump, Bruder.'

But I was already wedded to the private darkness of my theatre, the sweaty twilight inside the mask, the tight straps above my ears and around the back of my head. I was half drunk on the sweet fug of my own breath, and I absolutely would not accompany her out into the unfriendly light of day.

I remained alone in the kitchen dreaming vague dreams involving glittering cloaks and dazzling lights.

If there was anything to spoil my reverie, it was the knowledge that my mother had given me that mask against her own heartfelt principles. I believed that she loathed Bruder Mouse. And thus when she finally arrived, a good hour before the pie was ready, and I heard the sound of her heels cross the cobbles of the foyer, I lost my courage and removed the mask.

I did not reflect on the fact that my maman had been born in Saarlim. You are from Voorstand, so you know what this means: that as a child, on Harvest Sunday, she would have sat on a mouse's knee; that *the least of God's creatures* played their role in Easter and Christmas. They were illustrated in the Holy Cards – Ducks and Mice weeping at the Crucifixion of the Lord.

So no matter what her critique of Voorstandish hegemony, my maman obviously held more complex feelings for Bruder Mouse than she had ever admitted to the collective.

Indeed, it is obvious to me now, she was a creature of her culture. No matter that she denounced your country's intrusion into Efican soil, she was a Voorstander. You can see it in the Feu Follet acting style, which has its roots in the laser technology of the Sirkus. My mother pushed her actors into shapes more suitable for laser stick-and-circle figures than human beings with rigid skeletons. She would do the same to herself, contort herself at the expense of ligaments, bloat or purge herself, shave her head, willingly distort her perfect features. She could easily make her eyes appear too close together, her lips pinched and mean, her chin weak, her nose long, her feet huge, her legs shapeless, her chest flat and so on.

Indeed, when she arrived, at the end of the first day of her campaign, I recognized what had been so familiar about her image on the vid – she was nothing less than the Kroon Princess.* She had

* *In truth, I did not know the Kroon Princess at that time. In Chemin Rouge the character was named after the European fairy-tale character of Snow White who, as you know, does finally become a Kroon Princess.* [TS]

185

the huge eyes, the long neck, the pale skin of the character whom Bruder Duck always sought to wed. There was such intelligence and sexiness about her. When she stepped into that kitchen and stood there, her male secretary behind her, her PR woman at her side, Roxanna and Wally stood and applauded, their eyes bright, their faces shining.

She came to me, where I sat, on my blue stool. She put her hands under my arms and lifted me – I was heavy, too – into the air. I, Tristan, was the one she loved.

'We're going to do some acting,' she said. 'Right now. We start our classes.'

'What . . . about . . . Vincent?'

'What about him?'

'Isn't . . . he . . . coming . . . in?'

'He's outside. In the car.'

I had known Vincent all my life and there had always been, in his relationship with me, this slight distance, this reserve. From time to time I suspected that his reserve was caused by a disgust with my person, but then he would do something – hug me, bathe me, touch me – in a way that made all these fears ridiculous. But for him to sit in the car on this night was most peculiar, and because I felt guilty about the mask I got it into my head that this was where the problem lay.

'Is . . . he . . . angry . . . with . . . me?'

'Vincent? Angry with you? Why would he be angry?'

'Because . . . of . . . that . . . thing.'

'You don't have to whine, sweets. What thing?'

'That . . . *thing* . . . you . . . gave . . . me.'

'What thing I gave you?'

'Wrapped . . . in . . . yellow . . . paper.'

'The mask? It's from his collection. Sweets, it's a very special mask. It's two hundred and eighty years old. It's not a Sirkus mask. It's not plastic. It's made from pine resin like they did in the old days. He wanted you to have it.'

'Then . . . why . . . won't . . . he . . . talk . . . to . . . me?'

'It's made by the plain Volk. Do you know what I mean? It was made by good people who thought animals were Bruders to us all.'

'Why . . . won't . . . he . . . talk . . . to . . . me?'

'Please don't whine. He can't come up.'

'It's . . . because . . . I . . . ran . . . away . . . from . . . that . . . house.'

'For Christ's sake, Tristan, he is not angry. It's nothing to do with you. Not everything is to do with you. There are all sorts of things happening that are nothing to do with you. There is a whole country out there. Eighteen islands.'

'It's . . . the . . . mask.'

'Oh merde,' my mother said. She picked me up roughly.

'I'm . . . sorry . . . I'm . . . SORRY.'

But she was already carrying me and as we came into the gloomy foyer I could hear the rain spilling from the rusted down-pipes in the street. If my mother heard this, it did not slow her. She pushed on out into the rain, shouting Vincent's name.

'Talk to him,' she called. 'For God's sake talk to him.'

Vincent's car was nowhere in sight. She banged on the wet window of a station wagon.

'Talk to him,' she said.

There, through the rain-beaded window, by the light of the street lamp, I saw Vincent's pale beard, his bulging eyes. He was pointing a gun at me.


## 50

What bound Vincent to my mother was the shared belief that what you said could matter, might change the course of history itself, but when he had – two nights before – faced his trembling wife, it seemed as if his very life depended on what words he chose.

Natalie was pale, pretty, weak-mouthed. Her arms were thin, perfectly un-muscled. She had big eyes and short hair like a child. She stood in her husband's untidy book-lined study and folded her arms across her chest and clutched a white lace shawl which she more normally wore across her shoulders when dining in the garden. It was not cold, but her perfect little teeth were chattering. She pushed the base of her spine against the bookshelves.

'I'm going to kill you,' she said.

It was four in the morning. Vincent, who had crept home to pick up his cash parole, was sitting at his desk with his hand in his top drawer.

He found the cash card, slipped it in his jacket pocket. He began to stand, and then his wife dropped the shawl and revealed the long-finned barrel of a 9-mm Globlaster.

'I'm going to kill her too,' she said.

'Natalie, don't be silly.'

'I can do this,' she said. 'It's called a spurt-and-splatter. It just kills everything.' Her small bare feet were poking out from under the long white nightdress he had bought for her in Egypt.

'So I went away,' Vincent said. 'I'm sorry. I'm back now.'

Natalie's hair stood up on end. Vincent saw it lift, on her neck and the crest of her head. 'You think I don't *know*,' she said.

'Just put the gun down,' he said. 'Your hands are shaking.'

'I told you – it's spurt-and-splatter. You think I am a moron. You think I lie here every night and don't know you are *living* with her.'

He had to get himself standing, but it felt too dangerous a thing to do.

'Natalie . . .'

'Aren't you surprised your flighty little wife managed to actually buy a gun? Aren't you going to ask me how I did it?'

Across Natalie's shoulder Vincent could see through the window to the driveway. He could see the Corniche and my mother's face illuminated by the instrument lights. 'Natalie, I'm sorry. I'm so sorry. I've really been a shit.'

'*Oh Lord, I am a louse,*' she mimicked, curling her mouth in an ugly way that shocked him, not just for its ugliness, but for its heedlessness. '*Oh Lord, I am a worm.* Forget it. All that Catholic bullshit doesn't cut with me any more.'

As she spoke, her trembling increased, but the curl of her mouth warped itself into a small half-grin and Vincent saw, with fascination, that his wife had chipped a front tooth.

'I'll always look after you,' he said.

'You can't look after me if you're dead.'

'Natalie! Don't *say* that.'

'Dead,' she said. 'D-e-a-d.'

'If you kill me, Natalie, you'll go to jail.'

She shrugged her little shoulders.

'You *stole* my life,' she said. 'It's gone. You pissed on it. You stopped me working. You wouldn't let me have children.'

'Natalie, you know that isn't true.'

'You didn't want stretch marks on your china doll.'

Natalie did not have a chipped tooth. Did not speak like this.

'I let you lock me up here with all this crap, then you run away and live in your "house of few possessions".' She turned the gun towards his Lalique angel. He thought she was going to shoot it, but she merely used the barrel to tip it on to the tiled floor. It did not fall in slow motion. It hardly made a noise. It just changed itself into pale sharp pieces which rushed across the terracotta floor. Vincent rose and stooped towards the fragments but as Natalie turned the long barrel towards the angel's twin he swooped up and grabbed her, pinned her round the forearms, as she began to laugh.

'Oh dear,' she said, 'I guess it's just not perfect any more.'

The laugh was so natural, so relaxed, that he smiled too.

'Natalie . . .'

'You're going to die,' she sighed 'And so is she.'

He could feel the gun, still in her hand. He could feel it against his thigh. He walked her across to the settee. 'Drop the gun on to the settee,' he said.

She did. It did not go off.

'I can wait another day or two,' she said. 'I used to wait for you to go to sleep.' She sighed. 'Then I would go to the linen closet and take out the gun and bring it back and point it at you. Tons of times.'

He could feel her frail body. He held it tight, frightened to let it go, wary of what it might do. He turned her, so she was facing away from the window.

'I used to put the gun an inch away from you, while you slept. And you know why I didn't?'

'Natalie,' he said, 'you need help now. I'm going to get you help.'

'The only reason I didn't shoot you is that if you fucked me, I might have a baby.'

He could feel her crying quietly, feel her thin shoulders shuddering against his chest.

'Natalie . . . please . . .'

'I know you had a child with her, so watch out, buddy boy,' she said. He could see her face, bright, sharp, wet-cheeked, broken-toothed, shining at him from the mirror. 'Watch out for Natalie.'

Vincent was now so frightened of this pale, fine-boned woman, he dared not let her go. He imagined she would somehow stab him, murder my mother in the car. He held both her wrists in one hand while he telephoned his brother.

'I know who you're calling,' she said, 'but it won't work, no matter who you know.'

At five a.m. Natalie Theroux was a client in a psychiatric institution in Goat Marshes. Twenty-nine hours later she was free again, riding through downtown Chemin Rouge in a taxi cab.

This was why Vincent sat in the rented car outside the theatre while my mother went in to conduct the first of my acting lessons – he was keeping guard. He kept the car doors locked and sat low in the seat with his eyes on the rear-view mirror, and only after I had appeared, wet and frightened in the rain, and he, in terror, had nearly shot me, did he come inside.

If you witnessed Vincent (who could not even program his own vid-remote) sitting in the kitchen, reading a photocopied instruction manual for Natalie's Globlaster, you knew he would shoot himself or someone he did not mean to.

He had not liked the bulge the holster made on his jacket so he had spent the day shifting the gun from briefcase to clutch bag, from clutch bag to belt. At lunch he left it underneath his chair with the result that his secretary was forced to ring all the previous places on the morning's itinerary, asking noncommittal questions without ever mentioning the word 'gun'.

He was nervous that he would squeeze the trigger too much or not enough, and when he sat in the car that night, watching the taxis come and go in Gazette Street, he sometimes feared the tightness in his hand, the tension in his muscles, would make him squeeze off a shot when he had not meant to. He did not trust himself with the safety catch, so left it off.

When I tapped on the glass, Vincent got such a fright he nearly fired the gun, and then he was so shaken he had to give the weapon to Felicity. She took it in both hands and walked slowly back into the kitchen, where she placed it on top of the kerosene refrigerator.* When Vincent entered the kitchen he was holding me in his arms and pressing his bearded face against my neck and

---

* The frequency of power blackouts during the Efican Moosone means that the old kerosene refrigerators continue to co-exist with microwaves and vids.

kissing me. He had nearly killed me. He could feel his own heart thumping in his chest.

It was at this moment that Wally chose to serve his *Pigeon Patissy*.


## 51

I never tasted the famous *Pigeon Patissy*, or witnessed – as Vincent did – the effect the pigeon's flesh had on Wally and Roxanna. I had seen the candles lit in the kitchen. I had observed the brand new crystal glasses, the two bottles of champagne which Wally had 'found' for the occasion, but when my maman said that she and I must be excused the meal, it did not occur to me to be either apologetic or disappointed.

And I must ask you please, Madam, Meneer, to leave Vincent in his priestly black to be the sole witness to the lovers' meal, and to follow my strutting knee-walk across the foyer, and to take your seat inside the Feu Follet.

In the kitchen a cork popped, but in the soft sawdust of the ring I removed my shoes and tangled socks and felt the whole history of our national theatre between my liberated toes – Ducrow, Dubois, Millefleur, Smith. My maman also slipped out of her shiny black shoes and placed them, neat as quotation marks, on the wooden ring curbs.

My mother went into the workshop and returned with two wooden-handled rakes. She gave me one. She took the other. 'First we rake. You work that side of the shoes. I do the other.'

It is not often that you recognize a milestone in your life, but I knew that this was serious. I treated the vulgar sawdust like a zen garden.

When it was done, my mother took my rake and laid it down, together with her own, so it indicated a cord cutting across one side of the ring.

It was now two a.m. That day she had done three 'street walks', a press conference, eight interviews, delivered a speech, and seen her lover nearly shoot her son, but as she swept she became calmer, quieter in herself. She lost the pale political beauty of the Kroon Princess. She began to rebuild herself from the outside in, to define herself by her movements, to make her body a mould for her emotions. She became at once precise and tranquil. She arranged the two rake handles so they touched between the high-heeled shoes.

She removed her grey shot-silk skirt and folded it. She took it to the wings, and returned with two empty paint tins and a small black towel. Then she sat cross-legged – just in her jacket and panty-hose – on the black towel. She indicated that I should sit opposite her.

Then we meditated, for perhaps ten minutes.

'Now,' she said, at last.

I opened my eyes. My mother was very still. A smile – almost a smile – was on her face. All the focus of her eyes was on me. I felt a physical sense of expectation, a pins and needles in my limbs.

'We are going to do *The Chef of Efica*.'

'No!' The word escaped, a puff of disappointment – to hear her say something so common, so vulgar, was a great disappointment to someone with my ambitions. I had expected a text from Shakespeare, Molière, Racine.

'Oh yes,' she said. She leaned across and ruffled my head. Then she gave me one high-heeled shoe and an empty paint tin. 'This is your voice,' she said.

'I . . . want . . . to . . . be . . . LEAR.'

'This is your voice,' she said, placing the shoe firmly in one hand, the paint tin in the other. 'You can move however you like, but the only thing you can *say* is with this shoe. You bang it, or tap it. You are the Chef,' she said. 'I am the soldiers. You know the story.'

'It's . . . so . . . corny.'

'Corny or not – this is our play. I want to kill you, but you want to live. We soldiers are hungry, but cannot cook. We don't believe you are really a chef. We think you are lying to save your life.'

She picked up a shoe and banged it on the paint tin. As she did this, she changed herself. Her cheeks blew out, her eyes slitted, her stomach bulged. She sneered at me. Bang, bang, bang. She scared me.

'I'm talking,' she said. 'This is how I talk to you.'

I picked up the other shoe and banged the ring curb. My mother took it away from me.

'You are trying to persuade me not to *kill* you. Think what you need to tell me. First you smell the smoke, the burnt food. You hate

192

the soldiers. They have bright red coats with huge hats made out of fur. You are frightened of them. You have to tell them that you can cook their meal, before they kill you. Let's stand.'

She made 'the horse', i.e. the fighting stance, legs wide apart, knees bent. She crouched to bang her shoe on her tin can, then straightened, but her eyes never once left my face.

I banged my own tin can right back at her.

She stopped, shook her head.

'Listen to me, watch me, don't decide what you're going to do until you see what I have done. Come on, Tristan – you want to act. This is acting – the moment while you wait to hear what I say. While you *think* what to do – that's it. It isn't the lines, or the lights – this is what we give them: the energy, made by this gap which is made by you listening to me. Drama is a spark plug. Your listening is the gap the spark flies across.'

Then she sprang into the air and came down hard – the horse – upon the floor. She drummed a loud rat-tat, an aggressive, sneering territorial tattoo.

I tried to make the horse myself. Of course I could not. I teetered, fell. She laughed – not my mother – the soldier laughed. He laughed. They laughed, all of them.

My eyes welled up with tears. I showed them the shoe. It was empty.

She hit the shoe against the tin once, hard, a warning shot.

I began to make the food with the shoe, I was quiet and busy, I chopped.

They moved in on me, around me. They shoved, but also: they smelt the food. They became gentler, then fierce again: they said it was no use. They told me I would die.

I faced them. I held their eyes. I made myself be calm and then I persuaded – I used the shoe to sing them the recipe.

They faltered. They were like feral dogs. You could not trust them.

I described the dinner I would cook them – gravy – bubbles in a pot.

They told me I was a liar. They said they would split my head, burst my guts. I stayed calm. I watched their eyes. When they were still again, I described silky sauces, butter, gravy, things simmering on the stove. I promised them thick bread, treacle puddings. Time ceased to matter for me.

I was walking across a tightrope. I moved through the soldiers' defences until the moment, the famous moment, when they were sated, and I had the sharp knife in my hand.

'Bravo,' my mother said. 'Bravo.'

I looked, dazed. Wally and Roxanna were standing by the door to the foyer, swaying, arm in arm, their glasses raised.

'He actually has some talent,' my mother said, and hugged me.

Then Vincent stepped up into the ring and spoiled it all.

He fetched my mother's skirt. He held it out to her. She took it. He brought her case. He picked up my mother's shoes and placed them by her feet. He gathered the rakes.

My mother always hated to be organized by others, but when Vincent came on to the stage to take her away, she surprised me by being no longer angry with him.

'I left all my stuff in the hotel bathroom,' she said.

Vincent was so paranoid, not only about his wife. He lived in a world of secret agencies. VIA, DoS, conspiracy, misinformation, destabilization. Four days into the campaign he had my mother sleeping in a different hotel each night. 'It's all been packed,' he said brusquely. 'It's moved already. Come on, you have to *sleep*.'

My maman walked obediently off into the wings and came back with her skirt on. She was the Kroon Princess again – conservative, trim. She was about to kiss me goodnight but then I saw her soften, change her mind.

'Stand on the other side of the ring,' she told me.

'*Felicity!*' Vincent said.

One can easily sympathize with Vincent's agitation, but look at my mother – no matter what mistakes she may have made in raising me, you can never doubt her feelings for me. Now she was committed to making me an actor, she behaved as if each moment were precious.

'I'm so sorry, mo-chou,' she told Vincent.

Vincent looked at his wrist-watch and shook his head.

My mother looked at her own watch. 'Roxanna,' she said, 'would you help us?'

The older I get, the more amazed I am by the number of people who spend their whole life waiting for a chance to jump on to a stage. Before my mother had finished speaking, Rox was inside the ring, kicking off her shoes, tugging down her skirt, fluffing her hair, looking for a place to put her champagne glass.

Vincent went and sat on a starbuck. My mother's eyes never lost their focus on me. 'Tristan,' she said. 'This is an acting exercise you can do without me. OK?'

'OK.'

'You can do it as often as you like. What I want you to do is move very slowly towards each other. I want you to look straight into each other's eyes. When you reach a point where this makes you uncomfortable, I want you to stop and explore the feeling. Then, when you are ready, come on forward again. Roxanna, maybe it would work better if you could kneel too. Could you manage that?'

'Sure,' Roxanna said. She kneeled.

'You're wearing stockings. Take off your stockings.'

Roxanna stayed stubbornly kneeling.

'You'll wreck your stockings.'

But Rox had her ankles hid in sawdust. 'Listen,' she said, 'leave the stockings to me. OK?'

'OK,' my mother said.

As Rox and I edged across the ring towards each other I was, at first, aware of everyone. It was half past two in the morning. I could feel Vincent's agitation, Wally's happiness, my mother's exhaustion.

Roxanna came towards me, smiling crookedly, holding her skirt in an odd little curtsy.

I looked at her eyes. I concentrated. I could feel her so personally. I felt myself being looked at. When I stopped, it was not from calculation.

'Explore it,' my mother's voice said.

'It's like a pain,' she said. 'Get used to it. When you can stand it, come closer. I'm leaving now,' she said.

I was now in the scary world of Roxanna's eyes. It was like holding your hand in a flame. My ugliness was all around me. I was vile, on my own stage, in my own home.

I did not even hear Vincent and my mother leave. I did not see her walk out into the dangerous dark.


## 52

Roxanna had promised herself she was going to marry a rich man, and there was nothing on earth – not *Pigeon Patissy*, not sex, not

French champagne, not the tender feelings she had begun to engender in her breast towards Wally Paccione – nothing that would make her change her mind.

She was going to marry a rich man. She was going to meet him at an auction – it was all she had lived for for two years, and yet, after five minutes in the auction room, Roxanna believed that her plan had failed.

She stood in front of two flat lead figures – soldiers of the French Colonial Native Cavalry. She knew these figures from the catalogue, but now she hardly saw them. She was sick, disappointed, angry. She had spent two years of her life preparing for this, and the thing was: she was so damned stupid. She had bought a pig in a poke, a cul in a sac.

Her new dress was black with thin shoe-string straps and a camisole top. Her stockings were seamed. She had a small clutch bag. Her hair had been cut, coloured, permed. She had spent every penny of the 650 dollars for this moment, but when she walked into the wide echoing room, she was very disappointed to be the most dramatic person in it.

The auction room was filled with nerds, wimps, frumps, stooped men with leather patches on tweed coats, women with string bags.

She had not allowed for this, had not even considered the question of the husband's face, body, personality. She had not thought of sex. She had thought it was frivolous, unimportant, but now, as she walked around the exhibits with her annotated catalogue, she began to panic.

A calmer personality might have thought that she should wait a minute or an hour, to see what other fish might enter the trap, but a calmer personality would not be in the place Roxanna was now in, would not have married Reade, torched the house, travelled to Chemin Rouge, accepted a proposal of marriage from Wally Paccione and then rejected it next morning.

Her hands were damp. She could feel sweat between her shoulder blades. She looked at the lead figures and thought she would like to melt them, see them droop and bend, see the red paint drown and burn inside the bubbling metal.

When she felt the attentions of the collector next to her a shiver of irritation passed up her spine and into her hair. She felt him move around her, stand on one side of her, then the other. He was a guy.

He was doing the guy-things that her entrance had encouraged him to do, but Roxanna was not attracted to these nerds.

'So what do you think?' the man asked. He spoke English with a Voorstandish accent, but she did not look at him. She could feel him at her side, in her space – short, tweedy.

'Think of what?' she said. She was so pissed off.

'The Hilperts,' he said.

He meant the figures.

'Don't look like bloody Hilperts to me,' Roxanna said.

She had seen few Hilperts in life, but many in photographs, and when she looked at these two figures in the harsh neon light the precision of the colour and the details of the moulding confused her.

'The curator says they're Hilperts.'

'Bully for him.'

'What do you think they are?'

She looked at him more closely. He was wearing tweed, it is true, but not in that nerdy way. He was wearing very precise cuffed corduroy trousers and soft Italian slip-ons. He was, in short, the image of a rich man on a Saturday. Also, now she looked at him, she saw he was actually good-looking – he had chiselled lips and intense, dangerous, blue eyes. He was looking at her, up and down, but subtly at least. 'It says here' – he held up his catalogue – 'that they're "bloody" Hilperts.'

Roxanna felt herself blushing.

'I'm sorry,' she said. 'I was angry about something.'

'You think it's not Hilpert?'

And then she saw: it was working, it was really working, even though she used a swear word, it was happening like the book promised it would. Nothing in her life had ever worked out, but here she was, talking with a rich man. She knew stuff he didn't know. He was looking at her tits.

'What year did Herichsen start business?' she asked him.

'Your calendar?' he said. '240.'

She knew it was 236. She did not want to show him up. She knew the answers. She knew the questions. She felt everything, her destiny, at her fingertips.

'It's very detailed,' the man said. 'There's that – the detailing on the musket.'

'I didn't mean that. I mean – there was no native cavalry until after the native wars. And the native wars did not end until 249, and then they put a few survivors in a uniform.' Reade would have died to see her answer. He knew her, or thought he knew her, back in Jonestown High School: never knew the answers, purple lip-stick, black eyeshadow, Bad Girl, Fast Girl, I'll-cut-your-fucking-face-Girl.

'Are you sure?' he asked her. He was cute. His accent was cute. He had the suggestion of a smile, a wonderful cool, almost scary blue about his eyes.

'Of course,' she said. 'Then they shipped them off to fight in Europe, and they died.'

'So,' he said, 'that's very bloody astute.'

Roxanna giggled.

The collector smiled.

She liked him, she liked him anyway. She wanted to touch his mouth with her fingers.

'Could I buy you lunch?' he said.

And it was done. They had met.

When, exactly three hours later, she went with him to his hotel, she guessed it was too fast, that you should not conduct this sort of relationship like that. She knew a lot about him, but. His mother was a waitress. His daddy was missing. He grew up in a little town where they used poisonous snakes to prove their faith in God. He was very high up in a bank. If you sat in his office you could look across at the Skyscraper Cathedral, and down to the Bleskran. He was not married. He was funny and kind of wild. She thought: whatever happens, happens.

As she walked into the elevator in the Ritz she wished Reade could see her.

Reade would have been frightened to walk into a hotel like this. She too, once. But she read a book and here she was. She was in a daze, and only once – the moment she entered Room 2302 – did she feel a crackle of anger, out of nowhere: the unfairness of it, that there were women who lived every day of their lives in places like this.

Wealth was not like she had imagined – no dark panelling, no gilt – all these different pearl greys, dove greys, this velvety, almost colourless luxury with its single big bed, crisply turned down, and its antique writing desk and the big bathroom with its phials and canisters and silk kimonos, and this wide, deep anger lay glowing beneath a silky sheet of pleasure and gave her that dangerous ecstatic feeling she knew she should not encourage in herself.

'Would you like an Aqua?' Gabe asked her now.

Eficans never used the word. It was as exotic and beautiful to her ears as a glass angel.

'Oh, yes,' she said in the breathless little voice which she had learned from Irma.

He went to the bar and she sat at the writing desk. Probably it was called a bureau, something unexpected. She ran her hand over the leather desk top. She thought: there are people who do this every day of their lives.

He brought her the drink. She took it without looking at it, half giddy with what she had done.

'I have to go soon,' she said.

He smiled at her.

He was not very much taller than she was, but he had a broad strong body and a handsome olive-skinned face with a neat, short haircut and a cute grin which showed the edge of one slightly (only slightly) crooked tooth and made his eyes crease up. He was forty, maybe forty-five.

She tried to sip her drink slowly, but something inside her made her gulp at it. She squeezed her eyes shut against the bubbles. When she opened them he was smiling at her and she knew he thought she was cute.

'Tell me more about your job in the bank,' he said.

'You're the one who's got the job in the bank.'

'I know.'

'Then I can't talk about it.'

'But I love the way you talk,' he said. 'Talk to me about anything.'

She loved the way *he* talked. She liked the bright, clean confidence of his voice and that three-showers-a-day smell, all soap and steam and light spicy after-shave.

It made her giddy, gave her that feeling, made her laugh more than she might have otherwise, and when he came behind her and put his hand on her thin straps she curled her shoulders up and let the straps slip down over her soft white shoulders, and she turned and bowed her head a little and pulled up her hair to let him see the tattooed dove she had hidden on her neck.

He did not go away. Indeed, he kissed her there, and made a little moan in her ear, and in a moment that 450-dollar dress was on the floor like a great black bloom fallen on to the soft grey carpet and he was telling her he was crazy about her lopsided smile.

Now the dress lay on the floor as if it were nothing better than a pair of shucked-off overalls. She should hang it up. She should say, well, honey, you're just going to have to *wait*. But he already had his jacket and trousers lying there beside the dress and if she was going to insist she would have to stand up and walk across the room in her pants and bra and she didn't want him lying there and looking at her. She was prettiest when closest, so she left the dress where it had fallen, but it stayed in the corner of her mind, this big black worry which had cost her all her capital.

She just wanted to hold him against her, feel herself sort of folded into his chest, but whenever she reached for him he was not where he had been – his face was in her stomach, at her knees for Chrissake.

Now he was at her ankles. She blushed bright red and tugged away.

'No.'

'Babe,' he said reproachfully.

'Let go.' Her ankles were like meat, fat, pork-chop, ugly.

But he took a hold of them, against her will. That really pissed her and she suddenly felt that sort of distance – she just *watched* him as he kissed them. He was kneeling on the floor and kissing her ankles, taking off his wrist-watch while he did it.

'Please don't.'

'Please,' he said. 'Babe, please.'

'I hate my ankles.' Her voice caught on the word. She hated to have to say it out loud.

Gabe ran his tongue between her toes.

She felt the tears run down her face before she even knew she was crying. It just came out of her as if she were a thing, a sponge, soaked with too much moisture.

'Hey, hey.' He crawled up towards her. Oh thank God, she thought. He held her. It was like she wanted. 'Don't cry, hunning. Daddy's here. Why are you crying?'

She held him hard. She pushed her face into his neck and sobbed. She could not say.

'What did I do?'

She shook her head.

'I love your feet,' he said. 'I just love your feet.'

'Don't mock me,' she said.

'These are the kind of feet I like.'

She looked up at him, tear-smeared. 'Really?'

'Really.'

She snorted. She could not help it. It was not quite laughing, but that's what it became.

'I mean it,' he said, blushing. 'There are leg men and breast men and feet men. I am a foot man.'

'Gabe, my ankles are ugly.'

'What do you know?' he said. 'These are beautiful feet.'

'Really?'

She was too tensed about everything – her impetuousness, the 450-dollar lump of dress she had left lying on the floor, this dizzy, unconnected feeling. She wept then. Once a whore, she thought.

'Tell me what to do,' he said, rubbing her neck. 'Just tell me what to do.'

'Hang up my dress,' she said. 'Please, would you do that for me?'

He looked at her incredulously. At first she thought he was going to laugh, and then his eyes narrowed and she thought he would tell her to hang it up herself.

'Please.'

He shrugged his head down into his shoulders and splayed his hands. He hung up the dress. She did not look at him do it, because she would not have wanted him to look at her.

When he came back into bed he held her head between his hands and kissed her on her eyes and then softly, repeatedly, on her mouth. She felt herself open up to him.

She had done everything wrong. She had lost the plot completely but for this long at least she did not give a damn.


# 53

When Roxanna confessed to Gabe Manzini that she was a pyromaniac, he felt a give-away smile appear on the edges of his small, pretty mouth. He kissed her neck to hide it and felt the coarse tickle of her thick, strong hair. He inhaled her smell, whisky, barley. He rubbed his nose against her little rough tattoo and he was happy. God damn: she fit the specs. She had the look. He had *known* her when she came into the auction room – slightly bruised but golden, small-waisted, heavy in the legs, they were always similar, each time, and here was this thing – pyromania this time – it clicked into place like the keystone in an arch. Whatever it was he was repeating, he did not want to stop. He was going to have a perfect gig in Efica.

'What is it?' she said, snuggling up to him.

'You're my good-luck charm,' he said.

All his girls had some kind of craziness – kleptomania, agoraphobia, always something that would later be a pain in the ass, but which would also be part of their sexual fizz. Sometimes he tried to think how their personal craziness matched the craziness of the country, but pyromania, no, please, not Efica. Pyromania was more applicable to Indo-China, South America, time-warp Marxists, Jesuits with blazing eyes.

Gabe Manzini liked Eficans. They were dry, ironic, uncomfortable with dogma, suspicious of high-sounding rhetoric. Their small population, their geographic isolation, their lack of natural riches, their tiny GNP, their historical military dependence on both the French and the English had helped forge a pragmatic people, not easily given to visions of bloody revolutions or even rosy futures. Yet, for all that, they were presently engaged upon a full-scale national misunderstanding – that they could renegotiate their alliance with Voorstand.

If this had been a major nation, one would be irritated, but this was not a major nation. This was Efica, for God's sake, with neither military nor economic power. You would imagine that after three hundred years they would understand their position, but suddenly they did not get it – not just the intellectual minority, but an infuriating 51 per cent (October), 52 per cent (November), 50 per cent (December) were responding to the current Blue Party rhetoric. If the Blues won the upcoming elections, Voorstand would be directed to remove its devices from Efican soil and Efica would become 'friendly but neutral'.

In the world of realpolitik, this was fantasy, not because Efican territorial waters supplied 25 per cent of Voorstand's fish, or even because the northern islands provided a safe storage place for chemical waste. It was fantasy because Efica's southern granite islands were now host to fifteen vital subterranean defence projects. Eficans would not be permitted to reject their twenty-five-year-old alliance with Voorstand.

And this, of course, was why Gabe Manzini was here. It was his job to make sure the status quo was maintained.

'So,' he grinned, 'you're a pyromaniac? You burn things, right?'

'Oh, don't be horrible.' Roxanna lifted her face from his chest and showed him her wide, moist brown eyes. She was delicious.

'Isn't that what you were telling me?'

'You tricked me into saying it. It isn't fair.'

'So I should I hide my matches from you,' he teased. 'No flambés.'

'It isn't like it sounds. It isn't really that at all.' She paused. 'What's flambé?'

'We could have room service, right now.'

'What *is* it?'

He loved the way she flushed and the way her lips parted. He placed his hands under her plump arms and pulled her further up his chest. She moved up with a soft grizzle like a puppy and kissed him with that huge soft open mouth. He checked the clock from the corner of his eye. 'I'm a lucky guy,' he said. He kissed her on the nose. 'Those other fellows in the bank will be out whoring and making themselves miserable.'

'Mmmmm,' she wriggled against him.

'I just hate I've got to go to sleep.'

'Me too,' she yawned.

Gabe sat up. 'Roxanna. I'm not permitted to do that. I can't actually sleep with you.'

'Oh *listen* . . .'

'It's not personal, Roxanna.'

'*Listen*, I was just playing a game with you. You told me you were dangerous. I just said it to trump you. I don't even know what a pyromaniac is, not really. Do I really look like a crazy person?'

'This is policy . . .'

'I wouldn't do anything to you, honey. If you knew how much I loved being here, you wouldn't send me away. Please let me sleep here, Gabey, please. All I want to do is sleep, and wake up, and then I'll go away.'

'If it was up to me . . .'

'But it is up to you.'

'If it was up to me you could stay a week.'

'Who is it up to?' she said, sitting up.

'The bank.'

'Some guys don't like to fall asleep with women, I know that. Maybe they're Catholic or something – they just want to call the girl a cab. If that's what it is, just tell me. I can take it.'

'We have a policy,' he said. He pulled her reluctant body towards him and kissed that delicious little ink-blue dove under her hair. 'We have a policy, in foreign countries, to protect our executives. Guys in my job get kidnapped, killed, colleagues of mine.'

'This is *Efica*.'

'So if you just give me your driver's licence number or your ID, they'll check you out and then we can sleep.'

'I have to give you my ID?'

'You don't have to do anything.'

'I guess this is a foreign country,' Roxanna said. 'I guess I seem as foreign to you as all this does to me.' But she got out of bed and found her ID and gave it to him and watched while he wrote it down. 'Now I take a cab, right?'

'Now you take a cab.'

She took her ID back and opened her wallet.

'Damn.'

'What?'

'I left my cash at home.'

For a moment it occurred to him that she was on the game. He felt a bitter disappointment, a kind of anger. It flushed into him like speed when it enters straight into the vein. It changed his face, slitted his eyes, thinned out the bow in his lips.

'So,' he said, 'what do you need?'

She was looking at his face and her own was pale. 'Five,' she said. 'If you don't have it, it's OK.'

He laughed then, and gave her the 5 dollars. At the door he kissed her again. He was in a good mood. He kicked off his shoes, poured himself another glass of red wine, and then he rang through to the Voorstand embassy to have them send over the latest communiqués.

## 54

Gabe Manzini is the man who ruined my life. I had no idea that he existed, or rather I knew only that 'something' had arrived which threw a shadow across Wally's countenance, that had him sitting by his bed at one a.m., waiting for Roxanna to come home.

It was this nameless 'something' which also made Roxanna so gentle with Wally, and had her performing small domestic tasks for which she had no aptitude – she darned his socks (once), ironed his trousers (twice), and cooked meals and sandwiches for him continually.

Roxanna was no cook, believe me, but she performed these sad services for Wally in recognition of her role in his silent pain, and Wally, sitting with his rough-skinned elbows resting on the kitchen table, observed her crack eggs inexpertly and did not seem inclined to criticize.

I had never heard or read Gabe Manzini's name, but I knew he was out there, on the other side of the dusty windows, a *something* in the night. I intuited him.

This was the man who would end up as Direkter of The Efican Department at the VIA, but let me tell you, Meneer, Madam, your man did not intuit us, not by computer or any other method. His ID check on Roxanna used data banks in four continents, led him to arson in Melcarth, but not to Gazette Street. The part of Roxanna's life she lived with us was unknown to him.

She had sex with him (and champagne and chocolate mousse). With me, she studied acting. Ostensibly she did this as a favour to my maman, to pay her rent, but when you saw her kneel upon the sawdust to play *Exits and Entrances* the light shone out of her. She did not 'act', which is what amateurs usually do. She had the capacity to 'be' which is a gift, not something you can learn in drama school or acting workshops. She was great at exits, at being about to kiss, about to die, about to stab her enemy. Sometimes she seemed paralysed by her own intense feelings, and when she moved it was as if she had to tug herself free of them. She was sometimes obvious in her choices, but there was always something eccentric in her enactment of these choices, a quirkiness which made her interesting to watch. She was technically ignorant, and occasionally sentimental in her tastes, but she had it – the thing that makes you watch an actor on the stage. No one told her she had it. No one said anything to her. But I saw my mother, who had begun by thinking of Roxanna as a whore, soon begin to treat her very differently. As for me, she quickly became my intimate friend and fellow student.

Who knows how our lives would have been if there had been no Gabe Manzini. There is no reason, for instance, why Roxanna might not have become the actress my eleven-year-old heart imagined. We might have reopened the Feu Follet – why not? There is no doubting her raw talent or her enjoyment of the exercises she did with me on the stage.

Roxanna, however, wanted very specific things for her new life: a country house with a park, peacocks, a fountain. She wanted a white carpet, a brass bed with lace-covered pillows of different sizes, and she had persuaded herself that Gabe Manzini could provide these items.

I do not need to point out how naïve she was, on every level, but she had no previous experience of even moderate wealth and she trusted the appearance of his hotel room, the cost of the restaurants he took her to.

She would arrive back at the Feu Follet just after midnight, no ring on her finger, still muggy and musky and happy from love-making. Then she would join me in my mother's master class – do her entrances and exits, pass through her circles of concentration, frighten and amaze herself, earn herself my maman's warm embrace.

At two o'clock my maman had to leave. I never knew where she slept, only that it was a different place each night and that she was afraid. I did not know the person she was afraid of was Gabe Manzini. No one knew his name in those days, but I could always feel him – I did not know it was the same thing, the same person – the one who was there in the night, the one who gave Roxanna her puffy eyes, Wally his morning melancholy.

After breakfast Roxanna came with us to the fish markets.

Then we would come back to Gazette Street and Wally would fillet the fish. At around noon he and Roxanna would begin to drink beer. They would argue about food or sing folk songs in rough harmony.

Sometimes Sparrow sang with them. He had a good baritone

which he liked to use and he would have come more often, but he found a job in a music-hall restaurant. His employer was a Mr Ho, an Efican-Chinese who, whilst undemanding about many things – he was sloppy in dress and careless about hygiene – had such reverence for the text of his Victorian melodramas that he twice dismissed actors for departing from the written word.

'You would think it would be easy,' Sparrow said, 'but it is just exhausting. The guy is a maniac. He sits in the restaurant following the script with a flashlight.'

The city had election fever. The light poles were wreathed in red or blue streamers made of crepe paper which bled in the rain each afternoon. Ice-cream vans with loudspeakers on their roofs prowled the suburbs. As the day of the election drew closer, more actors began to visit us. It was incorrect, they said, for the Feu Follet to be dark at this moment in history. They offered their services. They wanted to do something for the election – a review, a fund-raiser, street theatre. They sat in our kitchen and judged us. They looked at Wally's depressed demeanour, Roxanna with her Irma hair-do, me in my Mouse mask. They saw only surfaces. They did not see history lurking in the dark.

## 55

It was half past eleven at night. Roxanna was with Gabe Manzini, having her ankles kissed. I was lying on my mattress. Wally was sitting on his bed, a blue-lined notebook resting on his knees, his upper body contorted around the pivot of his pencil. He erased constantly, seemingly more words than he wrote. The wattles of his pendulous ears glowed pink.

'What . . . are . . . you . . . rubbing . . . out?'

'Nothing.'

'A . . . letter?'

'None of your business.'

There was a time when Wally would not have risked being seen writing in a notebook. It would have been too much like his early days at the Feu Follet when he had fraudulently represented himself to Annie McManus as a 'prison-poet'. But now there was no other witness but me and I had no memory of the prison-poet. I imagined him composing a love letter to Roxanna. I napped, dreaming about Roxanna and Wally getting married.

When I felt hands on the buckles of my mask, I was not alarmed – I imagined Roxanna had come in and was doing what she often did before our acting class. I felt the buckles undone, the straps loosened, the mask removed, and my sweaty face meet the coolness of the draught from the open window.

And then: this shriek.

I awoke, my hair on end. The lights were blazing. Beside my mattress, kneeling on the floor – a pale-skinned, slim woman with short hair. My eyes met hers. She shuddered, hid her own eyes, shrieked again.

Maybe I screamed too – how do I know? The woman by my bed was so thin I could see the bones in her chest above her breasts. Once she had finished one scream, she began another. She put her hands across her eyes, but I could see her chipped front tooth, her pink epiglottis. I watched her as she gulped, screamed, gulped, screamed.

You would imagine all this fuss would bring Wally leaping from his bed, but he continued sleeping. He lay on his back with his exercise book on his chest, his mouth open, his arms flung sideways.

A taxi began to toot its horn outside. Still he did not stir. When the woman finally stopped screaming, he turned on to his side, his back toward me.

'You're it?' the woman said. She lowered her white, red-nailed hands to her lap. She looked at me as if I were a source of light so bright that I might cause damage to her sight. 'You're his *son*?'

She scared me. Everything about her scared me. She had her handbag open. I could see a gun inside. It was quite clear, undisguised, lying amongst crumpled tissues and a rent-a-car agreement.

'Are you Vincent Theroux's son?' she quavered.

I was too afraid to answer.

She put her hand into the bag. I thought she was reaching for the gun. I screamed. I threw my mask at Wally and it smashed into the bridge of his nose and brought him leaping out of his sheets, white-legged, outraged, his hand clutching his injured tarboof. The woman dropped her handbag.

Wally was in no state to understand anything quickly. He stared at the woman as she picked up her handbag and ran out the door. I could hear her on the stairs, laughing.

The front door banged shut – Wally flung up the window but she was already driving away.

'A crazy woman,' he said, patting my hair. 'That's all, just some old crazy woman.'

He helped me back on with my mask, making the buckles as tight as I liked them, biting hard against my skin. He wrapped some blankets around my shoulders, tucked his exercise book into his back pocket.

'Some old crazy woman, that's all.'

'She . . . was . . . going . . . to . . . murder . . . me.'

'No.' Wally's hair was standing skew-whiff on his head. His face was pale, drawn. His nose was turning purple around the small cut the mask had made. 'She wasn't going to shoot you, son.' He hugged me into his cigarette-smoke shoulder. 'You scared her, that was all. You frightened her.'

'She . . . came . . . to . . . kill . . . me.'

'You both scared each other, that's all.'

But he began to busy himself around the room, gathering blankets, a kettle, the vid, and when he was completely loaded up with all these things he stooped, grunted, and brought me into the tangle of hard and soft things in his arms. 'We'll have a little kip up in the tower.'

The tower was now empty. Everything that had marked it as my home was now gone and it had, instead, a rather depressing dusty appearance, but it still had the same heavy bolt my mother had always slid across when making love, and when Wally had set me on the dusty floor, the first thing he did was drive that old bolt home.

I stood on my ugly stick-thin trembling legs, shivering. I tugged my mask straps one notch tighter.

Wally plugged in the kettle and the vid and arranged them beside each other on the floor. He inserted a pirate recording of Irma. While the show began he wrapped me in two blankets and made a hood for my head.

'There,' he said, 'that's cheerier.'

He squatted beside me for a moment but when I looked across at him I saw he was writing in his exercise book again.

'Aren't . . . you . . . calling . . . the . . . Gardiacivil?'

But Wally did not feel free to call the Gardiacivil about Vincent's wife. He held his handkerchief to his injured nose and turned his bleak grey eyes on me.

'You're . . . writing . . . her . . . description?'

'She's gone,' he said. 'The door is locked, OK? We don't have to tell the Gardiacivil about her.'

'What . . . are . . . you . . . writing?'

'I'm staying awake with you, OK? I'm writing because I'm staying awake.'

'But . . . what . . . is . . . it?'

'NOTHING,' he said. 'Just watch the vid.'

'You're . . . writing . . . a . . . *play.*'

Wally looked up at me, his eyes accusing, his mouth uncertain.

'Watch the vid,' he said, but I knew I had got it right. He was writing a play for me. I was at once excited, but incredulous. My legs became itchy and kicky. Could he write a good play? I watched Irma on the vid. She splayed her small white fingers, bent her wrists backwards.

'Never, ever tell anyone, right? Not till I say it's OK.'

'OK,' I said, but I could not stop my legs drumming on the floor.

'What I can do,' Wally said, 'is write parts for them.'

'Actors?'

'Animals,' he said.

I looked at him sharply.

'I know about animals,' he said. His eyes were bright, aggressive. 'You can't have a circus without animals.'

'Wally . . . '

'Shut up,' he said. 'You don't know shit. We can open this theatre without your mother. You don't know shit about all this stuff, so just listen to me. We've got to make a living. You can be in it, and Rox. We can have a good life here,' Wally said. 'That's what you've both got to realize. We can make it out of what we have. She doesn't have to go outside. She doesn't need peacocks.'

'What . . . peacocks?'

'Parks, peacocks, all that crap,' he said. 'She's going to see it's totally unnecessary.'

But someone opened the big door down on the street. It let in a draught which came all the way up the stairs, under the door, and shifted the dust around.

'What's that?' I was afraid.

'Mollo mollo.' Wally went to the door and unsnibbed the lock. He stood there for a moment with his head out.

'Your maman,' he said.

I began fiddling with my straps, unbuckling my Mouse mask. Wally ejected the vid of Irma and slipped it into his back pocket. I could hear the footsteps on the stair – not one person, a crowd – fast and purposeful, hard leather soles.

I rocketed towards the door, through a crowd of trousers and stockings and high-heeled shoes, my mask held in my hands.

'There . . . was . . . a . . . crazy . . . woman . . . here,' I said, but my maman was anxious, did not hear me.

'Why are you up here?' she said, disentangling me. 'What happened?'

I tried to answer but Mother's team were pushing in around us, men in suits, women smelling of perfume and instant coffee. They had tiny computers, miniature telephones, French battery chargers with complicated adapters. Vincent was there too, pasty-skinned, pouchy-eyed, talking to someone on his telephone.

When he had finished he came and kissed me.

'A . . . crazy . . .' I began.

'Shush,' my mother said. 'Be quiet. Be calm.' She squatted on the floor beside me. 'My darling,' she said, 'your maman has to tell you something quite upsetting.'

I looked into her face and saw how the make-up sat on the surface of her skin and how the skin beneath was tired, how there were lines beside her eyes, beside her mouth, and how the eyes themselves seemed clouded.

'Roxanna?'

My mother shook her head. She opened her purse and took out a folded front page of *Zinebleu*. On the front page there was a photograph of Vincent and my mother kissing. I had seen this photograph before, beside my mother's bed, pinned on to the moulding beside the very window where I now sat. It did not seem 'upsetting'.

'Darling, there are things I must tell you. I can't tell you here.'

She held out her arms to me and I clung to her again. I buried my

211

face in her neck, ashamed that everyone could see my ugly legs sticking out of my pyjamas. Then she carried me downstairs to the bathroom and sat me on the toilet. Then she carefully wiped my nose and turned on the taps, in the basin, in the bath.

Then she squatted beside me and put her mouth against my ear. I thought she was going to kiss me, but instead she spoke.

'You saw that picture in the paper?'

'Yes.'

She looked at me and blinked. She put her mouth back against my ear and started whispering fast. 'We are about to win this election, and now there are all these stories which are going to hurt your maman.'

She took the crumpled paper out from her purse again and held it up to me.

'They stole that from the house,' she whispered.

Steam swirled around the black ink picture.

'They broke into my house and *stole* it,' she hissed. 'Can you read it? They're saying I hurt Vincent's wife.'

'How?'

'Sssh. Talk into my ear too. They say I took Vincent from her.'

This was nothing more than she had already told me.

'We think they have microphones in here, to listen to us.'

'Who?' I asked, looking up at the dripping yellow walls.

'The water stops them hearing what I say to you.' The steam was causing her make-up to run. 'For Chrissakes, listen to me. Please. They are going to start now in earnest. Some of it is already with the newspapers. They are going to say things about your mother that are not true. You must never believe what they say about me.'

'What . . . will . . . they . . . say?'

'Whatever they think will hurt us the most. That I'm a thief, perhaps, that I tell lies, God knows what else. When we win, we close down their facilities. We send them home to Voorstand. The alliance is over, mo-chou. They thought it could never happen to them – that's why it's all happening so late, but what is happening now is like their play – they've written stories about me, Vincent too.'

'About . . . me . . . too?'

'No, sweets, not about you.'

Her arms were white, hard, stringy, her nose sharp, her skin hot and red with the steam.

'The Voorstanders are very bad,' she said. 'This is what I've always tried to tell you. I know Wally tells you other things, but Wally doesn't know some things, OK?'

'OK,' I said, but I held my mask tight in my lap, in case she tried to snatch it from me.

She wiped my face with Roxanna's towel. 'We are going to go upstairs now and we are going to hear people making plans we do not intend to follow. It's a performance – do you understand?'

'Like . . . a . . . play.'

'Like a play, exactly. We think they listen to us, somehow. We don't know what they can know or how they really do it. Maybe they can hear all this. We don't know if they can hear or not. Tristan, darling, your maman doesn't know how to fight them when they're so unfair.'

All of this had its effect on me, of course, but not nearly as much as the news that she planned to trick her enemies by staying the night at the theatre. I hugged her and kissed her, and told her I would look after her.

She turned off the bath and the basin taps and mopped the condensation off the floor.

I wanted to put my mask on to face the crowd upstairs, but I could not wear it with my mother present. I went upstairs and faced them with a naked face, a rag mouth. Vincent came and brought me a sandwich and a glass of milk. He looked very old behind his beard. His eyes were bloodshot and his suit looked like it had been slept in.

'There . . . was . . . a . . . crazy . . . woman . . . here,' I said.

## 56

Gabe Manzini sat in a car in Gazette Street and watched the old Circus School. He had been awake all the night but his tanned skin was clean and taut. He felt light-footed, clear-headed, alive to the pleasures of the sunshine on his shoulders and the light salt breeze which ruffled the sleeve of his grey and white checked shirt.

The clarity of the Efican light was electric, dream-like. He enjoyed the bright, almost two-dimensional façade of the Feu Follet

213

building, the extreme clarity of its rusting steel-framed windows, even the obvious warp and weft of the twelve tall Blue flags which floated gently in the cloudless sky, the bright, clean reflective surfaces of the red and silver taxi cabs parked in a chain along the street.

There was a way in which all of this was so much in keeping with his mood – clean, cool, ordered – so much in contrast to the murky, panicked mood presently prevailing in Saarlim where Analysis had once again misread the Efican political climate.

It was the historical mission of Analysis – this was what he'd told his own guys at one o'clock this morning – to screw things up and therefore make Operations look good. He said this to motivate them, but he also believed it. Analysis thought Efica was already lost to the Alliance.

Gabe had been grateful to be given this task, nineteen days before polling day, and he enjoyed this feeling now, with just nine days to go, that he could save Efica without a single shot being fired, keep the Red Party in power with the sheer force of his will.

On the seat beside him were the newspapers, not just those from Chemin Rouge but from all over La Perouse, from the other islands, too – Inkerman, Nez Noir, Baker, tiny islands like Shark that no one in Saarlim City ever heard of, all of them carrying the one story, his story, fresh, hand-made – the suicide of the wife of the candidate's lover.

Before this happened, Smith had been ten points up in a vital seat. Now he sat in his car to watch her cop the bad tomatoes. The guys from *Zinebleu* were parked across the way, right in front of the steps. They were gutter hounds, pit-bull terriers. He had released her location to them, exclusive. You could rely on them. Their front-page photograph would make her look sleazy beyond belief.

Of course, Analysis would call this luck. What they never did appreciate was that things only fell together with a great deal of assistance. Operations had not induced the wife's mental state, but only an amateur would call the action lucky. It was the result of detailed knowledge, of discipline, and the ability to act swiftly, cleanly, without hesitation. Natalie Theroux was unstable. She had a gun. The gun now bore her prints. The bullet in her brain was from this gun.

You could not have this sort of 'luck' without happy, well-motivated people on the ground. Gabe had these people, not by accident, but because he personally selected them, trained them, and flew thirteen-hour flights in order to visit them regularly. They were a particular type – active by nature, intelligent, but able to endure weeks of drudge work. They were more than this – they were like this driver who sat beside him now, a Uzi strapped inside his coat, a man who picked a bag of apples from his own tree before he came to work at four a.m.

Now, as he waited for Smith and her campaign manager to emerge from the front door of the building, Gabe bit into one of these small pale yellow Efican apples. The skin had the golden translucency of a yellow plum, the flesh was very white, slightly tart.

'Good?'

'Good.'

'Best damn apples in the world.'

He was not wrong, Gabe thought, washing down the white sweet apple with hot sugarless Efican coffee. This was also good, heavy, characteristically fragrant, slightly furry on the tongue, and he thought how much he always enjoyed what was particular about every country he had ever worked in.

He smiled and contracted his thigh muscles, recalling his three-hour R&R with Roxanna Wonder Wilkinson, her honey-salt taste, her adventurousness in bed, her soft baby tears and her easy need. He had thought about her all through the long night afterwards. She had lain there like a promise.

Indeed, he was thinking of Roxanna, gazing across at the building, listening to the flapping flags, admiring the way the sun seemed to glaze the chipped and flaking white wall of the Feu Follet, when he saw, framed perfectly in a window, a woman so exactly like her that he gasped.

He poked his close-cropped head a little out of the car, and squinted up towards her. The woman was rubbing her scalp and yawning. As she yawned, her eyes closed up, but as the yawn ended, the eyes opened. She saw him looking up at her. And he understood, not so much because of her appearance, which was clouded by the filthy window, but by the frozen guilty moment that came before she ducked her head, that it was Roxanna.

215

He shut his eyes and exhaled.

When he opened his eyes, a man and woman were walking out the front door of the theatre – the woman was in a yellow dress, the man was bearded, all in black; it was Smith & Theroux. The boys from *Zinebleu* came in from the flank. Their flash gun was popping from fifteen feet away, but Gabe could no longer enjoy it. He opened the car door.

'Tell Cantrell advise the CRTV,' he told the driver.

'Who?'

'Cantrell.' He was already heading for the theatre door. 'Hurry. There she goes.'

As he crossed the street, a terrible feeling took control of him. He had been set up by a woman. He could not believe something so humiliating was happening. He prayed, as he entered the rank foyer with its whining little notices pinned to the wall, as he ran three steps a time up the stairs, that he was somehow mistaken about what he had seen, that the woman at the window had just looked like Roxanna because he was thinking of her at that moment. But even while he prayed this he could see, in his mind's eye, the results of the residence check he had run, but barely looked at – Gazette Street. God damn.

On the second floor he discovered a line of deserted offices. He was light on his feet and he moved down the corridor with the careful grace of an athlete, but he felt ill-prepared, clumsy, like someone drunk called into combat. He had been sloppy, complacent, second-rate – everything he despised. His only weapon was the box-cutter which he now transferred to the palm of his hand, still closed. He opened one door after the other – not following procedure, but with a deliberate carelessness – a challenge to fate to prove his fears unfounded.

The rooms whose doors he so casually opened all had that particular potent emptiness he equated with stake-outs, sniper posts. They were like sweaters with their labels torn out – they taunted him with their lack of information.

In the last room he found three mattresses on the floor, a fug of blankets, sheets, socks. The door banged back when he kicked it. Two of the mattresses were empty but on the third he could see a small white wrist showing from beneath a pile of blankets. He wrinkled his nose and passed his broad hand over his clipped hair.

'Roxanna?'

The blankets stirred, and then her tousled blonde head appeared, caped in a tartan blanket.

'Gabey?'

Even now, in extremis, a part of him was touched by her, moved by the white softness of her flesh. She was sleeping naked, and as she kneeled he could see the pronounced curve of her belly, and he could imagine the smell of her warmth, the feel of it against his face.

'You stupid bitch,' he said.

'Gabey . . . '

'What amateur trick is this?'

'No, Gabey,' she said. 'No trick.'

She pulled the blankets around her shoulders like a shawl. She squatted, frowning up at him. He could see her little foot, her ankle, her chipped toenails.

'I'm poor, that's all.'

He went to the window and looked down. Everyone had gone.

'I am respected, all over the world,' he said. 'Peru, Burma, China – they know me in these places. They know I am the best. I write their fucking history books, Roxanna. People stand in my way, Rox, I kill them.'

'I don't understand what you're saying.'

'Read the paper, bitch. Look at the front page of today's paper.'

'Gabey, don't be angry. What's in the zines, honey?'

'You tell your people, Rox – they're dead. They're fucking history.'

'What people, Gabe?'

'So what did you get?' he said. 'Why would you risk it? What the fuck could you get anyway?'

Roxanna stood up and walked to her handbag which was sitting on a milk crate underneath the window. She opened her handbag. His neck bristled when he heard the sound of small objects, clinking. Then he saw what they were: small Ritz shampoo bottles, moisturizers. Oh my God, he thought, the bitch has wired me.

'Put them there.' He pointed to the window ledge.

When she had arranged all the items on the sill, she stepped back. He stepped forward, picked up the shampoo. It seemed heavier than normal to him. He opened the cap, poured the goops of shampoo on to the floor, peered inside, then stopped. He was being an amateur himself.

There was a plastic shopping bag amongst tangled dirty clothes on the floor. He picked it up and swept the little bottles into it.

'We could never let them win the election,' he said. 'Don't you see that? Do you have anything else?'

'You're not a banker,' she said. 'What are you?'

'Very funny. Do you have anything else?'

She stooped and lifted up the corner of her mattress. Turning, she held out a big menu from the Ritz dining room. He dropped it in the plastic bag.

'I would never have picked you,' he said.

'I picked you.' She smiled uncertainly. 'I thought you were the answer to my prayers.' He saw her smile collapse, and the tears begin to run. Resisting the desire to embrace her, he turned and went out the door.


## 57

I could feel suicide all around me, viscous, shameful, wrong. I could see the inside of Natalie's mouth in my mind's eye, the broken tooth. The odour of death lay in the hallways. It got mixed with pie, cinnamon, sugar, pigeons' throats, vents opening, closing, was overlaid with a persistent vision of the dead woman's bony chest – birds' bones, white translucent skin.

Wally would not let it matter. He was a sergeant-major, stamping and stomping in his big suede boots. He brushed my teeth. He made me gargle salt and water. He combed my hair with his comb, digging its sharp tortoiseshell teeth into my scalp. He strapped on my mask and sent me down into the leafy courtyard where old Ducrow got eaten by his lion.

'Do your warm-ups,' he said.

'Are we going to do a show?'

'Just do what I say.'

He was hectoring and impatient with Roxanna too. He bullied her into going out for coloured chalk. I had not seen him treat her this way before. I did not understand it, why she let him, why he wanted to do it. I did not know why she was so upset – she had less connection with Natalie Theroux than any of us.

She had a little lambswool cardigan she had found in Props. It was a size too small. She buttoned it to the neck and folded her arms across her breasts. Her eyes were weepy, her nose red, her shoulders were rounded, but she went out to buy the chalk and came back to the courtyard where Wally, having swept the cobblestones fastidiously, was now running a long orange power-cord to one of the stolen vids he always had around the place.

Roxanna, in giving him the chalk, made a small noise, a sob.

'Don't dwell on it,' was all he said.

As for me? I could not warm-up. I was too disturbed. Whenever I closed my eyes to begin my breathing I saw the crazy woman's face – her throat, her tooth, blood, gore, ooze.

Then Wally turned on the vid.

Roxanna sat heavily on the garden bench. She held out her arms for me. I sat in her lap and pressed my body hard back into her.

The weather forecast was on the vid. Wally began to draw white and yellow chalk marks on cobblestones. The chalk did not always take well, but he was not prepared to wait. Following his blue-lined exercise book, he made a series of loops, arrows, arcs, all with the greatest urgency, but when my mother's face appeared on the screen, he stopped. He tucked his chalk back behind his ears.

'Shush,' he said, but the only voices were crackling from the slightly damaged two-inch speakers. 'This is it.'

What they were saying was – my maman as good as killed Natalie Theroux, and when I saw Felicity's ghosted image on CRTV4 it seemed as if she really had. I watched her mouth, her eyes, the 625 lines across her face, at noon on 20 January, in Chemin Rouge in the year 382.

'*This is political*,' she said.

It did not seem the right thing to say. They wanted to talk about her and Vincent. I pushed further back into Roxanna's breasts. I tightened the buckles on my mask and stared at my mother through the slits. She was scared. She laid her hand briefly against her throat. She tried to smile. It did not seem the right thing to do.

My mother swallowed. She touched her hair. I could feel her shame behind my own eyes, a cold, cold pain like ice.

The camera showed the interviewer with his head on one side, stern, judicial.

My maman was irritated, angry.

*'This was a political assassination.'*

'No,' said Wally, 'she doesn't need to say that. She shouldn't say that.'

Then she started to talk about 'military and security elements in Voorstand'.

'No one wants to hear this,' Wally said. 'She makes herself look bad . . . '

'Shush,' said Roxanna.

'She should not be saying this,' Wally said. 'She looks as if she doesn't care about Natalie.'

'Shut up,' Roxanna said.

*'This was a political assassination,'* my maman said. *'Natalie Theroux did not break the laundry window of her own house in order to kill herself from one foot away . . . '*

'OK,' Wally said. 'That's that.' He turned off the television.

'Gabe did this,' Roxanna said. 'This is what he did.'

'That's history,' Wally told her. 'It happened in the past. Now we've got to deal with the future. Whatever happened between this Voorstand jerk and you, that's one thing. What happened with Vincent's missus, that's another. It's all in the past.'

'What are you so scared of?' Roxanna said. 'What aren't you telling me?'

'You've got to keep it clear in your head,' he said. He was back at work, drawing on the cobblestones with chalk. He moved across the courtyard like a monkey, on his haunches. He had sticks of chalk behind his big lobed ears. He looked only at his exercise book and at the floor, never up at us. He made a dotted line.

Roxanna pushed her eye into my hair and rubbed against my skull. 'Wally, you can't see yourself?'

'I'm drawing lines for toucans . . . '

'You are drawing lines for toucans. What the fuck is that?'

'I can train them,' Wally said. 'You know what I do. You've seen my birds.'

'I am sure that what the mother says is true. I *slept* with this little creep, do you understand? He was the one at the Ritz. Why won't you listen to me?'

When Wally turned he looked as if his face had been slapped.

'Don't you see what's happened to me?' Roxanna said. 'I know

220

him. His name is Gabe Manzini. I was going to marry him. He's the one I picked. He as-good-as told me he did exactly what the maman says.'

'He *as-good-as* told you?'

'He said, *Tell your people that they're dead.*'

'That could mean anything.'

'No, no. It was very clear. He's not a banker. He said, *we could never let them win the election.* Can't you even imagine how I'm feeling?' Roxanna said. 'Can't you see what's happened to me? Can't you imagine how bad I feel, how stupid I've been?'

I looked at Wally. I had known him all my life, known the freckles and hair on his arms, the mole on his neck, the pouches under his grey eyes, but when I looked at him across that spray-wet sawdust I saw, for the first time, what his life had been like, how he had been in prison. He squatted on the floor, cold, cruel, like a dog, face drawn, hatchet-shaped.

'Just shut the fuck up,' he said. 'All you're doing is getting yourself in a panic.'

'All I want is a cuddle, Wally,' Roxanna whimpered. 'Is that so much to ask? Do I deserve to have you tell me shut up?'

Wally laid his chalk down on the cobbles. He put it down so slowly you could feel all his fear in the action. He laid the chalk as if it were precious crystal that might fracture, a bomb that might explode. He came and knelt beside us. He was stiff, contained. He put his hand towards Roxanna's shoulder. She flinched from him. He lifted his hands up, away, flat-palmed.

'Take responsibility for yourself.'

Roxanna held me tighter. 'Why are you so horrible to me?' she said. 'I *am* taking responsibility. I'm saying it's my fault. But what the maman says is true.'

'We have to get on with our lives,' Wally whispered. I twisted my neck to look at him. He was very close to me. I could see the fear swimming in his eyes.

'We make our lives out of what we have, out of what's possible.'

'Out of *toucans*?'

'This is Efica. We've got to be realistic.'

He reached behind his ear for another length of chalk.

'We can make a decent life,' he said. He knelt and began to draw a long yellow arc across the stage. All this was happening in the last twenty-four hours of my mother's life. No one told me it was so. I thought I would have her for ever.

# 58

If Natalie's suicide had damaged Felicity more, she might have lived.

Her support dropped seven points – not quite enough for safety's sake. They came and put a rope around her neck, and pushed her off. She hung and kicked above the sawdust ring, her own damn stage. She pissed, she shit, she bled, she died. Tristan's mother, a young woman in a yellow dress, forty-three years old.

Vincent was in the car outside playing with his gun. Tristan, Wally, Roxanna, were on the floor above her. Friends all around her, seconds from her side.

The maman loved Efica but she was born in Voorstand. The Voorstanders did not hate her personally. They stole her life – Manzini, the VIA, someone. It was not personal. They took her life from Tristan, not personal. They did not think through the consequences. They did not even think that when the boy found his maman, at two a.m., they were presenting him with a horror he would carry all his life, the picture of his mother dead and ugly, hanging from a bright green rope.

Tristan came down the stairs because he heard a noise, thought his mother's master class was about to start. His green rope was missing from the stairs. He came down a step at a time. Slowly. He heard the scuffling. Theatres are always full of scuffling, shouting, cries – it is the business of the theatre: life, death, catharsis.

Until this happens to you, you have no idea how the brain works, how it refuses to deliver the bad news, how it seeks anything but the truth, runs naturally away from it like water running down hill.

Tristan saw his mother hanging dead inside the Feu Follet theatre. Her handbag was on the floor. Her eyes bulging, her jaw slack. His brain lied to him.

*It is a mask.*

Then: *It is an exercise.*

Then: *It is someone else.*

Then: *It's Natalie.*

Only the smell. Forget it. It was a smell. I cannot go to the bathroom without remembering my maman's death.

The night my mother died, other things were happening to the Blue Party – land scandals,* money scandals,† they rose like mushrooms after rain. I did not know Gabe Manzini's face or name, but he was an ace, the best. One scandal one day, a new one the next. He made the Blues appear both incompetent and corrupt.

In the history of Efica my mother's death is an adulterer's death. She is remembered in the morass of shame that Eficans feel about this time.

Me – I never doubted what had happened – not for a second. Even before I saw there was no stool, chair, ladder, I knew. I could not reach her but I cut my mask off my face with a box-cutter. I could not reach her but I smashed Bruder Mouse with a brick. Wally was there then. Vincent was there.

It was Wally, goddamn, dear Wally who got the ladder.

I ground the mask, pulped the wood, paint. My real face was snot, tears, drool. I brought it into the lights of the vid camera and screamed at them.

I did not appear on vid. Edited out. Not part of the story.

---

* *Hélène Rivette, the Shadow Minister of Finance, was alleged to have been a beneficiary of an illegal subdivision in Berthollet. Documents 'proving' this were in all the zines on the day after my mother's death. A week after the election it was shown that these damaging charges had no substance.* [TS]

† *A series of faxes (first published by Zinebleu) which seemed to prove that Jack Mifflin and St John Theroux had received $100,000 each from French aircraft manufacturers. These documents, later shown to be false, did much to discredit the Blues' platform on armed neutrality and, of course, helped further destroy the party's credibility.* [TS]

# BOOK 2

## Travels in Voorstand

Great Voorstand

### Bruder Mouse saves Oncle Duck

Meneer Van Kraligan, as everybody knows, was the name of the Saint before he was a Saint. When he was a sinner he used to follow the old ways, and he would keep a Bruder prisoner, and lock him in the cage.

On this occasion he got old Oncle Duck and he was feeding him corn like nobody's business, feeding him millet pollard mash, brown peas, even the leftover warm milk and miller's bread his own children left on their plates.

Oncle Duck was eating – he could not help himself – but he was weeping. He would eat and weep, eat and weep, and the more he ate the worse he felt for he knew he was going to be murdered by and by.

The Saint was sitting by his fireside thinking of our Oncle's flesh – his head chopped off and so on. He was thinking terrible thoughts with perfect happiness when Bruder Mouse appeared to him in all his furry finery.

One mo nothing, next minute there he was, buttons gleaming, as solid as a yellow oak on a Monday morning. His black ears were sharp. His teeth were white. His eyes as bright as an angel of the lord.

One minute nothing. Next he was as solid as a miller's wheel.

'Hello, Meneer Van Kraligan,' he said to the Saint who was not yet a Saint.

'Hello, Bruder,' said the Saint. 'What you doing here?'

'I'm going to make you let go that Oncle Duck,' the Mouse said.

'Oh, are you now?' says the Saint. 'I do not think so.'

'It is a sin to keep a Bruder prisoner,' said the Mouse.

'What you're talking is a heresy,' the Saint said. 'And I know it is heresy, for it was declared one by the Pope and it was why they exiled that whole monastery to Voorstand in the first place. I don't suppose,' the Saint said, 'the Pope has told you something different?'

'Not the Pope,' said Bruder Mouse. 'But I was sent by the Archangel Gabriel to show you this.'

Then Bruder Mouse rose off the ground. Then he spun himself five times, in acrobatic harmony. Then he bounced up and down on the table on his little head, and as he went up and down, farting as he went, fart, fart, fart, fart – he made the Saint start laughing.

He looped and fell, on his stomach.

The Saint thought this about the funniest thing he ever saw, a little mouse doing Sirkus on his kitchen table.

'You wait there,' he said. 'I'll fetch the Kinder.'

And off he went, laughing and sighing and scratching his big backside.

And when the Saint came back, he saw his duck was gone. There was only the Mouse standing in his place.

One mo there he was, buttons gleaming, cane tapping, as solid as a yellow oak on a Monday morning. His black ears were sharp. His teeth were white. His eyes as bright as an angel of the lord.

One mo there he was, as solid as a miller's wheel.

Next mo he was gone.

Tales of Bruder Mouse, Badberg Edition

Rat Man, Fat Man

Rat man, fat man on his roost,
Grabs the neck of the golden goose,
Rat man, fat man, dust and dogs,
Dirty snakes and licky frogs,
Make a cake and have it iced,
Pray to rats and Jesus Christ.

Efican folk song *circa* 301 EC (Source:
*Doggerel und Jetsam: unheard voices in the
Voorstand Imperium*, Inchsmith Press,
London)

# 1

I am not one of those Ootlanders who wish to blame you personally for everything your government has ever done, so let me say it clear: I know you are not responsible for my mother's death. Indeed, I write this assuming your individual innocence, believing you unaware of Gabe Manzini or any of his criminal activities.

If I will believe that of you, then please believe the following of me: that when, a whole *twelve years* after Voorstand agents murdered my maman, I made the dangerous voyage to your fatherland, it was *not* – as Mrs Kram would still have you believe – to do your nation harm.

It is true that I entered Voorstand illegally, but the illegality was created by your government's refusal to place the appropriate stempel in my passport, a situation produced in turn by my own actions – certain offensive tracts I had written, and published, many, many years before, in the period following my mother's murder.

I understand that no one wishes to have their country called a 'poison gland' or a 'vile octopus'* but imagine, please: my world was shattered.

Everything that had allowed me to sustain my problematic existence, the illusion of my talent, my safety, my power, all this died with my mother. One day I was Napoleon. Next day I was a coward.

I was afraid that I also would be murdered. I was afraid of the street, afraid of uncurtained windows, unlocked doors, noises in

---

* 'If we let ourselves imagine this is solely a question of military defence, we are deluding ourselves. Our greatest defence is our culture, and the brutal truth is – we have none. The terms of our alliance with Voorstand means we are prohibited (for instance) from placing a 2 per cent tariff on their Sirkus tickets to subsidize our theatre. They call this unfair trade, yet we know that every ticket we buy to the Sirkus weakens us, swamps us further, suffocates us. If we wish to escape the vile octopus, our escape must be total. For some time we will need to be poor, defenceless and, yes, bored.' From 'What will we do?' by Tristan Smith.

231

the night. And yet I would not be a *total* coward. Through my teenage years I continued to write the political pamphlets and letters you still cannot forgive. I believed you were watching and listening, and I was not wrong. I kept the doors locked and my fear simmered and bubbled and I skulked and fretted like a cockroach inside the mouldy Feu Follet, and when no one came to kill me it did not matter because by then I was afraid of the air on my skin, of the sky itself.

Is it grandiose to say I too feared assassination? Then let it be: I was grandiose.

I still rehearsed my circus swings and tumbles, juggling, a whole illusionistic repertoire, but I did it with a shame that came from knowing that I lacked the courage to be the Great Figure I had previously imagined. I ate too much. I slept. My pale white stomach began to bulge while my legs remained as thin and twisted as they had ever been.

It was Wally who stole the Axis 9iL computers from the University of Chemin Rouge. His motive was simple entertainment. He imagined I would play *Cat & Mouse*, *Chessmaster* and *Battlefield*, and I did play these games, and others, but my lethargy did not finally disappear until I discovered that I could use Axis 9iL to make money. Then my life changed overnight.

While boys and girls of my age were kissing each other, twining their legs around each other in the back seats of their parents' cars, I was sitting white-eyed at my terminal, plugged into Financial Data Services like 'Voorstand-on-line' and 'Uptrend'. I was a teenage share-trader.

I never did get any higher than level 5 on *Cat & Mouse* but the Bourse was another matter. I persuaded Vincent (the executor of my maman's estate) to release a portion of my inheritance to establish an account. I had a shaky start, but two years later I was producing returns of between 5 and 10 per cent per month. This was from 386 to 393, years of the great Bull Market, and I was one of those so called pin-ball sorciers* who brought the market crashing down – a Momentum Investor. I played the game a kid can play so

* Literally, Pin-ball Wizard, a derogatory term for the traders who were held responsible for the computer-driven selling frenzy which produced the crash of 7 May 393.

well – pure mathematics, trends, swings, surges in stock. Did I make money from toxic waste? Perhaps. Did I buy and sell in Sirkus stock? Who knows? I was interested only in the momentum of the equities.

At first I used my profits to make the Feu Follet safer. I engaged a security guard. I put bars on the windows, installed an electronic security system. But then I began to seek safety in money itself. You might say that Mammon became my maman. I do not need to point out what a betrayal this entailed.

Of course it was not just Tristan Smith who was scarred by the events of 20 January. All these years later Efican politicians have not forgotten what happens to those who oppose our great and powerful ally. Even the Blue Party has become, to say the least, pragmatic. Thread all the navigation cable you wish inside our caves. Leave your poison water wherever it suits you. Our government will give you no trouble.

Following my maman's death, I sought wealth in a way that would have upset her dreadfully, but life is never simple and I remained loyal to some of her ideals while I betrayed others. So even while I rode the powerful surges of the Bull Market I was active in the January 20 Group* and I wrote my pamphlets and letters to the editor.

And this, I can only assume, is why, two days after my twenty-second birthday, you refused me a tourist stempel. This is why you still suspect that a great political *cause* had me drag my blinking share-trader's face out into the bright sun. You still want to know why, *why really*, did I abandon my safe house and trundle down the No. 25 wharf in my wheelchair. What is the real story? Why did I allow myself to be thrown from a heaving fishing trawler on to a Morean Beach at dawn?

I, of course, would rather tell you how Wally, Jacques and I crossed what you like to call '*the great historical sea*' and how we entered your Voorstand by tunnel, in the company of thieves, how we met Leona the facilitator, how we saw the altars to the Hairy

---

* *Radical nationalist group named in commemoration of Felicity Smith's death. In 387 two of the group's members were charged with possession of firearms and sentenced to jail for five years, in one case, and seven years, the other. From that time on the group was thought to be toothless.*

Man beside the highway, how we crossed the great plains of Voorstand, across the mighty earthworks, dams, lakes, and saw the huge Sirkus Domes rising from the earth, everywhere, like mushrooms after rain.

We had some high old times before the thing came unstuck in Peggy Kram's trothaus, higher than Drs Laroche and Eisner ever thought when I was born. Love, joy, adventure – all these things are there ahead of me, and you too, but I know, I am avoiding your question.

You want to know why I left the place where I was safe. Why I felt it necessary to smuggle Wally Paccione into Voorstand in the first place.

To tell you this I must – I am sorry – walk you back into the dark closed world of the Feu Follet at a time when it smells not only of death but also of rotting sawdust, of stale orange peel, of spilled wine, of old ham sandwiches. I will seat you in a starbuck. I will do the show – act out for you the parts of WALLY, ROXANNA, TRISTAN too.

*The year is 382. It is March, and the wet season has just finished. Felicity has been dead for nearly two months.*

*The lights come up to reveal ROXANNA and WALLY dancing. TRISTAN watches them from his chair.*

## 2

It is eleven o'clock in the morning and the streets of Chemin Rouge are white and blinding, sticky with the smell of honeysuckle. The bougainvillaea is puce and purple on the sagging veranda roofs, and the papaya are once again orange enough to tempt the crows to strike their beaks deep into their seed-jewelled bellies.

Inside the dusty, darkened Feu Follet, ROXANNA dances with WALLY. She wears a red dress which is tied around the neck and which shows the small black mole in the middle of her soft white back. She wears small gold heart-shaped earrings with little red stones in their centre. She has black high-heeled shoes with a complicated series of straps which secure them to her sturdy unstockinged ankles. She rests her crisp, permed hair against her partner's white cotton shirt. They are now a couple. They have walked though a fire and each has been imprinted by the other just as you see the warp and weft of dress fabric scorched into the skin of people in intensive care.

They dance while I, YOUNG TRISTAN, watch them. It is so long ago. I am another person, sitting in my club chair with my skinny arms held tight around my chest. My white gold-flecked irises never leave them as they dance. It is a foxtrot, no music, sawdust on the floor.

Inside the ring is the crumpled pink tissue Roxanna has used to wipe my spittle from her face.

Beyond the tissue, half lost in the folds of the black velvet curtain which separates the theatre from the foyer, is the reason I have spat at her – the picnic carton. In the carton is bright orange cheese, a loaf of fresh white walloper, apples, jelly beans, croix cakes, a bottle of very cold beer wrapped in sheets of newspaper, glasses. She has a folded blanket. She has altered my dead maman's red sundress and imagines no one recognizes it. Wally has his nose against the skin behind her ear. She can feel him inhaling her, like he does when making love, breathing in the air out of her pores.

I say nothing. I have stared at the dress when she walked in, but I say nothing. I sit in the middle of the ring on the club chair they have placed there for me. I hold a banned book in my lap. It is called *Without Consent – Voorstand's Secret Agencies in Action*.

Since my maman's murder I will not sleep in a room with a window. That is one problem.

Roxanna is going crazy, that is another. Also: she has promised God that she will do whatever is needed to diminish my pain. She is giving herself to my restoration.

I have barely left the theatre since my maman died. If that is what I want, that is fine with Roxanna. After all – she is my nurse. In real life, however, the building presses on her, sits on her. It is like having a fat spanker pressing on your face. She has asked God to please give her air, but what can He do?

She is twenty-five years old, had thought herself past saving, but on that night of the murder she felt herself turn into something shining. She took me, the other me – YOUNG TRISTAN – the whimpering child – she took me into her bed, rocked me in her arms, bathed me, towelled me, sang to me, oiled my dry, scaly skin, made up my terrible face with blue and gold and silver. She was a nurse, a nun, someone finally to look up to.

Then the dry hot weather arrived, two weeks early. You could feel the warm, salty northerly on your skin and you could stand on the steps of the Feu Follet and see, across the tops of the high weeds in the vacant block across the street, the skipjack boats heading out of the port three miles away.

She prayed for my health, she packed me a picnic, with jelly beans and croix cakes. I agreed to go. I thought I could go. Then I stood on the steps and my breath stopped breathing. I thought I would faint. I could not go. When she tried to pick me up against my will, I spat right in her face.

I would live only where my mother had died. Within fifteen feet of the place. Will you laugh in my face if I tell you I felt safest there? In the deepest, darkest hole on earth.

I sat with my book, always the same book. I did not understand it, but I would not permit anyone to explain a word to me. I was eleven years old, ferocious, like an animal.

ROXANNA looks over WALLY's sweet white cotton shoulder and there I am – her salvation, her nemesis, locked into my chair, my eyes blazing, my nose running, my loose maw dribbling thick saliva.

She has ironed Wally's white cotton shirt. When they dance, she can smell that sexy mixture of man and cotton.

She whispers, her mouth close against Wally's ear. Wally nods his nose against her neck.

'I'm not staying here,' she calls to TRISTAN SMITH. 'I'm going out.'

'Someone . . . has . . . to . . . be . . . with . . . me.'

'Come on, Rikiki,' Wally says. He breaks away from Roxanna, kneels at my feet. 'Come on, fellah, you're going to feel much better.'

'It's . . . my . . . theatre.'

'Of course it's your theatre,' he says. 'We're going to swim, in the ocean.'

'You . . . have . . . to . . . stay . . . here.'

'Wally does not *have* to do shit,' Roxanna says.

'He . . . has . . . to . . . stay.'

Roxanna looks at me and sees Phantome Drool – wide mouth dribbling. 'Wally's entitled to have his life just like you.'

'If . . . my . . . mother . . . was . . . alive . . . you . . . wouldn't . . . talk . . . to . . . me . . . like . . . that.'

Rox takes a breath before she answers. 'Come *on*, Tristan.'

She turns and walks towards the foyer.

'Where . . . are . . . you . . . going?' This is not ROBERT BRUCE talking, not NAPOLEON. This is a crow, a gull, something on a city dump. My voice is high and scratchy with anxiety. I make 'going' sound like 'gung'.

She says, 'I'm taking the food out to the truck now.'

She descends the front steps with the picnic box. She sees two chopped and channelled custom cars drive along Gazette Street, taking the short cut on to the Boulevard des Indiennes. Two boys in the front, two girls in the back. You can see beach towels on their rear window ledges, and they double-declutch as they come past the taxi base, and Roxanna, as she crosses the tar-sticky street towards the truck, skips, once, across the broken white lines. It is, like, normal life occurring.

She unlocks the truck, places the cardboard box behind the bench seat, opens the driver's side door, and sits behind the glove box, looking through the tapes for 'Beach Music'.

She hears me coming before she sees me – arms flailing, spitting, howling, shrieking like a cat. Roxanna jumps down from the truck and opens the door. Wally releases YOUNG TRISTAN into the cabin and I scramble, fight, claw like a native cat, clambering over the bench seat and into the darkness of the back.

My captors climb into the truck, turn up the music, loud.

I find picnic things and throw them: cheese, bread, apples.

They are not even into the Boulevard des Indiennes when the beer bottle smashes. Roxanna sees me – on my back, my arms and legs up in the air, rolling on the broken glass like a dog in the dust. Even as the glass cuts my skin, I keep my eyes on hers.

War.


# 3

When they got me back from hospital, Rox was very nice to me. She spread the picnic rug on the stage, right at my feet. She put soft pillows on my chair so I could lean back without making my cuts hurt. She unwrapped each of the small pink-iced croix cakes and cut them and spread them with blackberry confit.

Whatever she did to Wally's porpoise in the bed that night, it was more than she had ever done before. When he saw the angels, he made high, hard noises in the back of his throat. He went on and on. In the morning he whistled and drove all the way down to the port to buy some fresh bream for our breakfast.

The minute the truck's engine started, Roxanna got out of her bed and came into my room, pulling Wally's blue-checked dressing gown around her. She was still very nice to me, but her eyes were bloodshot and there was a hardness in her face I had not known before.

She took *Without Consent* from my hands and slid it under my pillow in a way that did not brook interference. 'It's a beautiful day out there, Rikiki.'

She cocked her head, as if waiting for an answer.

'Not a beautiful day,' she said. 'Obviously.'

She kneeled at my feet and opened her handbag. At first I thought she was looking for a Caporal, but when she turned back to me she was holding something in her closed cupped hands. Then she smiled. For a moment it was the old Rox. She blew across her intertwined fingers, like Wally in his magic trick. I could smell the sour wine on her breath. Everything about her was so familiar, so much a part of me, that even this smell, which had initially been so alien, now signalled comfort and security – breakfast, warm sheets, buttery toast eaten in her arms.

'Mo-chou,' she said. 'Did you hear me, Chocolat? You want to see my present?'

'OK,' I said. I sat up in my bed.

She opened her white hands – a small squish-mak frog, bright green with long yellow stripes, sat on her palm.

'Was . . . it . . . in . . . your . . . purse . . . all . . . night?'

'Look,' she said.

'I . . . know . . . a . . . squish . . . mak.'

'The world is beautiful.'

'I . . . *know.*'

'It's so easy to forget.'

'You . . . don't . . . understand . . . *anything.*'

Her eyes narrowed. 'You be careful, mo-camarad.' She held the frog up to my eyes. 'Look,' she said. She smiled again. The squish-mak was wet and shining, a kind of lime green. It had big wide eyes and long thin fingers. 'God made it, just like He made you.'

I did not answer.

238

'Well?'

I could see how tired she was, her skin, her red and yellow eyes. She had a red wine crust around her lips.

'Do you know what I'm saying to you?'

I did not know what I was meant to say. I shrugged.

'Do you want to ruin my life?' she said suddenly. 'Do you?'

'No,' I said, and it was true. I loved her, her lipstick-sour-wine smell, her frowning forehead, the fine blonde down which only showed when the sunlight fell on her neck, along her chin line, her chipped and bitten cuticles when she removed her red stick-on nails, the way she bent her small thin fingers back to explain a point, the bruises on her knees which she rubbed at with her fingers now, as if she might erase them.

'My life has been lousy up to now,' she said. 'Do you realize – I'm nearly twenty-six years old?'

'Your . . . life?'

'For Christ's sake,' she said. 'Your life is fine. Nothing is going to hurt you now. It's been two months, Tristan. Nothing has happened to you. Nothing will. You're not political. No one thinks that you're a threat to anything. If you're a threat to anyone, it's me. Do you realize what happened at the hospital?'

'Six . . . stitches.'

'They thought me and Wally cut you up. That fellow with the specs near-as-damn-it called the Gardiacivil. I'm the one who should be scared, not you.'

'I'm . . . sorry.'

'I already burnt a house down,' she said. 'It isn't smart to make me tense. Please say you'll let us go and live somewhere else. We could be happy, all of us.'

She opened her handbag and slid the frog back in. She snapped it shut, and caught the creature's foot between two golden metal clips. She did not seem to notice what she had done.

'You cannot do this to me,' Roxanna said to me. 'You can't.'

'Look . . .' I pointed to the frog.

Roxanna followed my finger to her handbag but did not seem to notice anything. 'I love that man, you understand? I know I didn't used to, but I do.' She looked up at me. 'He's a good man, and he understands me.'

'I'm . . . sorry.'

'I'm not going to lose him, Tristan. So I'm telling you, I'll be nice as pie to you while he's around, but either you suggest we go and live some place with light and air or . . .'

'Or . . . what?'

'Or I'll go away and I'll take him with me.'

'I'm . . . just . . . a . . . kid.'

'Listen, Mr Machin,* I'm a woman. He's a man. I can make him do whatever I damn well want.'

'You . . . can't.'

'I don't want to do this,' Rox said. She slung her handbag over her shoulder. The frog's fingers were not moving. 'I want us all to be together, Rikiki, but you've got to understand – if you want to fight me, I'll beat you.'

'I'll . . . tell . . . Wally.'

'You don't know who I am.' She ruffled my hair, just like she did when she was nice. 'I'll kill you if I have to.'


## 4

I never doubted Wally loved me, but I was up against blusher, eye-shadow, mascara, black lacy panties with a red slit in the crotch, suspender belts, little silver balls connected by a nylon thread. When I heard him whimper in their bed I believed she could make him do anything, including abandon me.

For me he would make french toast, but for her he would rise at five-thirty in the morning and go down to the port for those little fish she used to like deep fried on buttered toast. He bought full cream for her coffee. He began to steal again. He did not need to. It was his excitement. It was the feeling of youth Roxanna gave him. He came back to the theatre with his forearms bleeding and unplucked poultry in a hessian bag – ducks, geese, turkey.

He was conjuring for her, making a rich person's life from nothing. He made sauces with blood and raging blue brandy fire. He was like a crazy bird building a bower and stacking it with pearls and silver paper. New knives appeared, choppers, scalpel-sharp instruments with fat black handles. He produced them like a musico and dissected whole ducks in seconds, piled them on silver

---

* *Literally, Mr Thing.*

platters which still bore the imprint of the Excelsior Hotel.

He began to look different. He had his hair cut short and bristly, so his nose and chin seemed to grow bigger in his face. He 'located' more white shirts and came running into the theatre in his clean white sand-shoes bearing baked banana bread, his paternal vision fogged up by the steam of sex. He touched me and kissed me, but he really did not see me at that time.

When we were all together, Roxanna smiled and petted me exactly as before, but when he was away, she made it clear to me that she was going to move Wally out of the Feu Follet.

'Within a week,' she said. She held up a finger with a chipped and bitten red nail. 'Seven days.'

Even I could see she was not well. Twice she tried to light fires in the night – I did not witness this, but saw Wally dealing with the debris in the morning. She did not want peacocks any more, but she wanted apple trees and a vegetable garden. This was what she dwelled on – the impossibility of happiness inside the old Circus School. She showed me her skin. She had a rash along her back she claimed was made by being there.

I was not so well myself. Now I was not prepared to move from my club chair inside the circus ring. I shat there, peed there, was washed while still within its overstuffed arms. I did not know what your agents looked like then. I imagined them in shadows, their features masked by wide-brimmed hats. I forced the new lovers to sleep beside me.

Rox was not continually unkind, even when we were alone together. She would arrive with little egg creams she made herself, but then – while I devoured them – she would walk around the wooden ring guard, circling me, talking to herself about me, or praying to God to put me in a home. She said things in Latin I did not understand. At other times she disappeared. I would hope she had gone, but then I would learn that she had been on the front steps, getting 'clean air'.

I slept, I woke. I peed in the plastic bucket. Time began the grey, almost featureless continuum that was to be so much a characteristic of my future life. But always, at three o'clock in the afternoon, while Wally was preparing his evening 'surprise' in the kitchen, Roxanna would bring me a perroquet and then sit in Row B with a glass of ice-water and a zine.

241

At these times I tried to reach out and touch her heart. I had no idea how sick she was. I was a child, tried to arouse her sense of pity by making myself seem ill. I complained of aches and pains. I wept, hunched my shoulders, folded my arms across my chest. Sometimes she drew me to her breast and told me that she loved me.

And then a new stage arrived and it seemed that my organism had responded to my will. I became truly sweaty, really feverish. Roxanna held me and begged me to change my mind. Even when I began to vomit I imagined it was something I had willed myself.

Wally gave me dry toast and made me chicken soup, but nothing stopped me getting sicker and Roxanna crazier.

On the fifth or sixth afternoon, she stood herself up straight in front of the front row of seats, held her plump arms by her side, made her hands into fists, and began to scream at me. She told me she had been convicted of stabbing a man in the spanker. She said I was unwise to mess with her. She said she had Wally's tringler in her pocket. But as she said these things she got redder and redder in the face and she began to gulp and burp. She collapsed into a starbuck and put her head between her legs.

'Please,' she said when she regained her composure. 'Please don't make me do this.'

She began to frown. Then I saw that she was crying. The tears were very large. They made large round marks on the dusty duck-boards.

'Why do you want to destroy my life?' she said to me. Her face was crushed by howling. Her eyes were running black. 'You're the one who's going to lose,' she said. 'Can't you feel what's happening?'

By then I was desperately ill, racked by stomach cramps and diarrhoea. It was the first time I thought that I could beat her, but it was also as close as I came to witnessing my victory, for it was during this fracas that Wally, finally, realized how sick the little actor had become.

I never knew what happened until later, but when I was discharged from the Mater, Roxanna was gone from our life.

There is a mystery here, Madame, Meneer, which will all be settled in good time. But when I came back to the Feu Follet, nothing seemed mysterious.

Peace prevailed, long sweet unchallenged periods of silence, long dust-filled rays of light, the odour of sweet musty sawdust in the air. So happy was I with this resolution that it took some days to realize that Wally was now in pain himself. He had loved Roxanna. He had thought they were two sides of the same coin.

As the days passed this pain did not diminish. Sometimes he stole a little to cheer himself. Sometimes he cooked new and complicated recipes from gourmet magazines. Often he just sat at the kitchen table and watched the white train of his foaming bride as it spilled down the side of his glass.

As one week became a month and the month a year, his injury set hard. We were like two planets caught in mutual fields of gravity, each unable to break free. In this way my youth passed and he moved into old age.

And then, just when you would think that that was that – when we were, the two of us, like a pair of crippled eccentrics whose wasted lives would make you shudder, whose existence you might learn of only when one died and the other starved to death, I suggested that we take this trip to Voorstand together.

It was an unlikely thing for me to say, given that I would not go as far as the Levantine shop across the street, but when I saw how Wally responded, what life it gave him, I dimly realized that this might be our life-line and I began to inch my way timidly forwards, not towards the trip exactly, but into a more intimate proximity to its glow.

First we clipped the coupons in the advertisements in the zines, then we waited for the colour brochures. For a long time it was what we lived for – all those beautiful pictures of Voorstand in the mail. We were going on a Sirkus Tour of Saarlim.

All this was enough for me: the fantasy – but Wally was not going to let me get away with that. He set a date. He hired a new nurse. He bought the wheelchair. I watched him come alive, glowing in the reflected light of travel brochures.

I moved into a room with a window. I prepared.

## 5

My nurse on this journey was named Jacques Lorraine, and this individual, who turned out to be the most curious young man I ever met, had more to do with the course of events than any of us understood.

Jacques had distinguished himself, from the first interview, by insisting that he would do whatever it was we needed him to. This was an immediate relief to us. His two predecessors had had such strict descriptions of what the title *nurse* might mean: Phonella would not do the dishes or mop the floors; Jean-Claude would not make the beds. He would cook, but if there was no food in the house he would not go and buy it. Phonella was a Ph.D in Archaeology. Jean-Claude was a flautist, and was saving up to travel to the Old World.

In contrast to both of them, Jacques seemed to have no other ambition but to serve, not just me, but Wally too. He was a nurse. It was all he wanted to do. He was self-effacing, like a good waiter is self-effacing, but not meek, or subservient. Whatever misunderstandings we had about his true nature, we always knew, even while he cooked and washed and scrubbed and dealt with the intimate secrets of my body, that this was an attractive person with considerable reserves of self-esteem. He had an 'edge', and although we did not know just how much edge he had, we never called him pissmarie or prick-buttock, not even behind his back.

He replaced broken zippers, darned socks, even typed my essays and manifestos for the January 20 Group. When it was necessary that he learn to drive a five-ton truck – our only vehicle – he did it. It was in this truck that he delivered me, as curtained from the public gaze as a lady in a mobile-amor, to the Group's meetings. In this and other ways he made himself some sort of ideal figure in our lives.

He was below middle height, but handsome, with honey-coloured skin, large brown eyes and lashes that Roxanna would have died for. He was lightly built, but athletic. He squeaked around the dark rooms of the old Gazette Street building in fastidiously clean white running shoes.

Then he was merely our employee, but now let me make it clear – this next part of the story belongs to him as much as to me or to Wally, and not just to him, but to the extraordinary family that he came from – the father with his ludicrous passion for tropical snow, the mother with her martinis resting incredibly on the peeling front veranda of that lower-middle-class street.

However, on the spring morning we boarded the trawler *John Kay* in Chemin Rouge harbour, it did not occur to me that I might grant our recently employed nurse this importance in my own private history. I was so tense and frightened about everything ahead, and I felt – not incorrectly – that Jacques was secretly intolerant of my fear.

When he trundled my new wheelchair down past the skipjack boats on the No. 25 wharf, I was half dead with shame and self-consciousness. As we passed men filling their water tanks or loading gas cylinders, I pulled my panama hat low over my eyes. Though covered by clothes, by hat, I felt like a snail – de-shelled, slimy and naked in the vast and merciless light of day. We were setting out on a journey of 3000 miles and I was nervous, not just of 'logical' fears, like your agents, or storms at sea, but of the light, the air, the naked eyes of my fellow humans.

And although you, Madam, Meneer, now know me at a time when I have strode across the world and even been, for a moment, famous, in September of 394 I was still a prisoner of Phobos – I stood on the deck of the *John Kay* and felt like fainting.

Jacques, in this situation, was a master, managing to accommodate himself not only to my phobia but also my pride. He helped me on to the trawler, introduced me to the skipper.

I now know he had talked to this fisherman beforehand, had shown him photographs which had appeared in medical histories when I was born. But I did not know it then. So imagine my gratitude when the Captain showed no shock, looked at me as if I were human, held my eye, nodded. He may not have understood *every* word I said, but he knew I was the shapoh – i.e. it was me, not Wally, who was going to pay his bill. He shook my hand politely.

Not once in our five-day journey did this man ever treat me with less than respect. All this was due to Jacques. Also: as a result of his expert care, I arrived in the little republic of Morea a great deal calmer than I had been in years. Whilst continually subject to fits of irrational panic, I was now able to calm myself with Dr Fensterheim's breathing. I was well fed, freshly shaved, a little sun-tanned, with no more discomfort than that created by the 50,000 Voorstandish Guilders I had bound to my chest with adhesive tape.

We have fully automated credit systems in Efica. We use them daily, just like you do in Saarlim. When I entered Voorstand like this, without a cash parole or any type of credit card, with only cash strapped to my chest, it was not because I was naïve or ill-informed, or rather – not in the way you might imagine.

Wally and I had, at that stage, a high opinion of your efficiency, your expertise. We imagined Voorstand to be a web of co-ax, optic fibre, little chips with brains the size of elephants. We travelled with cash because we were illegal and wished to keep our names out of the computers, and that is why I was lowered on to the dinghy in Morea with 50,000 Guilders strapped to my body with surgical tape. A saboteur, of course, would have known that this was stupid.

The morning we arrived at the Morean tourist resort of Club Hedoniste, the air smelled like overripe papaya. I was down to one layer of white cotton but Jacques was still wearing his three shirts and long black jacket. He placed the panama hat on my head and set it at an angle.

The dinghy was already heading back through the surf to the *John Kay*. I was on the beach – small, exposed, but I was *there*, under that velvety sky, and I was dizzy, a little, but not panicked.

It was seven in the morning, and the guests, if there were any guests, were not awake to see me. They missed an interesting procession.

First came Wally. He had always been a little hunched, but like a ping-pong player is hunched, like a man listening to a story is hunched. Now he was like those old men you see in Efican fishing villages, bent over with the weight of long-dead tuna and skipjack. He was seventy-three years old, a pensioner. Most of his hair was gone, the rest he had shaved off, and he had covered his craggy nose and freckled scalp with glistening sun-tan lotion. He wore a camera case around his neck but, with his heavy eyebrows and gimlet eyes, he must have looked – to anyone who did not know his sentimental heart – like some cruel old bird, some kind of vulture in crisp white T-shirt and white canvas frippes. He led us up the cracked concrete paths, beside the empty swimming pool where exotic red fish dropped flaking scales of red paint on to a bilious puddle of old storm water.

I was also dressed in white – long white shirt, long cotton trousers, Italian canvas shoes, my white wide-brimmed hat. I came behind him in my wheelchair, my face in shadow.

Behind me was Jacques, his hands on my wheelchair, a big pack on his shoulders. He had dressed for tropical Zeelung exactly as he had for Chemin Rouge – the white tennis shoes, the three layers of spotted shirts, the wide-shouldered suit jacket, the black hair slicked back on his head, the two silver rings in his left ear.

You would think our distinctive group would make a strong impression in Morea, but the taxi man, who waited for us in the steaming gravel car park, did not seem to notice anything unusual. He was listening to a loud speech on the car radio and as the speech became more passionate he drove faster. The country was poor, hardly lived-in. There was some white sand, tussocks, a few fishing boats with inverted triangular sails. Then we were at the Zeelung border post.

The customs office was like a portable latrine on a parking lot but the soldiers, contrary to their reputation, were stone cold sober, wore pressed fatigues and were erect in their postures. The Captain – spit-bright, gold braid – was everything I had feared when I set out.

He looked at me with horror and disgust. He shouted. He crossed himself. He spoke volubly and abusively to Jacques in Old Dutch, but although I felt that sea swell of dread, I did not die, or even faint. I felt dizzy, yes, but finally he stamped my passport and we went, in *triumph*, Madam, Meneer, in total triumph.

Ahead of us was a bus station and a clay road with potholes and dark-eyed teenage girls roasting corn and selling small glass cups of tea.

We were in Zeelung. I was entering my second country in two hours. I had become an adventurer.


# 6


In Zeelung, we ran the gauntlet of the border hustlers, predators, buskers, owners of religious artefacts and flea-bitten hotels, all of whom, it seemed, were scoping us, trying to figure out a way to get at our wallets. They called to us in English and the local Dutch-Indian creole, but did not actually press in. They leaned and lounged against the chipped pale blue wall of the bus-shelter.

Then, right in front of them, Wally's new plimsolls came unlaced. 'Stop,' I said.

'No,' he said.

'You want to break your hip?'

He stopped.

The efficient Jacques was immediately by his side, taking his little pack, kneeling, intending to tie the lace himself. But Wally, typically, did not wish this sort of help in public, and he shooed the nurse away as if his offer was completely unexpected.

Phonella would have been offended by this dismissal, Jean-Claude would have fought to tie the lace, but Jacques gracefully retreated, reshouldering his own pack.

So we all watched – Jacques, me, the Zeelung predators – while the bony-headed old man stooped down, like a big old shell-backed turtle, to slowly tie up his shoelace.

On the periphery of my shaded vision I became aware of one of the Zeelungers, a white-shirted, dark-eyed Presence, leaning his bony shoulder blades against the bus-shelter wall.

I *felt* this man before I properly saw him. I felt a prickling on my neck, and even before I studied him I was twisting away from him in my chair, so I could discreetly slide my precious Efican passport down into the secret linen pouch inside my frippes.

No sooner had I got the passport hidden than Wally finished with his shoelace.

'OK,' he said, slowly straightening. 'Illico presto. Let's go.'

He began to walk, but my wheelchair did not follow him. I twisted my neck and found Jacques gone.

Then I saw him: in the bus-shelter. Surrounded by Zeelungers.

As I watched I saw him accept a cigarette from the Presence and permit the dangerous-looking man to light it for him. These local violinistes were short. Jacques was even shorter, but, in the midst of all those creased and weathered faces, he shone like something loved and valuable.

The Presence had dark, deep-set brown eyes and scimitar-shaped sideburns, and as I watched he held out a gun – black-nosed, white-handled – towards our young employee. The hair on my neck stood on end.

Wally called harshly, but Jacques did not even turn. The Presence was like a stage magician, a demonstrator in a department store on the Rue Tienture. As I watched I saw that this was possibly a deeply dangerous situation, but I also realized – and this made my skin tingle – that Jacques was not at all afraid.

As the man shucked cartridges from his revolver, I felt I had entered a dream.

'Jacques!' Wally clapped his big freckled hands together.

Jacques turned, and nodded. To the Presence, he said, 'Derthunken, un moment.'

He walked back to us, insouciantly pigeon-toed, across the gravel. I was so relieved to have him safe again, so easily.

'He's doing the prelude to Van Cleef's bit from *The Heroes' Sirkus*,' he said. 'He could never have seen it live, but he can do the bit. It's the show when Henk Van Cleef died.'

'You are working,' Wally said. 'You are not on holiday.'

'Any . . . way,' I said. 'This . . . looks . . . iffy.'

'Iffy?' Jacques smiled at me. I would not call it a pitying smile. I could not call it condescending, but he showed me the line of regular teeth in his handsome face. This was not someone who would stay locked in a dark theatre eleven years. I did not like him then. I was shocked to imagine he might not like me.

'It's like a *quote* this man is making,' he said to me, 'from something he never saw.'

And, damn it, if he didn't turn and walk back to them.

'OK,' called Wally. He sounded like an Inkerman sheep farmer calling up his dog. 'That's enough.'

'Good to meet you, Aziz,' I heard Jacques say to the Presence. 'Cut veer enloadei.'

Wally clasped his big hands across his slippery scalp and groaned.

'One more minute,' Jacques called to Wally, but even as he spoke he was slipping his slender finger into the trigger guard of Aziz's gun. He placed his feet apart. He held his left-hand index finger in the air. Then, with his right, he spun the weapon, and flicked it high into the air.

The slippered pimps and bare-footed thieves lined up along the bus-shelter wall must have been as stunned as I was, but when Jacques caught the spinning weapon by its stubby barrel they all burst into applause. It was clear to me then – not to Wally – that nothing bad would happen to him. The Zeelungers produced more guns and began to do the same sorts of Sirkus tricks themselves.

Jacques looked back at me and *blushed*.

Wally came behind my chair and began to push me away across the featureless grassless earth. After fifty yards or so, Jacques caught up with us, his cheeks red, his headphones slipping from his head.

'Sorry,' he said as he took the chair from Wally and repositioned his headphones.

'Listen, Jules,' Wally said in that dead quiet voice that had its roots in the violin, 'you play that trick again, I'll hurt you.'

In the silence that followed it occurred to me that Wally was perhaps too old to be making threats like this.

'You understand me?'

'I understand,' Jacques said at last.

'Now' – Wally jerked his head back to where the boys from the wall had gathered in a loose semi-circle some twenty yards back – 'unless you want those violinistes to cut your throat, you better push the chair.'

We were in a kind of clay-pan bus station with no buses and three roads leading out of it. We walked along the widest of them, between a grove of banana trees rich in the odours of human excrement. It was very hot by now, and spittering with rain. The man with the white-handled revolver, alone now, began to follow us.

'He'll cut your fucking liver out,' Wally said to Jacques.

'I'm sorry to have distressed you,' Jacques said.

Wally grunted.

We travelled on a little way, bumping over the rutted road.

'You just don't go talking to strangers,' Wally said, 'because you think they look like something in a vid.'

'Mollo . . . mollo,' I said. 'Let's . . . just . . . forget . . . it.'

But when Wally got mad about something he could not let it go.

'When you travel with us,' he said, 'you do what we say. You're too young. You don't know shit from jam.'

Jacques said nothing.

We left the banana grove behind and were now walking between fields of onions. Ahead we could see what may have been a chemical factory and a highway. The rain was beginning to fall again. We had no umbrella.

'They're following us,' Wally said. The more he talked, the

250

angrier he got. The angrier he got, the faster he walked. The faster he walked, the more his glistening head craned forward and the more hunched he became, and all the time he talked downwards to the road in his humming Efican accents. 'I can't believe you did that. Now they know we have money.'

Jacques stopped pushing. The chair stopped. It was a moment before Wally realized, and when he turned he was five yards ahead.

'I know you're upset,' Jacques said. 'But it is ridiculous to keep blaming me.'

'Look,' Wally said, pointing a finger at him.

'They saw us come across the border,' Jacques said. 'They didn't need to talk to me to know I was a tourist. Besides, you've never been out of Efica either. You're just as excited as I am.'

'Look,' Wally said, stamping his foot. 'Look behind you, you damn fool.'

It was the Presence with the scimitar sideburns. He was right behind us – small, neat, his hands clasped together in a rather beseeching way.

'You are walking the wrong way,' he said to Jacques. 'There is nothing there, no hotel, nothing but some small boys who will rob you.'

'We know,' Wally said, coming back to take charge.

'You need a hotel,' the Presence said. 'You are poor mens, I know, you do not want it too expensis.'

'That's right, camarade,' Wally said. 'Not expensis.'

'You want to go to Voorstand, let me help you. I make a good price with you.'

'Vat es der geld?' Jacques said.

'Keep out of this,' Wally said to Jacques. 'Just keep out of it.'

'We *make* the price,' Aziz said to Jacques. 'You cannot say what is a good price. We make it, together. You understand? You say one thing, I say the other. We make the price. It is something mens do together.'

'We don't do it that way in Efica,' Wally said. 'You give us a fair price, the hotel plus the guide.'

'You are from Africa?'

'Not Africa – Efica.'

Aziz pursed his lips, shook his head. 'One old man,' he said, 'one

sick man, one . . .' He looked at Jacques. 'One other, not so experienced perhaps.' He had small soft hands and delicate wrists. He
smelled kind of soapy. He kept walking with us. 'First, you need a
nice hotel. Not too expensis, but clean.'

'We'll . . . look,' I said. 'Tell . . . him . . . we'll . . . look.'

'Der enkelamade es der berzoomin,' Jacques said to the Presence,
'Derf hotel es becoomin nacht anajadin.'* To Wally he said, 'Is that OK?'

Jacques knew that neither of us spoke the language, but when he
asked his question his manner was as polite as if he were inquiring
about the water temperature of his bath.

Wally paused a moment. He looked at Jacques with his brow
pressed down upon his cloudy eyes.

'Yes,' he said at last, 'that's fine.'

# 7

Once we were on our way to the hotel, it was as if that clear sharp
moment of rebellion had never occurred. It was the original Jacques
who travelled with us in the back of that dirty old flat-bed truck –
professional, solicitous, attentive to our needs, even before we could
express them. He propped his dos-sack behind Wally's sore spine.
He produced glucose tablets, sun-screen, a ground-sheet to save our
clothes from the bouncing farm muck which littered the tray. He had
moist towelettes. He kept his sneakers clean.

What should have been a short journey was interrupted by two
flat tyres and some problem with the fuel-supply line. Such were
the delays along the roadside that by the time we finally arrived at
our destination it was dusk and we were too weary to understand
where we had come to – it may have been Sint Vincent, the border
town, or Gelukfontein, an industrial centre inland and to the
north.

The hotel turned out to be a store owned by relatives of Aziz. It
was not what we had expected, but we were too exhausted to
protest. Jacques and Wally carried me down the steps into the

* *Long the butt of jokes in Amsterdam, the so-called Vuilnisbelt pidgin of Zeelung has
recently begun to be seen as a language in its own right. For more examples of the rich and
poetic usages of Vuilnisbelt (lit: Garbage Dump) Dutch see* Songs of Zeelung *and*
South East Voorstand *by Prick Van Kooten (Potter Press).*

store. The metal concertina grille was padlocked shut behind us. We sat, and blinked.

Women in black dresses were in the process of dragging large rolls of bedding out from between delicately stacked cans of fish and cooking oil, but when I was brought in, still sitting in my chair, everything stopped. Bright lights were produced – three noisy gas lights, each with its own blue gas cylinder and long metal neck. Insects with long iridescent wings clustered around the light. Tristan Smith was illuminated without apology, but when I turned my big pale eyes on my hosts they quickly flicked their own eyes away, leaving me alone in my wheelchair, like some wet squid washed up amongst the seawrack on the beach.

From out the back, men came to stare at me and argue with Aziz. They were so like Aziz they could have been his brothers – they had identical sideburns terminating in a concave sweep, a crescent which indicated skill with a cut-throat razor. They had narrow hips and little backsides. They carried guns in their trousers, slid under the waistband, with the barrels pointing down to their coccyx. They had dark hands with pale palms which they held expressively when speaking. Their voices were feathery, caressing. The children, with their fine straight noses and their dark darting eyes, bore a resemblance to almost everybody who came in and out of the shadowed doorways of the store.

Diesel fumes drifted down from the roadway through the concertina doors and mingled with the foreign odours of dry fish and spices. Wally sat down on a sack of something, resting his head in his hands. Jacques must have been as weary as any of us, but the instant we arrived, he was on the job.

If he despised my anxiety, he also had the imagination to push my chair into the shadow, to give me some privacy before he began to explain to Aziz that this unusual beast was his employer and it was his job to give me a hot bath at this hour.

They seemed to say that this was not possible.

But Jacques, still wearing the layers of shirt and coat, his eyes bloodshot from diesel smoke and dust, insisted. I did not understand the language, but I was once again impressed by both his politeness and his tenacity. Twice he managed to make them laugh. He was obviously witty with their language and you could see they liked him for it, but there was, it seemed, some problem with the propane gas – there was not enough propane, or there was propane, but they could not spare it for hot water.

'Don't . . . worry . . . mo-ami,' I said.

When I spoke, all eyes turned on me, almost all eyes – not Jacques': he was the nurse, it was his job to bathe me at six p.m. and he planned to do it.

I turned to Wally, but Wally was sleeping, sitting on a sack of corn flour. He had unlaced his precious canvas shoes, removed his socks, and exposed his big pale wrinkled feet. His big high forehead was propped in his dry hands.

'Tell . . . them . . .' I said to Jacques. 'I . . . don't . . . need . . . a . . . bath . . .'

Six pairs of dark eyes returned to stare at me, the creature in the chair. I placed my large red-knuckled hands across my mouth, but as my mother would have said, 'That does not help at all.' Ashamed of my ugliness, I made myself worse – a praying mantis with red knuckles.

A grey-haired old woman crossed herself and then held a tea towel across her mouth. The men looked down at their bare feet and shook their heads.

No one looked at neat little Jacques. They all stared at the thing in the wheelchair until I was forced to stare back at them like I had once stared at Ultras in motel dining rooms.

While the lamps roared, the men began to argue again, their soft voices sliding upwards in glissandos of ever increasing indignation. The foreign insects gathered in suiciding swarms around the hissing lamps.

I stared out past my audience into the shadowed recesses of the store. In the corner, there was a large red table stacked high with car batteries. Beside it, there sat a pretty dark-haired girl of perhaps seventeen. While her family brought their attention to the problem of the amount of propane a bath would consume, how to price it, what to charge, she began to pull a blue plastic brush through her long straight hair. She closed her eyes against the blue-white light of the propane lamps. She put her oval face a little to one side.

I stayed in my wheelchair carrying my big knobbly knuckles in my lap. The girl brushed her long shining hair. I watched her, my heart aching at what I could not have – the small flat ears, the straight, slightly haughty nose, the high round forehead, a slight asymmetry in her lips, the dark hair on her pale olive arms, the green and yellow geometric print on her cotton dress. She knew she was being watched. She felt my eyes.

'All right,' Jacques called to me. 'Bath-time. Warm water.'

I did not wish the girl to see me nod and dribble. I put my forefinger along my cheek, my thumb under my chin.

My nurse wheeled me into a dark passageway, then bumped me down a step on to a cracked concrete-floored veranda which was piled high with cardboard cartons and sacks of flour. There were candles burning inside punctured tin cans, placed on top of the cartons. Banana trees pressed in from the outside and rested their torn leaves on the piles of produce. The air was sweet with honeysuckle, rancid with sewage. Jacques set up the expanding travel bath – clips, locks, five pages of directions. He filled it with water, folded a towel, and placed some soap in a saucer. Then he turned to me and began to undress me.

'Towel,' I said.

'No one wants to see your porpoise.'

'To . . . hide . . . the . . . jon . . . kay.'

'What?'

'Jon . . . kay.'

'Oh – jon-kay. Sorry.' He held up the towel so that as I stepped out of the chair he could arrange it around my shoulders. I held it closed around my neck, staring out into the strange-smelling night, while he slowly, secretly, like a photographer changing his film inside a black bag, began to peel off my bandage inside the cover of the towel, and let the Voorstand Guilders fall in soft parcels beside my curtained calloused ankles.

My skin was so sore, my limbs so tired. When the bandage was removed we let the towel fall on top of our money and Jacques lifted me, naked as a worm, into the bath. The water was hot and stung my torn skin, but it smelt of roses, and I could hear the brothers' voices, perhaps arguing, perhaps not.

What did Jacques really think of the creature it was his task to care for? It would be a good time yet before the truth would be revealed. For now he did his job, washing me in a way that did not make me feel ashamed. He was gentle, careful. I closed my eyes. I felt the warm water, inhaled the oddly perfumed soap. The banana trees rustled, and the leaves scratched at the tops of the cardboard boxes. The air on my face was warm, almost oily, and I realized, with some shock, that it was not triggering any phobic tremors. Perhaps it was physical tiredness, but it was most unexpected – to feel safer in this foreign land than I had inside my own home.

When the bath was done, he towelled me dry. He laid me on another towel and oiled my red bandage-sore back and then my stomach. I opened my eyes and saw, behind his shoulder, an audience.

The girl with the long hair stood in the doorway, a child in her arms. I was half drunk with massage, numbed, sleepy. She stared straight at me, expressionless, and my porpoise, I could not help it, slowly stood erect before her gaze. Our eyes met for a second. She did not shudder and contort her face but stared at me with an open kind of wonder. When she turned, she turned in her own good time, not modestly, but politely. She turned and she went away.

In the morning, when we were leaving in the truck, this same girl came out and gave me a small white flower. That's all. Wally argued about the cost of the accommodation. Jacques translated. The girl gave me a flower, and then we went.

Jacques rode in the cabin. Wally and I rode in the back of the truck, amongst hundreds of pumpkins. She saw me naked. From the total disinterested goodness of her heart, she gave me a flower. Then we rode in the back of a truck, quietly, in the world.

# 8

I sat in my wheelchair surrounded by green pumpkins, the flower clasped in my big bony hands, and everything I saw – the big-leafed trees, the dark little shops, the lolly-pink advertising signs – was new. The air was sweet and rank with diesel. Talcum-fine dust covered my skin. The sky was overcast, but soft and velvety. I sniffed the flower, brushed its fleshy petal on my upper lip.

'Here,' Wally said. 'Here, give it to me.'

I shook my head.

'I'll take care of it,' he said.

The truck sounded its horn and blew a neat column of black exhaust up into the pearl-grey sky.

'It's . . . OK . . .'

'It's just a weed,' he said. 'Look out – it's sappy.'

If it was a weed, it was a pretty one. It had fleshy creamy petals like a frangipani, and the stalk was – as he said – sappy. That flower was precious to me. It produced in me the most exquisite melancholy, a kind of yearning, a profound unhappiness, an erotic kind of grief.

'Come on,' he said. 'It's dripping. You'll get dirty.'

'It's . . . OK . . .' I said.

His back pained him, always, but now he stood up in the lurching truck, for no other reason than to take my flower away. I pulled it out of his reach. The poor old fellow tottered and fell backwards into the pumpkins. It must have hurt him, but he did not cry out or curse. When he had himself seated again there were ochre clay marks on his white canvas frippes, and his ear lobes were very red.

My dab could not leave his frippes like this. He balanced himself on a large green gourd and set to cleaning himself with his handkerchief, spitting and rubbing, fastidious as a cat.

The truck was what we call a Teuf-Teuf. Its rings were bad, its timing out. I could feel its broken springs through my spine.

'You . . . should . . . sit . . . in . . . the . . . cabin,' I said. 'Let . . . Jacques . . . sit . . . out . . . here . . . with . . . me.'

'Just throw it out,' he said.

'Sit . . . up . . . front . . . keep . . . your . . . trousers . . . clean.'

'It doesn't mean nothing,' he said, spitting on the corner of his handkerchief. 'She gave you a flower, that's all, a weed.'

'I . . . know . . . mollo . . . mollo.'

My dab folded his handkerchief carefully and jutted his chin at the landscape – red and yellow clay, bright green foliage, creepers with orange and red flowers growing over collapsing ramparts.

'It's . . . pretty . . . here . . .'

'Pretty?' he almost spat. His grey eyes, when they turned to me, were filled with upset. 'You don't even know their language.'

'The . . . creepers . . . the . . . trees.'

'Throw the fucking thing away,' he said. 'She couldn't even talk to you if she wanted to. There's no one here to sew you up if you go slashing yourself. Just remember that.'

'That . . . was . . . six . . . years . . . ago.'

'Give me the flower, Tristan,' he said. 'Don't do this to yourself.'

I turned my head away from him.

'I knew this was going to happen,' he said. 'There's going to be women everywhere. You're going to have to learn to deal with it. Look at me. You know what I'm talking about.'

What he was talking about was Phonella.

Phonella was my nurse from ages twelve to sixteen. It was because of Phonella we agreed not to hire women again. It was because of Phonella that we had Jean-Claude, lived all those years with sour-smelling men: whiskers, sweat, nothing in the vases. When the incident with Phonella occurred I was sixteen years old and she was twenty.

Phonella was passionate about the ruins of Angkor Wat. She had clear unblemished blue eyes and wild curling red hair. She was kind and soft with me, but when my porpoise stood on end she thought I needed to make pipi. I thought I was aware of myself, but I had no idea who I was. I fell in love with Phonella, completely, hopelessly. I could barely sleep for thinking of her. I woke at dawn, just waiting to see her sweet triangular face again.

'Girls like that, they do things and never think about the consequences. She gives you a flower – she doesn't think what it means to you. She's not thinking you're a man. It isn't on her mind.'

'Shut up,' I cried. I threw the flower at him. It was a poor twisted sappy thing. It fell into his lap and he picked it up and, as the truck swayed and growled up the steep rutted road towards the high saw-tooth silhouettes of the Mountains of the Moon, he dropped it over the side. The truck ran over it, I guess, squashed it, broke it.

'You wouldn't want to live here, son.'

I was too hurt and ashamed to speak.

'It's not so pretty.'

'I . . . don't . . . want . . . to . . . *live* . . . here.'

It was then we smelt the burning rubber. A tyre had blown but the condition of the road was so bad that no one – certainly not Aziz – detected it before the tyre was ripped to pieces and the truck was running on its rim. Wally stood – remember, it was not an easy thing for him to do – and began to strike at the cabin roof with his walking stick. The truck continued to roar and crash towards the border and Wally – hoping to attract the driver's attention – began to pitch pumpkins over the cabin. Three pumpkins later, the truck stopped, and Aziz presented himself at the tail gate, his eyes dark, shaking his finger, but not about damage to the truck.

'These are not my pumpkins,' he said.

'*Pumpkins?*' Wally jumped from the tray and landed on the roadside with a small cry of pain. 'For Chrissakes, mo-ami,' he said, grimacing, and holding his hand against his coccyx, 'can't you smell? You've got a blow-out.'

'They are my brother's pumpkins,' said Aziz.

'You don't drive on a blown sock,' Wally said to Aziz. 'Do you understand, Aziz? You fuck the rim. The rim, mo-ami.'

The roadside was no longer deserted. Behind Aziz there had appeared, from nowhere, three men with coarse black trousers, grubby white shirts, bare dusty feet and wide black hats. One of these men had a brand new wheelbarrow. Another (whose sideburns echoed Aziz's) carried an antique military rifle. There were also several small children, four or five of them – I did not count.

There was no house or vehicle they could have come from, but they were there, and together they stared, not at the smoking torn rear tyre, not at hunched-over Wally or handsome Jacques, whose white sneakers were enclosed in plastic bags. They stared at me, the monster in his wheelchair on the back of the truck, rocking back and forth as he tried to free himself from his nest of pumpkins.

'You have to pay for the pumpkins,' Aziz now said to Wally.

'For Chrissakes – you blew a sock. I was trying to get you to stop before you shredded it.'

'No,' said Aziz. 'The tyre is flat.'

'Yes,' said Wally. 'The rim is wrecked as well.'

The man with the rifle stepped forward so that, had he not been a good foot taller, he would have stood shoulder to shoulder with Aziz. 'We are poor peoples,' he said. 'He have only one tyre.'

Jacques spoke quickly to the man and listened carefully to his answer. 'He means there's no spare,' Jacques said. 'They wrecked their last spare yesterday.'

They gathered in a semi-circle, staring at the remnants of the ruined tyre.

'You give me Guilders,' Aziz said at last. 'I go to Droogstroom and buy a new one. I come back tomorrow.'

'OK,' Wally said.

But I was the shapoh, not Wally. I was the one whose money it was. And I did not want to stay in the truck, being a freak on exhibition. 'We're . . . all . . . going . . . back,' I called to Wally. 'We're . . . not . . . staying . . . here.'

Jacques began speaking to Aziz in creole.

'Shut up,' Wally shouted. 'For Chrissakes, shut up everyone.' Then to me he said, 'Don't make a dick of yourself. She just gave you a flower. She doesn't want you. She just gave you a fucking flower.'

'Shut . . . up . . .' I hissed at Wally. 'Don't . . . talk . . . to . . . me . . . like . . . that . . . in . . . public . . .' I was humiliated. My face was blazing.

'How much further to the border?' Wally asked Aziz.

'Ten miles, fifteen.'

Wally left the semi-circle and came to the back of the truck tray. He brought his shining bony face up against mine. 'I'm sorry,' he said quietly. 'I'm sorry how much this hurts, but I'm not taking you back near that girl.'

He turned. 'We'll walk,' he said to Aziz. 'Ask that man how much for the wheelbarrow?'

'What about my truck, the pumpkins?' Aziz said. 'It is not possible to leave them here.'

The tall man with the rifle then said something to Aziz. Aziz said something back. They spoke earnestly, quietly, for some time. They might have been judges in chambers – such was their gravity. When they finished talking they stepped back a little from each other. Then Aziz gave the tall man his pistol and the tall man gave Aziz the rifle. Then they both crossed themselves and spat on the earth.

'This will cost extra,' Aziz said. 'This is much more money.'

'All right,' said Wally. He did not ask how much. 'No problem, mo-ami. No problem at all.'

Aziz watched him with his dark intelligent eyes. 'It is ten miles.'

'No problem.'

'And I have to pay for the guard, and the pumpkins.'

'No worries, mo-ami. We need to purchase his wheelbarrow as well.'

'That's . . . my . . . money . . . you're . . . spending,' I said.

'I'm sorry,' Wally said. 'We'll be in Voorstand tonight.'

My face never coloured evenly. When I was upset my nose streamed. I dribbled, and my head jerked and rolled. Wally picked me up. He was seventy-three years old. He curved his body around mine, and pinned my arms around my chest. 'You want to get laid, son,' he said, 'it can happen in Saarlim. Anything can happen there.'

## 9

I am a passionate man, full of feelings and opinions, but I knew no woman wanted me and I knew no woman ever would. When I wanted to go back to Aziz's store it was for two sane reasons: number one: I did not want to be stared at; number two: I did not want to sit out there in the open with all that money taped to me.

But Wally could not forget something that had happened six years ago, and I was therefore punished all over again, and the memory of the humiliation and pain, the darkness of the nights and days when I never wished to live again – the past all came back, while in the present we were compelled to exhaust ourselves, to push on toward the border in a ridiculous fashion, without dignity.

The convoy travelled in this order: first, Aziz with his rifle; second, Wally riding in the wheelbarrow; third, a squat broad-shouldered farmer with a black hat and bare feet, engaged to push the wheelbarrow; fourth, me in my chair; fifth, my stylish, uncomplaining nurse. Three children also followed for a little way, but by the time we came to the first stream, they had gone.

There was more audience for this silly spectacle than for any of my somersaults or tumbles at the Feu Follet, more than you might believe such a deserted-looking road could have delivered. All along the way there were knots of people standing – if they were waiting for something else, I don't know what it was.

These people were extremely poor – you could see it in their skin, their clothes, but mostly in their dark, deep, recessed eyes and a sort of tension across their cheekbones that made them shine.

'Goeie daag,' Jacques said, not once, but many times.

No one answered him.

Occasionally a woman would cross herself. As we moved closer to the border the situation of these silent farmers seemed to become more desperate. They stood on their broad splayed bare feet staring at us, ammunition belts strapped diagonally across their chests, their eyes filled with awe, disgust, pity. They did not know that they were seeing 50,000 Guilders pass them by.

Aziz was angry to have been forced to leave the truck and now all his solicitousness had gone. He was cold and withdrawn. He strutted ahead of us, duck-footed, a second pearl-handled pistol clearly visible against his black trousers. He rarely turned around.

I could hear the distant crump of what may have been artillery, Jacques' rasping breath as he uncomplainingly pushed my chair up the hill, the crunch of gravel beneath our tyres. Wally, balanced in a wheelbarrow which jarred his spine and rubbed the skin raw, twice lost his balance and was tipped out on to the roadside. The first time he leapt up cursing, fast as a crab on an open beach. The second time he lay there, dry-lipped and exhausted. None of the bystanders stooped to help him. Indeed they stepped back, pushing back in amongst a small stand of maize, damaging the new crop rather than touch the old vulture with the bleeding crown.

I could not assist him, a hateful feeling. I will not dwell on it. It was Aziz who did it, although he spoke to Wally more as employer to employee and, when he did bend to lift him, displayed a kind of disdain for his injured person which would have been unthinkable an hour before. He locked his fine olive-skinned arms under the old man's, and lugged him upright. Wally's white shirt and trousers were now filthy. Aziz's mouth was fastidious. His dark eyes were furious. It was all to do with being forced to abandon his truck, the damage to his pumpkins.

By noon he had led us into even less hospitable country and, apart from a solitary farmer with a rough-handled hoe on his shoulder, we had no more witnesses to our journey. All this, I now know, was exhilarating for Jacques. In fact, I knew it then. I could feel it in my chair. His hands were blistered, his lips white and dry, but his eyes were small, bright, burning in the secret shadow of his brow.

The road was slowly rising and we switched on my electric motor to give my nurse some rest. It had perhaps three hours' range in this country, slipping, growling against the gradient and the loose rocks. Jacques walked behind me, steadying the chair. The country was becoming more open. The vegetation had thinned until you would have to call it desert – khaki grasses, small clumps of fleshy cactuses with long nicotine-yellow spikes. White limestone broke through the yellow clay of the road surface, which was also deeply scoured along its edges. The chair lurched and crashed, but I was not frightened.

As we came closer and closer to Voorstand, my irritability also seeped away. Colour crept into the soil, first in pinks which became more and more bilious, then in acid greens. We stopped to rest beneath butts as gorgeous and sickly as melted ice-cream. In the distance we could see the snow-capped Mountains of the Moon, inside Voorstand itself. Twice we saw the ice-cold lines left by fighter planes across the cloudless sky.

We pushed on, towards the Sirkus Tour of Saarlim.

Soon the air began to have an afternoon chill, and the road degenerated further – we had to find a path downhill over dangerous gutters and between strewn boulders.

Jacques called and pointed down into a gully beside the road, and there, in the gloom of the valley, I could make out what at first appeared to be a wireless station (antennae, satellite dishes, guy wires), but I soon saw was a series of huts all secured to the ground by a complicated series of guy ropes.

'Kan ons kakshtoop?' Jacques called to Aziz.

'What are you saying?'

'I asked, is there somewhere where we can take a shit,' Jacques said.

The road became softer, sandier. We came across a wide white glistening flat towards the cabins where the red and yellow Voorstand flag – the big moon, the sixteen stars – hung limply in the air. Standing below the flag was a figure dressed in navy blue – an overweight pink-white woman of perhaps sixty or seventy, dressed in a metallic flecked pant suit. She wore a peaked hat with gold braid. She had tightly curled blonde hair. She wore bright blue-framed glasses and shining leather lace-up shoes.

'Ah-zeez,' she called, as we approached. 'Ah-zeez, where in the Christ have you been?'

She turned on her heel and we bumped along behind her, towards the huts. As we went she talked, but she did not once turn her head.

'You ain't going to have them out the other side till three a.m.' The accent would have been familiar to you – she was a Voorstander, a trader, one of your people, a lone entrepreneur on the very edges of your law and land. 'When you make an appointment,' she said, 'you got to keep it. Next time, Ah-zeez, I'll just footsack you. I got other stuff to do out here sides this, you hear me?'

Aziz inclined his head in what may have been a sarcastic version of a bow.

'Good,' she said. 'I thank you.'

'Excuse me,' Jacques said. But she turned and led us into a small hut which proved to be nothing more than an ante-room. We passed up a small wooden ramp (me still in my chair and Wally still clinging to his wheelbarrow) into a little dusty cave with whitewashed walls. There were a number of rusty folding chairs facing a small lectern and it was obvious that we were intended to sit there. Wally climbed out of the barrow and sat in the front row rubbing at his hands and elbows.

'OK?' I asked him as Jacques pushed me in beside Wally. 'You . . . want . . . to . . . rest . . . here?'

His eyes were dull, exhausted. 'I just want to get there,' he said. 'How about you?'

'I . . . just . . . want . . . to . . . get . . . there . . . too.'

Jacques sat behind us in the second row. The farmer who had pushed Wally's wheelbarrow took his hat off and sat in the back row. Aziz remained at the door.

The woman took off her braided cap and placed it on the lectern.


10

That woman never looked at me, not all the time I sat there. She was not so easy on the eyes herself – she had a fleshy face, with large jowls and small eyes which distorted behind her thick lenses. She did not even glance my way. She looked down at her lectern, or over my shoulder at Jacques. I was not insulted. It was fine with me.

'This three-mile tunnel,' she said, referring to a stack of tattered index cards, 'was dug by a fellow wanted to get into Voorstand every bit as bad as you. Thanks to him you have this lovely tunnel. Thanks to his widow I have the pleasure of being its present owner.

'The man who dug this tunnel, his name was Burro Plasse. Burro Plasse was a posturer in Saarlim, Voorstand. Has anyone ever heard of Plasse's Knot?'

None of us.

'Plasse's Knot was the invention of Burro Plasse. He was a famous posturer. He could do the backwards and the forwards, both. Mostly, people who claim to do Plasse's Knot are not doing what he did.

'Burro Plasse was a posturer in Saarlim, Voorstand. Came home one night, just after midnight. It was a snowy night, mid-winter, and there was the Hairy Man sitting on Plasse's stoop, sack in his hand.

'"What you got there?" Burro Plasse said to the Hairy Man.

'"Just a little old sack," said the Hairy Man.

'Then Burro Plasse knew the Hairy Man had come to get him and take him down underneath the earth. He knew his time had come.

'But Burro Plasse – he was young and had a fancy lady sleeping in his bed upstairs and he was determined not to be took by no little black hairy thing, so he says to the ugly little creature who is sitting there, "I know you like the Sirkus, Hairy Man. How about I show you a few new tricks fore we go?"

'The Hairy Man had icicles on his beard and snow on his big eyebrows, but when he heard this he swished his tail and he said to Burro Plasse, "I reckon I seed just about everything there is to see, but why don't you go ahead? Don't make no difference to me."

'So that night in the snow in the Kakdorp in Saarlim City, while his fancy lady was sleeping in the room above his head, Burro Plasse did the best show of his life. He did it in the street wearing his blue singlet and his swimming trunks. He was thirty-three years old, which is old for a posturer, but that night he did knots for the Hairy Man no one ever saw on earth, or in the other place.

'When the show was done, the Hairy Man said to Burro Plasse, "I'll tell you what I'll do, on account of how you are just about the best posturer I ever saw. Instead of taking you below the earth I'll take you on to the other side of the Mountains of the Moon, and if you can dig through the mountains, you can come home to that fancy lady in the room upstairs."

'Now maybe you folks come from some parts like Pakistan where they never heard of no Hairy Man, and maybe you are thinking this is just a story I'm telling for the money. But you already paid your money to Aziz and I don't have to tell no one any story, and I'll tell you – there are folk who say he came here because he had TB, but if I have to choose between the Hairy Man and a fellow with TB digging three miles through solid rock, well, you tell me.

'Folks thinks his name is *Burro* cause he *burrowed* this tunnel, but that is not the case. He was named Burro cause he had this-here donkey. We call it a burro. He used to take that burro into Droogstroom once a month to get supplies. I knew Burro Plasse. As you'll see from the postcards he was a big old fellow with a long white beard.'

She removed the card from the top of the stack and placed it on the bottom. I looked across at Wally. His hands were cut and bleeding from the wheelbarrow.

'What is this horse-shit?' he said.

'Many folks,' the woman said, 'also think he digged the tunnel for smuggling purposes. Nothing could be further from the truth. He digged that tunnel to get back to that fancy lady, but by the time he got back there she was an old lady, eighty-five years old. Her name was Mary Anne Lubbock and you can see her grave in Saarlim Central Cemetery. She was the one I bought the tunnel from, and she was the one told me this story.'

'Why are we listening to this?' Wally said, loud enough for anyone to hear.

The woman fiddled with her index cards, but she did not look at Wally.

'Now if you come up here, I have postcards depicting Burro Plasse, two for each of you. One, I'd like you to take the trouble to mail to me, the other is a souvenir. Ah-zeez here will take you through the tunnel, but you can't ask him to lick the stamps. So I'm asking you. When you get to where you're going, send me the card. I like to know my customers got there safe and sound. I'm going to give you your cards and a flashlight each. Thank you for using Burro Plasse's tunnel.'

She opened a door behind her lectern. Wally stood and limped forward. It was only then I saw how tired he was. His grey eyes were empty, exhausted. His face was dust-caked, streaked with dry sweat.

'You . . . want . . . to . . . rest?' I asked him.

'Please hurry,' said Aziz.

266

Wally turned, he turned slowly, like an old turtle, craning his
neck up to bring his tight-lined jaw to the same height as Aziz's.
'Don't tell me to hurry. Don't waste my time with all this horse-shit
and then tell me to hurry.'

'Please,' Aziz insisted. 'You hurry.'

'Shut the fuck up,' Wally said.

Aziz's little shoulders seemed to shiver beneath the white cotton
skin of his shirt.

'Just shut the fuck up,' Wally said, climbing into the wheelbarrow. 'Can you manage that, mo-ami?'

Aziz lifted his chin, and his face, for the moment he looked at
Wally, was cold and shining. Then he ducked his head and passed
into the cold air of the tunnel.


## 11

Our extraordinary nurse had not expected to walk straight into the
tunnel. Even when the door was opened, he had imagined that
there would be an ante-room, toilets, perhaps even some bread, or
one of those yellow cans of herrings which he had seen on roadside
tables and which, although disgusting to contemplate at first, had
become more and more appealing as the day wore on. But there
was no food or water. The door opened – and there was a blue
gravel floor leading away into the chilly darkness of Voorstand.
There was no chance to prepare for it. He was in the tunnel before
he was ready. He felt the weight of rock above his head but also –
paradoxically – inside his mouth. The air was dry and cold. His
bladder was filled to bursting. He had to push the wheelchair hard
in order to keep up with the farmer and the wheelbarrow. His arms
ached. The blisters on his hands had burst, blistered, burst again,
and were now weeping for a second time. The floor of the tunnel
was uneven. Rough outcrops tripped him, stopped the wheelchair
dead and jammed the handles into his hip bone or stomach, and it
felt, almost from the beginning, like more than he could manage.

No matter what lies he had told to get here, no matter what long
strands of life led him to this point, no matter that it had seemed –
as recently as two hours ago when they first caught sight of the
Mountains of the Moon – as if this voyage was nothing less than his
destiny, now his body was traitor to his will. If he could have

resigned, he would have done it. (So it felt. So he feared.) He could have cried, but of course he could no more cry than piss, no more piss than he could resign.

It was the nature of his secret life. The whole armature of his body was, every minute of the day, pushed and pulled by the requirements of disguise. Even the way he walked had to be disguised. He had no training as an actor. He was an intellectual, a Ph.D whose prize-winning thesis had been entitled 'Orientalist Discourses and the Construction of the Arab Nation State'. To change his natural walk had not come easily to him, and it was difficult, when occupied with this performance, to be sufficiently aware of others. But to hide his true sex, to continue to be a 'he' when he was in fact a 'she', produced a kind of numbness, fits of absent-mindedness and stupidity. There were too many things to think about, things you now had to decide with your conscious brain – how you moved your hand, whether you smiled or not, listened or interrupted. To be a man was like driving a huge and complicated machine on manual systems, so even something as simple as urinating involved planning and subterfuge, asking for a place to shit so you could squat in private.

Wally and Tristan, Aziz, the farmer – we would pee just about anywhere. We had no sense of privacy and would wave our penises and splash our sour, luxuriant urine against the blue rock walls, flap our foreskins, squeeze them dry. But Jacqui thought of urine and its disposal like a desert traveller rationing a supply of water.

It had not been like this at the beginning. She had begun her association with me at a time when the risk was less, the stakes were lower, but by the time she was in the tunnel with her bursting bladder she was the real thing, an undercover agent, an operative of the Efican DoS in an operation which involved the secret agencies of both Efica and Voorstand.

For three years she had sat behind her computer terminal at her third floor 'pen' in the DoS 'Green House' on the Boulevard des Indiennes, a POLIT analyst, a long-haired girl who was remarkable mostly for her eccentric dress, her baggy pants, her Polynesian earrings, the geometric tattoos on her upper arm.

Fresh from the University of Efica she had applied for a posting in Operations. 'No angst, sweets,' the Section Leader said. 'We'll

268

transfer you when we have the opening.' But that was typical DoS bullshit – there were two women in Operations and no one was going to add another one. She visited her Section head twice a week for thirty-four months. She drove him crazy, flirted with him, bored him, infuriated him, made him laugh. She wrote a sign in Sirkus-style lettering – *Lost in POLIT*. She stuck it on her terminal: apart from her Section head (who smiled), only Daphne Loukakis found it funny, and she was in the same boat – a smart woman trying to get into Operations.

Jacqui translated and analysed trade journals, foreign press transcripts of newscasts in Tashkent and Quom. From her desk she liked to observe the unmarked cars of the operatives as they waited at the security gate to be admitted to the building. She never saw an operative on the third floor, never met one inside the building. They drove in and out of the security gate with their tanned male arms resting on their open windows. They hung around in the basement wearing shirtsleeves and shoulder holsters. They told jokes and threw medicine balls at each other. She knew this because she managed, through Daphne Loukakis, to get asked to the drinking parties at the Printemps.

In Analysis the operatives were thought to be barbarians. They were crude. They had words for penises that Jacqui had never heard before – wind sock, blood sausage, rifle, cyclops, middle finger, marrow bone, zob, tringler, drooler. They did not just take a shit. They laid a log or cast a bronze. But they were not half-hearted, or meek. They were alive. They took risks.

You had to discount a lot of things they thought – intellectually, politically, they were not far above the neighbours in her mother's street – but at the core they were the real thing. That was her opinion. They did not live as if they were in rehearsal. They lived like this was it. They did hard things, they suffered. They would walk off a cliff for you if you were their friend. They died for each other. They had nightmares and found it hard to trust their lovers.

And Jacqui, who feared only what was mild and reasonable, massaged their sweaty heads, pressed her face against their chest hair, driven by an anxious itchy sort of need that you could say, if you were being simple about it, went back to a cautious mother wasting her life behind a privet hedge.

She first heard about me when she was in the Printemps Inn with

Wendell Deveau watching the Nez Noir Grand Prix with the sound muted. Wendell was not her 'boyfriend'. She did not have a boyfriend. Wendell was a camarade. They had sex together. He was not an old man, no more than thirty, and he was still handsome, but he had already been through the fire-bombing of Blue's headquarters and he was now balding and pale and overweight as though bloated with the gas of secrets he could not release. He was wry and he could be a gentle man and he had a cute dimpled chin, but on each of the three occasions they went to bed he spoiled the night by being angry about the DoS and what it had done to him. On the day of the Nez Noir Grand Prix he had learned that he was about to be appointed 'baby-sitter' to a monster so notoriously ugly that the previous two operatives were said to have retched involuntarily on first encounter.

I did not know it, but I was their 'keyhole' to the January 20 Group. I was a low-level security risk, a boring, tedious report job. I had a 30-megabyte file filled with detailed examples of my unpleasant character, my ugly face and body.

So there you see it: her interest in me, at the beginning, was opportunistic, manipulative. I was so unattractive a job that others might just let her have me.

'No way,' Wendell said when she suggested she might apply for the post. 'The mark won't hire a woman. He falls in love.'

Someone else would have been discouraged, but this was Jacqui. She wanted me. And two days later there was a furore at the third floor 'man trap' when the guard tried to deny her admittance to her own workplace. She had chopped her long black hair and swept it back with mousse. She was wearing a wide-shouldered black jacket which had once been her father's. The layered look came later – on the first day, she wore just one shirt with a white tank-top beneath it.

The thing was: she fooled them all, not just the guard but everyone who saw her. She had practised with Wendell, had him walk and sit whilst naked, watched what his cock and balls did to his walk. And she got the walk, without exaggerating it. She did not go in for ball-scratching or leg-spreading or any of the mistakes you see so often on the stage. She centred her maleness on her eyes, and in her jaw. She led with her chest. She hollowed her cheeks, made herself dangerous and slit-eyed like a snake, and her body followed the instruction.

If the assignment had been politically hot, there is no way she would have got me. But although the January 20 Group had the publicly declared aim of attacking sites of Voorstand's installations in Efica, no one really expected anything more terrorizing than an essay or a letter to the *Chemin Rouge Reformer*. Jacqui got me because I was low-status work – demeaning, disgusting, safe.

Once she got me, she changed what I was. I was safe, she made me unsafe. I was inactive, she made me active. I was a thing to her, a maw, a streaming face, a line of gums, a pair of pale staring eyes. At the same time she was professional. She valued that quality almost as much as courage. And once she was my nurse she cared for me with almost fanatical dedication – washed my body, changed my sheets, fed me with a spoon when necessary. She was as discreet and complete as any butler, but at the same time this twenty-three-year-old young woman was fraudulently misrepresenting my activities to her computer.

In DoS terminology, she made me Sexy, that is, she loaded my file with interesting specs and features, until her superiors had no choice but to send her on this trip halfway across the world. They had no other choice, because it was her choice that they should not.

Likewise: it was her choice to speak to Aziz back at the Morean border, to accept the pistol when he offered it, to spin its six-pound weight on her single index finger.

When he walked beside her in the tunnel, illuminating the uneven floor with his moon yellow flashlight, it was her choice to keep going, to lean forward and put her full 102 pounds into the chair, to force it over the jags of rock. The blisters would heal. The pain would go. She could control her bladder, could carry this piss all the way to Saarlim City.

12

When she had spun the pistol on her finger it had been her choice, but it had not felt like it. She had walked towards Aziz on that gluey grey-skied day because . . . she was twenty-three years old . . . she had that jelly feeling in her legs, the warm soft heat behind her eyes. It had been a little madness, a frisson. But far from evaporating, as you might expect, this feeling had been dis-

tilled, condensed, intensified by almost everything she saw there-
after – even, for Chrissakes, the man's domestic life. The sight of a
wife, children – you would expect this to be a killer, but she
carried her crush in deep disguise, right into his home. She slit her
eyes, hollowed her cheeks, thrust her jaw, got a tingling at the
nape of her neck watching how this cool, elegant man with the
poker player's eyes was also the dab, the patron. She got numb
and icy in her sinuses watching how he exercised his power, how
he listened to his brothers with his dark eyes never leaving their
faces, how he nodded, gestured, settled a dispute about propane
gas by placing a hand against another man's cheek. Jacqui, who
hated the ordinariness of the lower-middle class of Efica, found
herself sympathetically imagining life inside that little grocery
store. She liked how they lashed the bedding on to the rafters just
before dawn, the way they scrubbed the cracked green concrete
floor until it smelt like a ship at sea; and although the men did
have Glock automatics stuck in their belts, there was also a
definite edge to the place she found almost religious – hierarchical,
ascetic, clean. She was not, herself, religious, but this slight
foreign man with weird-looking sideburns was that rarity – not
mediocre.

When she rode with him in the truck, he talked to her man to
man. It was almost unbearable, the intimacy. She twice had visions
of resting her palm on his bristly olive-skinned neck. He told her
frankly, in English, how they hi-jacked the big gasoline auto-lorries
when they crossed the border out of Voorstand. He would die not
knowing he had said these things to a woman. She did not want to
tell him either. That was the paradox. It was her business to hold
secrets, to retain them, to gain pleasure only from their tumescent
pressure, never their release.

Aziz made Wally Paccione appear more and more a spiv. He was
rude about the blown-out tyre, bad-tempered on the road, and
now, as they pushed on through the stale air of the tunnel, the old
Efican seemed to Jacqui to look like a Grand Duke by Bertolt Brecht.
Sometimes, when his wheelbarrow hit a bump, you could hear him
cuss. But he never did direct a human remark to the man who
pushed him. Jacqui had watched. She had not yet seen so much as
a smile or a nod pass between them.

In Chemin Rouge, Wally had been a reasonable employer, occasionally withholding, but mostly good-hearted. But neither he nor I – this was her opinion – made any concessions to the country we were passing through. We had not learned a word of Old Dutch and this, to a linguist, seemed both lazy and offensive. To her it seemed ill-mannered and provincial to continue to call a tyre a 'sock', a truck a 'Teuf-teuf'. In Zeelung our nurse began silently to judge us.

'Shut-the-fuck-up,' Wally had said, and Aziz, this so-called gangster, who could just as easily slit our throats, had sheltered us, fed us and abandoned his own truck just so he could fulfil his part of a bargain.

Jacqui could not bear that he be treated like this.

When he shone the torch for her, she thanked him in his own language: 'Dankie voor die flits.'

In the flickering yellow light she could see his mouth was compressed. His top lip was slightly swollen and this, with its intimations of both violence and grief, she found attractive.

'I am sorry,' she said to him. 'I know we have offended you.'

She had not really imagined he would hold her responsible for Wally's rudeness, so the darting hostility of his eyes, when he looked at her, shocked her.

'Het spijt ons als wij jou kwaai gemaakt,' she said, but he would not let himself be massaged by the language.

'There is no offence,' he said coldly.

'You must be concerned about your truck?' she said.

'Wat?'

'Ben jou worried oor jou auto-lorrie?'

'The auto-lorrie,' he said, shining the flashlight on a jagged tooth of rock which they both had to duck beneath, 'is gone.'

'Hey,' Jacqui laughed, not knowing what to say, but meaning, please, mollo-mollo, I'm not your enemy.

'Wat?'

'Relax, the truck is fine.'

'You are a boy. What can you know?'

'I heard you ask the camarade with the gun,' Jacqui said. 'You asked him to care for the truck. He is your family?'

'You listened?'

'Aziz, you spoke in front of me. You know I speak your language.'

'You are very rude boy,' Aziz said.

Jacqui felt her eyes burning.

'He is thief,' Aziz said. 'He take too much money. This man will take my auto-lorrie. The pumpkins, he sells them, then the auto-lorrie. Do you think I meet my *family* by the road?'

'I'm sorry but . . .'

'Sorry, sorry, I'm so sorry,' Aziz mocked, making his voice so girlish that Jacqui, chilled with fright, felt she could not hold her bladder a second longer.

'Please shut up,' Wally Paccione said. 'Push the chair.'

'You shut up,' Aziz said.

'I was not talking to you, mug-wallop. I was talking to the nurse.'

Jacqui saw the size of the offence. She saw the explosion coming like a bulge in a cartoon snake.

'Mug-wallop?' Aziz said, his voice rising incredulously. 'Mug-wallop?'

'It's not this camarade's business to talk to you,' Wally said. 'His business is to push the chair. It is my business to talk to you.'

Aziz called to the farmer. 'Jy mag nou wegdonder,' he said. 'Jy can die wheelbarrow vat. Hy kan die rest lopen.'

The farmer immediately obeyed. He stopped pushing. He stood immobile, his closely barbered head bent so as not to hit the ceiling.

Aziz was going to make the old spiv walk.

'Ik heb mijn geld nodig,' the farmer said, producing a blue cloth purse from his trouser pockets. 'Ik moes blijven tot ik mijn geld krijg,' the farmer said. He loosened the lips of the purse and waited.

'He needs to go,' Aziz said curtly. 'Now you pay him. Geduld,' he said to the farmer. 'Hierdie heer sal jou nou betalen.'

The farmer turned towards Wally, who began to struggle from the barrow which, being temporarily unsupported, tipped and sent him sprawling. He hit his head against the rock wall. When he stood up there was blood oozing down his temple and into his eye.

'I am an old man,' Wally said.

'My truck is gone,' Aziz said.

'Petit con.'

'Let me help you,' Jacques said to Wally. 'Let me interpret . . .'

'Your truck is still there, you ballot,' Wally told the glowering guide. 'Tell this man we will pay him when he pushes me to the end of the tunnel.'

'I have been very stupid,' Aziz said. 'I have been too stupid for anything.'

'Your truck is fine,' Wally said.

'The truck . . . is . . . fine,' Tristan said.

'This isn't necessary,' Jacqui said, but Aziz was already holding the slender flashlight with his teeth. Jacqui watched with a chilled sort of pleasure as he aimed the beam of the light at his revolver and fed small blunt-nosed cartridges into it. He took his time, as if he did not expect anyone to interfere with him. Indeed, no one did.

When he had loaded eight shells, he removed the flashlight from his mouth and, having held it fastidiously between thumb and forefinger, dropped it into his shirt pocket.

'Kom, staan agter mij,' he told the farmer.

Jacqui translated: 'Come and stand behind me.' No one seemed to hear her. The farmer scraped along the tunnel wall behind Aziz so that he was, of all the party, the one nearest to the exit.

'You pay me,' Aziz said to Wally. 'You pay for my truck. Or I take the money for myself.'

'Take it then,' Wally said. He pulled a crumpled handful of Zeelung currency out of his trousers and held it up towards Aziz. 'There is no more money.'

It was obvious to Jacqui: you did not deal with a man like Aziz in this way.

Wally let go of the money so it fell in a damp wad to the floor of the tunnel.

It lay there, beneath Aziz's consideration.

'You,' he said to Jacqui. 'Go back with them.'

She hesitated. He kneed her in the backside, pushing her into the wheelchair. 'You are a girl,' he said. 'Go back with them.'

Jacqui edged around Tristan's chair.

'Now you turn him around,'

It was hard to swing the chair around. Jacqui did it.

To the farmer, Aziz said, 'Geef mij jou mes.'

'He's telling him to get a knife,' Jacqui said.

The farmer lifted his wide trousers, revealing a bright red cloth tied around his calf.

'He's asking for a knife!'

275

From the red cloth, the farmer pulled out a long knife and gave it, handle first, to Aziz who, having moved his revolver into his left hand, accepted it with his right.

'Schijn het licht aan die veranderling.'

The farmer took the flashlight from Wally and shone it on me, Tristan Smith.

Aziz then knelt carefully in front of me. He put the tip of the knife inside the cuffed leg of the trousers which Jacqui had had made for me on the Boulevard des Indiennes. Then, with the confidence of a tailor, Aziz brought the knife upwards and parted the leg all the way to the hip in one clean straight rip.

What was revealed, of course, was the bandage. Inside the bandage you could see the fat wads of currency, sixteen different bundles each wrapped in oilskin.

Aziz cut the second leg.

'OK,' he said to me, 'perhaps you do not want your shirt cut.'

I undid my own buttons.

'We give you half,' Wally said. 'OK, fair is fair.'

But Aziz was already discovering the extent of the fortune hidden inside the bandages.

'You lied to me,' he said. 'You said you were poor. I was sorry for you. I tried to help you.'

I pulled the bandage from around my chest. When Jacqui tried to assist me, I shoved her hand away and pulled the bandage roughly away from my raw red skin. I gave the prick our assets, dry-eyed, giving him my mutant's smile.

When I spoke, I spoke slowly, carefully.

'I'm . . . coming . . . back . . . to . . . kill you,' I said to this man whom I would never see again. He had all my attention. All my animus. I did not notice Jacqui retreat into the darkness of the tunnel. We were like dogs fighting – she could have revealed her secret in front of us and we would not have seen her. She went two yards, three, ten. She lifted her jacket. She pulled her trousers to her knees. She rested her back against the rock wall, and balanced herself on her toes. As the steaming urine pooled amongst the cold blue gravel, we men continued making threats to each other. She could smell the testosterone, as strong as bacon cooking.

# 13

The tunnel had become a kind of open passageway or race, and from here I could see a flag, an exceptionally large Voorstand flag, hanging limply in the night sky above our heads. We were at our destination, but I was so angry I could not speak. We were in Voorstand, stone broke, unprotected.

'Relax,' Wally said. 'Look – the Voorstand flag.'

I heard a car door slam. My skin began to bump and shiver.

Then: a shout.

Then: bright white quartz lights. We were spotlit. I was blinded. My heart was beating hard enough to break. I was dizzy, blind, a rabbit in a hunter's spotlight. I was the Mutant entering Voorstand.

# 14

That night, the night we entered Voorstand, Leona had waited with the other facilitators. It was like any night at Plasse's Crossing – they had formed a semi-circle of trucks, cars, all-wheel drives around the exit from the tunnel. That was what normal life had become for her. You camped there with the other facilitators, waiting for the *Fresh Meat* to come out of the tunnel. That was what they called the travellers who came illegally into Voorstand. Good people used this disgusting term – artists, performers, brave people she admired, folk who could hang from their toes one hundred feet above a bed of nails. Leona used it too, in the end. Nine times out of ten the poor fresh meat was panicked half to death. It came out into the light, blinking, hardly able to see, and all around it were facilitators, tugging at its sleeves, grabbing at its shoulders, signing up the business with give-away motel pens.

In her native Morea, Leona had been a jahli, that is, someone who sings songs and complicated stories, the performance of which not only requires considerable musical ability, but also a memory capable of retaining as many as one hundred different family names.

In Voorstand she was, among other things, a facilitator. This was not a job she would ever have imagined taking, but it would have to do until she found a position as a Verteller in the Sirkus.*

* *The Voorstand reader will be aware of how unlikely this was, for although all Sirkuses originally had a Verteller – whose epic songs formed the narrative backbone of the Sirkus – at the time Tristan Smith arrived in Saarlim only three Sirkuses still used Vertellers.*

A few facilitators liked to frighten the meat. Others were the soothing ones, talking in big deep voices and just being calm in the middle of all that confusion. Some achieved good results just by being good-looking – Kreigtown Jimmy, Marvin Tromp, little Oloff – all these guys had to do was stand there being gorgeous and work would come to them. Others, like those Vargas girls, focused on price, cutting their margins to the bone, trying to get the signature on that little bit of paper.

Once you had it signed, that meant you could relax: the meat was yours. Next: you got them into Saarlim, got them registered as pre-dated POWs with whoever was your contact in the military. You got their little pink and blue registration card. You shook their hand. You maybe introduced them to some housing, got yourself a little extra folding for the trouble. Some facilitators, *allegedly*, got a percentage of the rent money for the first year, but facilitators were such bullschtool. They would say anything.

There was a gate at the tunnel entrance. It must have worked, some long time ago, but it sure as hell did not work any more. It lay on the ground, rusting into the red dust. This was the gate that my wheelchair bounced across on the night I arrived in Voorstand.

No messenger arrived before me.

When the first set of spotlights illuminated the tunnel entrance, my reception committee readied itself – car doors opened, radios were turned off. Then, no one moved.

There was only Leona – she alone – spotlit like an actor on a stage, walking towards me, holding a clipboard. She ambled towards the tunnel entrance where the earth was ground so fine and dry, like the earth in a cattle kraal. She was short, broad, rough-looking, in a battered brown leather jacket and baggy combat trousers with neck-ties knotted round the ankles to keep out the night chill.

I had just been robbed. My frippes were split. I saw her full lips, her sleepy eyes, her round coffee-coloured face, her orange-blonde hair cut close, in a fringe; I could not tell if it meant harm or safety for me.

She looked at me.

I saw her shiver. It ran in a ripple from her face down to her knees. 'I's OK, hunning,' she said. 'You're not the only one is frighted.'

I thought she meant that she was feared of me, but she was referring to the other facilitators who, now they had seen me clearly, were placing their clipboards back on the dash and slamming their truck doors closed. These facilitators did not want to touch anything sick. Anything just the tiniest bit viral, they would not touch it. They stayed with their windows shut, the air-kool on, their hunters' halogens shining on us.

Leona, for reasons I will tell you later, had to take this job. Even when she saw our remaining 39 Guilders, she had no choice. She pushed the crumpled notes quickly down into her pockets and signed us up, all three of us.

'My name is Leona,' the facilitator said to Jacques and Wally.

I signed my big and fancy signature – *Tristan Smith* – with special loops like on a bank note. When she saw my name she smiled.

'Welcome,' she said to me. 'My name is Leona.'

And there and then, in the middle of the desert, in a sea of white light, she began what seemed to me, with my history, like an audition piece. She declaimed to us, in a rich round voice. She had no rhyti or bhalam to accompany her. She did not sing as she might have as a Verteller, but she chanted thus:

> 'What you are looking at here is a Pow-pow.
> Lots of people don't like that term.
> They tell you, it demeaning.
> They tell you, don't insult me.
> I tell you,
> Be pleased.
> I am going to make you a Pow-pow,
> I going to get you that little medal,
> the one with the pink and blue writing on it,
> the one
> with POW in big grey letters
> right across your face.
> I tell you – be happy. I am a Pow-pow.
> It is the Pow-pows make this country great.
> Not the Dutchies, they're history.
> Not the Anglos – they lost the war.
> It is the Pow-wows who dance on the high wire with
> Bruder Skat.

Be pleased.
It is us Pow-pows who tell the story for Oncle Dog,
who dive through the air with Meneer Mouse.
We are the ones who keep the Hairy Man laughing.
Not the Dutchies – they're too fat.
Not the Anglos – they lost the war.
Alice de Stihl, Boddy Gross-Silva, James Featherfleur.
Laser-Art, Spray-effect, Symphonic Clowns.
Pow-pow Music,
Tap, Joy-dancing,
Sirkus Stomp.
Pow! Pow!'

We stood in the glare of the spotlights, like cambruces, hay-seeds called up into the centre ring. Leona blew the smoke off the end of the barrel of her imaginary guns, twirled them, slipped them in her holster.

'Welcome to Voorstand,' she said. 'Arts and Leisure capital of the world.'

I pulled my big white canvas hat down over my eyes and crossed my arms over my chest, but my trousers were slit and my bone-thin legs were naked to the light.

Jacques put his shoulders back, and poked his sunburnt nose at the heat as if he did not give a damn who looked at him or what they did to him.

As for Wally, I do not exaggerate when I say that the dear old turtle transformed himself. He uncurled like a paper flower in water. He lifted his face towards the light. He raised his freckled liver-spotted arm and *waved* at the unseen Voorstanders. He turned his ruined face towards me, his thirst-white mouth loose, but smiling.

'How about us!' he said, so pleased that he made me laugh. We were broke, penniless, without a cash parole. 'Hey,' my dab said, blood running down his forehead, 'how about us!'


## 15

This was my maman's country. This was her land, and in that sense it was my land too. It was most unfortunate that I should be forced to stand here as a pauper and an alien.

It was four a.m., but the clay-pan at the tunnel mouth was like a fairground – all the facilitators' cars and trucks with their different lights: headlights, quartz halogens, fairy lights flashing around their contours, the air smelling of diesel fuel, woodsmoke, ketchup, fatty food, sugar burning in the night.

The Big Dipper, my maman's stars, was overhead. There was liquor in the air, ganja stick. Life crackled around me like small-arms fire. We followed Leona as she hustled across the bare earth towards the headlights.

As we went, the facilitators called to her, 'Wear your mask, Leona.' They made voices of disgust. Baark. Baarf. Urrrrk. That is how you greeted me, Madam, Mcneer. 'Hold your breath, Leona-honey.'

'Don't mind them,' Leona said. 'They just ignorant. Here my Blikk.'

Blikk – it is your word, as familiar to you as your toothbrush. To me, it was a jewel from the crown of your songs and stories – alien, mysterious, far more than what we mean when we say 'car'. Leona's Blikk, although not new, was gleaming, studded with small flashing pinprick lights, not just on the bulbous fenders, or on the side doors, but right across its wide curving roof.

Wally turned and looked at me, his face cracked open in a grin. This response, of course, was exactly what I wanted when I imagined the trip. It was imagining this that helped me overcome my phobia – the thought that my will could make him carefree, happy, not weighed down by history or loneliness.

But when I had imagined this I had not expected to arrive a pauper in the desert, and now that was my lot, my breathing was shallow in my chest, and I felt light, faint. I could not be the joyous man I had expected.

'Come on,' he said. 'Who else do you know who has ever come to Voorstand through a *tunnel*.'

'We . . . lost . . . our . . . *money*.'

For answer he gave me a very distinctive, mischievous grin.

'NO . . . don't . . . even . . . think . . . of . . . it.'

'Don't what?'

'I . . . know . . . that . . . grin.'

It was the same grin he wore when he arrived home with stolen watches and unnecessary toaster ovens.

'This . . . is . . . not . . . Chemin . . . Rouge.'

I hated him to steal. Twice he had been detained overnight in jail. As a result I feared the police, the courts, all those in uniform.

'Don't . . . even . . . think . . . of . . . it.'

'Don't think of what?' he insisted, but then Leona interrupted.

'You ever see Gyro's Sirkus?' she asked us.

'Read about it,' Wally said. Now all his attention was focused on Leona. He thrust his hands into his pockets and pushed his eyebrows forward.

'Gyro's Sirkus,' Jacques said. 'I know what you're going to say.'

'What am I going to say, handsome?'

'We don't get the big Sirkuses in Efica,' Jacques said. 'But we get the Simulation Domes. I saw the Simulation. Three hundred and sixty degrees. Three-D. This is the car – right?'

'This here Blikk,' Leona said. 'This the exact same one they drove across the high wire in Gyro's Sirkus.'

We had exactly three Guilders left between us, and my companions were staring at the Blikk, smiling, the pair of them rubbing their faces with their hands.

'You want to take a photo,' Leona said, 'it's OK.'

Jacques had no camera, but Wally gleefully followed the facilitator's suggestion. His flash flashed. The car blinked its lights back at him, like a giant dung beetle talking to its servant.

Leona looked at me and winked. I tried to wink back, but all I was thinking about was how we were to get money.

'You can't wink,' she said. She blew gum from between her teeth and popped it. 'You done all tried,' she said, 'but you can't do it. I seed you *tried* to do it. I know you, I knowed your type.'

I could not even think about her. But for Wally, of course, she was a woman and she was talking to me, and I might misunderstand her and fall in love.

Suddenly he had no interest in photography. 'OK,' he said to me. He picked me up – my trousers were slit like rags, my legs were there for anyone to see. 'Time to go,' he said to Jacques and Leona as he struggled with me to the open seat of the Blikk.

'What's . . . your . . . problem?' I asked him. 'For . . . God's . . . sake.'

He said something to me, but it was drowned by the extraordinary roar of the Blikk's V12 engine. Leona was ready. She slammed her door and fiddled with the choke. Jacques tumbled in beside me.

'Bout dawn,' Leona called, 'you're going to see some stuff.'
Then, without warning, she drove, fast, bumpy, full gas.

## 16

Leona had smooth tan leather gloves. She loved to let that wheel
spin through her broad little hands. 'Wink, he ain't pleased,' she
called. She slid the Blikk on sandy corners and bucked it high on
rocky passages.

'Look at him. He pissed as hell.'

Why would I not be? I had ripped trousers, mutant legs. I was
three foot six, powerless beneath the big empty sky of Voorstand.

'I see him coming out the tunnel, ducking and diving, didn't
want to give a penny to no one.'

She looked at me. Every time I looked up those eyes were on
me in that wide rear-vision mirror.

'Didn't want to give no Guilder to me. So damned mad couldn't
even wink at me, ain't that right, honey? You was mad as two
fleas,' she said.

'Still . . . am,' I said. I looked right back at her. I could see her in
the wide-screen mirror: broad nose, handsome face, yellow desert
eyes.

'What's he say?'

'He still is,' said Wally. 'Not with you, with me.'

'When he signed the A22 form, you should have seed the loop-de-
loop. Don't Fuck With Me. That was what he wrote. Straight on the
page.'

'It's me he's loup with,' Wally said.

'Loop with?'

'Loup – mad, angry.'

'Oncle, I love the way you talk,' she said. She left me then. She
began to chew *his* bone. Soon she had Wally blushing about his
accent. She made him happy, glowing. When she switched to
Jacques, I saw it was her talent, her thing. She was facilitating our
entry into Voorstand, calming us, flattering us. And, indeed, when
our moods improved, she lapsed into silence. We travelled with our
fairy lights still winking from our metal skin.

The earth was spooky white, clay yellow, dust brown – not like
anything in Efica. It was the landscape of the stories Irma had
recited, the landscape my ancestors, landing on the *Pietr Groot* from

the Netherlands in 135 BE,* had travelled through. It was alien. It was in my blood, in my dreams. It appeared and reappeared at every bend and cutting – real, not real, familiar, foreign.

The distances were vast, far greater than anything we were accustomed to. So even the famous cactus forest at Neu Zwolfe, which we entered early in the journey, quickly became tedious to our eyes. Likewise in the Poorlands which followed after – the little blue churches, the stone roadside shrines with newspaper-wrapped offerings to the Hairy Man – were soon bleached of novelty.

We had no money. We were unprotected. My breathing became shallow. I began to dwell on the circumstances in which our security had been lost. It would never have happened if only Wally had been calm about the flower.

I do not mean to blame my guardian for everything that happened, but just the same – he lost me my money, my power, all because he panicked about some girl with a flower. That girl had nice strong calves, it is true. She was kind. She had large dark liquid eyes and she saw that I was a human underneath my horror. I would have chopped my hand off if it meant she might really care for me. I do not mean it poetically. I mean really chop – an axe, the danger. But chopping, cutting, mutilation – none of this would change the bitter truth. I was who I was. She was kind, that's all. She gave me a flower with a thick pulpy stem like a Nez Noir thistle. *I was not going to slash my wrists, for God's sake.*

If Wally had not panicked, we would have *driven* to the tunnel and arrived rested, cool, cucumbers. There would have been no conflict with Aziz, no robbery. We would have driven on to Saarlim in the expectation of security and comfort.

But Wally did not even seem to have noticed what he had done. Indeed, the moment my fortune disappeared, he began to shine, and neither travel nor sleeplessness seemed to diminish his good humour.

'It's the challenge, son,' he said to me as dawn arrived – a streaky melancholy grey and yellow sky over wide valleys dotted with very high pillars of yellow rock. 'And Oncle Wal is the right man for the job.'

---

* BE, *Before Efica, dating from Captain Girard's landfall at what is now Melcarth.*

'Ask . . . her . . . what . . . they . . . do . . . with . . . thieves . . . in . . . Voorstand.'

'Mollo-mollo,' Wally said. 'There won't be any thieving.' He smiled, sat back. He crossed his legs and began rolling a cigarette of rank Morean tobacco.

'That's a willow,' Leona said. I could see her eyes, creased, tired, in the rear-view mirror. 'See a willow, maybe there's a stream.'

'We have willows,' Jacques said, stretching. 'But not like that.'

'That's a spit-weed.'

'We don't have them.'

That's a creosote bush. That's a see-saw. Beside a dry creek bed a little below the road, she showed us a twenty-foot long shoe and a leg carved out of rock. The leg rose maybe forty feet into the air and then stopped. It was trousered, cuffed, had a neat pleat up its front, and careful wrinkles, all carved from the yellow rock.

'It's laser art?' Jacques said. 'What is it?'

'Not laser. Real.'

'What is it?'

'It's a shoe,' Leona said.

It was a shoe, but, size apart, it was not normal. It had an excessively wide toe and a high lump on the toe cap – a clown's shoe.

'You know whose shoe that is?'

'Bruder . . . Dog's . . . shoe,' I said.

'That is the Dog's shoe,' Leona said. 'Honey, it a *mystery*. How were they going to build the rest? It one of the *mysteries of the desert.** Ain't that something. Now you look over there you see it. The wire lead from the shoe to that there cabin with the machinery out its back. That was going to be an avocado farm. All those dead trees – them are what we call avocados. It a kind of vegetable. Why is that wire there? You tell me, Wink. The answer is to get the energy from the Dog and give it to the avocado trees. That is what I figure, but no one knows. Would have been an avocado farm if they'd ever

* *The Voorstand reader will be aware that Leona was misinformed, and that the abandoned statue of Bruder Dog, far from being the product of modern Sirkus-style capitalism, marks the site of a well-documented Free Dutch Church community dating from 65 BE. These remains are known as the Dry Creek Dog. For more information, see* Heretical Christian Art in the New World *(Thames & Hudson, London).*

found the water. They planted the trees, never found the water. Then they tried to get the energy from the Dog, but they couldn't get the Bruder built up in time.'

'We're going to do fine here,' Wally whispered. 'Don't you worry.'

'What happened to him, Mr Avocado? Maybe he figured out how to do some other thing. Maybe he was the one went drove down the road and blasted the guts out of the cabin there. Now look at that.'

She pulled the car up. We wound our windows down. There was a cabin with its insides blown away by gunfire. Its insulation hung out of gaping wounds.

'We're going to do fine,' Wally said, but when I looked at him he looked away. 'Mollo mollo,' he said. 'We're going to do fine.'

'This is the land of Sirkus,' the facilitator said. 'No one will tell you not to try. Some countries, they have rules, regulations, government telling the people how to live their lives. Say you was Japanese, Chinese – put you in jail for making a statue of Bruder Dog. Here, you take the risk, you get the reward. You walk the high wire, you die or you get the silver cup.'

'Can I ask you, sweets,' said Wally. 'How much money did you have when you arrived in Voorstand?'

Leona began a long story about her arrival. Wally leaned forward and rested his arms on the back of the driver's seat. I looked out the window, behind his curving spine. There, on the right, on a cutting, a three-foot high Mouse was running beside the car.

I said nothing, but I could not take my eyes off the hateful thing. Its white scarf was gone. Its bright blue waistcoat was hanging from one shoulder. Its soft grey limbs were torn, covered in clay dust. Its eyes were fierce and wide, its teeth small and pointed. It was running badly, tripping itself on its own large white boots, stumbling, standing, falling. Its arms were loose and slightly boneless in appearance. I was reminded of a blow-fly dying.

The cutting led us to a view over a wide khaki-coloured plain. A single line of highway cut right across its centre, and one could see the thin chalk line of road, our road, leading into it. At any moment the car would begin its descent and we would leave these nightmare visions behind us.

'Wink sees it,' Leona said.

'Meneer Mouse,' whispered Jacques. 'God damn.'

'Where you folks from?' Leona said.

'Stop the car,' Jacques said.

'You ain't never heard of Bruder Mouse.'

'Let's get it,' Jacques said. I looked at him. He was so alert, so handsome. His colour was high, his eye-white a lustrous greyish white.

'Bruder Mouse is something we have here,' Leona said.

'We know the Mouse,' Jacques said. '"*One mo nothing. Next mo there he was, solid as a miller's wheel.*" We know it, really. It's, like, it's our Mouse too. "*His black ears were sharp. His teeth were white. His eyes as bright as an angel of the lord.*"'

'That's the words of a song, right?' Leona asked.

'Tales of Bruder Mouse,' said Jacques. 'Badberg Edition.'

But Leona, it was obvious, had not heard of the Badberg Edition. 'The Mouse is something we have from the Sirkus,' she said. 'But not like this old fellow – this one is a machine, a Simulacrum. This old mouse, he's older than me, believe it. He's an *old* model.* Hey, Wink, you *seeing* this? Just watch that Simi go. This must be the last Simi left in Voorstand. You guys don't appreciate how lucky you are.'

The Mouse, coming closer and closer to the edge of the cliff, had stumbled and fallen in front of the car. Now, like a rabbit that you've wounded but not killed, it picked itself up and began its wild, unco-ordinated run down the road which now, as Leona followed, began a steep descent towards the plain.

'You want a souvenir?' she said.

Jacques smiled. He did not even speak. He sat back in his seat, and I could see his will, his alarming, shining will through the lashes of his slightly narrowed eyes.

---

* '*The original Sirkus Mouse was like six feet tall. You see these early Bruders in the paintings, Dogs, Ducks, Mice, all as big as football players. In the beginning, of course, it was very religious. All God's creatures, all that sort of thing. Maybe they was priests at one time but as long as I remember they were krakers, swartzers, thieves of one sort or another. Those Bruders did some awful stuff – murder, rape, terrible things. So now we have the Creature Control Act – no Bruder in a public place can be over three foot six inches. And so there are none.*' For more details of these forgotten Simulacrum Mark 3s, see Chapter 28.

'No,' I said. I hated that Mouse. I hated its face. I hated what it stood for in my life, my history, that I was ever fool enough to hide behind its face.

'Twenty mile an hour,' Leona said. 'Look it *go.*'

Black legs flying. A cloud of dust.

'You want it?' Wally asked me.

'You . . . know . . . I . . . don't.'

There was a thump, a bump. The car stopped. 'Got it,' said Leona. 'Got the little sucker.'

She stopped, jumped out. A second later she held the back door open. She threw the Simulacrum on to the floor. It was still smoking. Cotton wadding grew like bloom from its elbow. It gave off the smell of burning rubber, like a dishwasher about to catch fire.


## 17

My nurse sat beside me like a woman newly pregnant, her hands resting on her stomach, her feet astride the stinking Bruder Mouse.

I thought she was my employee, my man. It never occurred to me that I might be *her* man, *her* invention, but that was what the situation was – this slight, attractive woman with size five shoes had made me into a terrorist.

She had found a timid wretch living in a dank, dark hole. He had skin like a baby and pearly inoffensive eyes, but while he slept she had transformed him into something potent – still ugly, yes, but venomous, a spider in the dark of the Voorstandish subconscious.

She had not meant me harm. She had not meant me anything. She wanted something for herself and I was a member of a pro-scribed group. She therefore falsified three fax IDs to 'prove' that I, Tristan Smith, was a terrorist in touch with Mohammedan cells inside Voorstand. If it had not been for this, she would have been sent back to her grey metal desk in POLIT. She felt she had no choice but to go forward – she linked me with Zawba'a* and now she was an operative accompanying a terrorist to a possible meeting with other terrorists.

She connected me with Zawba'a because she had translated their

* *Arabic: lit., whirlwind.*

manifesto and knew they had connections inside Voorstand. She was a beginner, an ice-skater. She only had access to level 7 information, and therefore had no idea that Zawba'a were currently under intense scrutiny from the VIA.

There were eight other cells she could have chosen, and all of them would have left her stranded back in the dusty tedium of POLIT. But she chose the one group which had all of Operations suddenly dedicating themselves to her.

They had only one anxiety – not that she had faked some fax numbers, but that she was inexperienced and would therefore make them look bad with their opposite numbers in Voorstand. They took her to their bosoms. They coaxed her, cradled her, pushed her. They had her doing crunches and push-ups. They gave her intensive weapons training, then halted it when they found her attempting Sirkus tricks with her fifteen-shot semi-automatic Glock.

'What happens if someone shoots at me?'

'Believe me, Jacqui, you're safer without a gun.'

They took back the handsome Glock and spent the last week teaching her how to talk to the VIA. At this, she excelled. When she boarded the *John Kay* she was a candidate well-prepared for examination.

I was the centre of her fiction. Yet as we travelled down the El 695 with Bruder Mouse, I was as unaware of all this as I was unaware of the honey-coloured breasts beneath her three poplin shirts. I was the baby, the mark, the monkey. I fretted about the stinking Simi, money, privacy, the revulsion I might occasion at a gas stop, the humiliation of eating in the public gaze. Panic flitted like a bat across the periphery of my consciousness as we journeyed deeper and deeper into Voorstand. I had no idea of the risk my sleeping nurse had taken to make this trip, the cynical lies she had told to get there, or the looming consequences she had successfully obliterated from her consciousness.

## 18

When Jacqui woke it was evening and the shadows were long and the colours soft and the highway was sweeping around the edges of one more lake. When she opened her eyes she saw, in the mirror,

Leona's yellow bloodshot eyes looking straight at her.

It was only then the possibility occurred to her.

Could Leona be the operative she had expected to meet in Saarlim?

Whatever Leona had said when she had emerged from the tunnel, Jacqui had not really paid attention. She had not expected the operative until Saarlim. Perhaps Leona said the ID line and Jacqui had not heard.

Now, twelve hours later, Jacqui recited her ID tag: 'It's a nice night.'

And Leona said her line: 'Nice night to be in Saarlim City.'

'How many miles is it?' Jacqui said, feeling the blood rushing up her neck and flooding into her ears and cheeks.

'Tsk,' Leona said, and shook her head.

A different person might have been embarrassed. Jacqui would not be. She learned that very early at the DoS. Never show weakness. The 'meet' was meant to be in Saarlim. She stared right back at Leona and crossed her hands in her lap. *Fuck you*, she thought. This is not my fault.

I was sitting right beside her when this exchange took place. I saw the recklessness which was beginning to shine, to glow through the dull brown paint of our nurse's dutifulness. It was powerful, palpable. I felt the need to stop it.

'Throw . . . the . . . thing . . . out,' I said, and nudged her leg with my foot.

'Whatsit say?' Leona asked.

'He wants you to throw the Bruder out,' said 'Jacques', and smiled at me, not insolently. It was the look you see on monks – a calm and luminous neutrality.

'You want me to footsack Bruder Mouse, Wink?' Leona brought the car round a large banked curve and came on to a high wide bridge, below which you could see one more ribbon of highway: transports carrying their spherical gases, cylindrical liquids, bright sanserif type on their shining silver surfaces.

'I might footsack you first,' she said. She flicked on her super-charger in accordance with a highway sign. 'This here Bruder Mouse is like a Saint to us,' she said. 'He ain't just the Sirkus. He means stuff to us.'

'It . . . means . . . stuff . . . to . . . us . . . too . . . we . . . suffered . . . from . . . that stuff . . . already.'

'What does he say?'

'He'd rather not have the Bruder in the car.'

'Fuck . . . the . . . Mouse . . . fuck . . . the . . . Voorstand . . . Hegemony.'

'What's he say?'

'He . . . says . . . it . . . makes . . . him . . . sick.'

I turned to Wally, who had his bent old spine propped in the corner. 'You . . . want . . . this . . . stinky . . . thing . . . in . . . the . . . car?'

'It's their country,' Wally said, and closed his eyes, pretending that he was sleeping. 'We should respect their customs.'

Jacqui crossed the Simi's arms across its chest, and gently pushed down on its snout and up on its chin, so just the faintest trace of white tooth was protruding.

'"One mo nothing,"' she recited, '"next mo – there he was, buttons gleaming, came lupping, us solid as a yellow oak on a Tuesday morning."'


## 19

To be driven across the El 695 gave me a feeling in my stomach that was almost unbearable.

The thing was – the El 695 would not stop. It curved, looped, but it kept on rolling, now three lanes, now five, now one lane of congestion and construction, but it did not stop. In Efica, you could not drive far without coming to the sea. Even on a large island like Inkerman you lived with a constant sense of limitations, the thinness of soil, the hardness of the rock, the long sail-less expanse of the Mer de Lapenise.

Voorstand, in comparison, was terrible, like being tickled relentlessly or plunging in an elevator. We were forever arriving at the *this* 'zee' and the *that* 'zee', not actual 'seas' but great lakes whose further shores were lost in summer haze – which signalled, to my Efican sensibilities, the end of the journey. Now there should be a ferry. Now a wharf. But this was Voorstand, 2000 miles from north to south, 865 lakes, 10,000 towns, 93 major cities.

I watched the edges of the road slide past my ear, endlessly, limitlessly, and, indeed, it was in these very roadside verges that I would finally begin to learn the truth about Saarlim City.

I saw the first signs of deterioration some hundred miles from our destination. At first I did not take it seriously, but soon there was no denying it – the condition of the roads got worse, consistently worse – and by the time we were embarked upon the elevated entrances to the great city the verges were cracked and weedy and littered with abandoned pieces of cars and trucks.

For you, who imagine I came to cause you harm, it may be hard to believe that I found this decay so upsetting. Why would I, a member of the January 20 Group, give a rat's fart about the state of roads in Saarlim City?

Madam, Meneer, you are part of our hearts in a way you could not dream.

It is as if you, at your mother's breast, had imbibed the Koran, the Kabuki, and made them both your own. We grow up with your foreignness deep inside our souls, knowing the Bruder clowns, the Bruder tales, the stories of the Saints, the history (defeating the Dutch, tricking the British, humiliating the French, all this gets you big marks in the islands of Efica). We recite your epic poets for the same reason we study Molière or Shakespeare, listen to your Pow-pow music as we fall in love, fly your fragrant peaches halfway across the earth and sit at table with their perfect juices running down our foreign chins.

We have danced to you, cried with you, and even when we write our manifestos against you, even when we beg you please to leave our lives alone, we admire you, not just because we have woven your music into our love affairs and wedding feasts, not just for what we imagine you are, but for what you once were – for the impossible idealism of your Settlers Free who would not eat God's Creatures, who wanted to include even mice and sparrows in their Christianity.

As we Ootlanders approached the legendary capital of Saarlim on the crumbling El 695, we each, silently, privately, recalled the story of the farmyard Bruders coming to the city, the *Hymn of Pietr Groot*, the suicides of the captains of the first great insurrection. Yet just as your history came to inspire me, I was depressed to see the cracks, the weeds, the litter of radiator hoses, broken glass and rusted mufflers.

'They . . . should . . . sweep . . . up,' I said.

No one translated for Leona.

The cars around us on the road were not like the ones I had seen with starburst reflections on their chrome work in the zines. They were old, rusting, crumpled, belching blue smoke, dropping black oil. I had imagined that my own country was backward, provincial, but we would not have tolerated this in Efica. Cars that would have been dragged off the highway by the Gardiacivil – cars with rusted body panels, broken headlights – were permitted to cruise beside us unmolested by the Saarlim Police who moved through the junk-heap traffic in cars bristling with computers and satellite dishes, their roof lights perpetually flashing.

Yet the more extreme the neglect became, the more Jacques liked it. As we came closer to Saarlim, his colour rose, he began to beat his feet on the floor. He sat on the edge of his seat, one hand resting on the Simi's shoulder. The Simi stank of smoke, of melting plastic, of damp fur, of old rags left too long in a bucket. Broken wires stuck out from its elbow – probably infectious. It made me ill to look at it, made me weak in the arms and legs – insufficient oxygen, the early-warning sign of phobia.

Leona drove us into leaking tunnels, under rusting bridges. All around us were grim brick buildings, some with windows, some merely with broken glass, and where the glass was not broken it was dirty. In Chemin Rouge we like to keep things clean. In Chemin Rouge we do not throw our garbage out on the public highway. Saarlim City was littered with abandoned papers, cans, bottles, cars, mattresses, stuffed furniture.

'We're going to do just fine,' Wally said. But the old bird had a tired, strained look. He ran his hand over his bony head. 'This is going to be my kind of town.'

But we had no money and the light was tired, yellow, poisonous. We crossed a long high rattling metal bridge across grassy marshlands in which one could make out the rainbow-slick of chemicals. Through the yellow mist we saw tall buildings clustering on the horizon. It was the fabled city, but I would have given anything to be back inside the mouldy safety of the Ducrow Circus School.

Leona swung the wheel, hit the horn, braked, accelerated, cursed, and then, hitting the current as it were, accelerated along a long avenue, weaving in and out of the traffic, bicyclists, reversing rollerskaters, wheel-squirrels of every size and colour.

We Ootlanders became quiet, like chickens squashed into a metal box for market. Finally it was Wally who asked, 'Will we be near the Grand Concourse when we stop?'

'Near it?' Leona said. 'Honey, you in it.'

The Grand Concourse. The home of Sirkus. When we had planned our Sirkus Tour, I had expected a certain standard. I looked out at a grim and sweaty avenue backed by tall grey-brick apartment buildings, lined with street stalls, pawnbrokers, liquor stores, strip clubs, electronics stores. I did not know it would be like this. I knew your agents had murdered my maman, but I also knew, since always, that you Voorstanders were neat, professional. Even in the matter of that murder – it was not amateurs killed my mother.

It was through your charm and your expertise that you con-quered us, with your army, yes, and with the VIA, but you kept us conquered with jokes and dancers, death and beauty, holographs, lasers, vids, with perfectly engineered and orchestrated suspense.

If the government of Voorstand now imagines that I came to threaten it, tell me, please – where is my Mouse, my Dog, my Duck? I came with nothing, not even courage. When we got to the Grand Concourse where we would have to stand in line to get our POW cards, I did not even want to leave the air-kooled Blikk.

That's the sort of threat I was. I was too ashamed to face the public gaze. It was Jacques (our polite, attentive, self-effacing nurse) who grabbed the Mouse by its clenched white hand and yanked it out the car, and stood in the fetid air, spookily, electrically triumphant.


20

I was on the sidewalk, my back against the rear fenders of Leona's Blikk. Jacques – the person I thought of as Jacques – was three feet away, standing on top of a rusting grating.

I ordered 'him' – for I did not know how to read his tusch, his peach, his insouciant dance-hall walk – I ordered this 'him' to return the Simi to the car. I had to shout, but he heard me.

'No,' he said, like that.

There he stood – my opposite – his eyes big, electric, his cheeks flushed, his limbs kind of agitated, drumming. How handsome he looked to me, how strong, well-formed. How I envied him, admired him, and – when he picked up this Cyborg, this Simi, this

294

dead rat, and stood there holding it around its neck, tapping his foot – how I feared the consequences of his will.

Ticket scalpers, smelling blood, milled round us with their stiff cardboard tickets – pink, green, silver – displayed like feathers on their long split sticks. I was defenceless: a snail without a shell.

It was like the Zeelung border, but this time the whole food chain was alerted to our weakness – Burmese boys with fireworks to sell, beggars with rattling cups, pickpocket gangs with sheets of cardboard, and lice eggs under their nails – and there was all this damn press upon us, and whether I was not seen and trampled, or seen and reviled, one thing was as bad as the other.

I turned to Wally for help, only to discover that he too was lost to me: standing there with his mouth open, staring up at a neon sign. '*The Gyro Sirkus*', the sign said. '*Who will die tonight?*'

Me. Me. I will die tonight. The air was rank, sweaty, so loud with the noises of sirens and klaxons that my bones vibrated.

I said, 'Make . . . him . . . stop.'

Stop what? I did not say. Hardly knew.

'Mollo mollo,' Wally said. He was in a dream. He had his hands resting on his lower back, and he was leaning forward, staring at those stained and sweating Sirkus Domes – the subject of 10,000 Ph.Ds, the celebrated meeting of the Sacred and Profane, the High and Low, the New and Old, the Dutch and English. How tacky they looked, how tawdry.

I turned from Wally back to Jacques. His upturned little nose was peeling, his small flat ears were red, his large brown eyes were alive, almost hyper-thyroid, with defiance and excitement. I did not know if he was male or female. He held that Simi. He clutched it, holding it like raw meat in shark waters.

'Put . . . the . . . rat . . . back . . . now.'

Jacques smiled at me and buttoned his jacket.

Above his head, tied to the balconies of a stained concrete apartment building, was a flapping canvas sign: '18th INFANTRY. PRISONERS OF WAR.'

Leona was trying to unfold my wheelchair. Jacques was now holding the Mouse underneath its arms and pretending to make it walk. You see the problem – our nurse was a Voorwacker, a fan, a follower of the Sirkus and all its trivia. This was why he was here. This was his trip and this was what he wanted – Sirkuses, ancient crucifixes, early editions from the Badberg Press. He loved your country, Madam, Meneer, he loved you half to death.

He looked my way, cheeks flushed, eyes bright, defiant in his public passion. Then he turned his back and made off through the crowd. He was going to stand on the line, the line we had come to stand in. BUT NO ONE HAD TOLD ME THAT. I knew only that I would not permit myself to be disobeyed by an employee. I walked, as I had previously only walked inside the long dark hallways of the Feu Follet, with my disabilities raw and undisguised. I rolled side to side like a comic-strip sailor. Anyone could see that I was three foot six inches tall, bandy-legged, club-footed, rag-faced, as I came across the grease-stained sidewalk towards Jacques, lacerating the skin on my 'ankles', feeling the pain only as you hear a telephone ringing in another room. I was not in control – I was already shouting.

I was like a machine, a thing with a light flashing on its roof. The crowds which had scared me now parted before me. And even the queue of would-be POWs – Chinese, Malays, Afghans, Indians (no one Flemish, no one white like the crowds in the vids and zines) – whilst remaining locked fearfully in its proper order, flexed and shifted like a tail threatened with a red-hot poker.

I came straight at Jacques and grabbed at the Cyborg. The Mouse – designed so no adult male could ever fit inside it – was my height.* I got its round black nose and tried to pull it from its captor. The nose was hard and black and dense and weirdly cold.

'You . . . shit . . . snot . . . fucking . . . fool.'

Jacques held the Mouse with both his arms. I tugged at the nose, but it would not tear away.

'I'll . . . rip . . . your . . . throat . . . out.'

Jacques looked down at me. I saw a spark there. Something. I did not know what it meant.

'Throw . . . that . . . thing . . . AWAY . . . NOW . . .'

---

* 'The aforesaid Simulacrum design is approved for manufacture as a free agent WITH THE PROVISO that no model, whether working model, prototype or branded product, shall exceed the height limitations contained in Codicil CXVIII, amendment 6, to-wit no variant shall exceed forty-two inches in height. Infringement of these restrictions will incur automatic suspension of Manufacturer's Licence and a fine of 10,000 Guilders.' Approval Certificate of the Opus 3a Simulacrum.

'You want to go to jail?'

It was Leona. You could never say her face was white, or even pale. But it had a still, shiny, immobile look. 'You don't ever,' she hissed, pushing the wheelchair at me so I was forced to hold it, 'make a fuss in this line. That the only rule there is. Look it. They all so quiet. They like chickens when the snake get in the roost. You stand like them. OK. How you think I going to get you captured if you make this fuss?'

That woman scared me. It was not what she said, but how she stood, the wild fire in her yellow eyes.

'We got to get you *captured*,' Leona said. 'But that a figure of speech, a way of speaking, you understand me? It paperwork. You in enough trouble I would say – no sense you push it any more.'

'OK?' Wally said.

I climbed into the chair.

The balconies of the apartment buildings above our heads were filled with white soldiers, smoking, playing cards, sitting precariously on the crumbling concrete balustrades. As I looked up I saw one of them point at us. I looked down.

'You be quiet now, Wink. Just hush, OK?'

'What . . . trouble . . . am . . . I . . . in?'

I asked the question twice but no one ever did answer it. Jacques patted at my face with a paper handkerchief. 'I'm sorry,' he said.

'If . . . you're . . . sorry . . . ditch . . . the . . . Mouse.'

'I'm really sorry,' he said, but then fitted the Simi beneath my wheelchair, under my legs, where I was spared the sight of it, if not its rancid smell.

It takes ten to fifteen hours to become a POW.* Almost all of this time you spend in line. I had a wheelchair. I went straight to sleep.

When I woke at two in the morning, an hour when the kanal fog has already rolled out across the turbulent streets, I found Wally on a sheet of cardboard, wide awake and grinning. God damn – his eyes were all creased up – he was happy to be just where he was,

---

* *The official paperwork indicates that a much longer delay was once the rule: 'Please wait at least 90 days after application before inquiring. If this form is folded at the lines in the margins, the address of the POW facility, or the address of the applicant, will show through a standard letter size (Type C1) envelope. All information should be typed or clearly printed in the English language, using ballpoint pen.' Inquiry about Status of POW 531 Form.*

sitting on the banks of a river which was flowing with small-time crime.

Not five feet from where we sat there were three pretty little spin driers with tight skirts and fuck-me heels. By the news stand there were musicos, jugglers, riveters. Between the traffic lights, on the busy street crossings, there were young gypsy pick-pockets with dark brown blameful eyes and tatty sheets of corrugated board which they pressed against the bodies of their marks.

Everything that threatened me seemed to sustain my companions.

'We'll do just fine,' the old turtle said to me. 'You just breathe, the way the doctor said. Don't worry about nothing.'

He rocked forward on his heels. He seemed to me to be like a retired footballer called down from the grandstand ready to thread fresh white laces through his dusty boots, to don the jersey with the old number sewn on the back, to climb the picket fence, to make that famous stab pass, low, spinning fast, down to the forward line.

'Forget . . . it,' I said.

'We need money.'

'Please . . . I . . . don't . . . want . . . you . . . in . . . jail.'

Wally smiled. He retied his shoelace. He relit his soggy cigarette. He squinted through the acrid smoke. He had romanced so often about his days as a facheur that now it was easy for me to imagine what he was doing: studying the form, analysing how the money moved, locating the *runners*, the *soldiers*, the *post-boxes*, the whole secret mechanisms, social and structural, of the street.

A swarm of pick-pockets began working the crowd not three feet from the queue. They were ten, twelve years old.

I saw how he looked at them, the smile on his face. I could not do the things they did, not ever – I could not duplicate their normal faces, their bitter freedom, the light, careless way they split the scene, like a firework blasting apart – brown lithe legs flying through the alarm of horns and klaxons on the Grand Concourse.

'You can't . . . run . . . like . . . that . . . please . . . leave . . . it . . . be.'

'Come on.' He touched my hair. 'Don't fret.'

'You're . . . up . . . to . . . something.'

'Sleep,' he said. 'Breathe proper.'

Finally I did sleep. When I woke up Leona, who was always

appearing and disappearing, had gone again. The Simi – this was Jacques' idea of humour – was now sitting on the sidewalk on its own sheet of cardboard. He had arranged it so it sat cross-legged, had cupped its gloved hands open in its lap, pointed its bright blind eyes so they looked upwards at the passing crowd.

And as I watched a middle-aged man in one of those tight-fitting sixteen-button suits which marks the business-gjent in Saarlim City stooped and squatted right in front of Jacques. He folded a Guilder and tucked it in the Mouse's paw.

'Where you from, Bruder?' he asked Jacques.

I looked to Wally but he was asleep with his chin on his chest.

When I looked back the business-gjent was holding the Simi's hand, his slightly wet alcoholic eye looking directly at the Simi's dysfunctional electronic one.

'Where you from?' he repeated.

'Efica,' said Jacques

The man shook his head, squinched shut his eyes. That is the paradox: we are important enough for you to bring down our government, but you have never heard of us. You could see this gjent had no damn idea where Efica was. 'You know how long it is since I saw this fellow on a Saarlim street?' he said at last. 'Ten, fifteen years. Do you know who he is?'

'One mo nothing,' Jacques said. 'Next mo there he was.'

'It was a different country then, a different country entirely,' the man said. 'Parks were safe. Streets were clean. You never saw a street like this.' He nodded towards the POWs. 'It was a different country then.'

'My friends are culture-shocked,' Jacques said. 'They never saw anything like this before.'

'And you . . . you're unshockable, huh?'

'This is a great city,' Jacques said.

'It feels a great city to you?'

'Look at all these people in this line . . . they're in love with Saarlim City. It's why they're here. They love you.' Jacques clicked his tongue. 'How about that?'

The man looked at Jacques and frowned. He dug in his pocket and dug out a fist of crumpled Guilders. He pressed them into Meneer Mouse's lifeless hand and, as the coins dropped to the sidewalk and the notes fluttered in the air, he turned and walked away into the crowd.

Jacques gathered up the money, grinning. I did not grin back, but I saw then, straight away – it was very clear to me what had to happen now.

## 21

How we got our POW papers was as follows. We came to the head of the line. I was nervous. There was a rope. A man undid the rope. We passed through: the four of us. There was a woman behind a metal desk. She had a big chest with many medals on it. She took the papers Leona gave her. She stamped them. She signed them. She then filled out forms for half an hour. She would not speak to Jacques. She looked at me, but did not react to my appearance in any way at all. She did not once speak to any of us except Leona.

When she was done with us, she sent us to another queue. This queue was inside the building with black and white tiles on the floor and peeling paint on the walls. We were in this queue for two hours thirteen minutes. At the end of this time we were taken into a room where we were given a pink slip of paper* and instructed to place our right hand, underside upwards, on a silver cuff which was set into a wooden block. A machine was then clamped across the wrist. The wrist felt hot. When the machine was removed we had a number. Mine was A034571. My maman was born in Saarlim, but this was my status – a 'Guest' number – it gave no guarantee of residency or protection of the law but it was, just the same, there for life.

## 22

Using the Guilders the business-gjent had donated to the Simi, we purchased two nights at an hotel – the Marco Polo – in one of the rougher parts of Kakdorp. The room was large, but gloomy, backing on to a wide balcony on which robed men with blue-black skin and yellow eyes – landlopers – were living.

---

* 'You have come in chains and the Republic has cast off those chains. You come defeated and the Republic grants you the spoils of the victors. You come without home and the Republic offers you shelter. You are, at all times, a guest of the Republic.' The pink slip.

They were outside. They washed their clothing there, in a pink plastic tub, and spread it out to dry on the hot concrete.

I was inside, on the floor, trying to find a place where I could begin to unpick the body of the Simulacrum.

I sat next to Jacques, so close to him that his short cuffs brushed against my wrist, his hand against my hand.

'Not there,' he said as I fiddled with the Simi's blue sequin waistcoat. 'You'll rip it.'

'Mollo . . . mollo.' I tugged at the creature's white plastic boots.

'Don't hurt it,' Jacques said. 'This is worth a fortune in Chemin Rouge.'

'Worth . . . good . . . money . . . here.'

Wally sighed loudly. I looked up to him through my sweaty white hair. He was sitting on the rumpled bed and rubbing his bare feet. He stared belligerently at the Simi which he had once, so blithely, invited into our life.

'Please,' he said, 'don't tell me you're going to be a tin-rattler.'

'If . . . we . . . don't . . . have . . . money . . . we're . . . as . . . good . . . as . . . dead.'

'For God's sake,' Wally said, 'no one needs to beg.'

'You'd . . . thieve.'

'Yes, I'd thieve, I'd con, I'd be a lever man, if it was necessary.'

'I . . . don't . . . want . . . you . . . to . . . thieve.'

'I never said I was going to thieve. I said I'd rather thieve than beg.'

'The . . . Simi . . . paid . . . for . . . this . . . room.'

'You don't need the Mouse to pay the rent.' He was trying to catch my eye and hold it. I ignored that. I held up the Mouse's grey spongy paw.

'Our . . . meal . . . ticket,' I said.

'Our Sirkus ticket, more like it.'

'Yes . . . that . . . too . . . I . . . can . . . get . . . the . . . money.'

He shook his head. 'We're not going to the Sirkus.'

'You . . . know . . . that's . . . why . . . we . . . came.'

He shook his head. 'You hate the Sirkus, Tristan.'

'We've . . . come . . . to . . . do . . . the . . . Sirkus . . . Tour.'

'Bullshit.' He was all closed down, hooded and bony – narrow eyes, shining cheeks. 'Ten fucking years,' he said to Jacques. He took some beef jerky from his back pocket and bit down on it. 'Ten fucking years the Mouse was the devil. You would think it was Bruder Mouse killed his maman. He wouldn't even let me say its fucking name.'

'The . . . Sirkus . . . is . . . for . . . you . . . It's . . . my . . . gift . . . This . . . Simi . . . is . . . going . . . to . . . finance . . . your . . . Sirkus . . . Tour.'

'Bullshit.' Wally tugged at the jerky. 'You think I'd go through all of this for some Sirkus?'

'Not . . . for . . . only . . . *one*.'

'Not for a hundred. Let's stop playing games, Rikiki. Let's just admit it, we've come to Saarlim so you can make peace with your father.'

'NO.'

'Oh yes,' Wally said, passing his hands repeatedly over his bald skull. 'It's time to say it. We've come to see Bill Millefleur. So don't give me all this crap about the Sirkus. You hate the Sirkus.'

I did not answer. I was still trying to find some stitching, a seam that would allow me to unpick the Simi's skin. My hand was shaking.

'Tristan . . . just telephone him. That's all it'll take.'

'I'm . . . going . . . to . . . make . . . money . . . and . . . I'm . . . going . . . to . . . take . . . you . . . to . . . the . . . Sirkus.'

Wally sighed. 'You can't go tin-rattling with a Mouse,' he said at last. 'You know you *hate* that thing.'

'Please,' I said.

'You think it's legal, it's not. It's just as illegal as thieving.'*

I ignored him.

'You'll get sick,' he said. 'Is that what you want? You climb inside that stinking thing, you'll catch a virus. You want doctors poking at you in a foreign country?'

He watched me as my mouth began to dribble, my head to nod. I hated how I was, how I looked, how I trembled.

'You want strangers looking at you? Is that what you really want?'

---

* *The soliciting of alms in public places is prohibited by law in the Canton of Saarlim and is punishable by a minimum sentence of six months (the first offence) and twelve months (the second). All sentences to be served in Work Camps. No remissions or reductions of sentence can apply.*

'SHUT . . . UP,' I said. The words came out of me. Without warning, hot and shameful as shit itself.

Wally passed his big dry hand thoughtfully across his mouth. Then he stood, picked up his stick, and walked towards the door.

I called to him, 'Don't . . .'

He stopped at the doorway. He had his hand across his mouth again.

'Please . . .'

'Please what?'

'Promise . . . you . . . won't . . . see . . . him.'

'Who?'

He knew. He knew exactly.

'Bill . . . Mille . . . fleur.'

'So,' he said. 'You can actually say his name.'

He walked out. I threw the Mouse aside.

'What is it?' Jacques said. 'Can I help you?'

I was trembling. I shook my head.

'It's your father? Your father is in Saarlim? Then let's go see him.' Jacques pulled the Mouse to his side. He folded its grey arm across its blue metallic chest. He stroked its fur. 'We could borrow the jon-kay from him?'

'No.'

'Why not?'

I could not tell him. But now, I see, I must tell you, Madam, Meneer. I must return to that night, that death, the single event I spend my waking hours avoiding.


## 23

Bill had not been there the night my maman died. He had been in Saarlim City, eating cheese and herring for his breakfast. I had telephoned him after Wally cut the death rope with a box cutter, after I began to hit the Bruder Mouse mask with the brick, pulverizing it against the theatre's concrete floor.

There was the smell of the shit.

There was no sequence of events.

There was Rox arriving, before the rope was cut, after the rope was cut.

Vincent had been already in the theatre, had arrived by car soon after.

Wally had a definite memory of laying my maman on the saw-dust and of Rox fetching a stainless-steel mixing bowl of soapy water. She wanted to clean my maman.

She said, 'I am a nurse.'

Rox was not a nurse.

Vincent was in a terror, circling my maman like an injured dog, fearful of blame, angry with everyone around him. He would not let Rox touch the body. Everyone remembered that. Rox and Wally discussed it afterwards, often. Rox always said, 'What was he afraid of?'

My maman's body lay in the same place they had once placed old Ducrow's remains. So much for history.

Wally remembers me talking to Bill on the telephone. Was I left alone? Wally cannot remember. He can remember thinking: Bill will soon be here.

Wally did not like Bill, but Bill was my biological father and Wally had a strong sense of what was right and wrong – he thought he must be there.

Wally can remember Vincent trying to light candles on the stage and refusing to let Rox wash her, my maman, his lover.

'Don't touch,' he said. 'You must not touch her.'

Rox tried to get me out of the building. I would not leave. Maybe it was in response to this that Vincent covered my maman's face with a green plastic garbage bag. In any case, too late, too late – none of us would forget what we had seen before the bag came down – the bared gums, the bleeding eyes.

When the garbage bag was across the face, I was present. They gathered around me. I had talked to Bill by then. Bill was maybe on his way already, flying 30,000 feet above the frozen lakes of the Canton of Saarlim. Wally steeled himself against this intrusion.

Vincent's candles were finally burning. The police arrived. They asked endless questions about the candles.

I was like an injured cat. I did not want to be held or touched. Rox and Wally circled me like a bandage, a blindfold, a blanket. They stayed with me all through the night. Other things happened – police, doctors, sedatives, statements – but they all happened after this. At five a.m., against my wishes, my maman's body was removed on a stretcher.

I rocked back and forth, pounding the now hateful Meneer

Mouse with the brick, turning the balsa wood into a feathery pulp.

Vincent sat behind me. Sometimes he put a hand on my shoulder. He was so frail and guilty, unwashed, matted, so wan and washed out in his crumpled lint- and snot-marked black suit – no one could have guessed he would be married again before two years were out.

Bill arrived late the next day, the Tuesday.

He was tall, tanned, gravure-handsome, with huge padded shoulders and pointed snakeskin shoes with silver tips on the laces. He looked like the embodiment of everything the Feu Follet had fought – your culture, your Sirkus. He opened his arms and, with tears streaming down his crumpled face, fell on his tightly trousered knees. He pressed the snotty rag of my face against the puffy shoulder of his black silk suit.

Wally remembers this.

He remembers also how he swallowed hard, how he felt grief and jealousy combine deep in the darkness of his throat. His hard freckled body woodenly resisted Bill's embrace. Yet when he said, 'I'm pleased you came, mo camarade,' he meant it sincerely.

But on the following morning, when Wally walked into his kitchen and found Bill already there – holding me balanced on his shoulders while he dredged skipjack fillets, one-handed, in a plate of flour – he was no longer pleased at all.

He looked at how I clung to my father's neck and felt usurped, injured, insulted. He stayed in the doorway, fiddling with his cigarette pack.

Bill was wearing a loose crumpled white shirt with ballooning sleeves and a big collar. 'We're going to do some acting exercises,' he told Wally. 'We'll need the theatre for the morning.'

'Sure,' he said, 'a great idea.'

After breakfast, he drank two small tumblers of brandy and cleaned up the mess Bill had left behind him.

Half an hour later he remembers looking into the theatre and finding Bill and me kneeling opposite each other on the sawdust, inside the ring. We were both weeping. Wally walked quietly through the darkened house and climbed up to the booth, and there, sitting alone and unobserved, not even smoking, he spied on us moving about the stage.

I was not his actual son, but he loved me like a son. He put me to bed each night. He checked my breathing, bathed me during my fevers, talked to me when I had bad dreams.

The big glass window of the booth framed the illuminated stage like a vid screen. He switched on the house mike.

Now Bill was asking me to 'do' different funerals. What I performed were more in the nature of revenges than funerals – stabbing and shooting. I moved around the stage like a wind-up toy, rolling, walking on my knees, spitting, shouting, crying in a high wild voice Wally never heard before.

I remember none of this. Wally saw it all. He saw Bill and me begin to move around the stage, pretending to pick things up and place them in the centre. It was some minutes before Wally understood: we were collecting Bruder Mouses for an imaginary bonfire.

After we had set the fire alight, I became a little calmer, and soon I was loudly imagining the four of us, me and the three fathers, wearing white make-up to the funeral. 'Thick,' I said, 'that . . . zinc . . . stuff . . . thick . . . like . . . mud.'

'That's beautiful,' Bill said. 'She'd like that.'

'Would . . . she . . . like . . . that?'

'She'd like that very much.'

'Could . . . we . . . do . . . that . . . in . . . real . . . life?'

'We can do what we like,' Bill said. 'Anything we like.'

'Horse-shit,' Wally said, alone, to no one, inside the booth.


## 24

Vincent was standing outside the upstairs toilet when Bill found him. He had wet hands and did not immediately take the jar of Zinc 3001 when it was proffered.

'It's *Hamlet*,' he said, patting his trouser pockets in search of a handkerchief.

'How *Hamlet*?'

'Felicity had the mourners paint their faces for Ophelia's funeral. Zinc 3001 – *Hamlet*.'

'Then it is not inappropriate for us to do the same.'

Vincent finally located a wad of tissues in his breast pocket and used this slowly to wipe his square white hands. 'The vid news will be there,' he said at last. 'They'll have vans and cables. They'll have it on the satellite.'

He threw the tissues through the open door of the toilet, lobbing them into the wastebin.

'Catch!'

He turned to see the Zinc 3001 flying at him. He had no choice but to catch it.

'I do not *want* this,' Vincent said, pushing the heavy jar of make-up at the actor who made no move to take it. 'It doesn't help to treat this funeral like a Sirkus.'

Bill's mouth tightened.

'I didn't mean that personally,' Vincent said.

'I know,' Bill said, but he hooked his thumbs in his belt and did not take the jar.

'They won't tell the real story,' Vincent said. 'They're not going to say anything about her production of *Hamlet*.'

'Vincent, this is not about the media.'

'It's *us* they'll show. The weirder you make us look, the more damage you'll do.'

'Vinny, please. Don't make this part of your election campaign.'

Vincent had lost a lover and a wife and was now in the process of losing an election. 'We'll be on the goddamn news,' he said, his pale blue eyes now full of tears.

'This is mourning,' Bill said.

'Listen to me, fuck you,' Vincent shouted, his face screwed up, the tears already flowing. His voice echoed through the stairwell, in the empty corridors. 'You don't know what's going on here. You just fly in and start to meddle. An Efican citizen has just been murdered by a foreign power. You want to mourn something, mourn that.'

Bill frowned and nodded. He took the pot of make-up from Vincent.

'You're right,' he said. 'I'm sorry.'

Any reasonable person watching this would imagine that Bill was on his way to talk to me, to tell me that our ritual was not suitable. On the morning of the funeral, however, Vincent found Bill and me and Wally in the dressing room, painting our faces with Zinc 3001.

The funeral was as Vincent knew it would be – not to do with us

307

at all. There were journalists, politicians, camera teams, demonstrators with placards accusing Voorstand of the murder.

Every soup-server and spear carrier who ever walked through the doors of the Feu Follet was there – Claire Chen, Moey Perelli, everyone you would expect – but also actors from the Efican National Theatre, soap-opera vedettes, news readers. There were known DoS spies, Gardiacivil, ambulances lined up between the narrow driveways of the old French cemetery.

Bill was the most famous mourner there, and he picked me up, his son, the white-faced beast, and carried me on the long walk through the cemetery to the Unitarian plot.

Vincent was beside himself. And even those who knew nothing of the conflict, who saw only Bill Millefleur weeping by the graveside, thought him theatrical and self-important in his grief.

Wally, however, was not amongst them. Even though he did not like Bill, even though he felt self-conscious with white make-up on his face, he also saw what I saw – that Bill Millefleur was finally determined publicly to own me.

My father had come home.

## 25

Vincent did have a strong sense of right and wrong, but he lacked the empathy which would have given his moral sense more reach and subtlety. He judged Bill's theatrical appearance at the funeral to be beyond forgiveness.

It was Wally, that violiniste and small-time thief, who forced Vincent to see through the Zinc, to see Bill's courage, to see that he was swollen with grief and guilt and wanted nothing more than another chance to be Tristan Smith's father.

But as for Bill himself, he was never so explicit, certainly not with the adults.

With me he was a little more forthcoming, but most of the important things he had to say he said sub-textually. He held me hard. He blew his nose. In the penitential stoop of his broad shoulders, in the clarity of his gaze, in all the subtle grammar of his body, he gave the clear impression that life – his life, my life – would now be different.

He was my dab now.

He had twice deserted me but now he had come back. He did not say this, but it was definitely the impression that he produced. He gave himself to me as intensely as ever he gave himself to an important role. He was dedicated. He took on the most intimate matters of my toilette. He studied. He read books about 'The Special Child'. He played guitar and encouraged me to sing. He was obsessive. He sent Wally and Roxanna off to their own room. He slept on a mattress beside me on the sawdust stage. When I woke with night terrors, he was there. Twenty-four hours a day.

He had black silk pyjamas made for me. He *acted* with me. He found me an audition piece in *Hamlet*. He inspired me. We began a preliminary reading of a two-hander by Bardwell.* He cooked delicacies he had learned in Saarlim, feather-light crepes with apricot filling, Beanbredie and so on.

I was ill, still filled with horror and grief, fearful of my own survival, anxious for protection, overcome by my father's affection, beauty, belief in my abilities.

There was nothing innocent about me. I knew I was being seduced, stolen. I was fully cognizant of the pain all of this caused Wally. I saw his grey-flecked eyes, his tired skin, his nicotine-yellow eyebrows and I knew that I was ditching him.

He had Roxanna. I had my father back. I would not be an orphan after all.

Bill mourned my maman, there is no doubt. He could not forgive himself for how he left her, for having patronized her work, blamed her for his scar. He told me he had been a snot. He said he had run away from me. He said it was time for us, the pair of us, to face the real world. And in all of this he focused on me, his beautiful features so close to me, his bright blue eyes always on my face so that I felt, in turn, transmogrified.

We took excursions out across the Boulevard des Indiennes to the downtown mall. '*This is my son, Tristan Smith.*' That is what he said, in that clear melodious actor's voice. Every time he was accosted by an autograph hound, he introduced me. '*This is Tristan Smith, my son.*' He was not thinking beyond that point. He did not think beyond his character, or think that, for me, it would be different. I

* *Jacqueline Bardwell – contemporary Efican poet, playwright, essayist, most famous as author of* A Long Way from Anywhere.

basked within his golden aura. I fell in love with him, my actor dab. I imagined our life continuing – Shakespeare, Brecht, agitprop, audiences, reviews, a life. If this was naïve, Wally was no more acute.

'He is your father,' he told me when he found me coming out of the first-floor bathroom. 'He loved your maman. If he asks you to live with him, you should feel free to go.'

Vincent had no advice at all. Day after day the vids and zines brought news of more scandals in the Blue Party as the invisible Gabe Manzini did his job of maintaining the Voorstand alliance. He manufactured evidence of crooked land deals, bribes from foreign arms dealers and aircraft manufacturers, the normal VIA menu of destabilization.

Vincent was a ghost who came and went at unpredictable hours. Once, when we were alone, he held my head against his chest and stroked my hair and wept, but he never said a word to me about Bill and he was not there in the kitchen when Bill said goodbye.

Wally was sitting at the table peeling potatoes for Sunday's evening meal. Bill, who had already prepared the apple pie, was leaning with his back against the porcelain sink. I was sitting on the counter top beside him stringing beans.

Bill began talking about letters. He talked about famous letters in history, a correspondence between Manuel Grieg and Sonia Nuttall which had been published in Saarlim the previous season. He talked about love, growth, understanding. He began to talk about the letters we could now write each other. He talked about it for some time, the ideas we could now exchange, not by speech, which is lost like drama is lost, but by putting ink on paper.

I don't know what I thought or understood but I saw the weakness in his mouth, the anxiety in his eyes. I saw Roxanna and Wally looking at me. I saw myself put down the beans. My hands began to pat-pat-pat against my narrow chest.

'Bill,' Wally said, 'what are you telling him?'

'I've got a contract in Saarlim,' Bill said. 'You know that.'

I tried to say something but the words got stuck.

My handsome dab filled himself a glass of water.

'You're . . . leaving . . . me.'

'What?'

'You're . . . going . . . to . . . make . . . the . . . Voorshits . . . laugh.'

310

Bill drained his glass and placed it in the sink. 'I'm a performer.'

'No,' I said. 'You're . . . a . . . *traitor.*'

'Don't be ridiculous,' he said.

'My . . . maman . . . knew . . . you . . . didn't . . . love . . . us.'

Bill did not have a cool temper. It took nothing to get it going. 'Shut up, Tristan. Don't say things you don't mean.'

'They . . . killed . . . her . . .'

'*They* didn't do anything.'

'They . . . did . . . you . . . did.' I was beside myself, four feet off the floor. I jumped. I fell. I hit my nose. I punched his great hard thighs, pinched, thumped.

He jumped away. I grabbed his cuffs.

'Stop,' he said, trying to shake me off his leg. 'Stop now.' But he was guilty, angry. He picked me up and held me out to Wally.

'I'll speak to you later,' he said, his face crimson. 'After you have apologized.'

It took perhaps three seconds to pronounce this ultimatum. I watched it happen. I watched, like you watch a glass falling to the floor.

When my father's car left for the airport, at seven o'clock the following morning, nothing had been mended.

He left me behind in a client state that made itself the servant of your country's wishes. His letters arrived. Even their stamps were repugnant to me – their folk-art imagery, their clear-eyed Settlers Free.

Thus I lived fatherless through that shameful period of Efica's history as armies of our conscripts were raised to fight Voorstand's war in Burma and Nepal. I saw the great Efican health-care system weakened and demolished at the insistence of Voorstand's bankers. I saw the Sirkus Domes spread across our little islands and the Bruders appear to spread their stories, your stories, not ours, in every corner of my nation's life.


## 26

While Jacques and I fiddled with the Simi inside the Marco Polo Hotel, that secretive, stubborn old man with the shining skull set out to do the thing he had been intent on doing ever since we first discussed the Sirkus Tour.

He came down to the foyer and there, in a varnished vestibule beside the bell captain's desk, he spent five minutes peering up at a framed map of Saarlim City. He took a sheet of paper from his pocket and, leaning the paper against the yellowed map, made some careful notes. Then, with the paper still in his hand, he walked carefully across the stained and slippery marble floor to the revolving door.

Half a second later he was in a dark, hot, smelly, bustling street – the Jean Pitz Colonnade. Bicyclists and other wheel-squirrels sped through the crowds blowing shrill whistles, shouting warnings of their approach. Beggars sat against the dark distempered back walls rattling their cups.

If you are from Saarlim, this is life. If you are from Efica, it is terrifying. The old man was spun around like a paper cup dropped in a river. Twice he was bumped, three times abused. Then, as he turned to raise his finger to a stranger, he was bowled right over by a pair of Misdaad Boys and he felt, as he fell, their flickering fingers enter and retreat from four of his pockets – his three Guilders were gone.

He retreated to the musty air-conditioned chill of the Marco Polo where he sat for a very long time doing nothing more than nursing his bruises and watching the guests come and go. Soon, however, he began to tap his shoe, and then he thumped his cane twice on the marble floor, and stood. Then he set off into the Jean Pitz again. This time he stayed close to the outer rail and as he went he muttered and tapped his Efican oak stick. He was beetle-browed, vulture-necked, and although he felt a total Ootlander, he became without knowing it one of those belligerent street characters that Saarlimites know to leave alone.

Five blocks later he was through the Kakdorp. He crossed the small gilt bridge into the Bleskran and here, where the walls of the buildings were clad in marble and granite, his style could be more civilized. Now he paused to look in shops whose bevelled glass windows held expensive items of gold and silk. He crossed the colonnade so he could look down on the long sleek-hulled boats of the Bleskran Kanal, and then he wandered up Shutter Steeg to look at No. 35, the narrow Gothic house my maman had lived in until her seventeenth year. Then he followed Shutter Steeg back up to the top of the Bleskran where, at the point where Bleskran ends and

Demos Platz begins, he came to a tall wrought-iron screen stretching right across the colonnade like something in a Catholic church.

Here he stood, running a white handkerchief over that slightly dented bony skull, wishing he had changed his clothes. Through the grille he could make out the long mosaic title of the building which he knew was his destination. The letters ran in pink and gold from the top floor vertically to the canal: 'The Baan'. The 'B' was topped with a small gold crown. And after the 'n' were a pair of crossed sceptres.

'Jo, Bruder!'

Wally made no attempt to disguise the distaste he felt for the security guard who thus addressed him – the belly protruding above the belt, the rolled-up zine in the back pocket. 'I'm looking for this number.' He produced a crumpled postcard which he read with some little difficulty. '247 Demos Platz.'

'OK, you looked.'

Wally began to walk towards the gate. The guard then put a meaty hand on his stooped shoulder and, as he did so, pulled a walkie-talkie from his belt.

'Move, Bruder.'

'*You* move, mo-ami,' Wally said, stepping forward, pushing his neck forward and scowling.

The guard drew the night stick and held it in both hands, as if he intended to crush it into Wally's windpipe.

'For Christ's sake' – Wally held up his hands – 'all I'm doing is *visiting*.'

'Move.'

'Read,' Wally said, pushing the postcard at the guard. 'His name is Bill Millefleur. He's asking me to visit.'

'Footsack,' the guard said. 'Scat. Shoo-fly.'

'Footsack bullshit,' Wally said, but he saw it would not matter what he said. He turned on his heels, humiliated.

He came into the dingy hotel room with all his failure and embarrassment sheathed in anger. When he discovered that Jacques and I had progressed no further with our plan than to pick open the outer skin of the Simi, he exploded.

'Can't anyone do anything?' he said. 'Here. Give it to me.'

'No, no,' Jacques said. 'Just lie down. I'll run the bath.'

All I could see was that he had no money and was angry. He

snatched the Simi from our grasp and pulled his traveller's jack-knife from his pocket.

'Please,' I yelled. 'Be careful.'

'Don't hurt it,' Jacques said. 'Please, Mr Paccione. We haven't cut it because it's so easy to damage it. It's valuable . . .'

Wally ignored us both. First he used the big blade, cutting through the wire-reinforced rubber in a two-foot long slit. He put his hand inside and found the 'core' – a pink glutinous substance in a plastic sac.

'Oh God,' said Jacques.

The core was joined to the rib frame by six or so small plastic tendons. He snipped these with the jackknife scissors and flipped the sac out on to the floor where it lay like an enlarged liver, quivering on the blue and green striped carpet. Next he began cutting away at the thin plastic connections between the computer cradle and the wire-reinforced body. Where the servo-motor made its connections with the web of wire embedded in its rubberized inner skin, he used his pliers, cutting each wire as close as possible, feeling with his big fat thumb.

First his temper invigorated him, and then his pride in his expertise began to soothe him, and when it was finally done, and he had removed sacs of pink stuff from the head, and the articulated plastic rods from the legs, he tidied up the mess he had made, bundling everything into the trash can. He lay on the bed and let the pillows take the weight of his ruined spine.

'There,' he said. He felt better, more like himself. 'That's how you do it.'

Jacques, having just witnessed the butchering of his precious souvenir, was pale and ill-looking. I did not notice. I was too busy strapping wads of toilet paper to the side of my ankles. When that was done I stripped down to my underpants and lay down on top of the Mouse so my privately devastated nurse could fit me inside it. Then I rolled on my stomach while Jacques fiddled around with a needle and thread.

When I stood, I was already my new character.

BRUDER MOUSE stepped forward, bowed, moved to one side. I was quirky, quick, bow-legged, a little too weird to be a legitimate descendant of the Free Franciscan Church, but I held out my arms to Jacques, silently asking if he might like to dance.

## 27

Jacqui's precious Simi was now as boneless as a fish fillet, its insides reduced to pink gunk like the inside of an old-style golfball. In place of all this cyber-junk dwelt I, yours truly, Tristan Smith.

Jacqui had valued that Simi like you yourself might value your Delft, your Doulton, and you might reasonably expect her to be devastated by its evisceration, but Jacqui was an artist on a slack rope* and she did not have time to stop to pick up broken pieces. She was in Saarlim, undercover, and the very thought of this extraordinary fact was enough to bring back the glow to her skin, the brightness to her long-lashed eyes. *She did not know what would happen next.*

She grasped my hand – not mine exactly, but the gloved hand of the limping bow-legged Mouse, which looked like a creation of the laser board, twisted, exaggerated, but rolling, lurching, both comic and benign.

We stepped out together, two actors, both did our respective *walks* down the hotel hallway, through the stained marble foyer, deep in our respective characters.

Ahead of her she saw the deskmajoor. He was tall but pudgy, not like an operative, but Leona had not looked like an operative cither, and the cops on the street did not look like Gardiacivil. Any moment she could be contacted, perhaps by this very man. He was coming her way, and if this was the guy she was ready for him. She inhaled the foreign air in the Marco Polo foyer as greedily as she had earlier inhaled the diesel and coal smoke of the Grand Concourse.

The deskmajoor had a pencil-line moustache. He had big pouches beneath his tearful bloodshot eyes. Now he arranged the stained and dishevelled items of his dun-coloured costume and shuffled across towards us, plunging his hand into his trouser pocket.

Jacqui readied herself, slitted her eyes, made her face expressionless.

---

* *There is no 'death rope' in either our circus or our vocabulary, although we are aware of the uses of the dramatic presentation of the slack rope in the Voorstand Sirkus.* [TS]

'Here, Bruder,' the deskmajoor said, holding out a piece of folded paper.

Jacqui reached to take the paper.

The deskmajoor tugged it away from her.

'No,' he said. He had a crumpled smile on his badly shaved face. He was a poor man, his collar frayed, his skin dry and powdering. 'For Bruder Mouse.'

'It's a good day to go to Saarlim,' Jacqui said.

The deskmajoor frowned.

'It's for *me*,' Jacqui insisted.

'Bruder *Mouse*, bubsuck!' the deskmajoor said, his eyes narrowing, his lip curling. 'Meneer Mouse, OK?' And he passed the message – for that is what she thought it was – into the Mouse's open palm. She watched with alarm as the white-gloved hands unfolded . . . a violet 50-Guilder note.

So the deskmajoor was a *fan*. He bowed to the *Mouse*, in the middle of the foyer. It was ludicrous from an Efican perspective – the respect. No Efican would act like that to anyone.

Jacqui looked at me, but I was gone, submerged, consumed by Bruder Mouse, and she, who knew, intimately, what the Mouse was like beneath its nylon fur, suddenly could not see her wild white-eyed employer. She knew I was there, but it was like knowing that there is a colon, a lung, a brain beneath the human skin – you don't respond to the squishy viscera but to the externals. Likewise, the appearance of alert intelligence, the silence, the mystery, the lack of communication, the absolute Mouse-ness of her companion was so convincing that it was impossible to remember that I wore toilet paper padding on my misshapen feet.

Now I spoke, not words, not my normal voice – a high-pitched squeak. I saw her pick it up, the flash in her bright eye. She was already off and away – high on the weirdness of it, the absolute foreignness of it.

'He thanks you,' Jacqui told the deskmajoor, straight-faced. 'He is touched by your gift,' she said. She was, typically, on the brink of taking it too far.

The deskmajoor opened the door for us, clicking his heels.

Jacqui clicked her heels in return. She would have done more, but I dragged her out on to the Jean Pitz and there we stood, each of us in our costume, together on the sidewalk.

In the midst of the noise, of the heat, the diesel, urine, construction dust, the roaring of the traffic on the Helmstraat down below, we were not immediately noticed.

Two minutes later there were people pressed against us so tight Jacqui could feel the buttons of their shirts digging into her arms and smell the garlic or asafoetida or cardamom on their skin. It was alien, like nothing she had ever seen – blue-black hands, café-au-lait, golden brown, fluorescent Pow-pow ID's stamped across the wrists, reaching out to rub the Mouse's nose with their own. These were not descendants of the Hollandse Maagd, the heretics of the Free Franciscan Church. They were not engineers, masters of earthworks, citizens with their 'one good Bruder cow'. They were here, like Jacqui was here, by choice, by their will. They stretched their hands out towards the Mouse as if it would bless them with Sirkus jobs, parkside apartments, topsoil ten feet thick, and the Mouse – to Jacqui's astonishment – struck poses, rolled, tumbled, held its hands across its mouth in a giggle.

Before this moment she did not know I was my father's son. She never saw me roll. She never saw me tumble.

'Stay by me,' she shouted. She was worried that her voice was female, no one in the crowd was interested in her. They elbowed her in the throat, stood on her toes. It was Bruder Mouse they wanted.

They picked me up and held me in the air making a collective noise, a sort of sighing.

They were devotees, worshippers. They wanted to eat Bruder Mouse, to fuck him, smother him. 'Keep back,' she called. 'Keep back from him.'

But I was not frightened. How could I be? The pathetic creature who had skulked inside the Feu Follet was now the object of these people's love. I kicked my legs, a laser figure walking off a cliff.

While Jacqui had been prepared to use me, she was not prepared to have me killed. She got her arms around my neck and, in her efforts to save my life, damn near throttled me herself.

I squeaked, loudly.

'Stop it,' she shouted at me.

Stop what? She did not say, but such was the intensity of our

317

'moment' – theatre people will understand this – the crowd quietened. They watched: how I turned; her bright eyes. They felt our electricity.

I could have used that moment to walk away, but when I saw how my nurse had changed towards me, how all that energy, bravado, that life in her eyes was distilled, focused, now beamed at me, I walked toward it, sucked it into me.

There was a woman in the crowd with oranges in her blue string bag. I held out my hands for the oranges. I said nothing, but my admirers made a circle. I was the Oncle, the Bruder, the Meneer. As I received each orange I held it in the air.

This show I began for 'Jacques'.

First: 'showering' – the simplest action for a juggler.

I switched to 'cascading', and soon I had all eight oranges crisscrossing in the air. This was a Sirkus town. They knew what I was doing. Guilders fell like leaves in autumn. The crowd was like rough water and she had no choice but to let herself be carried by it, bumping along the street like an aluminium canoe over a rocky stream, and when, twenty minutes after leaving the foyer of the Marco Polo, she found us pressed together, tumbling through the doorway of the Chop House, it was not through her own design or mine. One minute we were in the tumult of the colonnade, the next we were dumped inside the dark, stale-smelling room and a waiter, a Euro with pale skin, was clicking his tongue and shutting the door against the crowd.

Her first thought was: is he VIA?

# 28

I tumbled into the restaurant with an orange still in my hand. My admirers were banging at the door. For you, maybe, this is normal. You are a Sirkus star, perhaps, or a death-walker. But imagine Tristan, Meneer, Madam – imagine his feelings as he witnessed the passion of his new admirers.

Jacqui had me by the hand. 'Oh my God, mo-frere. You were amazing.'

She was alight. Her big brown eyes were wide, her lashes long. I should have seen it then: she was a woman. Sure, she walked that walk with the imaginary porpoise between her legs, but even as she did the walk, she unintentionally subverted it. She took a handkerchief from her pocket and *patted* the perspiration from her lip.

She was a woman.

But I was hot, tired, disoriented. The restaurant smelt of smoke and fat and stale liquor. There were red leather booths and caricatures of actors on the walls. My admirers began to tap with coins against the glass.

'Where did you learn that stuff?' she asked.

The booths were empty. The clock behind the bar said ten past five. It was 23 September in the year 394 by the Efican Calendar. If what had happened was all that would happen, it would have been a busy day. But more, I'm sorry, was about to come.

We followed the waiter's fat round arse between the booths. I was in pain, naturally. My head could not turn easily. Also: my eye-holes were poorly placed and my vision was limited. At first I could only see that our rescuer had a white shirt, black trousers, that he was short, bustling, energetic. Then I climbed into the booth and I got my first good look at the guy's fiz: very Hollandish – a white, downy kind of face, smooth and soapy, although, for all its softness, there was also a grittiness there, a big-city hardness in his small yellow-brown eyes.

'It's a nice night to go to Saarlim,' Jacqui said.

'What?'

'A nice night,' Jacqui said, 'to go to Saarlim.'

'Don't turn crazy on me,' the waiter said. 'Pray God don't do that.' And he stared at my nurse, like you stare at something unstable that might yet topple over.

Jacqui blushed and buttoned up her jacket.

'Just don't,' the waiter said. And then he turned his back and walked through a swinging door to the kitchen.

'Christ, mo-ami,' my nurse said. 'Who taught you to juggle? You were amazing.'

I tilted my head, cocked my Mouse's ear – comic, tray amusant – she smiled at me.

'It was your mother? Felicity Smith, right?'

I was surprised to hear my nurse say Mother's name, but before I could think about this the kitchen door swung open and the waiter was walking quickly towards us on the heels of his dainty pointy-toed black shoes.

'Cyborgs and Pow-pows in the one day.' With one hand he mopped the wooden table top, in the other he held a big bowl of Beanbredie which he now placed on the table, but not in front of me.

'You want to eat?' my nurse asked me. 'You want me to unstitch you?'

I shook my head.

'You want to go back to the hotel?'

I shook my head.

'Very cute,' the waiter said to Jacqui. 'You're some gjent. Some damn gjent.' The waiter rolled his intense little eyes and folded his arms. 'That's some accent . . . you know that?'

'I'm from Efica.' Jacqui looked up, her lips shiny from the Bean-bredie. 'Everyone talks like this in Chemin Rouge.'

'But why in the name of God' – the waiter jerked his small blond head towards me – 'are you messing with this fire risk? Christ save me, Bruder. You were talking to a Cyborg, a Simi.'

I scratched my head, which is, as you know, a standard comic gesture for Bruder Mouse. The waiter could not see me, but I made my nurse smile.

'It's not so funny.' The waiter was so close to me I could smell his odeklonje and see the pores in his soft and sexless skin as he leant across the table towards my nurse. 'You buy this old Cyborg, maybe someone took advantage of what you did not know. You're an Ootlander.'

'Actually, Bruder, this one is not a machine,' my nurse said. 'I think we should let him get a drink. He's just done an incredible performance.'

'Hey,' the waiter said. 'It's me. I'm not some Pow-pow you're scamming in the street. I'm not some nigger from Nigeria.'

'This is not a scam. Hell, Bruder,' Jacqui coughed deep in the back of her throat, 'there's really someone inside.'

'Is that what they told you?'

Jacqui coughed again. 'No one told me, Bruder. This is no shit. There's a little person in this suit.'

'Bruder,' said the waiter, 'I'm sorry to be the one to tell you, but what they sold you is a Cyborg. It is not a person, it is a machine.

320

You may not have them in Chemin fucking Rouge, but we have them here.'

The waiter was looking away from me. I could therefore put my nose close to his ear without him noticing. This made my nurse smile.

'Listen, bubsuck,' the waiter said. 'It does not behove you to smirk at me. This is not some little sticksville country with a picture of a fucking fish on its flag.* This is Voorstand. I am *from* Voorstand. I am telling you something you want to know, minebroo. This Mouse you have presumably purchased is what we call a klootsac, a balls-up. The original Sirkus Mouse was like six foot tall. You see these early Bruders in the paintings. Dogs, Ducks, Mice, all as big as football players. In the beginning, of course, it was very religious. All God's creatures, all that sort of thing. Maybe they was priests at one time but as long as I remember they were krakers, swartzers, thieves of one sort or another. Those Bruders did some awful stuff – murder, rape, terrible things. So now we have Creature Control Act† – no Bruder in a public place can be over three foot six inches. And so there are none.'

'This is one.'

'This is a Cyborg, I told you. They made it three foot six so no adult male could fit inside.'

'Maybe it's a small person.'

'I'm sorry, Bruder,' the waiter said, his tone now more gentle. 'I'm sorry you spent your money, but I recognize this little fuck. It's an Opus 3a Cyborg. They made a thousand of them.'

'A thousand.' Jacques winked at me. 'Good heavens.'

'I don't know the numbers,' he said irritably. 'They made a lot. They made hundreds of them, and everything was fine, for about a week, and then they started to catch on fire. There were Cyborgs

---

* A reference to the Republic of Morea.
† 'It being hereby stated, in amendment to Codicil CXVIII, that it is an offence against the laws of the state of Voorstand and the Free Franciscan Church, for any adult male or female to assume the costume or to impersonate in any way God's Creatures as defined in Codicil III and further this amendment shall apply to those Creatures of the Saarlim Sirkus Corporation including Bruder Mouse, Phantome Drool ©, Busker Bear ©, in which case Manufacture shall be deemed to be, for the purpose of this law, an act of Impersonation EXCEPTING those Simulacrum or Cyborg facsimiles of the aforesaid God's Creatures whose maximum height is less than forty-two inches.'

running around Kakdorp, in flames. Or they got run over in the traffic. You'd see them on the news at night, some dumb crazy Dog walking out along some ditch, lost in space. So this here creature, Bruder, no matter what you paid for it – take it, sell it to a museum, someone off the plane from Chemin Rouge. And don't go hanging round the streets with Pow-pows. These are primitive people. They don't know how to take a kak in a bathroom. They steal. They carry firearms. They have diseases.'

'Oh, I don't think so.'

The waiter's face was very red and angry by now.

'Listen, I know so, Bruder. I know who you are.'

Jacqui began to blush. She looked at me, and looked quickly away.

'I'm watching out for you,' the waiter said.

'OK, I get it.' Jacques was *scarlet.*

I was thinking: *What is going on here?*

'You don't get anything,' the waiter said. 'You're taking all sorts of risks you don't even know about. I cannot let you continue. If you weren't a trannie I would not care, but I am. I live here. I know how ugly it can be.'

I did not know what a trannie was. Jacqui did not either. The fact was obviously showing on her face for our host now reached across and took my nurse's hand and placed it inside his own white waiter's jacket.

'Be careful,' the waiter said. 'This is a big city. Women like us get raped and murdered every day.'

Jacqui was looking at me, her mouth open.

'I'm sorry,' she said. She picked me up. She took my weight, all sixty-five pounds, and hefted me over her shoulder.

'I'm sorry,' she said. 'You've been kind.'

I put my hand over her shoulder. I was wearing my gloves, but I brushed it 'accidentally' – her breast, no question – 23 September 394 by the Efican Calendar.


## 29

Do children decide how they are going to grow? Jacqui always believed she had decided, that she had stood on the veranda of her home and made the choice.

She had watched her mother (standing with her arms folded across her chest, making small disapproving exhalations – *Phhh, sssht*) and decided – against all the strong physical evidence to the contrary – that she would rather die than be like her.

It was Christmas Day in the year 380 and Jacqui Lorraine was nine years old. Her mother was on the veranda with the tape recorder, watching her husband and his friend Oliver Odettes, a science teacher with a red face and a large black moustache, shovelling snow across the small front lawn. The tattered leaves of the banana trees flapped in the warm wind. The trunk of the twenty-foot high papaya rubbed against the water tank. Beyond the small privet hedge, the neighbours watched – not just adults, but babies with spilled snow melting in their puckered mouths, squirming boys with snow down their shirts, silent teenagers with their hurt and hostile eyes.

In a moment Oliver Odettes would put down his shovel and walk under the veranda to fetch Jesse Lorraine's chair. He would place his chair in the middle of the snow. This would not be the first time this had happened.

'Incredible,' Rene Lorraine said, as her husband leaned his shovel against the privet hedge. 'Ssst.' As if it were all new, as if it were not like this every Christmas, always exactly the same, starting on Christmas Eve when Jacqui's father would borrow a refrigerated truck and then, with a loaf of bread, a blood sausage, and two bottles of roteuse sitting in a cardboard box on the seat between them, drive with Oliver Odettes to the peak of Mount Cootreksea, 10,000 feet and 200 miles from the palm trees of Chemin Rouge, and there they would spend two hours sipping wine, admiring the light, and shovelling snow into the truck.

They always left at eleven o'clock at night and they always turned the corner of the street at exactly eight in the morning. Then they would open the wire chain gates and back the refrigerated van up the twin concrete tracks and – with all the neighbourhood children crowding the street – shovel the snow over the pocket-handkerchief size lawn at the front of Jacqui's house.

The two friends had done it so often – from the year Jacqui was three – and they took (perhaps excessive) pride in knowing exactly how much snow it took to cover the grass, right down to the 'glace', those last six shovelfuls of snow which Oliver Odettes would fastidiously heap along the privet hedge while Jacqui's father went to fetch his books.

Rene Lorraine did not like Oliver Odettes, whom she referred to, in her daughter's hearing, as a riveter and a chochotte. Oliver Odettes wore very short shorts and fur-lined boots, always the same pair, for the snow. Every year it was the same. Rene would stand with her tanned arms folded across her breasts and an expression, always the same expression, a mixture of incredulity and outrage, on her broad handsome face, and watch the science teacher tiptoe across the white lawn, as ugly as a drag queen. Each time she shook her head as if she would have nothing to do with so ridiculous a spectacle, and each time she played her part: she pushed the play button on the tape player and turned up the volume so that the kids back on the other side of the hedge could hear the sleigh bells.

When the sleigh bell introduction had played for thirty seconds, she stood and pushed the 'stop' button.

Then her elderly, shambling, increasingly bear-like husband – he was seventy-six the year Jacqui turned nine – would shuffle out from his tiny 'library' beneath the veranda steps and sit on the ridiculously small chrome and vinyl chair which Oliver Odettes had placed in the middle of the lawn; and each year the corrugations on Rene's forehead would deepen and complicate a little more.

Each year Jesse Lorraine would sit on the chair and acknowledge his wife and daughter and the neighbours. He would push his freshly opened bottle of roteuse down into the already melting snow, tuck the tartan rug around his shining shapely brown legs, and open the first of the books in his lap.

Then in an educated voice that did not belong in that street full of liver-brick bungalows, back-yard hen houses, and wheel-less Peugeots quietly rusting underneath the bougainvillaea, a voice which the tense woman on the veranda had fallen in love with, he would read the neighbours stories about snow, different ones each year.

The year Jacqui was nine, Jesse Lorraine sat in the middle of his sixty-four square feet of snow and, wetting his dry throat with a little roteuse, began in the middle of Chapter 43 of *Tess of the d'Urbervilles*: 'There had not been such a winter for years. It came on in stealthy and measured glides, like the moves of a chess-player.'

'Schhoot,' Rene said. 'Phhhhh.'

Then he read Anna Karenina on her train, about to meet Count Vronsky. ('With delight she filled her lungs with deep breaths of snowy, frosty air . . .') And he read how – this time Charlotte Brontë – 'I had closed my shutter, laid a mat to the door to prevent the snow blowing in under it.'

He sat on his wooden chair, his tartan rug around his legs, his woollen beanie pulled down over his lion's mane of grey hair, his beetling brows pressing down upon his light blue eyes, and the neighbours listened to him. They were not religious people. They did not miss God in their lives, but they were Eficans, and their history had given them another kind of nagging loss which the cold white snow temporarily eased.

The snow eased nothing for Rene. It made it worse, each year worse than the year before – the effort, the expense, the very fact that it melted, was useless, helped nothing. By the time Jacqui was nine years old, her mother's impatient foot-tapping on the veranda had turned into an angry tattoo. It was unbearable.

The mythology of the family said Jacqui was already like her mother. She had the same honey-coloured skin, the dark brown eyes, the neat arched brow, the strong straight hair that sprang up from the crown, the small well-shaped mouth, the raging chemicals which made the little girl prone to insomnia from the age of six. That was as may be, but on Christmas Day she decided she would be like her father. She looked like her mother, but she would *be* like the big man, the bear with his tobacco smell – not a man, she never wanted to be a man – but not fearful or mean or angry or small-minded.

Jesse was a handsome man with fine grey hair, broad-shouldered, a little stooped, but with the intense, undamaged blue eyes of a child, which incorrectly suggested a life of moderation. He listened to everyone. When you spoke to him he turned those clear eyes on you and you knew he liked you. He liked everyone. He had had many wives, and many children. He had eaten fabulous meals at great restaurants. He had photographs of himself, a young good-looking man in a red shirt standing on a road in China, in a blizzard in Voorstand, in a restaurant in Paris, on the wharf in Marseille where his great-great-grandfather, a

325

tin-tin who had previously imagined himself a fortunate man, had been forcibly shipped to that country which Louis XIV called Neufasie.

Perhaps these photographs had once been interesting to Rene, but the first time Jacqui saw them they were already taboo – Jesse produced the old manila envelope when Rene was at the supermarket. He had photographs of houses he had once owned, interiors, exteriors, one with a famous actor holding a tennis racket in a funny pose.

What had happened to the money?

Jacqui never asked. Jesse never said.

By the time her mother had fallen for him, he was living in a one-bedroom cook-sit in Goat Marshes and they were both working in the kitchen of the Restaurant Quatorze. Jesse had been the one person in that chaotic kitchen who had the guts to stand up to the patapoof who owned it. He had been the troublemaker and she had fallen for him, and when he asked her to 'appear in the *Gazette*' she said yes although he was already sixty-five. He was handsome, gracious, and he let her finish her sentences.

Two months after the wedding the Restaurant Quatorze closed down. There was a recession, and the only work Rene could find was peeling prawns at a cannery at the port. As for Jesse – no one wanted him, not anywhere. He had a doctorate from the Sorbonne but he was unemployable. And although his bride never thought this was his fault she was, just the same, irritated by his lack of guilt.

'What do you want me to do?' he said. 'I will enjoy my life. I have always enjoyed my life.'

And he did. While she peeled prawns at the port, he read *Liberation* on the veranda. He made it wrong for her to resent this: what did she want him to do? Rub ashes in his hair?

When she became pregnant he did not act like any man she had ever known.

'Have it,' he said. 'It's what you want.'

It *was* what she wanted, but when Jacqui was three months old it became obvious – if Rene did not go back to work, they would starve.

'I'll look after her,' he said.

And he did. What was wrong with that? he asked her. What

uld she say? That she felt her child had been stolen from her?

The father cooked the food, played with the baby, read her stories in French and English. The mother came home tense, jealous, angry about the floor not swept, sheets not washed, a shitty bandock sitting on the changing table.

All this Jacqui only learned when her father was dying and her mother shocked her by confessing that for most of her marriage she had prayed to God each night for Him to take her husband from her.

Jacqui found that hard to stomach.

Even then, when her mother's prayers had finally been answered, when her papa's lips were purple, when his breath smelled sweet and rancid, like sour milk, when his lungs were gurgling with the mucus which would finally drown him, he had more life in him than her. Her mother knew it too. She was frightened of his death. She would not come into the bedroom. She stayed in her rocking chair in the next room, sipping sweet vermouth and ice while the Moosone rain fell like glass beads from the overflowing gutters.

It was the daughter who sat up with the dying man, who told him she loved him, who talked him through the panic of his gurgling drowning breath. It was the wife who sat in the next room, crying, drinking vermouth.

When the refrigerated truck arrived at her father's graveside and the ageing Oliver Odettes stepped out in his short shorts and his red demi-bottes, Jacqui Lorraine produced her copy of *Master and Man* and began to read out loud.

'He twisted his head, dug a hole through the snow in front of him with his hand and opened his eyes.'

'Oh God, please Jacqui,' her mother said. She clutched her daughter's arm. 'Please, don't do this.'

A different daughter might have found room in her heart to pity her, but Jacqui was not that daughter.

## 30

I touched her left breast, that's all, by 'accident'. Nothing had happened between us, but even though she carried me, on her

shoulder, like a souvenir, out of the restaurant and into the lunc
time crowds of Saarlim, even though I was enclosed in sweaty fu
and rubber, even though I could not smell her skin or feel her
hair, I was – please do not be embarrassed for me – in love with
her.

All the powerful irritation I had felt when I had seen her, bright-
eyed, wilful, dragging the Simi from the car, all this passion now
roared through the bottleneck of love and I wanted her with an
ache and want so powerful, so exquisite, that I could never have
wished to be spared the pain.

I had been raised to love a woman like this – her guts, her
humour, the luminous power of her life which I had observed
slowly shine through the heavy glaze of her professionalism.

But how could I have fallen for so demonstrably devious a
character?

It was not deviousness I saw, Madam, Meneer. It was mystery,
and I loved her for that mystery. I sucked it in and forced it into the
mould of my own desires, and you are right to fear for me.

We returned to the Marco Polo from the restaurant, where we
found Wally sitting on the grubby flock velvet settee in our room.
When I saw his face I knew something important had happened in
our absence: he now had a secret, too.

His skin was tight, he had a pleased look, a stillness, a sort of
deadness which was how he was when withholding his joy. He
had showered and shaved. He had a clean white shirt and trousers.
I was certain he'd been stealing.

I looked around the room as well as the eye-holes would permit
me. I expected to see factory-sealed cardboard boxes, vids, electronics, wrist-watches, but there was nothing in sight. The old
turtle had a stillness, a foxy shine. He lifted his chin and tilted his
head. When he lit a cigarette there was a fastidiousness in his
smoking, his thumb and forefinger around the weed like
tweezers.

'What's up?' I said.

'Not much,' he said. 'How about you?'

'Not much.'

I never kept a secret from him before and the pleasure, the
pressure, was incredible. I could not keep in my skin. I had touched
her lolo, that is what I could not say to him.

My extraordinary nurse now sat down at Wally's feet. He barely glanced at her. He did not notice the perspiration on her exquisite upper lip. He did not see he was a she, that all those shirts were there to cover her, that the long jacket must disguise her waist, her hips, her peach.

Jacqui had had no time to count or arrange the money neatly, but now she spread it out and sorted it by denomination. I admired her hands as I never had before – their shape, their suppleness, the lovely olive skin, the delicate pink shell fingernails. She ordered the Guilders. The maroon, the yellow, the violet. She had a beautiful neck, slender, downy.

'One hundred and twenty-three Guilders,' she said.

'Tray bon,' Wally said. He was pleased, but like you might be pleased with a child who has brought home too many shells from the beach.

Then Jacqui went to run my bath. *But she could no longer bathe me.*

'What?' Wally said.

'Nothing.'

I looked at him, not knowing what to say. He winked at me.

'Give . . . me . . . my . . . bath. . . please.'

He jerked his bony head towards the bathroom, meaning it was the nurse's job.

'No . . . please . . . you . . . must.'

He shrugged. 'Come on then, get your suit off.'

I lay down on my face on the carpet with relief. Wally sighed and grumbled as he kneeled beside me, but I realized he was pleased to do it. He always like to be the shapoh, to make the lunch, to run the bath. It was only age and weakness made him hire the nurse in the first place. Now he was happy to open his knife and cut me free.

I felt each stitch give way, and then the air on my wet skin.

'You silly fucker,' he said. 'What have you been doing?'

'What?'

'You stupid little ballot,' he said. 'You can't do this.'

I tried to stand up, but he held me down with his palm flat on the small of my back, held me flapping like a fish on the wharf. 'Didn't you *feel* anything?' he said.

I had felt a lot of things. I had felt the crowd. I had felt her breast. I had felt the small solder points and amputated wires rubbing at my skin, but there is no analgesic like an audience, the way it comes out to you, envelops you, wraps you in its cocoon, is warm, alive, fits you like a glove, holds you like a fist, strokes you like a cat.

When you look like I do, no one touches you.

When you look like this, your whole body cries out for touch, like dry skin for moisture.

The last stitch was cut. I wanted to stay inside the suit until I got into the bath, but I was lifted out before I could protest. Wally held me in the air, my naked body covered with a glaze of blood.

Jacqui stood at the bathroom door, a big grey towel across her shoulder. I could have died, to be like that, in front of her.

'He was amazing,' she said.

I turned my face away from her. I was so ashamed, so grateful, I could have wept. My face was a rag, my skin as slimy wet with blood as a new-born child, my limbs so sad it would make you cry if you had half a heart.

'He performed,' she said. 'He juggled for them. He was astonishing.'

'You're meant to look after him,' Wally said. 'You're his nurse. That's why we pay you all that money. You're meant to stop him getting hurt.'

'For Christ's sake,' she said. 'He's twenty-three years old.'

'It doesn't matter if he's a hundred.'

'He was making money for you,' she said, her face red. 'You shouldn't be shouting at him. Is he complaining? Are you complaining?' she asked me.

Wally kicked at the bloodied Mouse suit. His toe connected underneath the head and the suit lifted and flew and thwacked against the hotel wall. Then he carried me to the bath, holding me under my arms, out and away from him, so he would not put bloodstains on his clothes.

When he lowered me into the water, delicate pink clouds rose from my lacerated skin. He ran his hands over me, searching out my injuries.

'That's the last time you're wearing that thing,' Wally said.

'You . . . could . . . fix it . . . so it . . . doesn't . . . scratch,' I said.

'You *hate* the Mouse.'

'You don't understand,' Jacqui said to Wally. 'He was a star.'

'You don't know shit,' Wally said. 'You don't know what that fucking Mouse is in his life. You bring this crap into the car . . . I'm sorry I ever let you. I'm sorry I didn't make you throw it out.' He turned to me and patted at my face with a corner of a wet towel. 'You won't be needing to make money. I promise.'

'I . . . did . . . a . . . show,' I said. 'I . . . showered . . . and . . . cascaded . . . with . . . six . . . balls.'

Wally clicked his tongue and shook his head. 'I know what you can do,' he said.

'I . . . never . . . did . . . six . . . balls . . . before.'

'He tumbled,' Jacqui said. 'Did you know he could do that?'

'Yes,' Wally said, 'I knew he could do that. Now will you please go and buy bandages and antiseptic.'

'He could be someone.'

'Go. Go now.'

Jacqui bought the bandages and antiseptic. She also bought sandwiches, a very large bottle of beer, and a pair of needle-nosed pliers which she did not reveal until Wally was well into the last quarter of his beer.

Then she sat cross-legged on the floor with the Mouse suit open on her lap. Slowly, one at a time, she trimmed the wires flush against the rubber inner skin. She did not explain herself to Wally, and he watched her for a long time without saying anything.

'I told you not to do this,' Wally said.

'I know.'

'When you look back on this,' he said at last, 'you're going to know what a waste of effort it was.'

When Jacqui had trimmed a wire she placed a small adhesive bandage over each connection, and felt each one with her finger. I watched her. Without knowing I was doing it, I began to sing. When I saw Wally watching me, I stopped immediately.


## 31

My life had been filled with sexual yearning, but yearning is not the same as hope. That is what Wally did not know when he saw me hold the flower in Zeelung. I was someone driven by impossible desire, someone whose very soul is shaped by the sure knowledge that his dreams will not come true. My mother could not have accepted this but it was so: I had learned to equate the pain of unrequited desire with pleasure. I had crawled into the same

331

pigeonhole as those who get their satisfaction from sniffing women's shoes or underwear, or learn to achieve secret bliss from having their hair cut or their back washed. She would have hated to think of me like this. She would have had me focus on the startling quality of my gold-flecked eyes, the baby softness of my skin. She would have believed that I could make myself attractive with sheer will, with breathing exercises, and such was my dear maman's enduring power that I continued to hide certain thoughts from her.

For instance, I kept all my excitements about the Simi hidden in the dark side of my brain, away from her. She would not have understood it. She would have felt it a betrayal.

Likewise, if she should have seen see me shadowing Jacqui Lorraine, she would have imagined I had become a creep. Perhaps I had, for when my nurse left the hotel room the following afternoon, I was right behind her, filled with yearning.

I told Wally I was going to the hotel lobby to buy a zine, yet once I was in the foyer I shot right through it, illico presto. My wheelchair was just two months old – light, fast, geared, the same model which Michelle Latour used in the paraplegic Olympics. The deskmajoor held wide the door and I went straight out on to the loud and stinking Colonnade, totally alone, completely unprotected, without so much as a hat to give me privacy. I sprang from the high board, hands together, toes straight – an arrow following a mystery.

She had said I was amazing. She had said I was a star. My hands were lacerated from yesterday's performance but my arms were strong and I gave the chair the full benefit of my strength. The crowds were close. I had no bell, no horn. I made myself a goose on wheels. I honked. I came through the hawkers and wheel-squirrels at twenty-five miles an hour and those Saarlim gjents and gjils with their wide trousers and their tattooed noses, they stepped aside.

I could see Jacqui, half a block ahead. She was still 'in character', walking like a man with her chin thrust forward, her shoulders back, but once you knew, you knew. She was a woman, a rare reckless shining woman – she had a round female backside, a little apricot between her legs.

I thumped across the missing cobblestones on the corner of Shutter Steeg, my maman's street. I had been to Shutter Steeg three times already, sat in front of No. 35 and stared up at its tall arched windows. But today I had no time for Shutter Steeg. I swung around the tall glass water filtreeders,* crashed down hard across the kerbing. What did I think was going to happen? Nothing.

*Nothing?*

Nothing but a pain that you, Meneer, Madam, would never think was pleasure. Nothing but a hope so wild I allowed it to draw me further from the safety of my room than I had ever travelled *alone*, in all my life. Was I mad? Yes, I was mad. It is this madness makes salmon leap and crash on to the rocks of rivers.

I summoned all my strength to follow her up the hard high ramp to an exceptionally tall building – a classic wolkekrabber with ornate gold and silver angels above the entrance-way. As I hurtled into the vast atrium I caused a pleasant-looking man with short blond hair and dark eyebrows to convulse – the very sight of me – like a victim of electrotherapy.

The atrium was cavernous, filled with tall columns, reflections, echoes. Jacqui was walking into an elevator car.

I sped across the shining granite floor, my wheels squeaking.

'Wait,' I called.

But my voice was lost in the clatter of steel-tipped shoes and my heart's desire was already inside the elevator.

As the elevator doors shut, I heard a walkie-talkie crackling and saw, reflected in the doors' shining surface, a burly man in uniform walking towards me. It was the deskmajoor. We can safely assume that he was driven by kindness, the desire to assist the lost and disabled, but I could not bear to see the effect of my monstrous self on one more normal face. So when the next empty elevator opened, I rolled inside. The doors closed swiftly, mercifully.

This time yesterday I had been a little god performing for devotees. Now I was a solitary mutant, trembling, carried upwards.

Then, damn it, the elevator's walls revealed themselves as glass, and I found myself levitated into the Saarlim sky. I closed my eyes. I tried to breathe. But the old Feu Follet panic settled on my frame, clutched my heart. I thought I would die of dizziness.

---

* *The polluted water table of Saarlim is cleansed by filtering through these elegant glass towers, which stand, on average, twenty feet in height and measure one or two feet in diameter. There is a famous 'forest' of filtreeders in the entertainment district but, more commonly, there is one filtreeder for each city block.*

When the doors opened on the fifteenth floor, I rushed out.

Only after the doors had shut behind me did I realize that the boarding passengers were carpenters and that I was on a building site, alone.

And there I remained for a good half-hour, pressing the button, banging on the doors, until the same men returned with coffee mugs and paper bags.

As I reboarded the elevator car, all amorous fantasies had left me. I had no other desire than to return to earth, to go to my room, but when I pressed the button for Floor 1 the damn car shot upwards, six storeys higher in the sky.

I dared not face the abyss beyond the glass-walled car. When the elevator stopped again, I was equally afraid to face the boarding passenger.

The boarding passenger was more afraid of me. She turned away.

The doors closed. I pushed the button for Floor 1 but the damn thing kept on going up.

It stopped on Floor 23 – men and women with labels on their sixteen-button suits. Seeking to avoid their eyes, I pivoted my wheelchair, barked a woman's shin. I would have apologized, but I did not wish her to hear my speech. I created a bad feeling. I could feel it in their silence.

Then I spied 'Floor 31 – Consulate of the Republic of Efica'. Abandoning all thought of Jacqui, wishing nothing more than a refuge from foreigners, a respite from dizziness, I climbed up on my wheelchair and pressed the button for the thirty-first floor.

As I rolled out of the elevator I was, technically speaking, home.

On a still-luminous old Efican rag-rug, there were arranged three bronze and leather campaign settees of the type used by the French officers who accompanied the tin-tins to Efica at the beginning of settlement. It was, in some sense, home.

Perched uncomfortably on these settees I saw various persons, the Eficans amongst them identifiable by their absorption in the pink and yellow zines from home, the Voorstanders by their irritation with the uncomfortable settees. No one seemed to have noticed me arrive.

An electronic buzzer sounded. Then a door opened beside the receptionist's desk, and three people walked out into the foyer.

One of them was Jacqui. The second was extraordinarily like Leona the facilitator. She had different hair than the Leona I had met – this hair was black, sleek, long. She had different clothes: stockings, a slick sixteen-button suit. She turned and walked right past me, click-clacking on her shining synthetic shoes.

'Hi,' I said.

She looked at me as if she'd never seen me before.

I looked back at Jacqui. Her gaze settled on my agitated face.

'Tristan,' she said coolly, 'what are you doing here?'

What could I say? Now I imagined the whole room was looking at me. My face was hot. My monstrosity was vivid, slippery with sweat. My whole sense of myself came crashing, crushing down on me until I felt I could not breathe. I made myself wheel closer to the object of my affections.

'This is Gabe,' she said.

I did not want to look at him. I looked at her troubled face.

'An old friend,' she insisted.

An 'old friend' held out his hand. I had no choice but to take it. The hand was smooth and dry, not large, but square and strong.

'Now living in Saarlim,' she said.

He shook the hand up and down. He smiled – a fiftyish man with a pleasant grin which showed the edge of one slightly (only slightly) crooked tooth.

'Gabe was just telling me there is a new Sirkus we have to see.'

I did not know he was a murderer. I thought he had been her lover. That is why I hated him so easily. I hated him for being normal, for being with her, for making dreck of all my fantasies.

'Must see,' he said.

'I'm taking you and Wally,' Jacqui said.

Gabe stared at me, not a little to the left or right, but straight at my eyes. He went right into me, like a gimlet, a corkscrew.

'The walls of the tent are made from water,' said Jacqui.

'The Water Sirkus,' Gabe explained, but I hardly heard what he was saying. I was realizing just how close to her he was standing, seeing the casual way he brushed his hand against her arm.

## 32

In the old days, Gabe Manzini would have automatically requested hard copies of the faxes which Tristan Smith was reported to have sent to the terrorist group. He would therefore have discovered Jacqui Lorraine's treason before she was permitted to depart from Chemin Rouge.

Yet when the Efican DoS had requested these same hard copies he had told them no member of Zawba'a had been wire-tapped at the time of the transmission. This was not true. What was true was that my maman's murderer had become a slightly pudgy man with a red-veined nose and a low-level clearance and this class of information was no longer available to him.

You may remember the *Scandale d'Orsay* – the case of the alleged VIA officer who was driven to the Paris airport in handcuffs, the beginning of that long rift between Paris and Saarlim. That alleged VIA officer was Gabe Manzini.

Once the French had uncovered him and deported him, the government of Voorstand, in attempting to mend fences with the French, found it diplomatically necessary to sentence their loyal servant to fifteen years in prison.

They had promised him a release in six months, but as relations with France remained both important and difficult, he was kept a prisoner for almost six years.

At the end of that time, they had made an angry and vengeful man of their loyal servant. He was difficult to place: too public a face ever to return to his old work, not academically or temperamentally suited to a senior post in the administration of the Agency.

Finally he was shunted off to head the small and unimportant Efican Department of the VIA, a bureaucratic position that would have been beneath his notice at the time when he was fiddling with the Efican elections. His lack of gratitude won him no friends.

The Efican Department was a sinecure. It came with a small tasteful office, a view of one of the better corners of the Bleskran, but no staff, no secretary – there was no need for them. For six years Gabe Manzini had had nothing much to do except quietly stoke his anger at those who had betrayed him. He played chess with his computer. He constructed complicated strategies of revenge. Twice a year he flew out to Chemin Rouge to meet with the DoS.

In Efica, at least, he remained someone of importance, but in Saarlim he had the smell of anger about him and no one wished to talk to him. In Saarlim he put on weight, took to drinking a bottle of wine with his luncheon. He became chronically depressed.

But then Jacqui Lorraine came into his life, linking Tristan Smith to the hottest target in the world of Voorstand Intelligence. Gabe Manzini latched on to the case as to a life raft.

If he had alerted Internal Security (by requesting copies of the faxes, for instance) they would have thanked him very much – the bastards – and used the information to make themselves look good.

No way was he going to tip off Internal Security. Indeed, so anxious was he that Internal Security should not discover Tristan Smith that he sequestered Leona Fastanyna from the Morean Department and sent her all the way to Neu Zwolfe to pick him up and bring him safely to Saarlim.

He had stuff on the Morean Department. He could therefore trust Leona to keep her information about Tristan Smith out of the Mainframe.

Such was his distrust of Internal Security that he met Jacqui at the Efican Consulate rather than the State Buro. And if she was unlike any DoS operative he had ever met or worked with, he did not have room to suspect her. He was more suspicious of Leona than of Jacqui. Jacqui was an Efican, a good guy. She was his link back into the game, the big game at the VIA, and he therefore desired her.

She was going to be his – this woman dressed as a man. She was cute, he could not bear it. She had sweet little flat feet, no more than size five.

'What you are going to do,' he told her, 'is wire him for sound. Have you ever wired anyone before?'

'No,' she said.

He hesitated.

'Ever been wired yourself?'

'I can do it.'

'This is an aA345 I am thinking of. A button transmitter. You would have to sew it with copper wire.'

'I can do it.'

'First I have to get the transmitter.'

'Fine.'

'Could take a day or two,' he said. 'You have them in Efica?'

'Some.'

'Could they dispatch one to you?'

'Wouldn't it be faster to get it from here?' she said.

But for Gabe Manzini to get his hands on an aA345 was not an easy matter. The wire-men he had known were gone, or dead, or unfriendly. In spite of which, he would get an aA345 somehow. Then they would wire the rabbit. Then they would let him go right down the hole.

If the rabbit got no information, nothing lost.

But if he did, Gabe Manzini was back in the centre. If he could get incriminating evidence of Zawba'a they would have to bring him back into the goddamn game. They would be furious, but they would have no choice, and then there were people whose ass he was going to kick from here to Neu Zwolfe.

As they left the meeting and returned to the foyer, he was enjoying these thoughts, thinking of the punishment, the pleasure of removing that big jacket from the young woman's slender shoulders. Then he saw Tristan Smith, rolling through the foyer.

What a creature.

'Leona, go! Quick!'

As the operative exited, Gabe Manzini watched Tristan Smith. When the very weird white eyes turned on him, he overcame his initial desire to turn away. He gazed into them, as into the eye of a squid. They were alarmed, passionate, electric.

'There's a great Sirkus on in town,' he said to Jacqui.

He felt the creature's hatred of him.

'The Water Sirkus.' He smiled at Tristan Smith as he folded his hands across his narrow chest.

*You horrid little slug*, he thought, *you're going to save my life.*


## 33

When the lights came up in the Water Sirkus, the BUSINESS-GJENT was sitting on a chair. As he opened his zine, SPOOK-GANGER DROOL materialized behind him, softly, subtly, like smoke. So deftly did he materialize that I was sure he was a hologram image, but then the ghoulish Drool snickered and

338

produced a very solid rope. How this was done I do not know, but the audience of Saarlim connoisseurs all whooped and whistled their appreciation.

Spookganger Drool was such a clown. I had not appreciated that in Chemin Rouge, where his character was synonymous with fear.* In Saarlim, he had the audience tittering even before he began to make the noose.

I sat in my seat, finally free from autograph hounds – hot, sweating, in pain, but also . . . well, she was beside me: my nurse, my partner, the inexplicable, unattainable woman with her little honey-coloured lolos hidden underneath three shirts. What sweet pain it was to sit beside her, to see her delicate profile as she lifted her eyes to the spectacle.

As the Dreadful Drool now looped the rope around the Gjent, as Wally cackled, Jacqui turned to me and smiled. Drool ran round and round until he had the man imprisoned. Using Drool knots he bound the poor fellow's upper arms against his chest. He knotted him to the chair, the seat, the back. The Gjent, it seemed, could not care less. He read his zine.

Drool slapped his hands together and slithered to one side of the stage where a toilet bowl suddenly appeared in the darkness. The spook unbuttoned. He peed. He rolled his eyes upwards in relief. Wally roared with laughter. This, surely, was better than the room in Gazette Street with its smell of fusty zines, all of them covered with words describing the great Sirkuses of Voorstand, the death-stalkers, posturers, contortionists, the ventriloquists, laser-dancers.

'Oh my,' he said, and wiped his head.

The Gjent in his chair tried to turn the page of his zine, and couldn't.

Drool's urine slowed, then surged. Every time he thought he had done, there was more to deliver. He continued this business on and on, until the smallest drip was enough to unleash a paroxysm of laughter from the audience.

---

* Over and over again, we find this is the case – once in an overseas market and therefore beyond the control of the Saarlim Sirkus Convention, Sirkus managers have a habit of changing names and characters to suit what they believe are 'local conditions'. This makes the Voorstandish Spookganger Drool into the Efican Phantome Drool and results in such fracturing of the character that Phantome Drool has lost all historical and

When, at last, he was finished, he flushed the toilet. He looked into the bowl with interest. We heard the noise of torrents of water, babble, discord. Then water began to bubble up from the toilet bowl. Drool looked guilty. He put the lid down. He sat on it. He clung to the bowl, but the lid was lifted upwards, and he with it.

While the water gushed forth from beneath the rising lid, Drool hung on, his long protoplasmic arms stretching until they snapped like rubber bands and he was catapulted high into the air and left dangling from the catwalk beneath the lighting rig.

Now a fountain rose from the toilet, bringing with it, from deep inside the bowl, the brawling holographic figures of Bruder Duck and Bruder Dog. Round and round they fought, on top of the geyser, twenty feet above the stage floor, quacking, grunting.

The crowd roared and shouted.

The knotted Business-gjent remained absorbed in the problems of his newspaper. As the water rose in a sheer wall before our eyes it became clear that the stage was walled, not with glass, but with some new Voorstandish invention, something glass-like that did not refract or reflect any of the multitude of spots now focused on the tethered Gjent. The water covered his ankles, then his calves, then his knees.

Bruder Dog and Bruder Duck fell in the water with a splash.* At first they fought, beneath the surface. And then as Bruder Dog began to flail and sink, Bruder Duck began to save him.

Jacqui grabbed my arm. Then her hands were busy clapping. Then she was cheering, standing, and then, as the lighting drew attention to the poor Gjent, she gravely took her seat. The water was up to the Gjent's neck.

There was a great silence, and the sound of water, one drop dripping like a metronome.

The level rose over the Gjent's bearded chin, over his tightly clenched mouth. As his eyes stared at us across the surface of the lake, there was some nervous giggling, but for the most part that whole dark space was totally quiet and 2000 people watched the

---

*mythic connection to the Deuce and the Hairy Man.*
* *This being my first Sirkus, I was no connoisseur, so as to whether they were holographic images (as I believed) or Class IV Simis (as I now think possible) I am afraid I cannot say with any accuracy.* [TS]

performer subjected to a total immersion which could not but help recall the Waterhouse of ancient Amsterdam.

We Eficans were Ootlanders, but we knew – as all the world knows – that death, the possibility of death, is always on the menu in your entertainment.

We saw the bubbles come out of the Gjent's mouth. We saw his hands begin to grapple with the Drool's knots. We saw his eyes widen, as the water now poured in above his head through pipes as big as sewers. Soon even these were submerged and the entire performance area was like a giant aquarium. At the very top of this were chairs where the chorus (Bruder Dog, Bruder Duck, Bruder Mouse, Spookganger Drool, Heidi) sat, looking down into the water.

The Gjent had now been without air for minutes. We could see him panicking. We could see his hands flailing at the knots. We could see the bubbles coming from his mouth and now, as we watched, he opened his mouth in a silent scream and a great rush of air escaped – bubbles floating upwards to the Gods above.

His limbs jerked, his head rose, his hair floated.

He was free.

We roared. He was alive. He streaked upwards towards the air. He jumped out on to the catwalk above the water. He bowed to us. He stood in profile to us, turned and opened his mouth and, in a perfect replica of the De Kok sculpture, made himself a fountain – water poured from his open mouth back into the tank, and then he put out his hand and caught . . . a small goldfish.

Breathing deeply from his broad athlete's chest, he smiled at us, and held this tiny creature briefly by the tail.

'Meneer, Madam,' he said. 'We give you . . .'

He dropped the fish into the water.

'The Water Sirkus.'

And so the show began, a breathless, relentless entertainment – the man in the suit and bow tie walking through the water, looking for the fish with a flashlight. The huge fish that eats the man. The tiny man, no more than two feet tall, a Simi, of course, but it was endless. There was underwater dancing, great comic interludes, replicas of famous paintings, villainous creatures who seemed so real until they climbed from the water and then were hit by cannon and exploded in the air above our heads.

341

There was no plot, or shape, although there was the continual preoccupation with drowning that distinguishes Voorstandish art in general. There was no circus ring at all, and as such it would have damned itself, not only politically, but also theatrically, with the members of the Feu Follet. But few of the critics at the Feu Follet ever saw a Sirkus. Certainly not the Water Sirkus. They therefore overlooked one vital thing – the Sirkus is thrilling. Would it have captured half the world if it were not?

The last 'act' of the Water Sirkus was a performance of 'Pers Nozegard', the first ever performed beneath the water. The plot you know: the child whose beauty is boasted of by its mother in the hearing of sea spirits, the capturing of the child, and its life under the sea with mermaids while its parents mourn above, thinking it drowned, the funeral in the world, the child's christening in the water etc.

In this production the performers said their lines underwater.

This was such a new development in the Sirkus that when the father turned to the mother and said the first words of the little play (*'Our child is dead'*) the audience hooted and stamped with appreciation.

I for my part assumed the actors were miming a pre-recorded sound track. But later, in the finale, as the holograms spun, as the performers made themselves into a great water wheel, hand to ankle, and spun at speed, and what looked like a real live dog walked calmly through them and wagged its tail, one of the performers bumped a bright blue coral reef which had been a feature of the show.

'Shit,' he said.

It was only then that I knew what everyone else in that Dome had known from the beginning – that these brave performers were really saying words underwater and these words were being broadcast to us in our seats. I had witnessed one of those technical feats, the invention of which had probably resulted in the form of entertainment we had just witnessed.

I was beginning to reflect on this, and what this meant about the Voorstand Sirkus generally, when I felt myself half strangled from behind. I turned my head. I saw the face. It took me three, four, five seconds to understand who it was, this man who was cutting off my air pipe by embracing me so emotionally. He had bronzed skin and jet-black curly hair. He had sequins on his shoulders. He shone like a king in the midst of the common folk in the crowd, and when he let go my throat and hooked his big hands underneath my arms, and picked me up, all sixty-five pounds of me, none of the Mouse's admirers disputed his right to have me to himself.

'Hello, Tristan,' he said in that big actor's voice.

Madam, Meneer – it was Bill Millefleur.

It was not that he had grown older – indeed, he was as young as ever – but that I had changed him in my memory. I had remembered his sneer, his spleen, the hurt and anger in his eye.

But here he was, my maman's circus boy – his handsome sun-lamped face – mint smell, flossed teeth gleaming – little crooked scar on his chin. He looked so soft, and beautiful, and burnished, shining. He was so big, had such good skin, such glossy hair. He stood shoulder high above the crowd, and although he was not as famous as I thought he was – he had the look of someone very famous indeed.

This was the man who had picked me up so many times before, and put me down and walked away each time I needed him, but when he held me aloft and smiled up at me, I loved him without reserve. I felt a sort of giddiness, a great surge of relief.

I had worked so long in learning not to love him, not to trust him, but all he had to do was hold me, and he melted me, the Sirkus man, like he melted my maman – such charm, such energy, such focus – so many times before. What it is – I wonder, do you know? – to be loved by someone beautiful.

I forgot about Jacqui and Wally. I felt a great surge of happiness, of completeness, as my father carried me above the crowds. The tide of my already turbulent emotions made me unobservant and it was not until much later in the night, when I was falling asleep on my father's dining table, that I saw, in my mind's eye, the crew-cut man named Gabe sitting quietly in row 3.

## 34

Seven o'clock on the evening of the Water Sirkus found Wally on a plateau of sweet emotion. Steam from the bathroom drifted out into the hotel room where he sat. He was no longer agitated, but almost serene. The tickets to the fabulous Water Sirkus lay beside him on the quilt – three long paper slips on onion paper inside an embossed silver envelope.

He had washed, showered, shaved. He could feel that clean cotton next to his skin. He had taken his beta-tene. He had taken aspirin, but not too much. The landlopers out on the balcony were singing. They had a violin and a drum. They were like crickets in the night.

At seven-fifteen he walked along the corridor to the elevator in his formal bow tie and tails.

This time he was prepared for the odours and confusion of the Colonnades. He held his nose and grinned and shook his head and when he walked he tapped his cane jauntily on the sidewalk. If the crowds had remained normal he would have reached the Sirkus in an excellent mood.

But he was in the company of Bruder Mouse and before we had gone twenty yards there were admirers stretching out their hands to touch the Bruder's grey furry face.

'Shoo,' he said when the crowd began to form. 'Go on – skat.'

But no one shooed and no one skat.

'Piss off,' he said.

But it was half past seven at night, and bow-legged Bruder Mouse was on the town.

'Tristan! Jacques!'

This was the first time we had a chance to show Wally the successful act we had spent the week developing – the cartwheels, the tumbling, the juggling with tennis balls or apples.

'Don't do that,' he said. 'For Chrissake.'

'Look at him,' Jacqui said. 'He's amazing. He's a star.'

'Just stop it,' the old man hissed.

'But why?'

'No reason – just stop.'

There was a reason – he had not planned it. It was not part of his secret. It upset him so much that, when that show was finally over and Jacqui and I escorted him along the streets of Kakdorp, his head was pushed forward from his shoulders, his brows down on his old grey eyes, and he looked so much like a bad-tempered old vulture, a predator, that he helped effect what physical force might not have done – the comparatively peaceful entry of Bruder Mouse into a Water Sirkus.

344

Once he had me in my numbered seat, the seat he had planned, he began to regain his old humour. He sat in his seat, crossed his legs, arranged his stick. He took pleasure in not looking round to the row behind where he knew Bill Millefleur was sitting.

Perhaps it was prison that did it to him, or perhaps it was that brutal childhood which left those pale and slippery circles forever etched into his skin, but a secret gave Wally pleasure – whether it was something as simple as the meal he had cooked for dinner, the origin of a brand new washing machine, or the real reason he wished to go to Voorstand. There was always a secretive air to Wally, and he could not give you the time of day without standing next to you too close and looking at the floor. He had the habit of whispering when he could have spoken normally, a habit of with-holding information from you.

When I had come along the wharf at Chemin Rouge, pale, fright-ened, a snail just come out of his shell, I had already been – without knowing it – on my way to see Bill Millefleur. Wally had written to my father. They were long letters which, while hinting much, revealed nothing, not even the date of our arrival.

It was this cache of secrets that had given Wally's cleanshaven face that tumescent shine all the way across the ocean to Morea. And when he had seen Aziz's long-bladed bone-handled knife move upwards, sharp and slick as a surgeon's scalpel, insinuating itself between my bandage and chest skin, all he could think was that I would have to seek out my father, if only for the money.

He had let me believe that I was taking him to Saarlim to indulge his passion for the Sirkus, but he was seventy-three years old and had a painful spinal condition which made even the most luxurious starbuck uncomfortable for him – he would never have set out across the world just to see the Sirkus.

Indeed, he felt most content at home in his kitchen or in the sandy streets around the port. There he had come to savour the preciousness of time, the sweet sappy papaya trees resting their heavy fruit on corrugated iron verandas, the smell of seaweed that still drifted up the Boulevard des Indiennes after the winter storms.

He could see Sirkus enough for an old man in Chemin Rouge. There was too much death in the Saarlim Sirkus and he did not wish to think about death. It pushed in on him everywhere these

345

days: there were tastes in his mouth, discomforts in his stomach, he was secretly convinced was cancer.

He wrote a will. He went through his zines and threw away a number that were pornographic. And, as his final act, he set out to extricate me from the Feu Follet and reunite me with my father.

It was this last project which gave him the glow, the light, the surge of stamina which I imagined had been produced by travel brochures.

And in the last few days before he finally led me to a seat directly in front of my most problematic parent, the days when Jacqui and I were tin-rattling in the streets of Saarlim, or standing side by side in Shutter Steeg gazing up at the handsome stone house where my maman had been born, Wally conducted secret telephone conferences with Bill, refusing to divulge my whereabouts until the 'right moment'.

This ponderous, controlling secrecy drove my father crazy.

'Just tell me where you are,' he said. 'I'll be right over.'

'You come right over, it'll all *be* over,' Wally said. 'If he thinks I arranged this, he'll walk away. He has to think it's all an accident.'

When Jacqui came home with the tickets for the Water Sirkus, that was the venue Wally chose for the 'accidental' meeting.

'People are always bumping into each other at the Sirkus,' he said to Bill. 'You get the seat behind us. It's beyond suspicion.'

'Mo-frere,' Bill said. 'You don't know what you're asking. This is the hottest show in town.'

'This will be perfect,' Wally said. 'No way could he believe we set him up.'

'I've got a dinner party that night. I can't get seats.'

But of course he did get a seat. He was sitting there now, exactly as Wally had planned he would.

Wally did not turn around. He looked up at the shimmering walls of the Water Sirkus, which changed colours constantly as the currents of dyed fluids rose and fell, plastic walls of a material which reflected or absorbed the light depending on no apparent process.

'Are . . . you . . . happy?' I asked him.

'Tray bon,' he said. Everything had this glow, this light – his secret. 'You bet your dye-pot.' And all through the show he held his secret to him.

Yet when the moment finally came, when Bill Millefleur, unable to contain himself any more, lifted his son free of his seat, what Wally felt was worse than nothing.

He saw the Mouse hold its arms wide, saw its cheeky Bruder grin.

The job was done. Tristan Smith was safe. Wally's life, he thought, was over.

Only yesterday he came out of Goat Marshes Violin and found little Annie McManus with her curly blonde hair sitting in the Boite down at the port. He bought her a glass of roteuse and told her he was a poet and God loved him and put words of poetry in his mouth. She took him home and fucked him and he could have loved her if she would have let him.

Only yesterday he saw the great Ducrow, his big lips marked with dry red wine, mount the slack wire and walk from the sawdust ring up to the box, his long silk gown flapping between his veined old legs.

He stood in his seat and began to follow me. He mourned me, even while I was still there. He grieved for me, when I was not six feet from him. He tasted his own death, not just the steely fact of it or its imminence or its inevitability, but tasted it inside his mouth, the shittiness of it, the sour and bitter waste, the deep cold loneliness, the abandonment.

He had no real energy to push through the crowd. He was overcome with the notion that he had not only wasted his own life, but that he had wasted mine. Bill would see, any moment, I had no education worth a damn. He had liked to sit, to just be, to drink beer with his arm around my shoulder, to pass the time.

Now time had passed. He lacked the will to fight the crowds. He watched Bruder Mouse's head as I moved towards the east side of the auditorium, and then down a ramp which led into the under-world beneath the stage.


## 35

Bill had been forewarned about the Mouse suit, but he had imagined that I carried a mask on a stick like Saarlim children do at Easter. He did not realize that he would not be able to see my eyes, my mouth, that even as the reunion finally took place he would still be in doubt as to whether he was forgiven or rejected. Even as he hefted me high above the crowd, his head was full of Wally's warnings about my enmity. No matter what the easy smile might indicate, he was ill with anxiety.

'Is this all right?' he asked as we started off down between the seats.

He meant: is it all right for me to carry you on my shoulder, is it demeaning? He did not express himself clearly, but I understood him.

Had he lived with me in Chemin Rouge each gurgle of my subsequent answer, each muddy slide of vowel, each slur of consonant, would also have been clear to him. But he listened to my answer like a stranger, and the crowd, bumping, shoving, tugging at the Mouse's dangling boots, only made it worse.

A smooth-cheeked Efican in an eccentric suit – he knew it must be Jacques the nurse – was shooing the fans away, but he did not pay attention to the nurse, or to Wally either. He sought peace, clarity, a release from chaos. He headed for the door underneath the stage – down amongst the humming underworld of pipes and pumps where, he had imagined, he might have a chance finally to be reunited with his son in private.

But when the heavy door shut fast behind him, he found himself intimidated by the enigmatic face of Bruder Mouse – the painted smile, the broken tooth, the whole withholding wall of character.

He seated me carefully on a humming grey steel box, a pump perhaps, thereby placing my eyes almost level with his own.

'Would you prefer to walk?' he asked. 'It's not so far to go.'

I began to answer but he interrupted.

'Don't get me wrong.' He gestured with his two hands, smiled – these phoney movements being the by-products of his enormous tension – 'I'm happy to carry you, mo-frere, from here to the Bleskran if you want it.'

'It's . . . OK . . . go . . . on . . . carry . . . me.'

'You can carry him,' the nurse translated. 'Mr Millefleur. I can't *believe* it's you. How do you know Tristan?'

Bill's handsome face shivered with incredulity.

'He's my goddamn son,' he said, turning to look at the nurse, 'for Chrissakes!'

'Where's . . . Wally?' I said.

My father swung back to me, all politeness. 'Say again.' He placed his hand tentatively on my shoulder. 'Say slowly . . .'

'You . . . left . . . Wally.'

'Oh Jesus,' Bill said, his eyes glazing over with tears. 'Are you saying I left you?'

'YOU . . . LEFT . . . WALLY.'

'Shit!' said Jacqui.

'What is he saying?'

'We lost Mr Paccione.'

'We?' said Bill, his voice rising, his famous temper showing in his eyes. He turned on her. He raised his hands up to his temples. '*We?*'

'I.'

'For Chrissakes,' he said. 'Aren't you the A-1 nurse they brought from Efica? Fifteen hundred Guilders a month? Is that you? The perfect Jacques? You're the one who looks after Wally and Tristan?'

'I'll get him. I'll get him now.'

'No, no,' Bill said.

'Yes,' Jacqui said, 'I'll get him now.' But as she turned my father brought his large hand down on her padded shoulder and turned her in her tracks.

'You stay right here,' Bill said in that quiet and dangerous voice that I remembered. 'And do not fucking *move.*'

He turned and left us, me and Jacqui. I folded my arms across my chest.

'What?' she said.


# 36

Jacqui knew my handsome father in a way that I did not. She had been to Dome Projections* of all his Saarlim horse shows. There she had seen him dance from back to back on Arab stallions, do Lucio Cristiani's somersault across one horse and on to the back of a third as they cantered round the ring. She had heard him speak the great lines of Voorstand's Epic Poet. She knew the pores of his skin,

---

* *The Dome Projection is naturally little known in Voorstand, where no one would waste their time viewing a vid reproduction of a Sirkus. In the rest of the world, Meneer, Madam, this is often how we know you. Chemin Rouge, for instance, now supports two live Sirkuses, which change their show every three months or so. In contrast we have sixteen different Dome Projection theatres whose entertainment changes weekly.* [TS]

349

the scar on his chin, the sweet rise on his lip, the dimple on his chin which she thought almost unbearably beautiful.

In short, she was his fan, and as she travelled with him through the crush, pushed against his glistening suit, being careful not to stand on his snakeskin shoes, she was in shock, not merely to have met him, but to have met him in these most peculiar circumstances.

Now she was *crushed* against Bill Millefleur, was carried along in the same tumbling river of fluttering pink- and blue-paged autograph books. She tumbled down the ramp beside him, went through a grey metal door that said 'Sirkus Staff Only', was suddenly in a world of huge brightly coloured pipes, compressors, pumps, the smell of marine paint, the cold of concrete – *backstage*. Bill Millefleur put his hand behind her back and guided her into a link-wired alleyway. (*You see*, she wanted to say, to someone, to her mother most of all. *You see?*)

But then a minute later she was revealed as an amateur, a fuck-up, and she wished no one to see anything. Bill Millefleur was furious with her. He turned away from her, went walking, beautifully, athletically, impatiently over the metal floor, back into the cavernous Dome.

And Jacqui was left there – boneless, a lump, all her normal resourcefulness sucked from her.

The sharp-toothed Mouse sat on the water pump and stared at her, its grey furry arms folded across its spangled blue chest.

'What?' she said.

'Nothing,' it said. It stared at her impassively, and she was embarrassed to have her weakness so clearly exposed.

Yet when Bill Millefleur returned with his arm around the old man's bent shoulders, she did not care who saw her apologize.

'You're right,' she said. 'I was an amateur. I didn't do my job.'

And the actor forgave her.

He held out his hand. It was soft and dry. As it closed around hers, she had a vision of her mother sitting in her kitchen wiping counter tops, the little plates of plastic-covered leftovers, some as small as a teaspoonful. (*You see?*)

'I had no right to shout at you,' Bill Millefleur said. 'I was so excited to see my son, I didn't even catch your full name?'

'Jacques Lorraine.'

The touch of his hand made her numb in the neck, produced

shame and gratitude in almost equal quantities, and as she followed his athletic body carrying my misshapen one back into the labyrinth beneath the stage of the Water Sirkus, her cheeks continued to burn.

She watched how he held yours truly in his arms, how he squeezed my arms, my legs.

'Don't . . . do . . . that.'

'Tristan,' he said, squeezing me again, grinding my sore feet in against his hip bone. 'We have to sit down without our masks.'

And Jacqui, rather than being embarrassed by his tacky talk, was much moved by Bill's love, his need, by his good looks, by my lack of the same.

She was a fan. She wished to be with him. Thinking her silence a mark of unworthiness, she walked beside him wondering what to say. Finally, she asked about the Water Sirkus, inquiring how the performers had been able to speak whilst underwater.

She saw even as he answered – 'It's a voice patch, Jacques, that's all' – that he did not want to talk to her. He wanted to talk only – this was so weird, so bizarre – to the snotty mutant that no one in the DoS could bear even to think about.

'Did you enjoy the Sirkus, Tristan?' he asked.

But Tristan Smith would not speak, and when his father turned to speak to Jacqui his eyes were weak with need, with shame.

'It's a voice patch, Jacques, that's all, a new gizmo,' he said. 'Soon every shop in the Kakdorp will have one in its window. But I loved,' he said, speaking loudly, as one of the performers walked past in a white bathrobe, his cheeks red, his eyes bulging a little with fatigue, 'I absolutely loved that bit of business with old Spook-ganger.'

The performer opened a door and closed it behind him.

'That was Dirk Labelaster,'* he whispered to Tristan Smith. 'Would you like to meet him? We could visit him at home. He lives just near us. Are you still interested in posturing? Tell me who you want to meet.'

---

* *You may be surprised to see that Bill Millefleur did not have to explain who Dirk Labelaster was. Labelaster is hardly a star, but he has a following among the Eficans. Dirk Labelaster? you ask. In Chemin Rouge? And I, in my turn, say to you: you have no idea of your effect on those of us who live outside the penumbra of your lives.* [TS]

For answer, Bruder Mouse presented his immobile cheeky grin.

We descended a steel staircase. At the bottom we arrived at a closed roller door, not unlike the one at the entrance of the Feu Follet. Bill pressed a button. The door rose noisily and we found ourselves outside the Sirkus, in the dank night air, by a small kanal.

The air was fetid. There was broken glass, a burned-out truck. A man in a leather jacket came out from behind the truck and pointed his finger at us.

'It's OK,' Bill said. 'Relax. He's not a Misdaad Boy.'

This man was the wheelmajoor, the pilot of a boat, a gondel, which was sitting in the iridescent water with its motor purring. And now, as our party walked towards him, he held out his hand to help us aboard.

'It's a nice night to go to Saarlim?' Jacqui said.

'Yes, Meneer,' he said, but she could see he was not VIA, and as the gondel nosed out of the back kanal, and into Bleskran Kanal, as the great spires and domes, the luminous filtreeders, rose high above her, Jacqui left the cabin and went to stand alone in the prow. Then Saarlim appeared above her, around her, like the fairy city of the vids. It was one of those rare moments when a city can suddenly, unexpectedly, appear to open its doors to a stranger, and take them from the dirt and heat of the streets into that other secret world it shows only its creators and intimates.

Yet this experience, far from bringing our nurse a little peace, produced in her passionate heart a fierce agitation.

*You see*, she told her mother, who could not see, was not here, could never know, even if she were told. *You see* – you do not need to live your life like a pinched-up piece of leftover in a saucer in the fridge.

She sat in the prow, looking at the skyline, accepting the glass of *champagne* – from *Bill Millefleur*, who came out on to the deck to give it to her personally.

She sipped champagne, and thought contradictory and agitated thoughts about that cautious street her mother still lived on, the genteel poverty, the suspicion, the habitual meanness which was thought of as caution, the damn leftovers, the frozen scraps with date labels three years old.

*I am going to wait in Saarlim for the snow.*

Through the glass she could see Bill and me and Wally in intimate conversation. And she was somehow persuaded about me in a way she had not been before.

She sat out in the fog looking in at me.

She sat in the prow as the gondel glided along the black silky waters of the kanal, beneath the golden gates of the Bleskran, under the great illuminated wharf of the Baan, where uniformed doormen waited to help us disembark.

She arrived on the private wharf with the champagne glass still in her hand, and walked in through the foyer in her now slightly soiled male costume as if she too were already someone special.

When she entered the carpeted elevator it was as if she did it every day. The elevator was, as appeared to be the Saarlim habit, glass-walled. As our little party rose into the night we were presented with this jewel-box view of the city, its water, its boats, the rippling glass towers of water filters, the glow of the Sirkus Domes, like so many Florentine cathedrals clustered densely around the Grand Concourse but then spreading away into the great dark night of Voorstand.


# 37

I had been pleased to see my father. I loved him, although I had spent many years insisting I did not. But each time he did not understand my speech, he emphasized our eleven years of separation. This was the father who could not do the time. He could do what was 'brave' and 'dramatic', go to the Mall and say, 'This is my son, Tristan Smith,' or paint his face with Zinc 3001, but he did not have the spine to be a father.

When I saw the flashy gondel bobbing at the wharf, I saw one more of his dramatic gestures.

Of course I now know that this was unfair, that a gondel is not 'flashy', that it is, in fact, a perfectly ordinary conveyance for a Saarlim bhurger. But when I was carried inside the cabin, I did not understand that gondels are hired by the hour by bank clerks and fishmongers, or that the liquors displayed so proudly in spotlit niches cost a very reasonable 3 Guilders a nip. Laugh if you like, but when I saw the black leather banquettes and small brass lamps, I thought he was trying to seduce me with his money, and by the time I sat on the banquette I was as depressed as Wally was, although for different reasons.

Bill, meanwhile, plunged anxiously onwards. He was in full gallop, round and round, smiling, laughing, juggling tall-stemmed glasses in one hand while with the other he eased the cork from a dripping wet bottle of Veuve Clicquot.

I declined the glass in sign language, holding my Mouse head to show him why I could not drink.

Then the damn fool began to fiddle with my suit.

If he had only thought a moment more he would have realized I might not wish to undress myself in public, to show myself to him like this. I pulled away from him and turned, not towards Wally who was staring mournfully out into the night, but towards Jacqui who was seated on my left. In our days of tin-rattling my nurse and I had finally become allies. In the Water Sirkus she had been my friend and companion. Twice she had touched my knee, once my arm.

'Stop . . . him,' I said. 'Please . . . get . . . him . . . off . . . me.'

But when I touched her arm she gave a small, apologetic shrug and slipped off the banquette away from me.

'Just . . . tell . . . him . . .' I said, but I saw she had become my father's friend. She walked out of the cabin and up towards the prow, and let me tell you – it was obvious to me then – as she walked up and down that little deck, she walked not like a man, but like a woman, and a damn frisky one at that.

You may be thinking, Madam, Meneer, that Jacqui left the cabin from a sense of delicacy, a wish to leave me alone for my difficult reunion with my father. Equally you may imagine that Bill Mille-fleur, in carrying champagne to her on the deck, might have been performing his role as a gracious Saarlim host.

I was in no state to imagine any such thing. I watched Bill and Jacqui, a man and a woman silhouetted against the lights of the filtreeders and wolkekrabbers.

It made me half mad with jealousy – this whole world that I could never enter.

I turned to Wally. 'Let's . . . go . . . back . . . to . . . the . . . hotel.'

But Wally had found a bottle of whisky and was pouring himself a generous drink.

'Take your suit off,' he said. 'Have a little drink. Enjoy yourself.'

'He's . . . a . . . creep.'

'Give him a chance.'

354

'He's . . . such . . . a . . . phoney.'

'Don't be such a fucking Bruder. Take your damn suit off. Can't you see he's pleased to see you?'

'Mr . . . Walk . . . Away.'

'Relax, he'll be back in a moment.'

'Fuck . . . him.'

But then Bill did come back, stooping under the low roof and seating himself beside me.

'Now, Tristan, speak to me.'

But he seemed so far from me, so far, far away.

'You . . . don't . . . know . . . what . . . I've . . . become.'

'I'm sorry,' he said, laying his hand gently on my shoulder.

For a moment I imagined he was apologizing for something that had happened on the deck, but then I saw it was the same old thing.

'I'm sorry,' he said. 'I didn't catch that first bit. Maybe if you took the suit off. Maybe then you wouldn't be so muffled.' It was typical of him that he did not ask me why I wore the suit, or what I was doing with it.

In any case – I did not wish to take my suit off, and suffer his misunderstanding, all the false pity in his eyes. I wanted to set it straight with him – I was a man. Thus I began to speak to him, slowly, very carefully.

'We . . . have . . . not . . . seen . . . each . . . other . . . for . . . many . . . years.'

'We have not seen your mother?'

'*No!*'

'All right,' Wally stood. 'Don't shout. Mollo mollo. Just say it again. Your dab will get the hang of it.'

But my father did not 'get the hang' of how I spoke, and thus I travelled towards the Baan, not deep in the intimate conversation Jacqui imagined, but in a misery of anger and misunderstanding.

## 38

My father, in returning from the Water Sirkus, was late for an important dinner party in his own apartment. He had planned this dinner party three months before, and once it was planned it could not be cancelled – this inflexibility being a reflection, not of his character, but of manners in Saarlim City.

As you know, Saarlim has its etiquette. One does not, as in Chemin Rouge, drop over for a roteuse and stay all day. One does not arrive with a round of cheese and a baton and expect to be welcomed. There is this surprising strictness, this lack of ease, which is disturbing for an Efican, and it co-exists with what feels like exactly the opposite tendency: it is not in the least impolite for a host to be absent from the greater part of his or her own dinner party.

If you are from Saarlim, you will find nothing unusual in all of this, but for the rest of us, let me tell you, Saarlim dinner parties at first appear anarchic – confusing empty chairs and inexplicably appearing and disappearing guests. It is not until somewhere around eleven at night, when the Sirkuses are finally dark, well after we Ootlanders have lost all patience, that the table finally unifies. The tablecloth is replaced. New silverware appears. Ornate candlesticks are brought from hiding, and the pudding is served with a formality that we in Efica reserve for a good pork bake.*

You know this already, Meneer, Madam? Then skip ahead. There are other readers, however, to whom this may be surprising, Oot-landers who have until this moment expected your manners to be just like Bruder Mouse's or Bruder Duck's. You think this is preposterous? Then let me tell you: you have no idea how you are perceived.

Elsewhere in the world, when they imagine your personal character, they expect to see you blowing bubbles in your soup. They have seen the Drool or Dog pee in the Sirkus. They have heard the Mouse fart and play the bagpipes. They draw the wrong conclusion, and not merely about your table manners.

Having passed their lifetimes spending one eighth of their gross incomes on Sirkuses, it is hard for some Ootlanders to accept that they are not attuned to the soul of Saarlim. They may never have visited Voorstand but they know the names of the steegs, the kanals, the parks, the bars, the Domes. They own programme notes from performances they have never seen. They can discuss tragic deaths you never heard of, minor performers you have long forgotten. But they do not live in Saarlim and therefore there is

---

* In Efica, unlike Voorstand, it is perfect manners to serve meat at a formal meal. [TS]

much that they do not understand. It might be difficult to convince someone from Ukrainia, for instance, that it requires a highly tuned sense of etiquette to live in a building like the Baan.

So for the Ootland readers, let me make this thing clear: in the Sirkus, Bruder Mouse could say 'gaaf-morning' to any of God's Creatures, whether they had met before or no, but in the Baan it took a whole necklace of introductions for Bill to engineer a meeting with his neighbour, Kram. It was a slow process – almost a year before he could put her, socially speaking, in check. And then another six months of toing and froing with the gold-toothed intermediary, Clive Baarder, before they could confirm a night which was suitable for both of them.

They lived in the same building, used the same glass-walled elevators, walked into or out of the foyers next to each other, and although she was a Sirkus Produkter and he a Sirkus Star, they might as well have lived on different planets, and even after the invitation was issued and accepted they waited until the dinner when they would finally know each other. This is one aspect of karakter.

You are always explaining karakter to us visitors, telling us it means politeness, manners, breeding – but even as you do so you let us know we can never hope to understand exactly what it is. It is in the blood more than in the language. It is a Saarlim thing and after twenty years in Saarlim City it was still a notion that made my father not quite easy.

Bill had a six-room apartment. Peggy Kram occupied an entire floor, a real Bleskran trothaus with topiary and library. She dressed in long flowing garments in various earth tones which you could wear down to the Kakdorp among the throng without being remarked on as anyone wealthy but which, in the muted lights of a trothaus with the lights and the little lasers dancing on the ceiling fibre, was obviously a Van Kline with a price tag of 100,000 Guilders.

Such was life in the society whose original Christian vegetarian heresies still reflected the character of the 'Sirkus with no prisoners'.

Bill's whole dinner party (the one which had been irrevocably set for the night when he would finally have the chance to reunite with his lost son) centred on Peggy Kram, and not because Bill thought her charming or even interesting – he feared that she was neither –

357

but because Bill's contract with the Sirkus Brits had finally been terminated and Peggy Kram was a produkter who not only owned twenty Ghostdorps (where she had whole families of actors playing out the 'The Great Historical Past') but also four Sirkus Domes in Saarlim City.

Bill needed work.

And when he returned to his own dinner party at half past ten he hoped that the family obligation which had made his absence necessary might further elevate Kram's idea of his karakter. And yet, as he had never been totally confident that he truly understood the nuances of karakter, he entered his own apartment with some trepidation.

What he saw there did not encourage him.

His lover of that year (Malide Van Kraligan, the posturer) was asleep on the sofa with her little rose-bud mouth open and her slender arm across her eyes. Peggy Kram, a little plump, but very glamorous with her mane of blonde curls, was loudly quarrelling with the English bottelier (hired for the occasion) about the temperature of her Mersault.

The rented antique lace tablecloth was rumpled. The glassware and silver was in total disarray and Martel Difebaker, a legendary posturer, a man known for his fastidiousness, was sitting nodding his head in a stricken sort of way. Clive Baarder (who had been the intermediary for the meeting) was filing his nails.

When Mrs Kram looked up and saw the enigmatic figure of Bruder Mouse, she stopped arguing about the wine.

I barely noticed her. I knew nothing of karakter. Nor did I know that she was one of the most powerful women in Saarlim. I was hot, tired, thirsty, irritated to find my father entertaining strangers on what he had three times declared an Important Night. So when the gold-toothed Baarder rose from his ornate chair and took a mock karate position in relationship to me, I had had enough. I walked out of the room.

In doing this, it was not my intention to damage my father economically. I did not understand his situation. And when he finally found me, dipping my snout into a basin of water in the bathroom, he still did not explain who Mrs Kram was.

'Tristan!'

I turned, with water pouring down my neck and wetting my

chest, in search of something practical to help me drink.

'Get . . . me . . . a . . . straw . . . please.'

Bill knew he could keep his Big Shot Guest waiting a moment longer – two minutes, maybe three – while he finally established his meeting with me.

'Please, please. Please take the head-bit off. We have to understand each other.'

'Go . . . back . . . to . . . your . . . friends.' I shrugged myself free of him.

'They don't have to see you,' he said. 'You can get back in your suit for them.'

'Mo-dab . . . I'm . . . just . . . so . . . thirsty.'

But he began to fiddle with the suit. Or that is what I imagined. Later, on the road to Wilhelm, he swore to me that he had done no such thing, that he was simply patting me, but the fluttering feeling of his theatrically ringed fingers awakened old feelings of anger and I pushed him, hard.

He looked so hurt I thought he was going to cry.

'Please . . . get . . . a . . . straw.' I wrote s-t-r-a-w in the air, slowly.

'Oh,' he said, 'a *straw.*'

He rushed out and came back with a whole damn box of straws. He had perhaps a minute before he had to go and be the host.

'Tristan, I have to work when I go in there,' he said. 'I just need to know that we're OK.'

At last I had a single straw. I began to syphon down the chlorinated water.

'Tristan, I don't know who you are in there.'

He did not know, because he had not been there. He did not know that I had hidden in the darkness of the Feu Follet for eleven years, that I had worked each day on all the tricks he taught me and then lost interest in, that I could do things no doctor could ever have predicted, that I could juggle, tumble, stand on one hand.

I wiped my wet synthetic fur with his dainty little guest towel.

'You . . . want . . . to . . . know . . . who . . . I . . . am?'

'I'm sorry,' he frowned. 'Mrs Kram is waiting.'

'I'll . . . show . . . you.'

If he had told me who Mrs Kram was, I might have acted differently.

## 39

Jacqui was sitting beside Clive Baarder, wondering if it would be rude to lean across the table and take the bottle of wine from in front of Peggy Kram, when she heard behind her a light bumping sound, like a baby falling down the stairs. Turning sideways in her ornate high-backed chair, she saw the Mouse tumbling.

I saw her see me.

I saw her embarrassment, the slow motion of her hand coming to cover her eyes. As she turned in her chair, I completed my gymnastic entrance, twisting in mid-air. I landed, feet astride, my back to her.

Chubby red-cheeked Clive Baarder – the gold-toothed gjent who had earlier faced me in karate pose – now retreated towards the sofa by the window.

The tall hollow-cheeked athletic man, Difebaker the posturer, stood in order to see me better.

But the queen-like Peggy Kram stayed seated at the head of the table – one jewelled hand across her pretty mouth, her other hand outstretched, grasping the slender neck of the Mersault bottle. This one, let me tell you, no matter what she hinted later in her deposition, was not embarrassed. She raised her glass and sipped the straw-coloured wine but her clear blue eyes never left me.

Thus Mrs Kram became my audience. She was awake, alive to the moment. As for the host, he had followed me into the room and was now behind me out of sight. I confess that I forgot him.

'Well,' the lady said in a small breathy voice, which still carried the glottal stops of the desert regions near the eastern border. 'Well, how about that thing?'

She clapped her hands together softly.

'Those *things* are dangerous,' said Clive Baarder, blinking anxiously.

He was now back on the sofa, his short legs crossed, an embroidered velvet cushion placed protectively across his pin-striped lap. 'You know that, Peggy,' he said. 'You damn all know it well as I do.'

But no one looked at Clive Baarder. They looked at me. What did they think I was? I did not know. I was kneeling, holding out my arms, looking straight at Peggy Kram's clear wilful eyes.

Clive Baarder felt himself compelled to stand, and, whilst obviously most reluctant to do it, walked behind Jacqui's chair to be a little closer to me.

'Last time I saw one of these things, Peggy . . . *Peggy.*'

'Yes,' said Peggy absently.

My knees were sore, and yet I feared to break the spell by standing.

'It caught on fire,' Clive Baarder said, 'in a gondel in the Kakdorp. I saw it. I was up on the Colonnade near St Oloff's with Dirk Juta.'

'Dirk will be there tomorrow,' Mrs Kram said absently.

'Yes, and it caught on fire. They pushed it off near the Dagloner Kanal and it floated down for miles, still burning.'

'Peggy,' said Martel Difebaker in the careful rounded tones of the professional Sirkus class. He was almost opposite me, next to Mrs Kram. 'One really must conclude that it is not a Simi.'

Mrs Kram broke her yellow egg-bread, and sipped her wine, still staring at me with such intensity that I began to blush inside my mask. Any moment, I felt, she would ask my father who I really was. But I did not know her history or her passions. She was from the Zeelung border where the Settlers Free first settled, where the Bruder stories are set, where we Eficans saw the sculpted feet of Bruder Dog rise from the desert floor. She was also a collector of artefacts, a connoisseur of folk art. She liked to show her expertise. 'This is absolutely not a Simi,' she declared.

Bill sat himself down next to the place where I continued kneeling. He talked over my head to Mrs Kram.

'I'm so sorry,' he said. 'This is totally my fault.'

What was he apologizing for? Peggy Kram frowned and pursed her lips.

'On every side,' Bill said.

'This is not a Simulacrum?' said Clive Baarder, now approaching the table, still holding the small black velvet cushion. 'What is it?'

'Easier to say what it is not,' said Martel Difebaker, arranging his long and supple fingers so they rested on the tip of his pointed chin. 'Not a Simulacrum. Not a child.'

This was the place where Bill Millefleur might have performed the formal introduction of his son. But now he feared that he had acted in bad karakter by bringing me to table in my costume. He shut his mouth and held on tight, hoping it would work out for the best.

'You're not a dwarf?' Peggy Kram said to me. Her hair was gorgeous, a wild tangle of a mane. As she spoke, she pushed it back from her eye.

It was then I heard Wally sigh. For some time I had been aware of him in the corner of my eye, but now he was glowing with a sort of fury, blowing out his cheeks and wiping his bald head with his big freckled hands. 'Don't make a fool of yourself,' he hissed.

This comment created a strange little silence while all the Voorstanders, Mrs Kram included, looked briefly at the tablecloth.

Then Martel Difebaker spoke. 'This is absolutely not a dwarf. I work with dwarfs – Serango, all those gjents. Can you imagine Serango's head inside that suit?'

'*Tristan!*' persisted Wally.

Again the Voorstanders looked down at the tablecloth.

'Who is Tristan?' Clive Baarder asked when they looked up.

I was on the brink. I saw it coming. I was the girl in the cake. Now I would be forced to unmask. It was then, before anyone could speak, that I leapt up into Peggy Kram's lap. I knew I risked offence, but I was walking on the slack rope. I had to go forward.

Peggy Kram squealed. And held her hands up. I would not have planned it, but the hands went up, the hands came down, and when they did my head was nestled between her generous breasts.

Jacqui closed her eyes. Wally held his bald head in his hands – everything I *saw* told me I had committed a faux pas, but neither Jacqui nor Wally could *feel* the heat of Peggy Kram. I could, right through my suit. I could smell her hair, her skin.

'A humorist,' she said.

In the mirror I saw her take my mouse's soft ear between her fingers and stroke it.

'But what is it?' said Clive Baarder. 'I'd want to know, Peg, before I let it put its nose . . .'

'Oh, that's a joke,' said Peggy Kram. 'That is a joke, coming from you. Of all the people to . . .'

'All right Peggy, that's enough.'

'Of all the people.'

'That's *enough.*'

'You know what the trouble is? We are all so knowledgeable. We know what makes rainbows refract light. Love is all to do with DNA.'

'Not really DNA.'

'Yes, DNA.'

Bill sat down and began to eat his bread, tearing it apart and slathering it with butter.

'DNA or not, this is obviously not the actual Bruder Mouse.'

I peeked a look at Mrs Kram. I snuggled back down into her breast. She put her hand around my neck.

'Peggy?' said Clive Baarder, his lips wet and wobbly, his voice rising incredulously.

Peggy Kram did not answer.

Clive Baarder began to arrange his cutlery with great fastidiousness.

'You believe in St Francis and Jesus Christ?' Peggy Kram asked him. 'You believe the birds talked to Jesus – that's what you believe – am I right?'

'Of course, Peg.'

'Well, I'll tell you this, Clive,' said Kram, leaning across me to take her glass of wine and releasing with this gesture a giddy rush of jasmine. 'We owned Simis. We owned two hundred of them. When they banned them in Saarlim, we bought them for the Ghost-dorps. This is not a Simulacrum. It does not move like one, or feel like one. And all I am saying to you, why do you want to explain it. . .'

'I wasn't.'

'Why do you have to ruin everything by making it less than it is?' She turned my head. As she did so I caught a glimpse of Wally and saw his old grey eyes looking at me sourly.

'I could take him home,' she said, kissing my nose. 'I really could.'

You can understand, I'm sure, why I was under the impression that I was a social success. I was elated, aroused, almost tipsy on her perfume, and so it took a little time for me to look beyond myself, to see my father's pale and stricken face, Malide's comforting hand on his thigh, and it was only then – when it was too late to change what I had done – that I began to fear I had done my dab some damage.

## 40

In Efica everyone imagined that Bill Millefleur was famous in Saar-lim, whereas, as you know, he was just one of perhaps two thou-sand performers employed in the Sirkus, and that particular show – the Sirkus Brits – involving as it did both drama and animals, was as peripheral to Saarlim life as the gentlemen from India who played cricket on the outskirts of the city on Sunday afternoons.

My father had worked hard to make a place for himself in his adopted city. He had worked as hard with history books in Saarlim as he had once, long ago, worked on politics in Chemin Rouge. And just as the scrawny circus boy had learned Rimbaud and Lukacs off by heart, so the handsome man with spangles on his suit soon knew Voorstandish history like a scholar. He knew the Bruder tales, the famous sites, the battlegrounds against the Dutch and British. He could recite 'Pers Nozegard' in Old Dutch, and yet, for all the passion he had expended, he was still an Ootlander, and no matter how much he pretended to the contrary, he found your etiquettes stiff and uncomfortable. He felt his own obedience to your customs a compromise, and when he watched me leap through the air and land in Mrs Kram's lap, he believed himself shamefully exposed: he was a fraud, an ill-mannered barbarian, an Ootlander, a host with poor karakter. He watched Mrs Kram coo, argue, play with my ears, but he had long ago learned that Saar-limites could behave like this and still despise you. And despised was what he felt.

When he shut the door on Mrs Kram and her friends at four a.m., he imagined his guests clustered together in the elevator, raising eyebrows, sighing, and what depressed him – and he was very depressed, you could see it in his slumped shoulders as he came back from the door – was not the loss of a possible employer but his own lack of authenticity, that he should have allowed himself to be placed in this position where their opinion of him would matter.

He was not a Voorstander. He never had been. As he began to walk back to the cluttered dining table he began to talk to us about a strip of land out at Goat Marshes where he had often gone riding with my maman – a lonely windswept place where a muddy estuary met the sea. He hardly paused to dismiss the two helpers in the kitchen, and then he produced a large bottle of very rough red wine which he poured for everyone, remembering (even while he described the Arab stallion he had once owned) to fetch me a straw.

His grief had the paradoxical effect of dignifying him. He still wore the slightly vulgar sparkling suit, the lizardskin boots, but when he brought me my wine in both hands, this shining actor's garb took on a priestly, or even kingly, aspect.

'To Efica,' he said, still standing. 'To us Eficans.' He began to raise his glass in a toast, then lowered it.

Malide reached out to him from her chair. 'Don't do this,' she said.

He swayed his body back, away from the reach of her long white fingers. 'Don't do *what*?' he said, his eyes suddenly slit.

'Everything's all right, hunning,' she said. 'I think she was charmed.'

'Speaking as an outsider,' Jacqui began, but Bill cut right across her.

'Bullshit she was charmed,' he said to Malide, so roughly that I saw her wince. '*Bullshit* she was. I know you people. You're so fucking Japanese.'

Perversely, it was then, when he was unlovely, that I finally loved him freely. It was this sadness that made me trust him and I was ashamed of my childish jealousy earlier in the night.

'I'm . . . sorry . . . I . . . behaved . . . stupidly.'

My father turned towards my voice, frowning and rubbing his hands across his wan and uncomprehending face.

I was ready, at this moment, to step out from behind my disguise, and probably would have had not Wally chosen to rise from his chair like an old vulture, all shining scalp and glowering brows.

'*Stupidly*?' the old man said to me in a voice as abrasive as the legs of his chair scraping across the floor. 'You didn't do anything *stupidly*. What you did was act as if your brain was in your baton.' He stood at his place, his arms out from his side, his elbows bent, glaring at me.

There was a silence. I looked at Bill. His skin had lost its shine. When he tried to smile at me, he succeeded in looking merely puffy. 'For Chrissake, mo-ami,' Wally said. 'This is your father's home. These were important people. Even I could see that. What you did was ugly and embarrassing.'

'Did . . . I . . . screw . . . something . . . up?' I asked my father.

'I'm so very pleased to see Tristan,' Bill said. 'Nothing else is so important.'

'Did . . . I . . . screw . . . something . . . up . . . for . . . you?'

'Yes,' Wally said, so agitated that he began to pile knives and forks on to the delicate blue and white Dutch china.

'Leave it, please,' Malide said.

But Wally was too upset to leave anything. He carried the dangerously stacked plates and cutlery into the kitchen, his head down, his elbows out, his shoes shuffling rapidly across the floor. 'You screwed it up,' he called back over his shoulder. 'It's pretty obvious, even to an Efican.'

'No, no,' Bill whispered.

Malide put her bare arm on Bill's shoulder and drew him into the empty chair beside her. 'Calm down,' she said. 'I don't think this was simply karakter.'

'It was totally karakter,' Bill said. 'She slummed it with us.'

'I think you may be wrong,' Malide said. 'I think Mrs Kram enjoyed herself.'

'Oh Malide,' Bill said. 'No, no, definitely not.'

Malide took Bill's head in her cool tapered hands and kissed him on the forehead. 'The more uncertain you are,' she said, 'the more definite you become.'

'Come on, liefling,' Bill said, 'don't patronize me. I've lived here twenty years.'

'I'm . . . very . . . sorry.'

Bill turned towards me.

'You . . . should . . . have . . . explained . . . to . . . me.'

'Please,' Malide said, standing. 'Let me make tea.'

'Was . . . it . . . for . . . your . . . work? . . . Did . . . I . . . screw . . . up . . . your . . . work?'

In the end, I did not drink tea. I went, at Jacqui's suggestion, to my bath. I had not meant to hurt my father. I had been more self-obsessed than ever he had been. I went in shame, and although I had only recently planned otherwise, I permitted my nurse to gaze once more on the unattractive truths of my pale and twisted body. We did not talk. We barely looked at each other. She swabbed me with disinfectant, bandaged me, hid me again inside the suit.

'This is too intense,' she said. 'I'm getting out of here for a while. Are you going to follow me?'

'No.'

'Do you want anything else?'

'No.' I did not look at her. I stayed sitting on the toilet, feeling foolish, waiting for the others to stop talking about me.

## 41

Malide had given Jacqui the famous addresses where she imagined a voice patch or gizmo might possibly be found.

These stores (23 Lantern Steeg, 101 Sirkus Straat) were all very close to the Baan, in the maze of little lanes between the Marco Polo and the Grand Concourse. There were hundreds of Sirkus shops, opening their doors when the last show shut and closing again around ten each morning. They clung to the edges of the Tentdorp district like mussels on to a jetty, all cheek by jowl, tucked away in basements, in courtyards filled with lumber and the refuse from blacksmiths' shops, on the tenth floor of decaying warehouses in which unglamorous locations you could find the latest laser circuits, French and German make-up, African feathers, Japanese buttons, and any of the craft and technical aids which the Sirkus industry required.

As Jacqui left the Baan a little after five, the deskmajoor tipped his hat and wished her a polite, 'Gaaf morning, ma'am.'

Out on Demos Platz the rubber-booted yardveegs were already hosing down the pavements in front of their respective buildings and the air was as sweet as it ever got in Saarlim, considerably sweeter than the air down in Lantern Steeg which Jacqui, swinging her arms, jutting her little round chin, turning up the white collar of her third shirt, entered at a little before half past five.

That the air here was malodorous, the pavements decaying, did not dismay her. Even the sight of a group of Misdaad Boys, with their bright red kerchiefs and their heavy boots, swaggering towards her, did not make her heart so much as skip a beat. She leaned into the air with her chest as if it were a shield, bone, muscle, and she felt, passing through their field of testosterone, invincible, free from fear, hiding the riches the Misdaad Boys could not have imagined she possessed: the Water Sirkus, the Baan, the dinner with Bill Millefleur, Peggy Kram, the doorman, the gondel, the champagne glass she had carried in the elevator; and she wished only that someone from home – she imagined Oliver Odettes in his demi-bottes – had been there to witness her entry into such glamorous society.

As she entered 23 Lantern Steeg she had to stand astride a sleeping landloper in order to push the button for the elevator. She would have been wise to be nervous, but she thought what other small-town gens have thought since time began: *Here I am.*

When the elevator came, wheezing and clanking, she pushed the button for the tenth floor, the showroom of Ny-ko Effects.

When she emerged half an hour later, the landloper was awake. He lay on his back staring at her with bloodshot eyes. She dropped some coins into his tin, and hurried out into the Steeg, heading westwards towards Marco Polo where she intended to write the first of her daily reports for Gabe Manzini.

She walked into the foyer of the Marco Polo with her hands in her pockets. She nodded familiarly to the deskmajoor who had, only a day before, pressed that money on to Tristan.

Then, looking out across the foyer down by the stained old marble fountain, she saw a man sitting in a straight-backed chair who was so like Wendell Deveau – Wendell whom she had made walk round and round the Printemps Hotel naked, crossing his legs, standing, sitting, so she could see why it was men walked the way they did, where their penis and testes flopped and fell. This man, it was the same man, now stood and walked towards her, frowning and smiling at once.

'Wendell?'

'Who else?'

'Why are you here?' she asked, already irritated by the petulant, put-upon expression on his face. 'So?' she said. 'You couldn't live without me, right?'

'Let's see your room,' he said.

'Let's get a coffee somewhere.'

But he clamped his big white hand around her elbow and propelled her towards the elevator.


## 42

After the dinner party for Mrs Kram had ended, Bill and Malide made a fuss about their 'Saarlim hospitality', insisting that Wally

368

and Tristan stay the night, but this, Wally soon learned, was a sham like everything else had been. The guests would have to sleep on the FUCKING DINING TABLE.

When Wally had tasted the rough red wine – rot-gut, household jumbler, case-latrine, dog piss of the worst kind – the penny finally dropped. The suit and shoes were a costume. The gondel was a prop. The Mersault was a con. The so-called Sirkus Star was one more unemployed actor trying to find a part, to do an audition, someone waiting by the telephone for the call that would let them survive another month. Bill Millefleur was in no position to take back his son.

And to return from the kitchen and discover Bill and Malide laying a mattress on the table where they had previously spread their ostentatious dinner sparked a powerful storm of outrage inside Wally's shining skull.

He squinted his eyes, pushed his fists into his kidneys, jutted his chin in the direction of his host, following all the sheet spreading and smoothing with an increasingly agitated air which Bill and Malide stubbornly refused to notice.

'I was the one who was meant to be the con,' he cried at last. He tucked his dress shirt into his black trousers and tightened his belt. 'All that stuff about the Baudelaire book you used to tell everyone. But here you are.' He nodded at the mattress. 'You always made us think you were the big baloohey, arriving in your limousines. The thing is, mo-ami, I believed you. I brought this son of yours across the world. The pathetic truth is, I thought you were a better man than me.'

'He *is* successful,' Malide said. 'But he's a Sirkus man. One show has finished. Soon he'll have another.'

'I know what the circus is, young lady. I grew up in the circus. I was the Human Ball.'

'No,' Bill said, 'I was very young when I said those things to you.'

But Wally had turned his back and was staring out across the park at the grey and alien dawn. 'We lost our money coming here,' he said. 'We had money. We lost our money. I didn't even care. I thought you had so much. When we were robbed, I thought, that's perfect – now he'll have to see Bill.' He turned. 'We're down to lint and cake crumbs, just like you.'

'It's the Sirkus,' Malide began.

369

'He should have been with you all the time,' Wally said to Bill. 'You should never have left him behind. You could have taught him things I never could. All this behaviour tonight, it should never have happened. You don't know how he pined for you. He did his exercises, the same ones you taught him, year after year. Even when he was making a stack on the Bourse, he would do his exercises in the afternoons. You were very important to him. You were the one who let him imagine he could be an actor.'

He sat down on the sofa, looking up at Bill from under his nicotine-stained brows.

'No,' Bill said. 'We never discussed acting. How could he ever be an actor?'

'Oh yes. It was you. You had an idea for some character in the *Sad Sack Sirkus*.'

'I don't think so,' Bill said, his face now very pale. 'I wouldn't have.'

'These things are nothing to you. You forget them. But the things you forget, mo-frere – those things are the centre of his life. You can say, "I don't think so," but he did those exercises for ten fucking years.'

'I wrote to him,' Bill said. 'I know what I wrote. Now he is here, we'll be fine. Whatever has been wrong, we'll fix it. It's not too late.'

'I always thought he would be better with you, but you've got no job, no bedroom. Do you have any idea of what we've risked to do this? I must tell you, mo-ami, I'm shocked.'

Bill wiped his hands across his face. 'He got my letters, though. You say he read my letters. How could he be surprised?'

'You made him love you,' Wally said. 'You came and you got him eating out of your hand. He gave me up. He took up with you, and then you just dropped him. It was very cruel, mo-ami.'

'Bill cares,' Malide said. 'He is tortured by it. He writes letters every week.'

Wally did not comment. He wiped his face.

'He got them?' Bill asked.

'Yes, yes, they arrived.'

'But he didn't get them?'

'I didn't say that I was perfect,' Wally said.

There was a long silence.

370

'I thought you were rich and famous,' Wally said at last. 'I thought you had everything. He was all I had. No matter what was wrong with me, I knew I would never let him down.

'It was wrong of me.' He picked white specks from the black trousers of his rumpled dress suit. 'I admit it was very wrong.'

Bill gave a small laugh, and then threw the pillow on the bed.

'I was a prick,' Wally said. 'I'm sorry.'

## 43

The lift button was cracked and the light inside it flickered. Wendell pushed it without releasing his hold on Jacqui's elbow.

'What a dump,' he said, and the mouth which Jacqui had once thought of as his best feature now looked spoiled and sulky.

The DoS had sent Wendell here – obviously. They had approved the expenditure, signed the forms, issued the air tickets, which meant that the whole case had now moved three or four levels higher than Section Head.

'Where are you staying?' she asked.

'You stay here, what fucking choice have I got?' His lower lip was droopy, almost pendulous.

'What floor are you on?'

'Come on, professor, you're meant to be an *operative*.' He slammed the button with his fist. 'Use your *head*. What floor do you think?'

The elevator arrived. They rode up together in silence, Jacqui looking earnestly at the numbers while Wendell stared at her malevolently.

'Anybody thinks you're an homme,' he said, 'must be blind.'

She led the way to the room, very conscious of her walk.

She opened the door, and Wendell, having hesitated a moment, went first. He was a big man and overweight, and inelegant in his clothes: and yet when he moved around the room now he did it with a certain dangerous grace: checking for people or bugs or bombs, who could guess. It gave Jacqui a small ambivalent chill at the back of her neck.

When Wendell had finished with the bathroom, he took from his briefcase a small electronic device – a little black box with a series of tiny amber and red lights flashing on it. She knew what it was: a brand new bug-blocker. He placed this in the middle of the room, but the device would not arm itself. The lights, which should have switched to green, remained stubbornly on amber. Wendell stood over it, staring down at it like a golfer at a golfball. Then he kicked it.

The device slid across the floor, fast as a hockey puck, and slammed into the skirting board.

'Fuck *you*,' he said.

He took off his suit jacket, folded it, and laid it on Wally's bed. He went back to the bug-blocker, picked it up, turned it off, threw it on the bed. Then he opened the briefcase and removed the faked-up numbers (a photocopy, not the original) which Jacqui had printed out from Tristan's fax machine.

Jacqui sat on the edge of the other bed.

Wendell held the photocopy in front of her.

'You're a fucking *child*,' he whispered.

She took the paper from his hand. She noted the small green stamp and date which showed it had already been through Analysis. There was also a small black key number which indicated it had been to CRYPT-IT. So, she thought, the game is up.

Wendell took the photocopy back from her fingers and replaced it in his briefcase. She was surprised to see how carefully he handled it, how he slid the photocopy softly into its red plastic folder. He turned, his face frozen in anger.

'Christ, Jacqui, what are you trying to do to us? Do you know what it takes to set up an action like this? The Efican Department sent someone to Neu Zwolfe to meet you. Not some fucking baby-sitter. A real Voorstandish operative. That's VIP treatment, do you realize that?'

He picked up his suit jacket. She felt alert, in danger, but then he turned to the closet and she realized he merely wished to place it on a hanger. Once he had done this he seemed a little calmer.

'You've now got Gabe Manzini on your case. Aren't you even smart enough to be afraid? You know who Manzini is?'

'Wendell, I know who he is.'

Wendell sat down beside his briefcase. 'This fax printout links the mutant with the Zawba'a.'

'I know.'

'I know you know, you stupid bitch. You retrieved those

numbers from your dedicated terminal and you fed them into Tristan Smith's fax machine and then you printed out the call report. We know exactly what you did. But what you did not know is that the VIA has a major operation on to round up Zawba'a. Gabe Manzini is very interested in your case. Mr Manzini is a good friend of Efica's. We'd really hate to have him as our enemy.'

'Oh,' she said.

Their knees were almost touching. 'Do you know how many years it took for us to persuade the VIA to take us seriously? They're New World people like us, but you would never know it from their patronizing attitude. They're worse than the English or even the French. Do you know what it took, the things we did for them so they would trust us? The shit we ate? Friends of mine got killed just so these fuckers would share information with us. So when some little spin drier . . .'

'Don't call me that . . .'

'I thought you were smart. Doctor, right? Am I right? Doctor of fucking Philosophy?'

She knew that she should not be so near him, but it was equally dangerous to move away.

'We can't trust you, Jacqui. You're acting like the enemy.'

He took her face in his hand. She tried to push the hand away, but he was too big, too strong. Her face was small, his hand large, and he held the jaw so hard, pressed his thumb so cruelly, she thought it would break through the skin, and she was frightened, not just of the pain now, but what the pain would grow to, of his size, his bulk, his pale, pale eyes, the level of resentment she saw there. But then his face softened, his hand loosened.

'Jacqui, Jacqui,' he said.

He touched her cheek gently. She made herself very still.

'Did you want to visit Saarlim?'

She did not know how to answer him.

'I hope it wasn't that. It's such a pile of shit.' He looked at her petulantly. 'Isn't it?'

She nodded.

'I never saw such shit,' he said. 'It stinks. It's full of niggers. Why did you do it, Jacqui?'

He had that sticky angry feeling about him. He gave off a smell – she had always thought it was sex, but it was anger.

'You don't involve the Voorstanders like this and not have a result. Now I'm here, we're going to have a result.'

Jacqui felt ill. 'What are you going to do?'

*'What are you going to do?'* he mimicked her. 'I'm going to have to kill Tristan fucking Smith before the Efican Department finds out the real story.'

Jacqui began to cry.

Wendell looked at her, shaking his head.

'You silly bitch,' he said. 'You're lucky they sent me.'

He put his arm around her shoulders and she laid her head on his chest, listening to his heart, the passage of dry air through his moist and gluey lungs. 'Your fax came true. You made the poor little fuck a terrorist.'


# 44

Jacqui was kneeling beside my bed. She was beside me, so close that I could smell mint toothpaste when she called my name.

I knew she was there, but I stayed asleep. In my sleep I was lovable. In my sleep I had not disgraced myself at a dinner party. In my sleep she had different colours in her eyes, small islands of translucent brown, in a sea of coral blue.

'Tristan, hurry!'

Even as I rose regretfully towards her urgent voice, she remained a mystery of nature, beyond explanation and, because of that, someone who might, one day, mysteriously, love me.

When I opened my eyes, I found her in a slightly dazed and dishevelled state, unwrapping a small parcel on the floor.

'Tristan, please.'

I had been asleep on Bill's dining table with Wally's feathery snore playing in my ear, the sheet up across my naked face. Now I allowed her to help me down on to the littered rug and out into the muggy air of the balcony, where I saw she had the Simi suit laid out upon the ground, its gloved hands pointing away into the potted plants and creepers. I pulled my nightshirt tight around me, looking at the Simi without enthusiasm.

'Put it on,' she said.

'Why?'

'We've got to leave.' She stamped her foot. 'Quick, quick.' Her very strong, straight hair was actually bristling, not just on her crown, but on the fringe as well.

My muscles were still suffering from the exertions of the day before, but I laid my weary body down and soon felt the familiar tug and slide as I was sewn inside, snug as potatoes in a sweaty sack. Before she closed the parcel tight, she slipped her cool dry hand in around my neck. A second later I felt a small adhesive plaster applied in the region of my Adam's apple. As she smoothed it down with her fingers there was a brief stinging pain, like the bite of a small black ant.

'Don't say a word, Tristan,' she said, kneeling by my head. 'Don't even squeak. Just trust me while I finish sewing your suit together, and let me tell you where I was while you were sleeping.'

I stared out through my eye-holes at the concrete floor, the blue glazed pots.

'You're not going to like me, Tristan, when you know who I am, but just the same, mo-frere, I wanted to do something nice for you.'

She turned my head again. I imagined I knew what she was going to tell me, i.e. she was a woman.

'It isn't much,' she said. 'I hope you like it, but if you don't like it, you can at least be comforted by the fact that it hurt like hell to pay for it.'

I could imagine her frowning while she snipped with scissors at her untidy needlework.

'I went to a shop called Ny-ko Effects,' she continued. 'Malide told me it was there, otherwise I would never have known – ten floors up in some crappy little alleyway, run by some little Greek man with hair on his knuckles. Be still . . .'

She stood and shut the sliding door. I sat up.

'Now, please . . . we haven't got an awful lot of time.'

'What's . . . that . . . thing . . . on . . . my . . . neck?'

My words were repeated by someone else. *What's that thing on my neck?*

Jacqui smiled at me. 'Not bad,' she said. 'Not bad at all.'

'You've . . . got . . . a . . . tape . . . recorder?' I asked.

A light tenor voice repeated after me, *You've got a tape recorder?*

'Do some Shakespeare,' she said. 'Quick. Do that bit from *The Tempest* that you like.'

'What . . . have . . . you . . . done?' I asked, sitting up. *What have you done?* The effect was seriously disconcerting.

'You're wearing a "Two-pin Vocal Patch" like the actors in the Water Sirkus. You have a one-inch speaker sewn inside the Bruder's snout, and it is recommended that you change the patch every week. It's what they call a "Mid-frame" voice. You should have seen it, the shop. You wouldn't believe the stuff they have there.'

'I . . . can . . . talk,' I said.

*I can talk.*

'Recite something. *My name is Ozymandias . . .*'

It's . . . very . . . weird.'

*It's very weird.*

'You sound like Piper McCall. Do the bit from *Henry V*, the speech before Agincourt.'

'Piper . . . McCall . . . is . . . a . . . great . . . actor.'

*Piper McCall is a great actor.*

'So are you, mo-chou,' she said, kneeling to pick up needle, thread, crumpled paper. 'So now you can speak to Mr Millefleur. You can say all the things that are on your mind. Speak with your lips closed. I've stuffed a lot of paper in the snout to muffle it, but you don't want the broadcast voice to compete with the lip voice. Come on, we're going now.'

'*Now is the winter of our discontent, Made glorious summer by this sun of York.*'

'You could be in the Sirkus. You really could. You could be a star.'

'*Thank you,*' I said. It was disconcerting to have my voice booming around me inside the Mouse head. '*Thank you.*' I had to work at keeping my mouth closed. Even then my perfectly enunciated speech had a muddy undercurrent.

'*Do I have an accent?*'

'Tristan, we can't hang around here,' she said, opening the door into the apartment. 'I have things I have to tell you.'

'*Tell me how it works.*'

'It picks up on the resonance,' she said, whispering, so as not to wake up Wally, 'the vibration on the throat. It has a little chip which knows how to convert this to properly modulated speech. But listen, listen to me . . .'

'*I want you to wear women's clothes.*' I said that. It was like a dream – I didn't know where it had come from.

376

'What?' she said, looking at me, blinking, her lips apart.

'*Dress like a woman.*'

She tugged at the sleeves of her jacket and did up a button. 'What exactly does that mean?'

A delicious bloom appeared on her cheeks and neck.

'What?' she said.

I did not say anything. I was in a daze. The world was soft and out of focus.

'I don't have any girl clothes.'

'*Malide does.*'

She looked at me, hiding her expression with her hand.

'Quickly,' she said. 'Go and wait out there.'

I went back on to the balcony outside. I paced.

I was Meneer Mouse waiting for Madam Mouse on a street corner. I was the beau with the bunch of flowers, the stage-door Johnny. I was not a target of assassination. Not as far as I knew. I was the inhabitant of a trothaus, on a balcony high above Demos Platz, a Sirkus star, waiting for a girl to come and join me. It was yearning, desire, the most exquisite kind of pain.

I heard the door, the soft slide of machined aluminium.

Madam, Meneer, she was so lovely. She wore a simple skirt, long and black, and a tight-fitting blue halter. But it was not the dress or her body, but some bright, high light in her perfectly boned olive-skinned face. She wore no make-up, her hair was ruffled, but she was electric.

'I'm so sorry,' she said. 'I've been a stupid person. If there was a hell, they'd have to send me there.'

I hardly heard her. I saw her. I was so happy. I knelt in front of her.

'*My speech,*' I said.

'There's no time,' she said.

I knelt beside her. I picked a little flower from out of Malide's window box. Wally would have died to see it – a sappy thing with a stalk like a daffodil. She took it from me, and held it in both hands.

'*I prithee, let me bring thee where crabs grow.*'

I was Caliban, of course. You should have heard me, Meneer, Madam. I was funny, ironic, mocking, and so *clear*.

'*And I with my long nails will dig thee pig-nuts,*' I said.

377

'*Show thee a jay's nest, and instruct thee how to snare the nimble marmoset . . .*'

She sat on the white plastic stool beside me. Only then did I notice her face, the tears welling in her eyes.

'*I'll show thee the best springs; I'll pluck thee berries.*'

'Tristan,' she said.

'Yes. What?'

I felt her hands fondle my ears. I could smell the flower, the musty dust on its stamen. I saw her wet cheeks and was filled with joy.

'We have to go,' she said. 'There's someone out there wants to kill you.'

## 45

Wally woke to find Bill, Malide and Peggy Kram all camped on his dining-table bed and talking volubly as if the dinner party had never finished.

The old man had thought himself in a private place. He had gone to sleep with his trousers pressing underneath the mattress. His dentures were in public view. His dress shirt and bow tie were folded neatly on the bookcase at the head of the bed. Now, as he struggled to button up the crumpled shirt, he was mortified to find his bare and withered chest displayed for all to see.

How this could happen in etiquette-obsessed Saarlim was as much a mystery to him as was the warmth being displayed by the hosts and their powerful guest towards each other.

Yet the implications of the visit were so clear to the Saarlimites that they did not feel they had to explain it, not even to a foreigner. If Mrs Kram was clambering over Wally's bed, it meant she had decided, for whatever reason, that Bill's apartment was *hearth* and that Bill and Malide were *hearth folk*. In other words, Mrs Kram had derived value from the dinner party, and my father, to his barely concealed astonishment, found himself elevated, promoted, saved.

'I thought about it all night,' Mrs Kram said. 'I was so aired-up, I could not sleep.'

'We felt the same,' Malide lied. 'We went straight out for chocolate. We talked about you for hours and hours and then, coming back across the Platz, there you were.'

'And there *you* were,' said Mrs Kram, who had not, in the entire dinner party, said so much as half a dozen words to Malide.

'We were talking about you,' Bill said.

'And there I was, my head full of *you*.'

'We were saying, how could we live so close to you all that time and not hear that you were *folk*?'

They were, as you can see, in too much of a giddy state of insincerity to notice anything as ordinary as Wally's chest or dentures. If they sat on the bed, it was because this is what you do in a situation like this. They were in such a rush, were so loud and pleased to kick their shoes off at the door, were so happy to show how thrilled they were with each other's company. It took them nearly three minutes to realize that the nurse had changed sex in their absence.

'Excuse me, young lady,' said Mrs Kram when Jacqui brought Wally's socks and shoes over to the bed. 'Did I drink too much, or were you a gjent last time we met?'

Bill and Malide echoed her laughter, but their eyes registered their own separate but discreet emotions: amusement and admiration in the man's case, serious alarm in the woman's – that was her 1000-Guilder skirt swishing up and down the apartment.

Wally retrieved his trousers from beneath the mattress and drew them on beneath the covers. Then, as Kram wiped her eyes, he swung his legs out over the bed and smoothed down his wild eyebrows with his fingers.

'What time is it?' he said.

'Ohmygod,' said Mrs Kram. 'Ohmygod, this apartment is better than a cabaret. I should move in here. It's so amusing.'

If I had recited the speech which I was forming in my head it would have been a good deal more amusing, but Jacqui somehow intuited that I was about to show off my new voice.

'Forget that now.' To Wally she said, 'We've got to go.'

Wally stared at her, open-mouthed.

'Mr Paccione, we *need to go*.'

'Then others want to use the bed?'

'Ohmygod,' said Mrs Kram. 'This is Saarlim, hunning. No one sleeps in Saarlim.'

And straight away, without asking permission from Bill and Malide, the Kram began to phone up to her own apartment to tell

379

her caterers that there would now be extra mouths to feed.

'For Christ's sake,' Jacqui said to me, 'let's go.'

'Do you like berries, Oncle?' Peggy Kram called to Wally. 'Do you like wild rice and chestnuts? Will you eat today, cuteling?' She beamed at me. 'Will Bruder Mouse come upstairs to see my little trothaus?'

I turned to Jacqui.

'That's it,' she said. 'Go with her. That's perfect.'

And that, of course, is how we made our escape from Wendell Deveau without even leaving the building. We rode the big glass elevator up to Mrs Kram's trothaus.

## 46

My threatened assassination was much less in my mind than I might have expected. I do not mean that I was brave. You know I am not brave – I hid from death for years on end inside the Feu Follet. I saw death, smelled it, let it invade me like a gas until it had occupied every corner of my empty soul.

But as I rose inside the glass elevator, I knew my life was about to change. I was about to become witty, sexy. I was about to speak clearly for the first time in my life.

My only hesitation was – what should I say? You try it – think of a sentence, now, that will express all your genius and charm.

Hurry, hurry. You are on the tenth floor. Time is rushing.

It is better – *fourteenth floor* – to keep it simple.

*Fifteenth floor.*

*Sixteenth floor.*

You can see the gondels clustered at the steps on Demos Platz. You can see the pigeons on St Francis fountain. You don't know what floor Peggy Kram lives on and you are ready to settle on asking, 'Which floor?'

At the seventeenth this seems stupid.

*Eighteenth floor.*

At the nineteenth you see a chance to link life and art, to comment on the view. But 'Like a De Kok' is not accurate, and you cannot think of the name of the Saarlim painter whom the view recalls.

'Do it,' Jacqui said to me on the nineteenth floor. 'Just Caliban.'

'What Caliban?' said Kram, instantly alert, her blue eyes flicking between the pair of us. 'What's up?'

The doors slid open into a mirrored foyer. I saw myself reflected in a gilded frame – a myth, a legend, a beautiful woman on either side of me, my entourage behind.

'What's up?' asked Kram.

There was nothing I could answer. Instead, I took the Kram's little hand inside my own. Then, with Jacqui walking behind in long black skirt and bright blue blouse, I walked in stiff, bow-legged majesty, head high to Mrs Kram's gold-belted waist. I left Wally and Malide and Bill to follow me into the splendour of our hostess's Saarlim life.

You have seen photographs, perhaps, of Peggy Kram's trothaus. On the page it is what you'd expect. In life, in my Efican life anyway, it was simply unbelievable: the elevator opening on to the marble lobby with a little dog-headed Saint inside an illuminated niche, and thence to the succeeding parlours, with their Dutch and Flemish Masters, on to the so-called Great Room with its high windows opening out on to a garden with trimmed hedges – high, deep green topiary in the shape of 'The Least of God's Creatures', the Dog, the Duck, the Mouse, their soft and leafy forms silhouetted against the pale blue sky above the fabled city.

Someone wanted to kill me?

Let them try.

We stood in the sunshine above Demos Platz while Kram's 'Man' (an elderly Egyptian whose loose-fitting, dun-coloured clothing reinforced his status as a POW) emerged from the throng of earlier arrivals and offered drinks to those of us tall enough for him to notice. Peggy Kram excused herself.

'Don't hate me,' Jacqui said as soon as she was gone. 'I'm going to get you out of this.'

Her anxiety was delicious. I felt it, smelled it, a kind of aphrodisiac. She leaned out and touched my arm. I felt the contact in my neck, my toes.

'Don't hate me,' she said.

Hate her? All I heard in her voice was her remorse, concern.

'We're safe up here for the moment,' she said. 'Please say something to me,' she said. 'Please.'

The two-pin voice patch had cost her every Guilder she possessed, as much as a Neu Zwolfe crucifix or a first-century

Bruder mask. Now she needed to see the power of the gift: she wanted to see it unwrapped.

I would have said something, but you should have seen her in the skirt, the line of her back, the erotic grief in her eyes. I feared my voice would boom out of me, too loud, too hot, and we were not the only visitors gathered on the terracotta tiles of Peggy's trothaus. Clive Baarder was there once more. Also Martel Difebaker. Dirk Juta, the Mayor of Saarlim, Frear Munroe the lawyer, the comedienne Elsbeth Trunk. You'd know the names, not personally perhaps, but from the zines. I heard the ascetic Martel Difebaker once again playing expert witness on my nature. But as it turned out, I was not the only curiosity.

The Mayor, Dirk Juta, being daily in the Bankruptcy Court, was also the subject of much attention, as was the celebrated lawyer, Frear Munroe.

This Frear Munroe was, as they liked to say in Saarlim, bigger than life. He had a broad chest, a deep voice, a slight Anglo accent, a ruddy complexion and fair hair which he parted to one side and which, with the daily application of pomade, had become slightly green in colour.

He stood over the Mayor who, unlike any Efican politician I had ever seen, was a *dainty* man with thin brown wrists showing from his crisp white shirtsleeves.

'So, Dirk,' Frear Munroe trumpeted.

The Mayor smiled sadly up at him.

'So, is our dear old Saarlim to be declared bankrupt or not? Will we have a police force next week? Or should we make some new Simi-cops and put them back on the streets instead?'

'I'm pleased this is amusing to you, Frear,' the Mayor said.

'You misunderstand me, Dirk – I was not joking.' Frear smiled, pleased with himself. 'Perhaps this is a mythic moment – don't you know your Badberg? The barbarians are not *without* the gates. They are *within*. The God-fearing are being set upon by unimaginable odds. Rape and pillage is a daily occurrence. If we were true to the beliefs of our fathers . . .'

He gestured to the Mouse, the sort of hammy gestures certain Saarlim advocaats like to make.

'One mo nothing,' he said in a rough dialect. 'Next mo, there was Bruder Mouse . . .'

'In all his furry finery,' said Martel Difebaker.

'Solid as a miller's wheel,' said Frear Munroe.

'Leave him alone,' said Wally. 'Do me the favour.'

'Solid as a yellow oak on a Monday morning,' said Elsbeth Trunk, whose dialect was considerably better than Frear Munroe's.

'There are various similes,' the lawyer said. 'But perhaps this is, Elsbeth, don't you think, the mythic moment? Your honour' – the lawyer turned to me, placing his veined square face very close to my snout – 'oh, little being,' he declaimed.

The others laughed. Not Wally. He did up the button of his now rather rumpled dinner suit. His eyes were closed to jailyard slits.

'Oh, small beast.' Frear Munroe knelt before me, mockingly, so close that I could smell his herring breath.

Wally tapped him on the shoulder. 'I'm sorry,' he said. 'I can't let you speak to him like that.'

Frear Munroe blinked at the stooped bald-headed man, but he was already in full flight and did not have time to ponder his significance.

'Oh Bruder Mouse,' he cried. 'Thebes is in such desperate plight that we have come to you, the least of all God's Creatures, that you might tell us what to do, oh little club-footed thing.' He stood, his face contorted with his own laughter. 'Oh dear,' Frear said, wiping his eyes and dusting off his striped black trousers. 'I don't know if those legs are mythic.'

As the offensive fellow turned his back Wally took two fast steps forward. 'Enough's enough,' he said in broadest Efican. Then he kicked Frear Munroe up the arse.

The lawyer lurched. His glass flew from his hand and shattered.

Frear Munroe, although gone to fat on port and hunning cheese, was still a well-built fellow. Now, as Bill Millefleur hid his bowed head in his hands, the lawyer turned to raise his fist at Wally.

It was then that Wally lifted his stick to ward him off, then also that I made the twelve-word speech which, I discovered later, was to be quoted all over Saarlim for a week.

'*One mo' step*,' said Bruder Mouse. '*One mo' step and I'll tear your throat out.*'

## 47

Jacqui had been waiting to protect me from the DoS. Now, as the lawyer raised his meaty fist above my head, it was no great stretch for her to pick one of Kram's small lead figurines from a niche in the garden wall. It was a statue of a mole, and when she closed her hand around the chunky little weapon, she felt her soul rushing towards the extremes of action that had attracted her all her life.

She took two fast paces forward before she had time to consider what she would do next. Frear Munroe was solid and slab-sided, much taller than the nurse. As Jacqui came behind him, he turned. His eyes were pale blue, small and lonely in that big red face.

It was something of a shock to see that he was afraid of Tristan Smith.

'Some Bruder,' he said, but when he tried to smile his lips were wobbly and misshapen.

It was such a moment, a beautiful moment, but there was no time to relish it for Peggy Kram came rushing out and ran right through it and ruined everything. She entered, her servant at her tail, all that golden hair shaking, laughing, a peach cocktail splashing over her ringed hand. Jacqui felt a great shiver of dislike move through her slender frame.

Kram took the Mouse by its gloved hand. Jacqui watched her kiss it on the nose.

'Ohmygod,' Kram said, 'you savage little thing.'

Her friends all laughed too loudly, but Jacqui could have slapped her face. She could not stand the proprietorial attitude towards something she did not understand. But Mrs Kram now drew yours truly to one side and squatted down before me. Jacqui watched me bow. She saw Frear Munroe grin and turn away to find a listener for a story about his threatened throat.

Then she watched me appear and disappear amongst the creatures of the topiary. As I was taken from guest to guest, she heard the voice she had given me. She saw me shake the hand of the Mayor and she imagined me, Tristan Smith, inside the sweaty suit, stinking like over-ripe apricots.

Wendell might be in this very building by now, bribing yard-veegs and deskmajoors, going through Bill Millefleur's apartment, reading through his appointment book. Wendell was not the sluggish person his gross body suggested. If he had said he would wipe out Tristan Smith there was every chance that he would do it.

In this field, Jacqui had no expertise. She stood with her slender back against the terracotta wall, facing the french doors of the Great Room, standing as she'd seen bodyguards in front of prime ministers and presidents, their hands loosely by their sides, their eyes always moving.

If they took my life, she saw she would have to kill herself. She screwed her face up as against a bright and painful light.

She had the statue of that smirking little mole you know as 'Singing Willie'.* She was now ready to use it against my assassins. When Wally Paccione approached her she could not spare him any more than her peripheral vision. He came slowly across the terrace, out of focus, black and white in his dress suit, tapping his cane, jutting out his unshaven chin. The aura of his own upset preceded him.

He positioned himself beside her, and began, immediately, to go through the elaborate ritual of rolling himself a cancerette. Jacqui could not look at him. She was staring into the dark of the Great Room where she could see figures moving in front of the paintings. A man in a sixteen-button suit came out into the light. If he had been an operative, she would not have known.

Beside her, Wally finally lit his lumpy cigarette. He inhaled, exhaled. She felt him turn his grey eyes on her.

Finally he spoke. 'I don't know who you are or what you want.'

The man in the sixteen-button suit was now talking to a woman in a blue-veiled hat. He accepted a glass of wine from the servant. This must mean that he was not an operative.

'You've lied to me,' Wally said. 'You jerked me around. You might think you're cute, but let me tell you, sweets – you know what you've done to him . . .'

'You've got no idea, Papa.'

'I've got every fucking idea,' Wally said, his voice rising. 'You think I'm blind?'

Jacqui scanned the party, the topiary, the waiters, the hazy skyline, she heard the Mouse's two-pin voice. ('*I live on air*,' it said.

---

* *Actually, Sinning Willie.*

*'I suck it in, I spit out the pips.'*) Peggy Kram was laughing, shaking her head.

The old vulture edged himself closer to her. 'You think that's cute?' he said, nodding at the Kram.

'No.'

'You think this is good for his *self-esteem*?' He stood beside her, whispering in her ear in that way of his which she had always found off-putting.

'If I'd wanted to hire a woman,' he continued, 'I would have advertised for one. I grew him up,' he said. 'We had one female santamarie, never again. God damn,' he said bitterly, looking Jacqui up and down, her breasts, her legs, her face. 'He has feelings.'

'You think he's fallen in love with *Peggy Kram*?' Jacqui turned to look him in the face for the first time.

'He's a young man, for God's sake. Sex is all he thinks about.'

'Is he *flirting* with her?'

'You don't seem to understand – this isn't funny.'

'Mr Paccione.' She turned and took his sleeve and held it. 'I am standing here because I am expecting a man with a gun who wants to shoot Tristan.'

She saw his mouth open, saw his coated tongue. She saw the eyes reacting like living things exposed to acid. Suddenly, he looked so old. He began to wipe his hand over his head. The colour drained from his cheeks. He was an old man from a little town, far, far, far away. There was a helplessness about him she had never seen before.

'He offended someone?'

'It's nothing he's done.'

'I hate this place,' the old man said. 'We should never have come. I put the idea into his head. We were happy where we were.'

'Mr Paccione, please, be calm. Listen to me: it's the DoS, the VIA as well.'

'Oh my God,' said Wally.

'They have an agent at the Marco Polo. I talked to him this morning.'

'We have POW numbers,' Wally said, his voice breaking. 'What does it matter if he wants to wear the stupid suit? Who is he harming?'

They stood together watching me. I was alight, aflame, drunk on celebrity and the smell of Peggy Kram's hair as it brushed the surface of my Simi-shell.

# 48

Jacqui and Wally were ready, on that night, to risk their lives to get me out of Voorstand. I should have listened to them, but I was like a drunk around a bottle. My death hung over me, and I would not see it.

Wendell Deveau, his belly sticking out in front, his shirt hanging down at the back, was prowling round the Demos Platz. Leona the facilitator was bugging Wendell's room in the Marco Polo. And Gabe Manzini was sitting in a gondel off the Demos Platz tracing Wendell's progress on an electronic monitor.

Mencer, Madam – my death did not disturb me. I barely noticed it. It was no more than the distant flutter of moths' wings before the roaring of my need. I was twenty-three years old, crazy for life, the smell of a woman's skin, the great bursting view through the topiary and down into the long shadows of Demos Park with its looping flights of red-winged pigeons.

I was standing in the place where Sirkuses are born, where the fabled city itself was either saved or damned. I was impressed. I was excited. Will the judges at the Guildcourt consider this when they attempt to determine my motive?

It is true I never revealed my true identity to those I met at Mrs Kram's trothaus. But Kram herself never wished to name me. She said, I'd like you to meet a friend of mine, and gave *their* names to me, never mine to them. This was not my deception. It was her respect.* This is how you introduce kings, princes, and stars of only the most dangerous types of Sirkus.

And they liked me, Kram's friends. I listened to them. They listened to me. I quoted Seneca. I told them jokes in my two-pin voice, jokes I made up on the spot, and delivered with a physical technique the opposite of anything Stanislavsky would ever have thought possible.

---

* Cf. Item 3 of the charges against Tristan Smith: '[that he did] wilfully, blasphemously, seditiously disguise his being and therefore lead others to believe he was Bruder Mouse . . .'

I was Meneer, or Oncle, or Bruder, the last of these to Frear Munroe, who gave me his card and asked me to come and see him perform in court where – he whispered this into the great dead prosthetic he imagined was my ear – he would be called in to represent special interests in the case against the hapless Mayor, accused of many things, including selling public streets and parks to French and English corporations.

Did I like Frear Munroe? No. I did not like his smell, his bad-tempered face, the violence I saw brewing behind his eyes. But he had currency – he told me things, in such a way, that I felt I had been beamed into the white-hot centre of existence.

So even though my bones were aching and my ligaments torn, even though I was faint with hunger and my skin was itching and aspirin was singing in my ears, I was – with the Kram's long hair brushing across the wall of my face each time she leaned down to tell me something – in some kind of wild heaven where I did not give a damn for anything except how to get more of whatever it was I had.

I did not think the next move. I took it as it came. I spoke the words and learned to trust the patch. It strained my face most terribly. It is no easy business talking solely from the throat, but the result: the bliss of eloquence. Meneer, Madam, did you ever have dreams of flying?

Peggy Kram smelled of herbs and wild honey. It was her golden Dutch hair, her French shampoo, waving through the air in front of me. She had good skin, slightly golden, and clear blue eyes that stood in total contradiction to her Mersault.

Her hands were small, not perfect, indeed a little plump, but who am I to speak to you about perfection? She touched my 'ears', held my 'hand'. 'I'm going to keep him,' the Kram said to beaming Bill, repeatedly.

Of course she knew I was not a mythic beast. On two occasions she clearly communicated her wish to not know who I was. Why was this? She did not tell me. She is what is called in Efica a stoppered bottle, a private person. She lived alone, so Frear Munroe told me, had no lovers, had her corporation boardroom in this trothaus, and the only thing he knew about her was that she had been a Sirkus widow who made her money, like so many, when her husband fell from the St Catherine's Loop and crushed his head in front of a house of two thousand.

'I want him,' she said to Bill Millefleur, and thus produced a peculiar expression on my father's handsome face.

It was not unnatural that my father should feel uneasy. He needed her approval as much as anything, and yet I was his son. He was galloping forward while reining himself in. He was on the slack wire, eighty feet above the ring.

'Well, Peggy,' he said. 'This is not for me. I really think you have to discuss this with the Bruder himself.'

'I want you here,' Peggy Kram said to me, directly, frowning, and pushing her hair out of her eyes. 'I won't permit you to go home.'

You see my porpoise rise, you think you see where this is leading. That is your history, perhaps, not mine. In my history there can be no climax, no conclusion, no cry in the dark, no whispers on the pillow.

'My dear,' I said, and my voice was so intelligent, so clear, so damn *sophisticated*. 'My dear Mrs Kram, you couldn't deal with me.'

'Oh, I could handle you,' she said.

I knew her, knew her imperious, self-doubting little soul. I whacked her on the bum, not gently either.

This made her face red, Bill's ashen.

'Is this how you act with Madam Mouse?' she asked me. Her eyes were wet and bright.

'Madam Mouse is dead,' I said.

'Dead?' she said, colouring more. There was a way she spoke, with the tip of her tongue always forward in her mouth. It gave a slight cloudiness to her diction but made her mouth, always, wonderful to watch.

'Quite dead,' I said to Mrs Kram, playfully elbowing my anxious father in the thigh.

'Mrs Kram,' said Malide to Wally, 'is asking, would Bruder Mouse here like to stay with her?'

'How did she die?' asked Peggy Kram.

'She was assassinated,' I said, 'by agents of a foreign power.'

There was a long, long silence on the roof. I saw Frear Munroe, standing by the parapet alone, turn his square head. 'They came and hanged her by her neck,' I said.

'Stay,' Wally said. 'It's too late to go.'

'He should definitely stay,' Jacqui said.

389

'Meneers, Madams,' I said, looking at them gathering around me, out to Frear Munroe and Elsbeth Trunk, 'do I not have voice to speak? Can I not speak on my own account?'

What I liked, what made me giddy, was the way not only my friends but six of the most powerful personages in Saarlim turned their heads, lifted their chins, parted their lips, how they listened, how they waited. I had no idea what I would say.

# 49

I had fallen asleep on the bed Kram's servant had, rather formally, introduced me to. I woke at two in the morning. I was stiff, hurting, hungry. I needed drugs: Sentaphene,* Butoxin,† Attenaprin,‡ but they were all in my bag in Bill's apartment.

The glowing thermostat beside my reading lamp was set at a cool 65 degrees, but it was stinking and steamy inside the suit.

As I tried to stretch my painful hamstrings I knocked an envelope on to the floor. It fell with a heavy thwack. Later I would discover it to be a letter from my father, but at the time I was too stiff to think of bending for it. I was more interested in anti-inflammatory drugs, a bath, disinfectant, a bed where I could feel sheets against my skin. I left the large tan envelope on the bedroom floor and shuffled to the bathroom where I used the zip Jacqui had expediently sewn in the previous morning.

That aside, I was imprisoned by the Mouse.

I went looking for someone to release me, but the layout of the trothaus was more complex than the blockhouse exterior of the Baan suggested. The passageways were full of nooks, crannies, alcoves, reading rooms, small libraries of Sirkus art and so on. Twice I found dark rooms in which I heard the sound of breathing, but I did not know whose breathing it was. I retreated, and was soon lost again.

Finally, in the lobby by the elevator, in an austere straight-backed chair, in a lighted alcove which had previously accommodated the

---

* *Diazephene.*
† *Anti-inflammatory of Efican manufacture.*
‡ *Enteric-coated aspirin.*

Dog-headed Saint, I discovered Wally Paccione. There he sat, like a Folkghost in white pyjamas, his eyes bright, his mouth dark and toothless, a piece of looped wire held in his ancient liver-spotted hands.

'Sssh.'

He jerked his head in the direction of the elevator. I could hear the car moving in its shaft. Together we watched the numbers light up above the door. They stopped at the fourth floor.

He held up the wire, grinning. The inside of his mouth was black, the sunken cheeks bright white. Now I know it was a garrotte which he had made from ivory chopsticks and piano wire. But at the time I misunderstood.

'The DoS piano,' he said. And I imagined it was a primitive musical instrument from Kram's collection.

The lift clunked and rose up to the fifth floor. 'Don't stand there. Get behind this screen.'

I did what he said. I moved away from the lift doors and pressed myself between a Neu Zwolfe triptych and the wall. From behind these dark, worm-eaten panels I could peer out across the roof garden and into the softly illuminated kitchen.

'Can you help me out of my suit?'

'Turn that stupid thing off,' Wally hissed. 'I can't bear you talking like that.'

'I can't turn it off.'

I heard him spit. 'You know what a mess she got us in, that spy?'

'Where is she?'

'How the fuck do I know? You sound like a fucking Voorstander. If she told you that sound was glamorous, she's working for the governor. I promise you, my son, we're getting out of here. As soon as I deal with this fellow, we're getting out. We're leaving all these spies behind. We're going home.'

'Which fellow?'

'*Christ!* Don't you pay attention to anything except your dick? There is an Efican stooge coming to kill you. I'm going to kill him.'

'No, Wally . . .'

'You think I can't? You don't know anything about me.'

'No, of course not.' I came out from behind the screen. 'Please, Wally . . .'

'Get *back*.' He screwed up his face, and the lights in the alcove made the wrinkles deep and black.

'I really hate that voice,' he said when I'd retreated.

The elevator clunked again. I was reduced to looking out through a crack between the triptych panels. I could watch the illuminated numbers as the elevator descended to the ground floor.

'No one knows the things I've had to do,' Wally said. 'Not your maman, not anyone.'

'You stole some stuff,' I whispered. 'You never *killed* anyone. I don't want you hurt.'

'Murder is much more common than you'd think.'

The elevator made a whirring noise, then stopped on the fifteenth floor.

'You don't know much about me,' Wally repeated. 'For all the time we've spent together, you don't know what I've done. When I'm dead, you won't know,' he said bitterly. 'You'll say good old Wally, but you won't know who "Wally" was. You don't even know where I was born.'

'You were the Human Ball,' I said.

'I hate that voice,' he said. 'You're like another person.'

'You never wanted to talk about yourself,' I said. 'You can't blame me. Who did you kill? Tell me now.'

'It was a long time ago.'

'It was the person who put the cigarette burns on your arms,' I said.

Wally said nothing.

'It was your father, wasn't it?'

'This is not the first time someone tried to knock you off. It's much more common than you think.'

The elevator creaked and we both heard the doors in the distant lobby close. I could see the lights as it rose towards us: 16, 17.

'There were two times in your life,' Wally said as the elevator stopped. 'The first time was when you were born. The doctors wanted to kill you then. They wanted to take you away, but your maman would never let them. They sent the Gardiacivil after you but that made no difference to her. So she saved you the first time. But you knew this.'

'How did she save me?'

'She never let you go,' he said. 'She never let anyone look after you except me and Vincent and Bill and her.'

'When was the other time?'

'You know the other time.'

'No, I don't.'

'Roxanna tried to kill you.'

'I cut myself with the glass,' I said. 'It wasn't her fault.'

'No, listen to me: Roxanna tried to kill you.'

'I know you loved her, Wally. I'm so sorry about Roxanna.'

'She tried to *kill* you with Thallium, you dope. You were so sick. I told you you had Cuban flu, remember? There was no fucking Cuban flu. There never was such a thing. You wouldn't leave the Feu Follet, so she began to poison you. She kept feeding you little sweets, chocolates. She was injecting them with Thallium. You were nearly damn well dead by the time I got you to the Mater.'

'When I came back she was gone.'

'Damn right, she was gone. She was gone to damn jail is where she was gone. Roxanna was insane, Tristan. She tried to kill you so I'd go away with her.'

'Poor Rox,' I said.

'Yes,' he said, and his voice sounded old and cracked. 'Poor Roxanna.' A moment later he asked, 'You wanted a bath? Is that what you were looking for?'

'I'm OK.'

'Why don't you ask Mrs Kram to give you one?'

'Very funny.'

But then the elevator was travelling again. I watched the numbers, my mouth dry.

'Listen,' Wally said when it had stopped. 'Please, don't flirt with her. It's embarrassing.'

'I'm flirting with who? Mrs Kram? You're embarrassed? Why would you be embarrassed? Don't answer, because I know. I know what's embarrassing.'

'It's not you,' the old man said. 'It's her.'

'It's like in Zeelung. You got in a panic about the flower.'

'She's not a normal woman. What woman flirts with a Mouse?'

'It was just a flower. You think I'm still fourteen years old. You got in a panic, and you fucked everything up. You ruined it. You know that, don't you, Wally? The truth is: we lost our money

393

because of you. You're in a panic any time I like a woman.'

'I'm standing here,' he said, 'protecting your life, and you're *blaming* me for getting robbed.'

'Forget it,' I said. I was in a passion. It was not pretty, not nice. 'If that's your attitude towards me . . . '

'You're *blaming* me?'

I stepped out, out from behind the screen. 'It was just a fucking flower.'

Wally threw his garrotte on the ground and walked out into the garden. I stood there for a moment, and then the elevator began to move and I went to my room. There was nowhere else to go.


## 50

All my life I had waited for my father to need me, and now there was a letter from him, needing me.

All I could *think* of, however, was Wally. I lay on the bed and read Bill's letter, but all I could see was Wally, his anger, his self-righteous face, the elevator rising and falling in its dark and deadly shaft.

Bill's words ran before my eyes like ticker-tape.

My dear son,

So sorry for the SCRAWL but am sitting in the Kram's krapper with pants around my knees. Apologies for crumpled paper, bad spelling, all the usual.

Also: please disregard the attached until you have read this.

I don't think I have any right to ask you what I am going to ask you. I don't know what you THINK of me. The things I project on to that Mouse mask . . . 'THE POWER OF THE MASK', eh? Remember when your maman did the Brecht with the Japanese masks?

I feel like I have spent a lifetime apologizing to you and I was just so prikkeled that you never got the letters I sent to you. What circle of hell is that? Where you apologize for eternity?

Should have stayed in Efica, that is my feeling now. It was certainly a better life in Efica. We are 'creatures of our place'.

Each night I dream of Efica. Those damn white trees, they really do break my heart. Again and again I walk through forests of them, touching their sticky bark with my hands and knowing I am not there.

Here I am an Ootlander, a horse rider, a barbarian. I STILL DO NOT KNOW THE NAMES OF THE TREES IN DEMOS PARK. But 'the train is on its rails' as they say in Saarlim.

Maybe I will end up playing the part of the Hairy Man in some shitty Ghostdorp.

Someone is knocking on the door.

Tristan, maybe it is news to you – my contract with the Sirkus Brits is finished. I have a back injury and a tin plate in my head. I can't go back to performing, and as for acting – I never really was an actor after I left your mother.

Begging for help. My only hope is to run my own show. Have been trying to get BIG WIGS to read attached business proposal. So this is it: my pants down: begging you: please can you use your influence with Mrs Kram?

Is this too opportunistic for you? Have I become a total Voorstander? If so, just tear everything up, nothing matters so much as your good opinion of me.

Oh Tristan, I really am so full of shit.

I folded my father's letter quietly, slowly, with extreme care. And I lay waiting on my bed, just as my mother must have waited. She must have felt her Voorstandish murderer inside the Ritz, the Feu Follet, must have heard him on nights when he was not yet arrived, must have listened to the rumbling of the building's guts, just as I lay now listening to the distant elevator. She did not know they would tell her to stand on a chair. She saw the green rope and never did suspect the plan they had for her.

This room Kram had given me was ornate in the extreme, with heavy drapes and old folk paintings with worm-riddled wooden frames. I had not been ready for this folk-art aspect of Saarlim life, the reverence for the uncompromised past with its Saints and Hairy Man and beans and Bruders.

There were perhaps fifteen lamps inside that room, all of them with heavy shades and low-watt ratings, all with different types of switches to the ones we have at home. I turned them on, every one of them. Then I lay down inside my sweaty suit upon the quilted bed.

I picked up my father's letter once again, and then it occurred to me that I was making myself vulnerable by leaving all the lights turned on. I put the letter and the document back inside their envelope and then set about turning off the switches: the ones with knobs, the ones like levers, the ones you pulled like toilet chains, the ones which could only be operated by crawling underneath the bed, the ones hidden on the rat tail of the power cord. When the room was pitch dark, I locked the door.

But lying once more upon the bed, I began to worry that I would fall asleep, and not hear Wally if he came to save me.

So I stood, one more stiff and painful time, and unlocked the door. Then I lay on top of the quilt, in the incense-rich dark, listening to the noises of my breathing inside the mask, my squittering heart, my acid-wash belly.

I fell asleep. I woke. The door was opening, slowly.

Inside my clammy body suit, my hair rose on its ends. My skin prickled. I could hear the tread of the intruder. God help me please, I was half scared to death. The assassin's step. No one could have told me it would be so delicate – a rubber sole pressed against an antique carpet.

In my terror, I dared not move.

In my terror, I thought, I will cut off my suit, reveal myself in all my horror.

My assassin moved towards me, as fluid as a ghost in the dark. I watched until I had no choice but to leap. I shrieked. I came up off the bed towards him, arms outstretched, and got him by the throat. And down we went.

Too late I saw it was Peggy Kram. I fell upon her, elbows, breasts, her fragrant silk and cotton.

'I'm sorry,' I said.

But the crazy woman was laughing, untangling her hair from my ears and nose.

'One mo nothing,' she said, then broke out laughing once again.

'What?'

'One mo nothing,' she said, 'next mo there he was, Bruder Mouse, as solid as a yellow oak on a Monday morning.'

She stood and wrapped her white gown around her. Then,

without any explanation, she took me by my big gloved hand and led me out into the hallway and then into the room on the other side which was, I saw, her bedroom.

I could have held on to my anger, but let me tell you, Madam, Meneer, I was very pleased to be changing my address. No one was going to come looking for me in Mrs Kram's boudoir.

Just the same, I took the precaution of returning to retrieve Bill's letter and then locking Kram's door behind me. When I stepped behind her heavy drapes, ostensibly to admire the view, I checked the hardware on the windows and put Bill's letter in a place where I could find it later.

When I emerged from behind the drapes, I found the mistress of the house already in her bed, her embroidered white coverlet right up under her smooth little chin and her hair lying on her pillow like Madam Van Kraligan herself.

'Bruder Mouse,' she said, 'would you please be kind enough to tuck me in?'

She asked me so sweetly, I was pleased to perform the service for her.

When I had done it, done it properly, the same way Wally taught me, the same way he had learned in the violin, I stood and waited, wondering what was to happen next.

Peggy Kram then patted the coverlet beside her. I thought she wished to hold my hand, but no.

'Sit,' she said. 'Sit up by me.'

I climbed up on the bed which, let me tell you, was mighty soft.

'Can you sleep?' she asked me, a peculiar question you might think, given what had happened in my room. 'Are you nervous?'

'I thought you were a burglar.'

'When I cannot sleep,' she said, arranging her fragrant hair on the pillow with both hands, 'I always find a story useful.'

Then she smiled at me. I was slow to understand her. Now I was there, now I felt safe, I wanted nothing more than to lay my head down on her pillow and go to sleep.

'Peggy wants a story.'

Then I understood.

'Bruder Mouse,' she said. '"Bruder Mouse's Beans".'

You know the story. I knew it too. My dear maman read me the stories from the Badberg Edition with its beautiful pen drawings by

397

Oloff Tromp. I knew the words by rote, but now I was being commanded to perform them for the most powerful produkter in Saarlim.

'I'm not an actor,' I said.

'Sssh,' she said. 'I don't want to know.'

So I did my best, reading in a country style that I hoped was appropriate for the material.

As for the produkter, she was a perfect lady. She sat there with her hands folded in her lap, a slight frown on her face while I narrated the tale in which Bruder Mouse arrived (*'One mo nothing. Next mo there he was, solid as a miller's wheel'*) to fight off the Hairy Man with no other armaments but black beans and rice. Like so many of the Badberg stories this one derived its terror from drowning and its humour from flatulence, although in this case, of course, there is flatulence and fire, combined.

I was not auditioning, but I was, as I said, indebted to Mrs Kram, and I felt obliged to give everything to the task at hand. This was only prevented by my exhaustion, and from time to time the produkter found it necessary to wake me with a sharp little push in the ribs.

Even as she drifted into sleep herself, the Kram would not let me stop, but held me with her hand so she could jerk me if she found me sleeping. In this way we got through three or four of the longer fables – including the one where the Mouse persuaded Oncle Dog and his friends to save the city of Saarlim by walking on their hind legs with rifles on their shoulders and masks on their heads. The one that ends, *'And so it was, the Bruders were free and Meneer Mouse sat down to eat cheese pudding.'*

When I woke, it was morning. I knew straight away, even before I opened my eyes, that it was very late. The heavy drapes were partly drawn, and so the curtains which locked light out of the apartment like water from a bottle now permitted a thin slice of white sunlight to stream into the room. A yellow, artificial light also entered the room, this coming from an open bathroom door from which clouds of steam billowed, flowing prettily across the hard edges of bright light.

As I slowly woke I began to be aware that my hostess was walking back and forwards between bathroom and closet wearing no other clothes than those her God had given her. I never saw a

naked woman before and I cannot imagine a more wonderful introduction to the phenomenon – set off by fragrant steam and morning
sunshine.

I moved and yawned, to let her know I was awake.

She looked across at me.

'Good morning, Bruder Mouse,' she said.

I did not say anything.

'One mo, there she was,' she said.

She continued to parade up and down, to enter the bathroom,
to come back to the closet. I could not, for the life of me, see what
she was doing in any of these places. She did not take clothing
from the closet. She did not perform any toilette in the bathroom.
She walked before me as if I were nothing but a dog, and I
watched her.

Was this exciting? Yes, damn it, yes it was. She was an attractive
thirty-year-old woman with her clothes off. She was not tall, and
she was a little thick in the waist, but she had big well-shaped
breasts and a firm backside. She had a soft bush of blonde hair.

From the bathroom she called to me.

'Bruder.'

'Yes.'

'Do you have thoughts?'

'Thoughts about what?' I said.

'Do you have anything to have thoughts with?'

'I have as good a brain as you,' I said.

She came out from the bathroom, her hand holding her hair up,
smiling. 'It was not brain I meant,' she said.

'Oh.'

'Does my hair look better up or down?'

'Come here,' I said, 'so I can see.'

'What about Madam Mouse?' she said.

But she came a little closer. She had not dried herself quite
properly. I could see beads of water on her little nest of hair.

'Come here.'

She shook her head. She walked away. She walked to the window and pulled those drapes closed. She went to the bathroom and
turned off the light.

The room was now pitch black: darkest, deepest, velvet night.
Yet I could feel her come towards me. I could feel her warmth. I

399

could smell her perfume, shampoo, soap, steam. I heard her small white feet upon her knotted folk rugs.

'Don't tell me,' she said.

'Tell you what?'

'Don't tell me anything, OK?'

She came into the bed. I held her, this woman who had no lovers. She held me hard between her breasts. You might imagine me inside my suit, locked in, smelling my own breath, distant from this stranger, able only to feel her desire as she moaned and dragged me between her legs, and you may, never having been in my position, be thinking of the humiliation and discomfort and forgetting, entirely, that Jacqui had given me a zipper and that I could, there in the fragrant dark, slowly ease my porpoise into her, and feel her soft pink muscles grip me.

'Ohmygod,' said Peggy Kram, her fingers holding on to my back, 'Bruder Mouse.' Lots more she said. She talked and sighed and laughed and begged me keep my secrets to myself. She squirmed and slid and exclaimed and made little bird noises high in her white woman's throat and, what with the conversation and all, we hardly heard the banging on the door and Jacqui's distant voice crying, 'Tristan, if you're there . . . '

'No Tristan here,' murmured Peggy Kram.

'Tristan, we've got to go, now.'

'You can stay right on my pillow,' said Peggy Kram. 'This is better than a man. I'm going to keep you.'

## 51

She would not let me go, Madam, Meneer. I know now, she was not well. It is obvious to you, of course. It was obvious to Wally. But for me the case was different. She wished to dress in front of me. I am a man. I was more than pleased to watch. She wished to play games in the dirty dark and put her mouth around my porpoise and call it names in French. Why would I think that she was *disturbed*?

Outside the door my nurse called and hammered, but Jacqui – no matter how I admired her weird and dangerous spirit – was there to get me out, away from Peggy Kram, out of the country, over the border, down long roads with high poplar trees standing on each side. All right, all right – she wished to save my life, and I, the monster, was like a dog licking its dick in the middle of the road.

Mrs Kram had other plans for me, and she could not let me go. This is what she told Jacqui, shouted at her, through the door.

'He's mine,' she said. I did not think this strange. It is not alarming to be found, at last, desirable.

She opened the bedroom curtains and showed me Saarlim. She talked passionately about its former greatness, its present troubles. She pointed out the five Sirkus Domes she owned. She pointed out the roads the Mayor had sold to foreign speculators. There were tears in her eyes. I did not doubt her concern.

Was I simple? Was I an opportunist? Both, I suppose, but to charge that '[Tristan Smith did] wilfully, blasphemously, seditiously disguise his being and therefore lead others to believe he was Bruder Mouse and that all this was undertaken with the express purpose of defrauding the citizens of Saarlim and depriving them of liberties granted them by God' – really, Madam, Meneer, you give me too much credit.

Yes, I came into your country with my secret rage. Yes, I lied to you and said I felt no rage. Yes, I acted as if my mother's murder were not a personal matter between me and you. But is that not, in normal circumstances, polite?

Your own agent was the one who ran down the Simi, the so-called theft of which is the subject of charge three.* I could not have planned this. Yet if I had not met the Simi, I could never have so charmed Mrs Kram. So common sense will tell you that I could not have entered Voorstand planning to climb into Kram's bed.

Almost a week I spent with her. During that time no one – not Wendell Deveau, not Gabe Manzini – could discover where I was. Metaphorically speaking, I was in another country.

We sat amongst her folk rugs (so many mice and ducks you never saw) with her photograph albums. So many black borders, so many dead people. So many terrible things had happened to her in her short life. She had witnessed her handsome husband's brains splatter against the front-row celebrities on opening night. She lost two babies in the home that caught alight while she was at the theatre.

---

* 'Unlawfully take into his own possession a Simulacrum Mark 3, model No. 234, the property of the Saarlim Cybernetic Corporation, and that he did, without proper permission, either orally or written, and contrary to the best interests of the aforesaid Simulacrum's legal owners, damage the aforesaid machine to such a degree as to make it without value.'

Other things, you may or may not know about, more things than should have happened to anyone, had happened to this woman, whose wealth and power were envied everywhere.

She is thought to be ruthless, I know, and is, I know.

But Madam, Meneer, this misguided woman's passion for the principles of your past, her vegetarianism, her prayerfulness, all this is genuine.

In each one of her Ghostdorps she had tried to create an ideal world – a model – where the actor inhabitants lived in accordance with the values of the Settlers Free. 'They ploughed, they tilled, hulled, they shucked, they ground, etc.'

She promised me she would find work for my father, that she would keep me in comfort all my life. She told me she would employ my nurse.

She told me about the Saarlim Ghostdorp. It was not my idea. How could it be? Could it be anyone's but hers? It was she who had assembled Frear Munroe, Dirk Juta, Clive Baarder, on her rooftop.

It was she who later took me into her trothaus boardroom and introduced me to Clive Baarder. Please wait, Madam, Meneer. In a moment I will tell you what happened in that room. But first a reminder of what you put my family through.


## 52

'You are asking me to betray my son,' my father said to Gabe Manzini, who was drinking Orange Pekoe tea from Bill's best art-deco chinaware.

'A little melodramatic,' Gabe Manzini said, 'even for the Sirkus Brits.' He lifted the saucer to read the mark and then placed it on the table very gently. 'All I asked you was, have you seen him or his nurse?'

Bill looked away from him towards Wendell Deveau. The big pasty Efican was looking out of the window, eating the ham sandwich he had brought with him.

'I can't do it,' Bill said, at last.

'Come on, mo-frere,' Wendell Deveau said, crumpling up the green sandwich bag. 'Don't stuff us around.'

Bill took the greasy paper from the DoS man and carried it to the fastidiously tidy kitchen.

'It is your privilege not to assist us,' Gabe Manzini called. 'Just as it is my privilege to ask if your immigration papers are in order.'

'You'd kick me out of the country, for not answering a question?'

'Again: I did not say that. But we are a rough lot, Meneer Millefleur. We get very impatient with details.'

'I've lived here over twenty years,' Bill said, seating himself at the table again. 'I've paid my taxes.'

'Come on, Bill,' Wendell Deveau said. 'Don't stuff us around.'

'Twenty years!' Manzini smiled, and what was unnerving to Bill was that it was a nice smile, the smile of a civilized man. 'You must like it here. This is a very nice apartment. I was admiring the De Kok.'

'I like it a great deal,' Bill said.

'As for your papers, to tell you the truth, I couldn't say if they were in order if you showed them to me,' Gabe Manzini said. 'We have a whole building full of lawyers who look at that sort of thing.'

'And what do you want with my son?'

'Well, as you can see, we have two parties with an interest,' Gabe Manzini said. 'And if I were a little *less* upset with my colleagues in your estimable DoS I might not say this to you – but if I were you, Meneer Millefleur, I would be working damn hard to let me have your son. I think Agent Deveau here has orders to *eliminate* him.'

'Come on, Gabe, all I want to do is interview him, just like you do,' Wendell said.

'Well, Meneer Deveau, the tapes will settle that question. My advice to you,' he turned to Bill, 'would be to let me talk to him. We Voorstanders are not always the villains.'

'I don't have to work in Saarlim,' Bill said. 'You refuse me residency, I'll go home.'

'You know,' Gabe Manzini said, 'I wouldn't advise that. Those DoS guys can be real pricks, especially when they've been made to look stupid. Just because they're sometimes unprofessional doesn't mean they couldn't hurt you. The opposite, really.'

'Could I have a second of your time?' Wendell said to Gabe Manzini.

Gabe Manzini looked up at Wendell Deveau and smiled pleasantly. 'Of course, Bruder,' he said. 'Later. We'll talk all about it at 583. For now, I think we should give Mr Millefleur a moment to reflect.'

403

Gabe Manzini rose and walked around the apartment. He stopped at a sandstone figure of the Dog-headed Saint. Picked it up. Turned it over. Replaced it. He was a neat figure, slim, athletic, with shining brown shoes and corduroy trousers. He was like a curator, not a murderer. Everything he looked at, the precious dining table, the art-deco china, the Badberg first editions, the De Kok 'Crucifixion in the New World', revealed a connoisseur's discernment and therefore an educated approval which Bill would, in other circumstances, have found highly flattering.

Indeed, my father had always prided himself that, no matter what his disappointments in relation to his acting, he was living a cultured life at the centre of the world. He had seen Michael Cohen play Hamlet. He had dined with Una Chaudry. He had seen the greatest actors of his time. He had shaken the hands of two kings, a mayor, a duke from England. He had skated on the ice in Demos Platz on Christmas Day. He had dined at Le Recamier, at all the finest restaurants in the city. He had been born in a leaking caravan in Efica, but he had spent his life with the very best of everything in the world.

But now he saw it was impossible for him to do what he was asked. He sat and looked at the possessions which had hitherto given him so much satisfaction and realized that he did not give a tinker's fart about them. He saw a whole wall of dominoes tipping and falling like a long black tail which led back to the ageing Circus School with the rusting roof.

In his mind he and Tristan Smith were already back in the seedy little theatre in Gazette Street. It was raining. Moosone. The drains were overflowing. A plastic rubbish bin was blowing down the street.

## 53

Wally had turned his back on me. Jacqui had brushed past me and ignored my greeting. But it was Clive Baarder who had been the most upset to see me when, nearly a week later, I finally emerged from Peggy Kram's boudoir.

He sat at the top of the long table in the trothaus boardroom with his back towards the grey gritty Saarlim sky. He placed a yellow legal pad in front of him and removed the cap from his pen.

'So what is this about?' he said to Peggy Kram, who had positioned herself right next to his elbow.

'You tell him, Bruder, hunning,' she said to me.

I looked up the long table from my seat. 'The idea . . .' I began.

'Wait,' Clive Baarder said. To Peggy Kram he said, 'Is this his idea?'

'Not exactly.'

'So why is he presenting it? Why is this . . . personage . . . sitting in our boardroom?'

'In the past,' Peggy said, resting her hand upon Baarder's rigid forearm and patting it, 'this would not have been unusual.'

Clive Baarder let her hand rest a moment. Then he withdrew his arm and made a neat black line across his legal pad.

'What past do you mean?'

'In the Great Historical Past,' she said. 'When Bruder Mouse walked amongst the Settlers Free.'

Clive Baarder looked down at his legal pad for a considerable length of time.

I had earlier imagined Baarder to be a kind of private secretary, but now I saw what all of Saarlim knows: he was a powerful man.

'A mouse is a little thing,' he said at last. He fitted his pen back in its cap and held it up between thumb and forefinger, as if it were a dead field mouse he was pinching by the tail. 'You know that, Peggy, in real life.'

Mrs Kram swivelled through 180 degrees and back again.

'Clive-ling,' she said soothingly, even flirtatiously. 'Dear Clive, you know yourself the great benefit of conducting business in one's home is that one's clever friends, like Bruder Mouse, feel free to contribute to our meetings.'

'Peggy, you conduct business from home because you are agoraphobic.'

My mentor said nothing, although her colour rose.

'Peggy . . .'

'I'd rather have Bruder Mouse than a man,' she said, and shook her hair.

'Oh Peggy, please, don't be embarrassing!'

'You're the last one to talk,' she said. 'I wouldn't if I were you. I wouldn't even *begin* to talk.'

'Just the same: this is not a mouse, Peg.' Now he turned and took her hand. 'We know that, don't we? A real mouse is not like this little gjent.'

'Let him outline the concept before you race to judgement.'

'Peggy.' Clive Baarder opened his pen again. 'What is this meeting for?'

'If you listen, you'll find out.'

'I only say this because I have another meeting starting in the Tentdorp in thirty minutes and I can see how tired you are.'

'I'm always tired, Clive. You know I never sleep. And don't think your cynicism is attractive.'

Clive Baarder smiled implacably.

'You think you can reduce everything to DNA, but you can't. I tell you, this is what the Great Historical Past was like. It doesn't really behove you to doubt me. History is my *business*. It was my business when you were an out-of-work Verteller buying drugs from scum in Kakdorp. Who else but me preserves the Great Historical Past? No one would know what happened *yesterday* if it wasn't for the Ghostdorps.'

'Peg, my dear, you are exceptionally tired.'

'And don't patronize me, Clive. I am not tired, and you have always had a rather smug attitude towards the Ghostdorps which I find offensive.'

'My attitude towards the Ghostdorps is totally to do with profit . . .'

'A Ghostdorp is a safer environment for women and children.'

'Peggy, please, not today. Let's fight when it's just us.'

'When the Saints walked Voorstand, that is how it was, just like it is in the Ghostdorps. We were decent people then. The Sirkus was not just an entertainment. Bruder Mouse was not a clown. We knew him when we saw him. We did not argue about which was wild flesh and which was Bruder's flesh. We did not have all these codicils and revisions to the old laws. We ate beans and rice and raagbol pudding. We did not rape and murder. We did not thieve. We were better then.'

'You know that I don't disagree.'

'Bruder Mouse , the Saints, they walked amongst us.'

'Oh Peggy . . .'

'Fuck you,' screamed Peggy Kram. 'Don't argue with me. Here

he is. Solid as a miller's wheel. He is looking at you and politely waiting to outline an idea that will have you planting bulbs and making toasts.'

'This is not a mouse.' Clive Baarder was shouting now, not at me, at Peggy Kram. He was standing up, gripping the long table like he wished to tip it over. 'A mouse is four inches long.'

'One mo nothing,' Mrs Kram shouted back, 'next mo there he was, in all his furry finery.' She sat down. 'Look out there,' she said, nodding her head towards the grey and humid sky. 'You are looking out on a corrupt and decaying city and you have lost the ability to believe in a future.'

'This is not Bruder Mouse, Peg,' Clive Baarder said between his teeth. 'And you damn well know it isn't. You don't want to admit that it's a man, but it is some kind of man, a dwarf.'

Neither of them was looking at me now.

'So what if you're right,' she said. 'What does that do for you?'

'For me?' He shrugged.

'It makes you right, that's all,' she said. 'You see the stitching on his suit. Hooray. I see it too. Is that the point? We see the gold paint on the Saint's crown. So what? The point is not the paint. The point is, we've lost our values. We're eating Bruder's flesh, we're putting animals in Sirkuses. That Efican sitting in my garden, what's his name, Millefleur – riding on horses, frightening lions. That would never have been permitted thirty years ago. He would have gone to jail for even suggesting it.'

'Last week he was hearth folk. You said you liked him.'

'I do like him. That's why he's sitting in my garden. I've been discussing his future with the Bruder and it will be my great pleasure to employ him in something decent for a change.'

'All right, Meneer Mouse,' Clive Baarder said sarcastically. 'Please tell me what the pair of you have been cooking up.'

'It all began,' I said, 'when Mrs Kram observed that the Mayor had sold many of the roads and parks to foreign corporations.'

'Entities,' he said. 'We call them entities in Voorstand.' He turned to Mrs Kram. 'Are you paying attention to this, Peg? Only an Ootlander could call an "entity" a "corporation".'

'His idea,' said Peggy Kram, 'is that we buy them back.'

'Oh Peggy, what is this?'

'Shut up, Clive. I know exactly what I'm doing.'

'Peggy, not even you can *buy* Saarlim, if that's what you have in mind.'

'Yes I can. God damn, I am sick of being afraid,' she said. 'I am sick that something bad will happen after dark. I'm tired of being afraid of sicko men with knives and poisons.'

'Peggy, you never go out.'

'But I want to.'

'You cannot run a city of ten million like a Ghostdorp. We cannot even run the Ghostdorps that we have. We cannot buy Saarlim.'

'Oh I can. I can buy the roads and parks back from the foreigners. The city's creditors will be happy. Everyone will be happy. It's a very patriotic thing to do.'

'Is this the *Wishes of The People*? Is this government by *Each Family Before God*?'

'I'm going to give the citizens of Saarlim exactly what they need. Clean streets. Well-dressed people.'

'Stop it, Peg. You're frightening me. You can't ask the bhurgers to be like actors in your Ghostdorp. No one will let you. I won't let you.'

'I'll let all the *decent* folk go about their business. It's quite legal, Clive. We talked to Frear Munroe.'

'Oh Christ,' said Clive Baarder. 'Peggy, you are not well. You really must deal with your own past.'

'When you say past . . .'

'I mean past.'

'No, no, you're talking code. You mean I want to do this because I was raped? Is that what you're saying?'

'No.'

'No? Good. Because I can run a clean Ghostdorp and I can run this city. I can have the parks safe all night long. I can have the streets tidy and neat. The grass in the park will be cut. It is so very simple. People will come from all over the world once again. We will be a great nation once again.'

'This is not your idea.'

'This bit is mine,' she said.

'And how would you make the streets safe exactly?'

'I wouldn't let unsavoury types walk on them.'

Clive Baarder nodded his head slowly. Then, for the first time since the meeting began, he turned and looked at me.

'Do you hate Voorstand?' he asked me.

'He loves Voorstand. Leave him alone.'

'He is an Ootlander,' he said to Peggy Kram. 'He uses Ootland words. Now he's trying to deprive us of our freedom.'

In answer to this charge, Bruder Mouse said not a word. He slipped out of his chrome and leather chair and walked in that rolling sailor's walk towards the longest wall of windows. Despite the comic nature of this walk, despite the broken tooth and the spangled blue waistcoat with the button missing, anyone could see this was a powerful figure. He stood and faced Clive Baarder. Behind his back was all of Saarlim, all its territories and municipalities, roads, steegs, platzes, freeways, overpasses, intersections, public bridges, all glowing pink and dusty in the late summer light.

Such was the intensity of this moment for each of the three people in the trothaus boardroom that, when Wendell Deveau's pistol fired twenty feet away, they barely noticed it. A sort of phhht, that's all.


# 54

Jacqui recognized that sound. She had heard it at the DoS in that long thin basement room on the Boulevard des Indiennes – the sound of a silenced Glock, like a fart.

'Tristan!' She ran across the glossy blue tiles, through the glass door, into the trothaus foyer. There, in that gloomy chapel-like space with its Neu Zwolfe triptych and big gilt-framed mirrors, she heard a peculiar drumming noise which she later knew was her old lover's heels doing their death dance on the tiles.

They were lying together, the two men: Wendell on top, Wally Paccione underneath. The old man had his piano-wire garrotte around the agent's throat.

As Jacqui knelt, Wendell's great fleshy legs twitched. One foot had lost its shoe. The sock still had a gold stick-on label on its sole. His arm flopped out sideways. She jumped back, her hand to her mouth, as his Glock clattered to the floor.

'Help him,' Bill said.

But there was no one to help. Wendell had finally managed to shoot Wally Paccione through the rib cage – the bullet had passed upwards and sideways into his heart. Wally was dead. He was tied on to Wendell's throat with a piece of grisly piano wire.

In their struggle, a chair had broken. A 200-year-old plaster statue of the Dog-headed Saint lay on the floor, his plaster crown in fragments on the floor.

I sat on the floor amongst the broken plaster. I looked at Wally's dead, dead face, the hollow cheeks, the dried lips, the wide belligerent eyes, the arms that held the gory garrotte, all the tendons standing out like lines of cable underneath his skin.

I could see the line of small round white scars along his arms. Those arms and hands had bathed me, swaddled me, taught birds to dance, gripped his knees while he was the Human Ball, perhaps not in life, but always, forever, in my mind.

I whispered in the big old wattle of his ear. I was so close to him, the little white hairs, the freckles. I was full of my own poison. I told him that I had been wrong, that it was not his fault that we were robbed. I told him that I loved him. I could feel Peggy Kram pulling at my bulky suit. I felt so ill. My mask was full of my own foul air. I told him he had more love in his heart than any of us.

'Don't worry,' Peggy said, trying to help me up. 'I own five Sirkuses. I can promise you, there'll be no trouble.'

'Peggy . . .' said Clive Baarder. 'Please watch what you say.'

'God damn,' shrieked Peggy Kram, 'this is family. I said we'd fix it, Clive. We'll fix it. You get the damn Mayor on the phone.'

'He's in court.'

'Get him out of damn court.'

'They're Ootlanders.'

I turned from Peggy Kram and caught sight of all our images in the great mirror. What a filthy frieze it was – that sweet old man and Bruder Mouse – a perverse Pietà. How I loathed the Bruder's grinning face, those floppy ears. My stomach clenched and I knew I was going to be sick.

'Bill, help me,' but no one heard me.

'This is murder, Peg,' Clive Baarder said.

Now I was retching inside my suit. The contents of my stomach rose up inside the mask, were sucked down my nose.

Suffocating, I tried to pull the Bruder's head off, but Peggy Kram got her little hands around my wrists.

'No,' she cried, 'no, please, I beg you.'

It was Jacqui who saved me. She was smaller, finer, lighter than Peggy Kram, but she yanked the produkter by her mane of hair and pulled her free. Then she placed her hands on either side of my Bruder head and dug her nails into the slit she had so diligently sewn up. And then she ripped, ripped my Mouse-head apart like it was orange peel. She tore the head off like a prawn.

In the mirror we all stood and stared at my true face. I turned, gagging, aching for breath.

Spare me, please, the memory of Peggy Kram's face when she saw my true nature.

## 55

'It's OK,' my father said. He was a well-dressed, handsome man, an actor. He was hearth folk. He came towards Peggy Kram, holding up his pale pink hands. 'Peggy, please. It's OK, really.'

But Peggy could no longer see him. She could see only the horrid creature that had put its red prong between her legs. She saw blood, snot, some ill-defined horror like a piece of meat, wrapped in plastic, left too long in the refrigerator.

'It's It,' she cried, crossing herself in front of me. 'It's Marchosias. God save us. It's the Hairy Man. God save us.'

If this was Efica we could have dismissed all this as 'just religion', but this was Voorstand and we were Ootlanders and my father therefore wrapped his strong body around mine. He lifted me into the air with his left arm. He held out his right hand to Jacqui Lorraine.

'It's Dagon,' screamed Peggy Kram. 'God save us.'

'Goodbye old man,' Bill said to Wally's body.

'It's Red Saatanil,' said Clive Baarder, and I swear he meant it. 'God save us.'

'God save us,' hollered Peggy Kram, throwing herself on her knees before the triptych.

We left the dear old Human Ball. We had no choice. We left him grinning, stretched out with his victim. The elevator was rising towards us, but Bill, fearing it contained more assassins, led us through the fire door to the stairs.

Why did we flee? We had done nothing wrong. Why did we

rush out the back way and abandon our belongings like criminals?

Because, Madam, Meneer, my father had studied your Great Historical Past, and when Mrs Kram began to recite the Thirteen Names, he recognized the ritual from the Geloof Trials of a hundred years before. He saw the way Tristan Smith's own history was moving.

A bright red rail spiralled down twenty storeys to a chessboard floor.

'Hoop,' Bill said, and knelt so he could pick up Jacqui Lorraine around the waist.

She was one hundred pounds. I was sixty-five. When he got astride the banister he had the hundred pounds over the stairs, the sixty-five above the abyss. There was no rehearsal, no net, and his balance was by no means perfect, but as Gabe Manzini rose inside the elevator, as Kram and Baarder screamed the Thirteenth Name down into the pit, we were speeding towards sanity at thirty miles an hour.

On the fifteenth floor we wobbled.

On the twelfth I thought we were dead.

'Ooop-la,' Bill cried, holding us both, spinning on his toes as we landed. He wore his grey silk suit with snakeskin patches. He wore his elastic-sided boots with diamonds in the heels.

## 56

If you registered motor cars, like any other country in the world, perhaps you would have tracked us as we ran from you.

But you are who you are, and we who we are, and we drove five days across some of the most beautiful country I have ever seen. We travelled across the dairy belt, up higher and higher into the Gelt Plateau. In other words, we travelled in the opposite direction to the one you had expected, into the country where they still hang the Hairy Man to make the corn grow. We drove through the night, through lone pine forests with no other habitation but simple miners' shacks with their kitsch folk figures in the barren front yards, with their neat stacks of yellow wood lined up along the high verandas, ready for the winter. As we went higher the cornfields were silver, gold, brown. And everywhere the flag, crimson in the morning, carmine in the shade.

After we left Highway 270, we took roads so small they often had no names. Then we travelled through a lace-work of little lanes and plateau towns where you could see tin cut-outs of Bruder Mouse nailed to the barn doors.

Each night we slept in the car, fogging the windows with our life stories – Jacqui and her drinking mother, Bill and I and all those long-lost performances at the Feu Follet.

In the early mornings, before dawn, Jacqui left the car and went stealing. You know, by now, exactly what she stole: the three blankets, the raisin buns, the whole round of cheese, the red woollen shirt, all that drearily itemized account which is the sub-stance of the charge against her. But I doubt you know, Meneer, Madam, that damn cheese weighed twenty pounds and she dumped it on the roof of the car at five a.m., scared us shitless, laughed herself silly to see Bill Millefleur dancing round the steering wheel trying to get his pants on.

Jacqui had returned the long skirt and blue top to Malide. Now she had another black skirt, a loose grey sweater, and a white singlet. As we travelled higher, as the cornfields grew gold and silver, she also became burnished. Her eyes (perhaps they were always like this, but I only saw it now) became flecked with colour like an opal, beads of soft brown in the hazy blue light, and there was a calm about her, a passivity I had never seen in her in all the time I knew her.

She, whose life had been marked by the sharp snapping of her fingers, her need for risk and action, now sat calmly for hours on end. I do not mean to suggest that she travelled silently. Indeed she talked rather a lot.

The more I listened to her, the more exactly she painted the picture of her childhood, the less I felt I had known her, and the more attractive she became.

She who had entrapped me, used me, was the same person who came through the high wet grass at six on a misty morning carrying three bottles of milk clinking in a canvas sack.

Raw eggs we ate, by streams in sunlight, mung beans by the handful, hard corn intended for cattle.

A twilight comradeship developed between the three of us, a friendship marked by great intimacy, small kindnesses. It was a

413

tender plant that I, at that time, did not expect to live into whatever night might lie ahead. It was not equal, of course – there were three of us, and my father was a handsome man, Jacqui a good-looking woman.

I think I said I was accustomed to pain, that it was, in my case, almost synonymous with pleasure. But now, it seemed, the pain was less, the pleasure greater. My experience with Peggy Kram was quite enough, in every sense, so although I had begun the journey in the front seat, I soon sought out the back.

There, wrapped in a blanket which I was forever ready to pull around my face, in fear of my life, surrounded by animus, taunted by the dangling effigy of the Hairy Man at wayside shrines, I was more alive than ever in my life before.

By now you know where we went. We drove right up into the *Arctic Circle* where the temperatures were low enough to give you frostbite in a second and in a hunting lodge on a lake three miles from Port Wilhelm I sat in a bathroom and watched Bill and Jacqui dye their hair blond.

At the very hour Peggy Kram gave her deposition in the Bhurgercourt,* we sailed from Voorstand on the *Nordic Trader* bound for Bergen. Jacqui was dressed as a man. Bill carried me on board inside the Mouse suit, disguised as a souvenir. At that time, although I did not know it, my unusual life was really just beginning.

Chemin Rouge, 426

---

*      Deposition given by Margaret Kram, Produkter, to the
                Bhurgercourt of Voorstand

*It came to me disguised as one of God's Creatures. Its true nature was monstrous, like the Hairy Man, the thing with scales that Bruder Duck saw in the woods, the little black thing that swished its tail and stamped its foot with rage.*

*It was charming, ingratiating, with numerous stories and songs. It walked upon the public street, moving without let or hindrance amongst the folk. It performed many tricks, some with eggs and spoons. I never saw it eat or heard it complain of hunger. It would never show its face.*

*It said it had no wish to come to Voorstand, that it came only to see 'My Father'. It lived inside the skin of the Mouse. It spoke with the voice of a man. It said it lived on air. It said it was born in 'the Shadows of the Sirkus'. It said it had drunk 'the Light of your Dreams' and lived 'in the Penumbra of your Lives'.*

*For a brief time, to my great shame, I fell under its spell. When I saw its true nature, I asked it, what have we done to you that you should bear us such enmity?*

*It had no reason.*

# Glossary

**angels** *to see the angels*, to have an orgasm

**ASM** Assistant Stage Manager (standard English)

**avvert** newspaper advertisement, particularly a small or 'classified' advertisement

**bandock** nappy or diaper. From Voorstand English *banddoek*

**ballot** idiot, jerk. From French *ballotter*, 'to shake up' – thus, one who has had his brain shaken up

**baton** penis

**bazooley** 1. that which you are passionate about. 2. a prize, jackpot, winning bet. Also: *bazoohley*

**Benny bouftou** From French colloq. *beni-bouftou*, lit: 'a blessed eater of everything'

**biche-la-mar** sea cucumbers or trepang. Also: *bicho do mur*. Corruption of French *bèche-de-mer*

**Bride** pint of beer, so named for its foaming white 'train'

**brique bleu** unusually large molluscs (of the Gastropod class) harvested by first century EC Efican dyeworks. A source of 'Efican Blue'. Lit: 'blue bricks'

**cambruce** a hick, farmer, an inhabitant of Nez Noir. Probably a corruption of French *cambroussard*

**cancerette** cigarette

**case-latrine** poor quality red wine. From French *caisse poitrine*, lit: 'chest-breaker'

**cash parole** automatic teller machine card

**casserole** a spotlight

**couchette** a small bed or crib, sometimes a small bedroom

**Croco cristi** untranslatable expletive with origins in first century EC cant. *Christi* possibly from Sacristi or Holy Cow, *Croco* from Crocodile

**croix cakes** round poppy-seed cakes. The *croix* (French 'cross') may have its origins in the cross-hatched pattern of icing

**dab** father, dad

**demi-botte** gumboot, Wellington. Also: *demi, demon*

**dos-sack** back-pack

**dreck** shit. From Yiddish

**Enteralis** any tree of the predominantly Efican genus *Enteralis*

**facheur** thief. Corruption of French *faucher*, 'to steal'

**frere** comrade

**frippes** trousers, threads. From French *frippes*, 'wrinkles'. Also: *thrippes*

**ganja** dried leaves of the Indian hemp plant *Cannabis sativa*. From Hindi *gaja*, from Sanskrit *grnja*

**Gardiacivil** police

**gazetted** to be married. From first and second centuries EC, when civil marriages were published in the Government gazette

**gen** a man, a gent

**governor** *to work for the governor* is to work for the ruling class, to be a stool pigeon, to be untrustworthy

**illico presto** immediately; hurry it up. From Italian *presto*

**jon-kay** money. From French colloq. *jonc, joncaille*. Also: John Kay

**Jules** man in general

**Lasto-net** synthetic bandage developed in Efica 370 EC. Lasto-net is the registered copyright of Hellas Enterprises

**Leko** an ellipsoidal reflective spotlight

**lever man** a burglar specializing in forced entry

**lolo** breast. Most likely from French child's cry for milk, '*lait, lait*'

**loup** mad, rabid

**meccano** equestrian rig invented by Spencer Q. Stokes to train bare-back riders. A central post supports an arm like the jib of a crane from which the student is suspended

**mo-ami** my friend. Corruption of French *mon ami*

**mobile-amor** sedan chair

**mo-chou** common endearment. Corruption of French *mon chou-fleur*, 'my cauliflower'

**mollo mollo** relax, take it easy

**Mongrel Day** a warm, overcast, windy day

**mo-poulet** common endearment, lit: 'my chicken'

**Moosone** the wet season

**mouette** a gull-like bird indigenous to the southern islands of Efica

**Muddy** Member of the Efican Democratic Party

**mug-wallop** untranslatable abusive term. Probably cant, from first century EC

**musico** a flatterer, a crook. Also: a musician

**parsley** pubic hair. *To put the asparagus in the parsley*, to have sexual intercourse

**patapoof** a fat person

**pea and thimble man** a fairground con-man

**penguin** policeman

**perroquet** a green drink made from crushed ice, green lime cordial, seltzer. From French *perroqet*, 'parrot'

**petite tente** small tent used by family circuses in islands of Efica

**petticon** little cunt (esp. vulg.). Corruption of French *petite con*

**pissmarie** a nurse (vulg.). From *santamarie*

**playing card** small fish, usually silver bream

**porpoise** penis

**rak-rok block** three-dimensional jigsaw invented in Efica, now manufactured under licence in Europe and Voorstand

**rikiki** the little finger, an under-sized person, a 4 fl.oz. glass of beer. Corruption of French *riquiqui*

**ringhard** a bad actor. From colloq. French *ringard*, 'a real zero'

**riveter** a homosexual (vulg.)

**roteuse** any effervescent wine, sometimes champagne. Possibly from French *roter*, 'to burp'

**santamarie** a nurse

**shapoh** the boss, the person in charge. From first century EC, most likely from French *chapeau*

**shooting star** prostitute

**skipjack** fish of the genus *Pomatomus* common in Efican waters

**sorcier** (as in *Pin-ball sorcier*) a share trader who uses computers to make buying and selling decisions

**sock** car tyre

**soup server** an actor who plays small roles

**spanker** backside

**Sparrowgrass** common name for a tall thin person

**spin drier** a woman who extracts money from men. Very strong connotation of 'drying' as relating to male ejaculation

**starbuck** first two rows in the Efican circus, traditionally marked with stencilled stars. These seats have backs, hence also: *starback*

**tarboof** nose

**Teuf-teuf** onomatopoeia for sound an old car makes

**tin-tin** a dyer. First century EC, from French *teinturier*

**toubib** a doctor. From Arabic

**tringler** penis

**valsir** backside. From French *valseur*, lit: 'waltzer'

**vedette** a celebrity

**vert-walk** narrow band of mown grass between footpath and kerb-side in Efican coastal towns

**violin** prison

**violiniste** an ex-con

**walloper** see *gardiacivil*

**zine** any printed journal or news sheet. From English *magazine*

## VOORSTAND ENGLISH

**air-kool** air-conditioning

**Beanbredie** bean stew, a dish much beloved of Bruder Mouse in the Badberg Tales. See recipe in *Bruder Mouse and the English gjent*

**bhalam** a string banjo favoured by many Pow-pow musicians, but not known in Voorstand until last century

**bhurger** a citizen (Voorstand spelling of the standard English *burgher*)

**Bhurger-court** one of the two courts of Voorstand; the other, higher, court is the Guildcourt

**blikk** 1. a car (colloq.) 2. a tin can

**bottelier** wine waiter

**bullschtool** bullshit

**Cyborg** see *Simulacrum*

**deskmajoor** the concierge in a hotel or apartment building, a role often taken by retired soldiers of the Voorstand Armed Forces – hence *majoor* ('major') from Dutch. See also *wheelmajoor, sparkmajoor*

**Dome** a specially constructed theatre for the presentation of the Voorstand Sirkus

**facilitator** someone who earns their living by 'facilitating' the illegal entry of aliens into Voorstand

**filtreeder** a water filtration tower designed to cleanse the polluted water table of Saarlim City

**Folkghost** spirits in the Badberg tales who often appear in times of crisis to impart wisdom to the Bruders

**footsack** to go away; (trans.) to kick away, dismiss. Originally *voertsek* from Dutch *voert*, 'a foot'

# THE UNUSUAL
# LIFE OF
# TRISTAN SMITH